CIRCLE 7

OF SEVEN

CIRCLE 7 OF SEVEN

CLAY JACOBSEN

BROADMAN
&HOLMAN
PUBLISHERS

Nashville, Tennessee

0-8054-2283-8

Published by Broadman & Holman Publishers, Nashville, Tennessee

Dewey Decimal Classification: 813
Subject Heading: INVESTIGATIVE REPORTING—FICTION /
PUBLIC OPINION POLLS—FICTION / MASS MEDIA—FICTION
Library of Congress Card Catalog Number: 00-036044

Unless otherwise stated all Scripture citation is from the NIV, the Holy Bible, New International Version, copyright © 1973, 1978, 1984 by International Bible Society.

This book is a work of fiction. Any references to real events, businesses, organizations, and locales are intended only to give the fiction a sense of reality and authenticity. Any similiarities between the characters and persons, living or dead, is coincidental.

Library of Congress Cataloging-in-Publication Data
Jacobsen, Clay, 1956–
    Circle of seven / Clay Jacobsen.
      p. cm.
    ISBN 0-8054-2283-8 (pb)
    1. Investigative reporting—Fiction. 2. Public opinion polls—Fiction.
3. Conspiracies—Fiction. 4. Journalists—Fiction. 5. Mass media—Fiction.
I. Title.
  PS3560.A2584 C57 2000
  813'.54—dc21

00-036044
CIP

1 2 3 4 5 04 03 02 01 00

*To God's greatest gift to me beyond that of his Son,
and the most precious women in the world—
my wife, Cindy, and our daughters, Sharayah and Shelby—
thank you for being my greatest joy.*

ACKNOWLEDGMENTS

I've often said that it takes a great cast and a talented crew to pull off a quality television production—no matter how good the director might be. I believe that philosophy holds true when writing a novel as well. So with that in mind I wish to express my appreciation to those who helped me complete this project.

Dan Lovil, who worked with me through the first draft (the hardest one) and brought some wonderful ideas to the table.

My brother, Wayne Jacobsen, who helped me immensely, especially in keeping my characters real.

Steve Wark, whose diabolical political mind came in handy with plot ideas.

Gary Chapman, for his friendship; and to Gary and the workers at Averitt Air Charter for their expertise with helicopters.

For those who helped while I was researching the polling process: Deronda Wheeler, David Warnick, Ron Sellers of Ellison Research, and John McLaughlin of John McLaughlin and Associates, all of whom disclaim any endorsement of the plot lines I created.

Brent Bozell and the Media Research Center for their valuable information.

LuAnne Tilson, Director of Counseling and Client Services, Cumberland Crisis Pregnancy Center, for her wisdom and advice.

John McLendon of Creator Media for his expertise on Web site design.

To the great staff at Broadman & Holman who have become friends through the process.

Vicki Crumpton, for her wonderful insight as we worked through the editing process together.

My agent, Sara Fortenberry, whose wisdom and friendship is a blessing.

And most of all to my wife, Cindy, who stayed up hour after hour helping me work through plot ideas while giving me the perfect balance of her creativity, her encouragement, and especially her unconditional love.

PROLOGUE

Six men sat around the oval conference table; the seventh chair remained empty. No one spoke. They had arrived within five minutes of one another. Each had stepped out of a limousine driven to the back door of the Drake Hotel in downtown Chicago, walked directly down a dingy hallway to the service elevator, stepped in, and pressed the button for the top floor.

Now they waited. The warm room contrasted with the icy weather blowing off Lake Michigan outside. Three men smoked: two puffed cigars, and one dragged on a cigarette. Of the others, one sat quietly with his hands clasped in his lap, another tapped his fingers on the table, and the last one nervously bit at the cuticle of his left index finger. Each of them was rich beyond blue-collar comprehension. But their meeting wasn't about money. It was about power.

Down below, the final black stretch limousine turned off Lake Shore Drive, its tires crunching through the ice before stopping beside the service entrance. The door opened and a blast of snow flew into the vehicle. The man smiled at the discomfort as he made his way out of the limo, through the biting wind, and into the hotel.

1

Walking down the same darkened hallway the others had taken just minutes before, he reflected on the path that had brought him to this place. In the beginning, he wasn't sure if his scheme would work, but it had—beautifully. With each small success, the vision had changed; his goal had grown to a magnitude he couldn't have dreamed possible when it all started.

The six looked up with expectation as the main door to the conference room opened and he stepped inside. None of them knew why the meeting had been called. They had assembled only once, when their association had begun. Everyone knew the risk was too great to be seen together—at least, it had been until this night.

He made his way to the head of the table and began. "It's been many years since we first met. Since then, I've turned each of you," he paused, dramatically emphasizing his next words, "into millionaires."

The men held their gaze on him. Several nervous smiles adorned the faces around the room. It was true. Each of them had accumulated great wealth and even greater power, all because of their loyalty to the man standing before them. In different situations, the six men seated around the table would control any room they occupied. Not here.

"I don't expect any great accolades," he continued, "but I do demand your unquestioned loyalty." A smile creased his lips as his eyes scanned the room. Within this group, names were never used. From the moment of the group's inception, each had been assigned a number—one through seven.

The man seated directly across the table did everything within his power to remain absolutely still. The leader's eyes stopped as he looked directly at him; the intensity of the stare pierced through to the man's soul. Number Four felt his stomach drop. Beads of perspiration began sliding down from the pits of his arms underneath his starched white shirt. *He knows,* he thought in total fear. *After all I've done to be so careful, he knows!*

"We've accomplished unbelievable results with our affiliation," their leader acknowledged. "I couldn't have done it without each of you." His six-foot-three-inch athletic frame seemed to stretch taller as pride welled up within him. He looked upon the group seated around him as if the men were family. Closer to him than his own son had been, these were men he'd mentored over the years and made what they were today. It made his next step that much more distasteful but necessary nonetheless.

"Before we get down to business, let me offer up a toast to all of you." He reached to the table in front of him where a glass of champagne rested. There was a similar glass placed before each of the men around the table. He picked his up. "Please, stand with me."

The men scooted their chairs back and stood. Number Four was the last to move, finally finding the nerve to join the others on his feet. *Maybe he doesn't know after all,* he thought.

The leader beamed as he brought the glass up high toward the center of the table. "To each of you—may we forever be successful, rich beyond our wildest dreams, and so powerful that no one can touch us. To the Circle of Seven."

"The Circle of Seven," they responded in chorus. Each brought the glass of champagne to his lips, taking sips with all the honor and pride that could only be found in belonging to this most secret of groups.

Time stood still for a moment as each man proudly smiled around the room, acknowledging each other's success. Suddenly, the sound of shattering glass filled the room.

Number Four's hands suddenly clutched at his chest. A searing pain overwhelmed him. His face turned a dark shade of red as he struggled for breath. The terror returned. He thought about all that he had put in jeopardy: his company, his wealth, his wife, his daughters, and grandchildren. He loved them so much—then his fear-struck eyes locked onto the man standing at the head of the table. The stricken man caught a glimpse of the smirk that crossed Number One's face the second before he crumpled to the floor.

Not a soul moved.

Their leader broke the silence as two men quietly entered the room and quickly carried Number Four out the door. "As I said earlier, I do demand your unquestioned loyalty."

He slowly took in the five men left standing around the table. Each nodded a sign of allegiance as his eyes passed from one to the next.

"Now, gentlemen," he continued without missing a beat, stretching his arm out toward the door behind him, "I'd like to introduce you to our new Number Four."

The door opened and in stepped the newest member of the Circle of Seven. Without fanfare, he walked around to the end of the table and took his position.

"Let's get down to business," their leader smiled.

CHAPTER 1

WEDNESDAY, FEBRUARY 7
HOLLYWOOD, CALIFORNIA
NATIONAL STUDIOS
10 A.M. PACIFIC

"OK, everybody, let's settle," Frank Russell called out over the noise of the crowded room. The weekly "pitch" meeting for the staff of *Across the Nation* was being called to order. Russell, a former down-in-the-trenches reporter for NBC News two decades ago, was now the executive producer for National Studios's live Sunday night newsmagazine show, the new network's answer to *60 Minutes* and *Dateline*.

"First on the agenda—we're heading into sweeps," Russell bellowed as he took his seat at the head of the table. "That means we're pulling out all the stops—titillation and sensationalism galore. I don't need to stress to you how low our ratings have been, do I?"

The men and women assembled knew all too well the importance of ratings. The show was in its first season, barely holding onto its Sunday night time slot. If the National executives hadn't been so busy creating an upstart network after the success of its flagship late-night *John Harold Show*, their jobs might already have been lost.

Russell ran his hands through what little hair still clung to his scalp as he looked around the room. *They are all so young,* he thought. Trying to rally his team to the level of the competition challenged him. Russell knew he had good people producing a solid show, but they needed a break—that one sensational story that would scoop all the networks and put them on the map. That would give the show, and just as importantly, his career, the boost it desperately needed.

Around the table, along with his personal assistant and the script supervisor, sat the bulk of his creative force—four teams, each consisting of a producer and an investigative reporter. Lacking the budget of the major networks meant that each of them had to complete a segment for every show, so they were constantly researching three to four stories ahead while still completing their current one.

"Anybody have any problems with Sunday's segments?" Russell paused as he glanced across the room for any response.

"We're having difficulty getting footage out of India," Stan Jeffries spoke out. Stan's assignment for Sunday was the massive earthquake that had struck the heart of India the week before, adding to that nation's tragic struggle with its worst drought in over a hundred years.

"See me after the meeting," Russell instructed. "I've still got some friends at NBC. We'll get something. Anybody else?"

No one spoke up, so he continued, "Good. Then let's hear some ideas for sweeps."

Samantha Steel spoke up first. "Jeff and I have been mulling over one," she said, acknowledging the producer assigned with her. Their team primarily covered entertainment stories—profiles on celebrities, hit television series, or the behind-the-scenes action of a motion picture.

Russell grinned. It was like her to be the first one out of the blocks. Sam had a drive to succeed like no one he'd seen before; she also had a lot to learn. But she hadn't been hired for her journalistic expertise, Russell knew, because he'd made the decision. She became a member of his team for one reason alone—the magic that happened when she was in front of a camera. He saw it last year when he caught her on the ABC affiliate, covering the murder of a prominent Hollywood director. Samantha had a presence about her that was sensuous—the full head of blond hair hanging down to her shoulders and framing the exquisite face combined with a body that had the right number of curves in all the right places; yet on the air she exhibited amazing poise, intelligence, and grace. What had astonished the studio executives were the high marks she received from the females in their focus groups, uncommon among on-air talents with her beauty.

"If we really want to get some ratings," Sam continued with a devilish grin, "let's do a story on adult Internet sites by creating our own Web page." She paused, watching the reaction around the room. Everyone seemed enticed by the idea except for one reporter, Mark Taylor, who had lowered his head into the palm of his right hand and rubbed his temples.

"Internet porn is huge." Sam's producer, Jeff Edwards, picked up the sales pitch. "What we want to do is create a Web site, nothing hard-core, just nudity. But advertise celebrities—starting with our own Samantha here. It'd be a great hook."

Sam glanced around at the staff with a huge smile. The boost this story could give to the show's ratings was just a small portion of her plan. She hoped the stunt would also increase her chances of breaking into the acting career she desperately craved.

"I guess I asked for something sensational," Russell responded dryly, "but what's the story angle? Not that having Sam unclothed wouldn't be marketable."

A few chuckles could be heard around the room, but Sam kept her somber tone. She was prepared for Russell's question. "We want to see how many hits a site like this gets. If we can work it out with legal, we also want to set up a pay area to see what kind of income can be generated. We can donate the money to a charity or something . . ." Samantha accented with a wave of her hand.

"Plus, we've got a computer whiz kid who's helping us design a survey as well. I'm sure we'll get some interesting demographic information on those who visit the site. Once we've analyzed that data, there's no telling where the story will go."

Repulsed and intrigued at the same time, Russell wondered how the journalism profession he had grown to love and respect over the span of his career had come to this. But as an executive producer for a struggling show, he had to look at what could keep the show on the air. It was the perfect story to promote for sweeps. "Jeff, I want this plan checked out thoroughly by our lawyers before I'll give the green light." He turned toward Sam with a sly grin spreading across his face. "Are you sure this—exposure—won't adversely affect your credibility as a journalist?"

Sam shook her head. "Not if I handle it right. I actually think it will do just the opposite."

Russell nodded. If anyone could pull it off, she could.

Mark sat across the table, his gut churning. He was appalled. He knew he should speak up—protest somehow. He squirmed in his seat, trying to think of a way.

"Is something bothering you, Mark?" Russell asked him.

"No," he blurted out nervously. "I guess if we want titillation, that would do it."

"I think it's a great idea." Tad Forrest, the show's male counterpart to Samantha's model-like beauty jumped into the conversation. Young, tall, and slim with jet-black hair, Tad had the GQ look and a wonderfully smooth delivery on the air. He was also gay. Ironically, the network had pegged him as the perfect reporter to bring in the female demographic. "It seems like it'd be a perfect hook to grab some viewer attention and maybe get our show out of the ratings cellar. You know, I might do some modeling as well."

Mark looked around the room as heads nodded. There didn't seem to be anyone who felt about the issue the way he did. He sighed and let the matter drop—as usual.

Mark Taylor had started with the studio as a production assistant fresh out of the Marines after Desert Storm. He'd always wanted to be a television journalist, and this job was his first big break. He didn't have Tad's elegant features. He was shorter and stockier, with a slightly crocked nose from a bone-crushing collision trying to tag an opposing player at home plate during a high school baseball game. His wavy brown hair wasn't always combed to perfection either, but his determination and drive made him a formidable reporter.

The idea of allowing the integrity of the show to be compromised for the sake of ratings angered him. And it wasn't just the impassioned journalist in him crying out. Mark was a Christian, but he'd learned quickly in Hollywood that things went a lot more smoothly when he kept his spiritual convictions to himself. Not a person in the room knew about Mark's faith, not even his producer, Jennifer Williams. He wasn't proud of the fact, but he thought it was what was needed to keep his career on track.

"Did you have any ideas for us, Mark?" Russell asked.

Mark looked down at his notes. "Well, I've been taking a look recently at how politicians appear to be catering to opinion polls."

In contrast to the enthusiastic response the group had given Sam's idea, Mark's listeners now sat in stoical silence. Samantha eyed him. A sarcastic edge rose in her voice. "A political story—there's something new. What angle could there possibly be that we or some other show hasn't already run into the ground?"

"Well, I'm not sure yet. I haven't had time to sit down and work this through. If you look at the headlines lately, it seems like everything is being run by the polls. Instead of leaders with ideas, we've got politicians taking surveys before they make up their minds on what to order for dinner. Nobody is taking the firm stand of doing what they believe is right. They just look for what's going to give them a favorable approval rating.

"You can't watch the network news without hearing that some percentage of Americans approve or disapprove of somebody or something . . ." Mark paused, searching for words. The idea had been brewing in the back of his mind for weeks, but his thoughts weren't solidified yet. He wasn't ready to pitch it; he was blowing the opportunity.

"Well, if you can come up with a new angle, go for it," Russell said, unconvinced. "But while you're at it, I need you and Jennifer to handle this." He slid a folder across the table to Mark.

Written across the top in bold letters were the words "Promotional Department/*The Single Life*." Mark knew what was inside the folder before he opened it. *The Single Life* was one of the new sit-coms on the network—an ensemble cast representing the young Generation X. From his point of view, a rip-off of *Friends* but with less morality. Mark shook his head and looked at Jennifer for help.

"You want us to do a piece on one of National's own shows?" Jennifer asked.

"It came down from the head of the network as a strong recommendation, if you catch my drift," Russell said. "They're pushing this show during sweeps and want us to do a profile on it. All you gotta do is go out and shoot some backstage footage—a few talking heads—maybe do a bit of background on any of the cast who had recognizable credits before this show. Remember, it'll be for sweeps, so you know what angle to look for."

Mark fumed but tried to keep his temper under control. "I thought this was Sam's area. Why are you throwing it to us?"

Russell looked at Mark over his bifocals. His classic posture communicated, I'm the boss, don't argue with me.

"Samantha's going to be busy making this Internet thing work," he said coldly. "This will help lighten the load for her and give you two something to do."

Mark knew that was the end of the discussion as he opened the folder and thumbed through the information. This wasn't how he dreamed investigative journalism would be. He'd never watched an entire episode of *The Single Life*. His fingers flipped from page to page as the biographies and glossy photographs of the cast flashed by, but his mind went elsewhere—working to find the right angle for the polling story. In spite of the disappointment he held in his hands, he felt a trickle of excitement—the kind that came when working on something that mattered, something that took some digging to get to the truth, something big.

WHITE PLAINS, NEW YORK
2:54 P.M. EASTERN

Tears streamed down Virginia Franklin's face. Dr. Weston had just told Laura that she had lost the baby. They'd done everything medically possible after the accident, but the damage had been too great. Virginia was shattered. She'd watched Laura grow up from a little child—every weekday from two to three in the afternoon on her favorite soap opera. The telephone interrupted her moment of grief.

"Hello," she managed to get out through her tears.

"Hello, is this Mrs. Franklin?"

"Yes, it is. Who is this?"

"My name is Tami, Mrs. Franklin. I'm with Research International, and we're conducting a nationwide opinion poll. Would you have a couple of minutes to answer some questions for us? It'd be very helpful."

Virginia sniffled, "You're not trying to sell something, are you?"

"No, ma'am. We just have a few questions to ask you, that's all. It'll only take a couple of minutes."

"Well, I guess it's OK then. I don't get too many calls, you know."

"Fine," Tami answered as she looked at the first question on her computer screen. "Are you a registered voter?"

"Of course I am," Virginia responded proudly.

"Did you vote in the last election?"

"Well, no, I didn't. I think I had car trouble or something that day. Yeah, that's what it was."

"OK, I understand," Tami responded. "Now I'm going to mention some names, and I want you to tell me whether your impression of the person is favorable, unfavorable, or you don't know enough about the person to make a judgment. The first person is President McNeil."

"Well, I'm not sure what you mean?"

"I'm not able to give you any help, Mrs. Franklin," Tami said. "I'm just supposed to read the questions, not explain them."

"Oh my, well, I guess he's all right," Virginia finally responded.

Tami clicked the favorable box on her computer screen, then continued down her list of names, most of which Virginia didn't recognize, but she managed to throw in a couple of favorable and unfavorable opinions along the way so she wouldn't look too silly.

"And the final question, Mrs. Franklin: In light of the fact that Social Security is in danger of going bankrupt, would you say you have a favorable or unfavorable opinion of the job Congress is doing?"

"Oh my," Virginia nearly dropped the phone. All she had left was her Social Security since Edmond had died two years earlier. "I would definitely say unfavorable. I couldn't live without that money."

Tami smiled as she checked the final answer. "Thank you so much, Mrs. Franklin. You've been very helpful."

NATIONAL STUDIOS
12:30 P.M. PACIFIC

Mark sat at his desk, partitioned from the rest of the staff by three gray temporary walls that reached only halfway to the ceiling. The cubicles resembled a newsroom more than a modern production office for a television series. It was Russell's design, a throwback to the heyday of early print journalism. Mark couldn't picture Dan Rather or Diane Sawyer working in similar conditions.

He was still seething from the pitch meeting. How could Russell have assigned him that ridiculous segment on *The Single Life?* A fluff piece like that should be shown on a show like *Entertainment Tonight*, not on *Across the Nation*. And if National Studios had to cover it, Sam should be the one assigned to it, not him. The more he thought about it, the angrier he became. He stood up and looked over his "wall" to the corner where Russell's office was located. Samantha had just stepped out, sporting a huge smile. *That woman gets everything she wants around here.*

He was on his feet and walking that direction before he knew what he was doing. He found himself knocking on Russell's door without having a clue what he was going to say.

"What is it?"

Mark opened the door and peeked inside. "Do you have a minute?"

Russell stopped scribbling on some papers and looked up. "That's all I've got. I'm supposed to be at a meeting across the lot."

Russell had the only real office. A window looked out over a grassy area near the studio's day-care center. Impressive pictures of Russell with presidents, studio executives, and high-profile entertainers decorated the walls.

Mark stepped into the room and closed the door. "I'm having a hard time with something."

"What's that?"

"I've got some reservations about the story Samantha proposed."

Russell set his pen down and looked right at Mark. "OK, let's have it."

Russell's undivided attention added to Mark's anxiety. He swallowed hard, then began. "It's just that I think it cheapens the show's credibility. If we're trying to establish *Across the Nation* as a serious journalistic presence, how do you reconcile putting her story, pictures and all, on the Internet, much less on the air?"

Russell looked down at his watch and shrugged. "Have a seat," he said, waving to the chair in front of the desk.

Mark sat down, hoping he hadn't made a big mistake. Russell leaned back in his chair and let out a long sigh. "I admire you, Mark; I really do. You're young enough to have an idealistic view of this business."

Mark squirmed in his chair. He suddenly felt like a sixth-grader being called in by the principal.

"I, unfortunately, am not," Russell continued. "You have a great deal of journalistic integrity, and I want you to do everything in your power to hold onto it. Because in the midst of this business, you're going to be stretched and pulled all sorts of directions you don't want to go. You're going to be told to cover stories you loathe, just like the one I stuck you with a few minutes ago."

Mark agreed but said nothing.

"And do you know why?" Russell paused.

Mark remained silent.

"Ratings, that's why," Russell answered his own question. "You see, if we don't generate ratings—if people aren't tuning into our show—then we won't be on the air anymore. Don't fool yourself. We're not journalists; we're salesmen."

Mark's eyes darkened. The last line caught him off guard.

"We sell soap, cars, beer, cereal, even vacations to Tahiti. You take everything we do around here, and it all boils down to that—we sell things. We do a show and companies use it to sell stuff. There was a time years ago when I first started with NBC that the news division was separate from the entertainment division, and the bean counters kept to themselves. Unfortunately, those golden days of TV journalism are over. We're all salesmen. Do I think Sam's idea is worth a hoot as a journalist? Of course not! And don't insult me by thinking I would either."

Mark opened his mouth to speak.

"Hold that thought for a second and let me finish," Russell continued. "But will Sam's idea create some controversy? Will people watch just to see how much of her body we're going to put on the air? Will the ratings go up? A resounding 'you betcha' on all three accounts. I don't make the rules; I've just learned to follow them. We've got a struggling first-year show here. If we're going to have a chance at a second year, we need to get people watching. It's that simple."

Mark faced a flood of emotions. In the six months that he'd been working on the show, he'd grown to respect Frank Russell, the journalist. Mark had not seen this side of him before, and the cynicism was frightening.

Russell got out of his chair, stepped around the desk, and sat on the edge facing him. "That's reality, Mark. You've got a wonderful passion for journalism. Don't let it die. You've done some good pieces since we started this show. But you've got to learn to drudge through all the garbage and put up with whatever it takes to keep this show going. Then, when 'the story' comes along, the one that will create a fire in your gut so hot you won't be able to put it out, we'll still be on the air, and you'll have the platform to present it. Do you understand what I'm saying?"

Mark was speechless, so he just nodded an affirmative.

"Good. Now you let me worry about Samantha's segment. And as much as it may displease you, you're still assigned *The Single Life*. It's a fluff piece. Take advantage of it."

Russell stood up again, pulling Mark by the elbow and leading him to the door. "Use the time wisely. Look into this polling thing you mentioned. See if you can find the right angle. Then, with any luck, we'll still be alive for you to get it on the air."

Mark's mind was still reeling as he walked past the sound stages on his way to the cafeteria shortly after one o'clock. At National, the commissary was split into two sections. The door on the left led into a beautifully decorated restaurant with menus and full-service waiters; it was generally reserved for the top executives and the celebrities. The door to the right opened onto a typical cafeteria-style lunchroom. Mark took the door on the right.

He ordered a sandwich from the deli line, then picked it up with a Pepsi and a bag of chips, and made his way to the cashier. Stepping back out to the seating area, he scanned the room for a free table, hoping to eat alone. Just his luck with the way the day was going, there wasn't one.

"Mark, over here." He heard his name called over the low hum of conversation. A few tables away sat Rick Treadway and Cassie Petterson at a table for four. Rick waved Mark toward the seat next to him.

Mark forced a smile and headed their way. Rick and Cassie worked on *The John Harold Show*. Rick was the director, Cassie was the producer, and a more attractive couple would be hard to find. Cassie's wavy brunette hair hung gently over her shoulders, and large hazel eyes accented her girl-next-door face. Rick was taller than Mark, stretching just over six feet. His dark hair, which was usually ruffled from what he termed "headset hair," gave him a boyish charm.

"Thanks for the invitation," Mark said as he set his tray down. "I don't think there's an empty table in here."

"You're welcome," Rick answered. "I think there are a couple of films in production this month. We had to wait for this table."

Mark angled his head toward the next table at a man attempting to wolf down a cheeseburger while wearing a strange costume that looked like some kind of extraterrestrial amphibian. "From the looks of it, I'd say one of them is science fiction."

The three laughed as the actor reached for some salt and the fin on the arm of his costume scattered his french fries across the table.

"How's it going, Mark?" Cassie asked, still giggling.

"It's going OK," Mark lied. "We just got out of a long pitch meeting looking ahead to those exciting sweeps."

"I know how that can be," Rick said.

"I'm sorry to have to run so quickly," Cassie apologized as she scooted her chair back and stood up. "But I've got a talent meeting in a couple of minutes. It was nice to see you, Mark."

Rick stood up with her. "I can stay a few minutes; we don't go on camera until two. I'll walk Cassie out and be right back."

"Good-bye, Cassie," Mark said, then bit into his sandwich as the two headed toward the door.

"He's down about something," Cassie whispered to Rick.

"How do you know that? He said everything was fine."

"Trust me. Call it women's intuition or the Holy Spirit, but he's troubled." She reached up with her hand and brushed Rick's cheek as she smiled at him. "See if you can help him—he might need a friend right now."

Rick smiled. "You're amazing," he said as he gave her a brief hug and kiss before she headed for their office. He paused to watch her walk away. It never ceased to amaze him—whenever he thought he couldn't possibly love her more than he already did, she'd do something like this to prove him wrong.

The two had been dating exclusively since they had first met last March. Cassie had been the assistant to the producer on the *Harold Show* when the previous director turned up dead from an apparent suicide. Rick landed the vacant job, and their relationship developed quickly, even during the intense time when it was discovered the previous director, Wade Bennett, had actually been murdered. They found themselves thrown into the center of the mystery. Now less than a year later, Rick couldn't imagine life without Cassie by his side. As she turned the corner and disappeared from view, Rick felt an acute sense of loss even though he'd see her again in a few minutes. *Funny how she affects me that way,* he thought.

Arriving back at the table and sinking into his chair, Rick didn't waste any time. "So what's bothering you?"

Mark looked up in surprise. "What makes you think something's bothering me?"

"Cassie." Rick grinned, realizing she was right again. "She has a keen sense for these things, you know. I can't hide anything from her."

Mark smiled. Rick's lightheartedness was infectious. "It's just this job sometimes…" he sighed. He had wanted to have a quiet lunch to get away from his frustrations, but maybe it would be better to talk about it. He'd developed a casual friendship with Rick, running into him on the lot occasionally. He seemed to have a sympathetic ear.

"I can't believe what's happening with our show over this ratings thing."

Rick laughed, taking Mark by surprise.

"I'm sorry," Rick apologized. "It's just that as bad as our meetings can be during sweeps, I can imagine what it would be like with your type of show. Lots of sex, violence, or both?"

"Mostly sex this time. Do you know Samantha Steel?"

Rick nodded his head. "Oh yeah. I've run into her a time or two."

"Oh, Rick, I'm sorry. I totally forgot," Mark said slightly embarrassed, forgetting about the history between Rick and Samantha. It was during the time of the investigation into Bennett's death that Samantha had erroneously reported that Rick had committed the murder.

Rick laughed it off. "Don't worry, that's ancient history. What about her?"

"She's got this crazy idea to have our show run an adult Internet site, with her as the featured model."

"That sounds like Sam," Rick smiled.

"Yeah. I was upset that our show would even consider it. But everyone there thought it would get fantastic ratings."

"The problem is, they're probably right," Rick added.

Mark continued, encouraged to be able to talk with somebody who agreed with him. "I think we're really crossing the line to cover a story like that just for ratings."

"Did you say anything?"

Mark lowered his head. "No, not during the meeting. I wanted to, I really did. I just didn't know what to say or how to approach it. No one would have agreed with me."

"Don't let it get you down," Rick said. "That's a tough time to speak up. I know a year ago, I probably wouldn't have said anything either."

Mark looked up, their eyes meeting. "You're kidding."

"No, actually I'm not," Rick answered, holding his gaze. "Let me ask you, why do you think you didn't speak out if it bothered you so much?"

Mark thought for a second. "I've always been afraid . . ." he paused as he noticed a man coming up behind Rick.

Rick turned around as a hand touched his shoulder.

"Hey, Rick," Chad Overton, Rick's associate director, said. "Hate to interrupt, but we'd better get back to the stage. We're on camera with Shania in a few minutes."

Rick looked at his watch. "Thanks, Chad. I didn't realize how late it was." He turned back to Mark, smiling as he stood to go. "Shania—speaking of ratings, huh? Look, Mark, we need to spend some more time on this, but I've got to run. Do you want to get together after the show?"

Mark was surprised to realize he was disappointed they couldn't talk more. "Yeah, I'd like that, but it depends on how things go at the office. I'll stop by the show if I'm free."

"Great. You know Reggie, don't you?" Rick asked. Reggie was the lead security guard assigned to the *Harold Show*—a former football player on the Los Angeles Rams teams of the 1980s and a great friend to Rick and Cassie.

Mark laughed. "Everybody knows Reggie."

"You're right. I'll tell him to expect you then. I hope it works out. If not tonight, then soon, OK?" Rick turned to follow Chad.

Mark agreed, picking up his Pepsi and taking a long swig. He hoped the rest of the day would brighten up. Right now, he felt as if he had fallen into a deep, dark hole, and getting back on top seemed next to impossible.

CHAPTER 2

RESEARCH INTERNATIONAL
NEW YORK CITY
4:10 P.M. EASTERN

Tami Hawthorne hurried down the plush hallway leading to the executive suites of Research International, one of the most successful polling companies in the nation. She opened the large door to her employers' inner chamber. The dramatic shift in décor—from the gold-plated chair railings to the great works of art adorning the walls—always had the same effect on Tami. *I will have my office in here someday,* she thought.

Olympia Pearson, the executive receptionist, looked up from her desk. "You may go right in, Tami. Mr. Palmer is expecting you."

Tami stopped for a moment to glance into a mirror and check her appearance before she continued into Palmer's office. She noticed Olympia's attention was back on her computer, so Tami took an extra second to hike her already short skirt up a bit more, then stepped through the doorway with a smile.

"Here's the final data from the weekend survey," she said as she entered.

Mike Palmer glanced up from his computer, enticed by Tami's appearance. He received the papers from her with a grin, then scanned to the bottom of the summary page that she had laid on top of the stack, just the way he liked it.

"Good, uh-huh," Mike acknowledged as he scratched his chin. "The client should be pleased with these results."

Tami smiled. "That's an understatement if I've ever heard one. They should be ecstatic."

"We have to make sure the client gets what he pays for." Palmer chuckled. He was having his best day ever professionally. His first as president of Research International, and he was loving it.

"By the way, I'm so sorry about Mr. Dawkins's heart attack," she said. "It was so unexpected."

"Thank you, Tami. He was a wonderful man, and we'll miss him around here," Palmer intoned with just the right amount of sorrow.

"He sure was," Tami agreed, "but I'm sure you'll be a great president, taking this company to even greater heights."

Palmer broke into a proud smile, the sorrowful expression quickly disappearing. Gaining the presidency at forty-seven was even faster than his ambitious goals had prescribed. But who could account for the unexpected tragedy that had struck his predecessor?

Tami matched his smile with a sexy one of her own. "If there's anything at all I can do for you, Mike, don't hesitate to ask."

Palmer greedily eyed the woman standing before him. "Don't you worry, Tami, I won't."

NATIONAL STUDIOS
1:45 P.M. PACIFIC

"Start your move, Chuck, and take six," Rick said, accented with a snap of his finger. The technical director punched the appropriate button on the switcher, putting the picture of Shania Twain's drummer on the line just as he rolled through his set of toms, ending with a hard cymbal crash.

Chuck Smith stood behind the twenty-one-foot arm that cradled camera 6 at the opposite end. On Rick's cue Chuck began moving, swinging the camera away from the drummer. As Shania made the rehearsed move up stage toward her band, the camera armed close by, revealing her in its frame as it swept past and out to a wide shot taking in the whole stage. Just as the camera completed its move, the band hit the final beat in a flourish.

"Take one," Rick snapped again, putting a waist shot of Shania on the line for her bow. "I'll probably want a reverse here, Teresa," Rick continued, talking to one of the handheld operators. "I'm sure the audience will be going wild."

"OK, Rick, you'll have it." Teresa's voice came back through the intercom system.

"The song looks great, everybody," Rick said into his headset while looking back through the script pages of the lyrics. "I just have a couple of notes. Dirk, on shot seventeen, let's add a dolly to it as you work into her waist shot. I think it'll add some nice movement there. Also, I'm going to lose shots twenty-four and twenty-five. Harold, that means I'm just going to stay with your close-up longer on shot twenty-three. She's the money."

Chad, Rick's associate director, erased the mentioned shots from his script as the camera operators in the studio did the same thing on their shot cards.

"Shania's clear, Debbie," Rick said to the stage manager, giving her permission to release Shania from the stage. "You can take her back into audio."

The John Harold Show allowed its musical guests to listen to a recording of their performances after rehearsal so they would be comfortable with how they would sound on the show that evening.

"That's a five, everybody," Rick called out to the stage. "Dan, cue up that last pass for me please. I'd like to take a look at it." Dan was the videotape operator working in a room down the hall. Rick liked to video the rehearsals so when time permitted he could look back over the performance and make sure he was happy with the camera angles, the lighting, and the audio mix. As Chad and the show's technical director made their way out of the booth, the phone in front of Rick rang.

"Control room," Rick said, picking up the receiver.

"Looks good, Rick." Cassie complimented from the other end. As producer, she had a monitor in her office, allowing her to keep track of what was happening on the stage from across the lot.

"Thanks, but she makes it easy," Rick responded. "She sure knows how to play the camera."

"She looks fabulous, and that's even before makeup."

"Really? I hadn't noticed," Rick snickered.

"Yeah, and if I believe that, you've got some swamp land somewhere in Florida ready to sell."

"OK, I'll admit she's beautiful, but I'm a professional and will act accordingly. Besides, my heart's already taken."

Rick could picture Cassie blushing. Even though they were dating, on the job they tried to keep their personal lives at a distance. And it worked—some of the time.

"Ah, that's sweet," Cassie responded tenderly, then it occurred to her how Rick's sense of humor operated. "You are talking about me, aren't you?"

"Of course I am," Rick assured her. "My heart belongs to no other. Now how can I help you?"

"I wanted to let you in on something about the monologue." Cassie slipped comfortably back into her role as producer. "We're going to plant one of the writers in the audience as a heckler. So you'll need to let audio know and have a camera ready for it."

"No problem. I'll warn them. Anything else?"

"Not at this point. Oh, wait. How did the rest of your time with Mark go?"

Rick laughed. "You're just wondering if you were right about him, aren't you?"

Cassie took Rick's challenge. "Oh, I know I was right. I was just wondering what was bothering him."

"What does the Scripture say: 'pride goeth before a fall'?" Rick teased.

"Actually, it's 'destruction.' A haughty spirit comes before a fall," Cassie responded lightly.

"Wow, you're sharp today, aren't you? OK, you were right; he was pretty down. I'll tell you this much; it involves sweeps week and Samantha Steel."

Cassie sat up straighter in her chair. "I think I want to hear the rest of this story."

"So do I, but I had to get back to rehearsal before we could really delve into it. I'm hoping Mark and I can get together after the show. I think he needs to talk this out with someone."

"But what about the sponsor dinner? Aren't you coming?"

"You don't need the director there, do you?"

"Officially, no, but for personal reasons it would be nice," Cassie answered in a softer voice.

Boy, this is hard, Rick thought. "Well, I'd love to be with you, Cassie, but if Mark responds, I feel I need to hear him out."

He heard Cassie sigh on the other end. Her understanding of Mark's needs didn't diminish her desire to have Rick by her side. "I guess we'll play it by ear then. I better get back to work."

"OK, see you later," Rick said as he hung up. He had no desire to attend the dinner, but he hated letting Cassie down. Using Mark as an excuse had come in handy though. He had other plans for the evening—important ones.

Rick grabbed his headset. "Dan are you still there to roll that tape?"

Almost instantaneously, the video played, and the downbeat of Shania's song filled the control room.

When Mark returned to the *Across the Nation* production offices, Jennifer Williams was waiting for him. He'd taken a short walk around the lot, hoping to clear his mind and calm down from the frustration of his latest assignment. It hadn't worked.

"You ready to get to work on the *Single Life* piece?" she asked. Jennifer was a bit older than Mark. He guessed somewhere in her late thirties, but he'd never asked her. She had a lot more experience, coming from print media before stepping into television. She kept her black hair cut short, just below her ears. For Mark's taste, she was overly thin, but the high cheekbones combined with her dark green eyes made for an attractive face. Her inexhaustible work ethic benefited Mark on numerous occasions when her thorough research had made him look good on the air.

Mark looked up at her, tempted to say what was really on his mind, but thought better of it. "I guess we'll have to."

Jennifer took a seat on the edge of his desk as Mark slumped into his chair.

"You're not very excited about this, are you?" she asked.

"Of course not. Are you?"

"Oh, Mark, it won't be that bad." Jennifer moved to a chair in the opposite corner. "Look at it as just a break from our normal routine."

Mark groaned inside. She had a better attitude than he did. *Who is the Christian here?* he wondered.

"I'm glad you're taking this so well," he smiled at her, "but as I tried to argue in the pitch meeting, this assignment should have been given to Sam."

"Now on that one I definitely agree with you. But I wasn't too upset. I love *The Single Life*. I can't wait to meet the cast."

Mark had an idea. He rolled his chair closer to her. "Jennifer, listen—"

"Oh, no," she interpreted, reading the expression on his face. "Whatever it is, no!"

"Just hold on a minute and hear me out," Mark pleaded. "You've got an interest in this show, and I've never been able to sit through an entire episode. Russell's given me permission to find an angle on the polling thing, so . . ."

Jennifer smirked as she completed his thought. "Why don't I do the legwork for the promo piece, which will give you more time to pursue your story?"

Mark laughed. "You're just too smart for me, aren't you? So what do you say? Wherever you want the story to go, it'll go. When we get to the studio, I'll ask whatever questions you want. Deal?"

Jennifer took her glasses off as she studied the pattern on the carpeted floor. Mark was afraid she wasn't going to go along with it. After a moment, she glanced back up at him. "Look, Mark, I'm not sure exactly what you're looking for in your polling idea. It seems like a waste of time to me. But if splitting up like this will help you, OK."

"That's great. I'll owe you one."

"Which reminds me," Jennifer said, "we need that interview to finish up this week's piece on the abortion lawsuit."

A group organized by Planned Parenthood was suing some people who ran an antiabortion Internet site. The Planned Parenthood group was attempting to blame them for the murder of an abortion doctor after his name had been identified on the Web site's hit list.

"What's the update on that?" Mark asked.

"The judge just handed it over to the jury, so we should have their decision soon. If I'm handling this," she reached over and grabbed the folder Russell had assigned them, "then you need to follow up on that interview. What was her name, some woman from the Anti-Abortion Advocacy Group, or something like that?"

"I remember. I'll call her and set it up for tomorrow afternoon. Is that OK with you?"

"Perfect," Jennifer agreed as she stood to leave.

Mark spun around in his chair to once again face his desk. He dug through the clutter for a notepad, and scribbled a reminder to call the woman for the interview. His eyes caught sight of the overturned *Los Angeles Times*; its headline stared up at him:

President's Plan for Economy Receives Broad Public Support

An overnight poll conducted by the *Times* states that 73 percent of Americans are in favor of the economic package President McNeil presented in his White House press conference yesterday.

Andrew McNeil, the former senator from Illinois, surged into the public spotlight when he challenged, then defeated Vice President Al Gore for the Democratic nomination. He'd kept the momentum going right through to the presidential election in 2000 and won the presidency by narrowly beating the Republican nominee. Mark scanned the article, looking for any additional information on the poll. At the bottom he found what he was looking for: "...612 people were polled with a margin of error of plus/minus 4 percent." This kind of reporting piqued Mark's interest. How can slightly over 600 people give an accurate portrayal of what 275 million Americans think about the president's economic package? Where do these people live? What were they asked? Who asked them? How?

Mark leaned back in his chair as he pondered his questions. In the upper corner of the room hung a television set, constantly tuned to CNN. A full-screen graphic caught his eye:

CNN/*USA Today* Overnight Poll
75% Approve Economic Package
17% Disapprove Economic Package
8% No Opinion

Mark squinted but couldn't read the small print at the bottom of the screen to see how many people the poll had questioned. He stood to get a closer look, but before he could get out of his cubicle, the screen changed back to the news anchor.

He dropped back into his chair, turning to the computer beside his desk. It was time to start digging.

MALIBU, CALIFORNIA
2:05 P.M. PACIFIC

As mansions go along the Pacific Coast in Malibu, this one was unique. It impressed all who saw it. Rising four stories from the tops of the rocky cliffs along Malibu Colony Drive, it was unsurpassed in modern architecture. Eight bedrooms, ten bathrooms, three dining areas, two kitchens, six fireplaces, a private screening room, a swimming pool, two Jacuzzis, a six-car garage, two helipads, and an elevator that connected the estate with a private beach—not a bad place to come home to after a hard day's work.

The owner sat in his plush office on the top floor overlooking the breathtaking view while keeping an eye on nine television sets placed within the woodwork of the south wall. Three of them were always tuned to the major networks; four to the cable news services: CNN, CNBC, MSNBC, FOX News; one on C-SPAN; and the final one on the new National Network. A control box at his fingertips allowed him to switch any of the programs to the Bose surround system hidden throughout the room. He thought back to the simpler days when he needed only three television sets to keep pace with the country's media.

Beside his desk sat three portable computers with information running across their screens from the major stock exchanges around the world. Although he paid others handsomely to oversee his huge stock portfolio, he still held a personal interest in every one of his investments.

His concentration was interrupted by the chime of the special phone line that came only to this office. He picked up the receiver sitting beside him, making sure the scrambling device was activated. "Number One here."

"It's me, Luis," he could hear from the other end of the phone. "I thought you'd like an update on Number Four."

"Old or new?" the man asked.

"The dead one," Luis answered dryly. "Everything in New York has been completed according to plan. His body was cremated this morning as per his wishes—or at least that's what his widow believes. All evidence he had accumulated has been destroyed."

"Wonderful," the head man responded. He'd hesitated at first in taking the drastic step required to eliminate the problem, but the former CIA operative had proven to be quite adept at solving life's little surprises over the years—a valuable asset to the Circle of Seven.

"Any chance he talked to somebody?" Number One asked.

"So far it looks like we're clean. If anything turns up, it'll be taken care of."

"I'd expect nothing less, and the new Number Four—everything working out for him as well?" he asked.

"He's taking to the new position quite well and enjoying some of the new perks of leadership."

Number One smiled. "Excellent, but let's keep an eye on him for a while. You understand?"

"Perfectly, Number One. Perfectly."

CHAPTER 3

The last hour had gone by incredibly fast for Mark. He'd done several searches on the Internet for information on polling, public opinion, politics, and political surveys. He'd looked at election polling results dating back to the 1920s. Recent years showed an amazing increase in their use. In 1972, the media conducted a total of three polls in connection with the presidential race. By 1992, that number had jumped to 125.

Mark's research showed it wasn't just the media that became enamored with polling, but politicians as well. The Clinton administration's obsession with public opinion brought new levels of polling to the White House in the 1990s. In his first term of office, Clinton had commissioned nearly two million dollars' worth of polling or focus groups, more than President Bush did in all four years of his term.

Mark also found many articles about the successes and failures in polling history. A report on the 1936 election between Franklin D. Roosevelt and Alfred M. Landon caught his attention. The *Literary Digest* magazine had conducted its usual straw poll mailings to predict the presidential winner. That year, the magazine sent out over 10 million ballots. The returns indicated that Landon, the Republican nominee, would win handily.

Roosevelt won the election by a landslide.

However, Mark's continued research revealed that errant election predictions were the exception, not the rule. Generally, they were very accurate.

As he made his way through the current data on polling, the names of three successful companies kept coming to his attention: Research International in New York City, Nationwide Polling in Chicago, and American Research Institute in L. A.

Mark rubbed his eyes as he backed away from his computer screen. He decided it was time to contact one of the companies for a firsthand look at the process. The obvious choice was the closest one: American Research Institute.

AMERICAN RESEARCH INSTITUTE
LOS ANGELES, CALIFORNIA
2:54 P.M. PACIFIC

The reflected rays from the sun glared off the mirrored windows of the Reynolds Building, blinding all motorists traveling north on Grand Avenue through downtown Los Angeles. The noise from the street below—sirens, horns, and jackhammers—could not be heard by the lone figure looking out of the corner office window on the sixty-fourth floor.

Tracy Reynolds mindlessly watched the traffic pass. Her musing was interrupted by the sound of footsteps.

"Tracy, turn on CNN," her secretary, Brenda Martin, said. "They're doing a report on your grandfather."

Tracy reached for the remote on her desk and turned on the television. The screen showed her smiling grandfather shaking hands with the president of the United States. Reynolds stood majestically, his silver hair gleaming in the sunlight as he waved to the crowd. His lean frame extended two inches taller than President McNeil's, and even though he had a good ten years on the president, Reynolds appeared vibrant and more youthful than the leader of the free world.

"You should have gone, Tracy. The White House. Meeting the president . . ." Brenda teased.

Tracy's eyebrows went up. "I probably should have for Papa's sake, but that's just not me . . . he's starting his speech. Hold on." Tracy hit the volume button.

"Thank you, Mr. President, ladies and gentlemen." Jason Reynolds spoke cordially as the applause within the East Room subsided. "I didn't come here today to be in the spotlight but to shine that spotlight on a great injustice. For the last several years, the funds we allocate to the United Nations have been given with strings attached. The money cannot be used in any way to promote safe, sound family planning around the globe. I, along with President McNeil, think it's time to do something about that."

Reynolds's last words grew in intensity, igniting thunderous applause from those invited to the ceremony in anticipation of what was to be announced. He didn't keep them waiting long.

"That's why today, in the name of all that's decent and what used to be right with this country, I'm making a private donation to the United Nations, to be specifically used for international family planning, in the amount of fifty million dollars."

The small crowd was elated, cheering wildly as the scene switched to the anchor back in the Atlanta studios. "Jason Reynolds made his fortune over the years in various industries including television, radio, newspapers . . ."

Tracy hit the mute button as Brenda let out a gasp. "Fifty million dollars! I had no idea, Tracy. Did you know it was going to be so much?"

Tracy laughed as she sat back into her chair. "Yeah, he called me yesterday when he was flying back after the ceremony. But remember, it's my grandfather we're talking about. He doesn't do anything small."

"He looked so natural standing with the president. Has he considered politics?"

"We've talked about it, but he's always claimed he's got more power doing what he does now without any sacrifice to his personal life." Tracy kept her eyes on the television as a picture of her grandfather and President McNeil filled the screen. Her eyes sparkled with pride.

"It's great to see you so close to him. We need more families like yours in this country." Brenda's voice brightened as she spoke.

The moment was interrupted by the ring of Tracy's phone. Brenda picked it up.

"Tracy Reynolds's office," she answered.

She listened for a moment, then said, "Just a minute, I'll check." She reached over and put the phone on hold.

"The receptionist has a reporter on the line with a show called *Across the Nation*. Do you want to take it or let someone else deal with him?"

Tracy's smile continued. "It didn't take long, did it? He's probably looking for a quote about Papa. I'll take it."

Brenda handed her the phone, put the call back on the line, then headed out of the office.

"This is Tracy Reynolds."

The sound of her voice brightened Mark's mood. It felt nice to be speaking with an actual person instead of surfing the impersonal Web. "Hi, Ms. Reynolds. Thanks for taking my call. My name is Mark Taylor. I'm with *Across the Nation* and I'm doing a story on—"

"Yes, I know," Tracy cut in, "on my grandfather."

Mark paused, not sure how to respond. "No . . . actually I'm not."

Tracy felt foolish for interrupting. "I'm sorry, Mr. . . ."

"Taylor."

"Taylor, but with the announcement yesterday and all, I just assumed you'd be calling to get a comment from me."

Mark was missing something, and he hated that feeling. Then his eyes caught the end of the CNN story from the monitor in the production office. He couldn't hear the sound, but he could see the image of a man with a graphic added to the screen identifying him as Jason Reynolds, who had donated fifty million dollars to the UN.

Thank you, God, Mark thought. "No need for you to apologize, Ms. Reynolds. I could see why you'd think that's why I was calling. Fifty million dollars is an unbelievably generous gift." Mark recovered quickly. "You must be very proud of your . . . grandfather?"

"Yes, my grandfather, and, as a matter of fact, I am." Tracy responded. "But if that's not why you're calling, then what can I do for you?"

"You know, now that I'm talking with you, I wonder if our show should be doing a piece on him. It's not often a private citizen is so generous to the United Nations."

"You're being very kind, but I know that's not why you called, so please don't patronize me, Mr. Taylor." Tracy's voice stayed pleasant, but there was no mistaking her annoyance.

I'm not getting off on the right foot, Mark thought.

"Please don't think I'm patronizing you." He felt an urgency for her to understand. "I'll be honest with you. I just heard about your grandfather's announcement, and I didn't connect your name with his until you mentioned it. You're probably thinking if I was worth anything as a reporter, I'd know who I'm calling, right?"

Tracy smiled; at least he seemed to be honest.

"Well, the thought did cross my mind. I'll tell you what, Mr. Taylor, why don't we start over, and we'll see where this leads, OK?"

Mark let out a sigh of relief. "I'd love to do that." Pausing for effect, he continued, "My name is Mark Taylor. To whom am I speaking please?"

Tracy couldn't stop herself before a giggle escaped. "My name is Tracy Reynolds, Mr. Taylor. I'm the vice-president in charge of media relations for ARI. How can I help you?"

"Well, Tracy." Mark was enjoying himself now. "May I call you Tracy?"

She couldn't resist joining in the game. "I guess that would be all right, if I can call you Mark."

"Excellent, please do. I'm a reporter with *Across the Nation* on the National network, and the reason I'm calling is to research a story I'm preparing on polling. It's come to my attention that ARI is one of the leading companies in the field, and I was hoping I could arrange some time with you or someone on your staff to help educate myself on the process."

"I think that can be arranged. What's the angle of your story?"

"I'm not quite sure yet. It seems to me that more and more our culture is being inundated with the results of public opinion polls. I thought I'd take a look and see if there's a story."

"Well, as far as a story for your TV show, it may not be all that exciting. We're just a bunch of researchers here. But you're welcome to come take a tour of what we do, if you like."

"That would be wonderful. Would tomorrow be too soon?"

Tracy looked at her schedule for the next day. "I've got a fairly busy afternoon. Would ten in the morning work for you?"

Mark jumped at the chance. "Ten would be perfect."

"Do you need directions?"

"No, I'm sure I'll be able to find you. And by the way, Tracy, what your grandfather did was pretty spectacular."

"Why, thank you, Mark," Tracy said with a smile. She liked the way he'd casually brought the conversation back around to where they'd started. "I'll be looking forward to meeting you tomorrow."

"As will I. Have a nice day."

NATIONAL STUDIOS
3:15 P.M. PACIFIC

The small conference room set aside for the staff of *Across the Nation* was just that—small. There was barely enough room for an oval table with six chairs placed around it. In one corner a credenza held a small monitor and a VCR. Samantha Steel, her producer, Jeff Edwards, and their computer expert, Peter

Lovil, sat around one end of the table, working intently over Peter's portable computer.

"We can put your head shot here." Peter was explaining the design for Sam's Internet page. "Now when someone moves their mouse over it, the border will gleam, and I can make you smile—letting them know that if they click on it, we'll send them to your pictorial. And when they do, with this program, I'll be able to add some great sound effect or music as the screen changes. Cool, huh?"

Sam was growing impatient with all the technical elements. "Look, Peter, you know more about this than we ever will. Can't you just design the site—giving it all the latest bells and whistles that you think appropriate—then we can make small adjustments when we see the finished product?"

Peter lowered his head dejectedly. He couldn't understand why Samantha and Jeff weren't more excited. "If that's what you want, sure," he responded, "but you're missing out on all the creative parts."

"That's OK, Peter," Sam said, placing her hand over his arm. She felt as if she were back in high school, flirting with the class nerd just to get the answers she needed on an algebra test. "That's why we have you with us—to make this project come alive."

Peter broke out into a cold sweat. His glasses slid down over his nose. He broke the contact to reach up and push them back into place. Beautiful women always made Peter nervous, and Samantha was definitely no exception. "I'll do my best, Ms. Steel," he said.

"Please call me Sam. We're going to be working together, so we might as well be friends, right?"

Peter nodded nervously.

"If we have the pictures done by Wednesday, when can we get this site up and running?" Jeff asked.

"Once you approve the final design, I'll have it up within twenty-four hours. But to do that you'll have to pick your site name today so I can submit it and have it all ready to go. That takes three to four days."

Sam looked at Jeff. "I hadn't thought about a name, have you?"

"How about samsnudes.com?" Jeff suggested.

Samantha giggled. It was concise and accurate and carried her name. "Sounds good to me, as long as that name isn't already used."

"I'll check tonight. If there's a problem, I'll get back to you. Now in the description I'll add all the buzz words for porno." As he was talking, Peter started typing phrase after phrase of filthy, vile words.

Sam was a bit embarrassed around the two men as the words started filling the screen. "What's that for?"

"It'll guarantee that when somebody is searching for a sexually explicit Web site your page will be included."

Jeff whistled. "Wow, I never knew. We'll make sure legal doesn't see this part, won't we, Peter?"

"Well, some of this language will appear under the heading in the search list, but it's the only way to ensure exposure," he answered.

Sam smiled. The controversy might add to the story. This was working out better than she thought.

"What pictures are you guys going to put on the site besides Sam's?" Peter asked.

Sam and Jeff exchanged puzzled looks. They hadn't thought that far ahead.

Sam finally said, "Tad offered to pose—"

"Look, you've got to have a lot of names offered on a celebrity site to get hits," Peter interjected.

"How would we ever get clearance for that?" Jeff asked dejectedly.

Peter laughed. "Clearance? You think any of those sites have clearance for what's out there?"

"If we have to get clearance for anything from legal, we'll be dead in the water." Sam paused to think. There had to be a way around this. "So let's get them out of the loop." She smiled as she placed her arm around Peter's shoulders. "Peter, this is now your Web site. We'll just be the behind-the-scenes observers of how these sites get created and who visits them."

"That's brilliant!" Jeff was enthusiastic. "Russell will go along with that."

"Ah, I don't know . . ." Peter stammered.

"Don't worry." Sam edged herself closer to Peter, now inches away from his face as she spoke in a sensuous whisper. "We'll make it worth your while. Won't you do it for us?"

Peter tried to think of all the reasons why that wouldn't be a good idea, but the proximity to Samantha made coherent thought impossible. Finally, he just nodded his head.

Sam pulled back slightly, getting back to business. "Now what about analyzing who's looking at the site? How does that work?"

"Well," Peter began, "it's easy to tell you how many hits a day your site gets, what time they log on—all that kind of stuff. The hard part is getting the information on who's hitting you. I'm going to be putting cookies out to everyone who—"

"Cookies? What are they?"

Peter smiled, happy to describe the technique.

"In terms we can understand," Sam added.

Somewhat deflated, Peter continued, "A cookie is a small file we'll be able to place on everybody's computer that looks at your site. It will help us track anyone who hits the site a second time. We'll know what pages they looked at, in what order, and keep a log of everything they do while there. If they answer the survey, all that information will be stored on the cookie as well so we can keep their profile current."

Sam was intrigued, in spite of the techno-babble. This was where she wanted the story to go.

"What about knowing their specifics?" Jeff interrupted. "Their ages, location in the country? Any demographic information we can get will help me with the story."

"That's a lot more difficult," Peter answered. "You'll have those that respond to the survey, but you never know if their answers are truthful, especially from a porno site. I'll run a thorough check on any E-mail addresses we get. See if I can turn up anything."

"The more information, the better," Sam said. "I'm not baring all just for someone's perverted kicks. I want a story here."

Peter sat quietly, secretly looking forward to the pictures himself. "I'll get everything I can, Ms. Steel."

"I'm sure you will, Peter, and thanks." Sam smiled as she placed her hand on his cheek. Peter nearly melted.

Mark was headed to his desk with a cup of coffee as the three made their way out of the conference room.

"How's the new story going, Mark?" Sam teased.

It was going to be a contest between the two, Mark could tell. "I'm still in the research stage, but I'm intrigued with what I've found out already. How about yours?"

"We're just going over the site design." Samantha moved Peter closer to Mark. "This is Peter Lovil. It's amazing what he can accomplish with a computer. Peter, this is Mark Taylor."

"Nice to meet you, Peter," Mark said.

"My pleasure," Peter returned.

"He really is incredible, Mark," Jeff interjected. "If you ever come to a dead end on something you're researching, Peter could probably find what you need."

Peter's face turned crimson.

"I might need that service someday, Peter. Do you have a card?" Mark asked.

"Sure I do," Peter said, fumbling in his pocket and nearly dropping his laptop. Finally, he came up with his card and handed it to Mark.

"Thanks, Peter. I just might be in touch." Mark continued to his desk.

Samantha and Jeff walked with Peter toward the door.

"When do you think you can get back to us with the final design?" Sam asked.

"I could be here Friday if that's convenient."

Jeff looked at Sam. "That gives us tomorrow to worry about the photo shoot. That'd be great."

"Good, then I'll be here. Same time?" Peter asked.

"We'll see you then, Peter," Sam responded.

AMERICAN RESEARCH INSTITUTE
4:21 P.M. PACIFIC

"Here are the phone records you've been waiting for," Cindy said as she entered the small room three floors below Tracy's office.

Kevin Spencer had been paging through the data from a survey conducted last month. He took the papers from Cindy Gardner, his secretary.

"Thanks, Cindy. I hope these will help."

"Why are you wasting your time on this?" she asked. "It wasn't even one of your surveys."

"I know, but Bob asked me to check something out," he lied.

Cindy didn't ask any more questions but made her way back to her desk.

Kevin kept looking through the information on the screen in front of him. It didn't add up. ARI had been sanctioned to do a poll last month on the current public opinion of homosexuality. It had been assigned to Bob Carpenter, another one of ARI's survey managers. It'd sparked his curiosity because most of the social opinion polls were handed to Bob, and the results of this one had surprised him. Between 65 and 75 percent of those polled, according to the information in front of Kevin, endorsed a wide range of homosexual behavior. The questions covered gay marriages, gay adoptions, special protection for sexual orientation in the workplace—that one got a whopping 81 percent approval rating. The numbers seemed impossibly high to Kevin.

He'd joined ARI two years ago, just after completing his master's in sociology from Stanford. Kevin had always thrived on numbers and statistical analysis. One of his earliest memories was counting the checkerboard pattern on the kitchen floor when he was six years old, then telling his mother there were forty-seven black ones but only forty-six white ones. She wasn't impressed.

Kevin took his job seriously, going through every detail of his surveys, making sure at each step that it was as impartial and scientifically accurate as possible. He knew polling was not an exact science. Correct results didn't depend on the number of people questioned, although he always pushed for at least a thousand polled to get into the plus or minus 3 percent range. An accurate poll depended on unbiased questions and an accurate sampling of the target population.

He'd been suspicious of some of the polling results published by ARI for quite some time. The results of this poll were unusual enough to push Kevin into a closer examination. He'd found out that a similar poll had been conducted by a New York firm, Research International, with amazingly similar results—results that Kevin wasn't buying.

He had made a call to the other company, attempting to get any information on how its poll had been conducted. He was unsuccessful and got the standard brushoff that "all data was strictly confidential and not available to the public." He had been shocked when a few days later, he received a follow-up call from someone named Lee. He remembered it well.

"This is Kevin. How can I help you?"

"I understand you called recently concerning a certain Research International poll?" the voice had said.

"Yes, I did. Who is this?"

"Just call me Lee," came the terse reply.

"All right, Lee. I had some questions about a recent poll on homosexuality."

"Those results haven't been released to the press yet."

"I know. Neither have ours," Kevin responded.

"Is this an official inquiry from ARI or something of a personal interest?" Lee said guardedly.

"Oh, this isn't official at all. As a matter of fact, I'd appreciate it if you would keep this call confidential," Kevin answered.

"I understand. What exactly were you looking for?"

"Well, I'm not sure where to start. You see, our company did a very similar poll recently, with pretty much the same results."

"Then I don't understand your reason for calling. Doesn't that validate both polls?" Lee asked.

"I've been looking at the data from ours and . . . This is going to stay just between us, right?" Kevin asked.

"Yes, I promise."

"Well, I'm not comfortable that our poll was accurate. The wording on some of the questions was very leading. So when I heard your results were the same, I wanted to compare notes."

There was a long pause, then finally Kevin heard, "I'll get back to you," and the call was disconnected.

Over the next day and into the following weekend, Kevin tried to find any employees for RI with the first name of Lee. Only two possibilities presented themselves; one was a woman named Leigh Bennington, and the other was Lee Fitzgerald, a janitor. Kevin couldn't imagine that either of them was his mysterious caller.

The second call came early on Monday morning. Kevin recognized the voice immediately. This time, Lee was asking the questions.

"How goes your search into the gay poll?" Lee asked.

"Lee, I'm glad you called back. I haven't had the time to look any further, but my curiosity is still up." Kevin spoke loudly into the phone. It was hard to hear. A lot of traffic noise drowned out Lee's voice at times. He must have been calling from a street pay phone.

"Check the phone logs, compare them to the computer data of the random select phone numbers. Also, look at the questions. See if the survey asked this: 'In light of the fact that homosexuals have made great contributions to our modern civilization, people like: Walt Whitman, Truman Capote, Rock Hudson, Elton John, Greg Louganis, and Ellen DeGeneres, should a homosexual lose his or her job because of his or her sexual orientation?'"

Kevin was floored. "How did you know? We had that exact question." It would be impossible for a poll designed internally within ARI to exactly match the complex question.

"Check the phone logs like I said. I'll get back to you." Lee nearly yelled to be heard over the sound of a truck driving by.

"Wait, how do I get in touch with you? What's your last name?" Kevin tried desperately to get more information.

"You know too much already. Just be careful."

That had been two days ago, and Kevin had not received any more calls from Lee. Looking through the computer data on the survey, Kevin thought everything looked just as it should for accurate random sampling. The program had correctly picked phone numbers from across the country during the three-day time period it took to complete the interview process.

Now with the telephone data in his hand, maybe he could find out what Lee was referring to. He scanned through the rows and rows of numbers called from the phone bank, looking for the exact time and day that the poll in question had started. Then he found it on the fourth page. He scrolled the computer data to the exact date and time of the first phone call and began comparing the two lists.

They didn't match, at least the numbers called didn't match, but the time of each call did. Only about every fourth number on the phone company's records matched the number listed on the computer. Kevin kept scrolling, not believing what was right before his eyes. It was impossible. The computer program randomly selected the area code and prefix to be dialed from ARI's vast data bank of each state's local access prefixes. It then randomly selected the last four digits, a fail-safe way to ensure random sampling. For a nationwide poll such as this, the area codes should display a cross-reference from all over the country. But a quick scan down the list brought Kevin up with a start. He wasn't sure of the exact percentage, but a large number of the area codes on the sheet came from either San Francisco or Miami, two areas known for large homosexual communities and both with decidedly liberal populations.

Who could he go to about something like this? Bob? Certainly not. It was his poll. He was sure to be behind the deception. Who could Kevin trust at the executive level? Who in this company had the expertise to rewrite a program so that the number listed on the computer screen was a completely different number from the one called? He needed to talk with Lee again.

Kevin closed the program and quickly saved it and the new poll Bob was working on to a personal disk. He placed it in his briefcase along with the telephone records.

He had to move; sitting at his desk suddenly felt suffocating. He got up and walked out of his office, passing Cindy without saying a word.

He blindly walked down the hall. He passed by the phone bank, a room filled with people sitting at computer terminals and chatting into their headset microphones. At the end of the hallway, he saw Tracy talking with Bob Carpenter.

He continued walking, but the closer he got the more difficult he found it to breathe. He suddenly remembered what it felt like as a kid when he'd stolen a cookie before dinner, then got caught by his mom before he made it out of the kitchen. But why did he feel guilty? Someone around here should, but it was not him.

He willed himself forward, attempting to act normal. As he got closer, Tracy's secretary rounded the corner from the opposite direction.

"Tracy, I just heard," Brenda was saying as she approached the two. "The president of Research International died Monday night."

Tracy gave Brenda a surprised look. "What happened?"

At the mention of Research International, Kevin stopped and casually stood by the group, hoping to look innocently drawn into the conversation.

"Evidently, a heart attack. He was working late. They found him the next morning slumped over his desk. Guess who's taking over?"

Research International was one of ARI's closest competitors, so any upheaval in the RI organization was of interest to Tracy. She pondered the question, then suggested, "You're not going to say Mike Palmer, are you?"

"The one and only," Brenda replied.

"Oh no!" Tracy reacted, "He's such a—" She remembered Bob and Kevin were standing with them. "Well, let's just say we'll now stand alone as the most respectable research firm in the nation."

Bob laughed, and Kevin tried to join in with a chuckle.

"So he bends the rules slightly, huh?" Bob asked, which Kevin thought ironic. "By the way, who was the president?"

"Leeland Dawkins," Tracy answered as Kevin's face turned ashen white.

CHAPTER 4

Mark sneaked quietly into the control room as the final moments of the *Harold Show* were being recorded. Shania Twain was on the screen singing her latest hit. Rick sat in front of six different black-and-white images generated by the cameras in the studio.

"Shot thirty-five on one," Chad, the associate director to Rick's left, called out.

"Ready one. One!" Rick counted off with a snap of his finger to the beat of the music. The image on the color monitor above switched to camera 1's close-up of Shania.

"Thirty-six on six," Chad prompted.

"Here we go, Chuck. Start your move. Ready six, six!" Rick snapped again and just as Shania finished her last lyric, the image of the drummer filled the screen. The camera pulled back, sweeping past Shania as she countered the move with the upstage walk, ending in a beautiful wide shot as all the lights focused on her in a magnificent ending.

"Great job, Phil. The lighting's super. Ready one, one!" Rick snapped again, placing Shania's close-up back on the screen.

"Ready five, five!" The reverse shot showed the audience members rising to their feet in a standing ovation as John Harold, the show's host, came walking into the frame to thank Twain.

"Ready two, give me a two-shot, two!" Rick called as John went into his closing copy.

Mark watched from the back in fascination. Before long, the credits were rolling, and Chad was counting them to black.

Rick thanked everybody, then realized that Mark was standing in the back.

"Mark, good to see you. How long have you been there?"

"Long enough to be impressed. I'll have to come in and watch a complete show sometime. I didn't realize what you guys go through in here. Our show is so cut-and-dried."

"Well, you're welcome anytime." Rick laughed, "This show is a little different from yours."

"Yeah, we just sit at our desks and talk. This is much more exciting."

The door opened behind Mark, knocking him forward a couple of feet.

Cassie stepped into the room. "Oh, I'm sorry, Mark. I didn't realize you were in here."

"That's OK. That's what I get for standing in front of a door."

Cassie looked at Rick. "Great show. I really liked the lighting at the end of Shania's second song."

Rick smiled, so had he. "I'll tell Phil you said that. Thanks."

Then from the hall they could hear, "What an awesome show! You guys did a wonderful job on Shania." John Harold walked in as he talked. "She looked like a million bucks."

"Thanks for the compliment. I'll pass it along," Rick responded. "John, this is Mark Taylor, a friend of mine and a reporter on *Across the Nation*."

"Hi, Mark. Seen your show. Love it," John said, extending his hand.

Mark shook it. "Thank you, I'm a big fan of yours as well. I was also admiring Rick's performance in the booth tonight."

"We're lucky to have him. He does a great job," John said, finishing the handshake and slapping Rick on the shoulder. "Well, we've got that sponsor dinner. I'll see you later."

"'Bye, John." The three seemed to say in unison.

Cassie looked at her watch. "I've got to get to that dinner too. You're still not going, Rick?"

"No, I'm sorry, Cassie. Mark and I have plans."

Cassie shook her head disappointed. "I'll miss you. Good to see you, Mark."

"You too, Cassie," Mark returned.

"'Bye, hon," Rick said reaching over and kissing her lightly before she turned to leave. "Have a good time."

She turned around as she paused by the door. "At a sponsor dinner? Sure!"

"I hope I didn't interrupt your plans tonight, Rick." Mark spoke as Cassie made her way down the hall.

Rick laughed quietly, "No, it's perfect that you're here."

"Well, I don't want to be in the way. You've got quite a girl there."

Rick looked down the hall, making sure Cassie was gone. "You've got that right."

Rick stepped back into the room, leaned close to Mark, and lowered his voice. "I'm glad you're here. It gave me the perfect excuse not to go with Cassie, but I've got something I forgot to tell you about. If you don't mind, could we hang here for a little bit and chat? I've got a little project I'm working on that I need to put together."

Mark found himself lowering his voice as well, "OK, but why are we whispering."

"Because I don't want Cassie to know. It's kind of a surprise."

Mark nodded. "Oh, that's why you waited for her to leave. It's fine with me as long as I'm not interrupting."

"Not at all." Rick pulled a folder out of his briefcase. "Just make yourself at home. I've got some pictures I've got to take to the stage."

Mark sat down at the back counter and pulled out his organizer. He looked through his notes from the day. It dawned on him he'd never made that call to set up the interview with the right-to-life woman. He searched frantically through his notebook, then he remembered he'd placed her card in his wallet.

There it was—Sara Medford, Right to Life Advocacy Group. The card had her office and home numbers on it. Since it was after six, he tried her home number. He reached her and set the interview up for one o'clock the next afternoon. That way he wouldn't be rushed with his time at ARI. When he went to put her card back into his wallet, he noticed Peter Lovil's card. Mark reached for the phone again and dialed.

"Yeah, this is Peter," he heard after the third ring.

"Peter, hi, this is Mark Taylor from *Across the Nation*. We met this afternoon when you were at the office with Samantha Steel."

"Sure, I remember. What can I do for you?"

"I was wondering if I could hire you to do some research for me."

Mark gave Peter the names of the top three polling companies he had found from his Internet search, asking him to particularly focus on ARI. He didn't know exactly what he was looking for, but Peter might come up with something useful.

He was just finishing the call when Rick stepped back into the control room and dropped back into his chair.

"Make sure the feed to the rest of the lot is killed," Rick told Milton, the technical director to his right. He wanted to make sure Cassie didn't see anything on the monitor in her office before she left for the dinner.

"OK, let's get these on tape so Harold can get out of here. Thanks for staying, Harold. I really appreciate it."

"No problem," the camera operator answered over the headset.

For the next few minutes, picture after picture of Cassie appeared on the monitor—from earliest childhood, through high school cheerleading, to current ones of her working with John Harold.

Mark waited, trying to figure out what Rick was up to. Finally, his curiosity got the best of him.

"What exactly are you doing, Rick?"

"I wondered how long it would take you to ask me," he said, laughing. "I'm producing a little video for Cassie. If I can get this completed, I'm planning to ask her to marry me Friday night over a romantic dinner at my house."

Mark was speechless. He could see that Rick was in total concentration on his project when he asked the audio engineer to cue up a CD he'd given him earlier. Mark smiled and decided to sit back and enjoy the process.

Rick turned back to him. "This won't take much longer. Do you mind waiting? Then we'll get a bite to eat and have a chance to talk."

Mark didn't mind at all. It wasn't too often he got to see behind the scenes of a marriage proposal.

BEVERLY HILLS
6:45 P.M. PACIFIC

Rush-hour traffic had been a nightmare as Tracy wound her way into Beverly Hills. She'd left her office with what she thought was plenty of time to drive to Gioni's to meet her grandfather. Now she was fifteen minutes late. Not being able to judge how long it would take to get across town at any given time was one of the things about Southern California that drove her crazy.

She pulled her silver convertible Mazda Miata into the circular drive in front of the restaurant. The parking attendant opened her car door immediately. The maitre'd met her at the door and escorted her to her grandfather's table.

Jason Reynolds was seated toward the back at his usual table overlooking a lavishly landscaped courtyard. He smiled as Tracy walked up.

She stepped into his warm embrace. "You looked great on TV, Papa."

"Thanks, honey," Jason responded. He helped Tracy into her seat, then took his own. "I really didn't like the whole press conference thing. That was the president's idea."

"I'm sure you must have hated it," she teased. "But if you wanted to give away fifty million dollars, why not give it to your favorite granddaughter?"

He laughed. The view from across the table took him back to when Tracy was five years old, batting her eyes at him so he would buy her that new doll in the store window. That was twenty some years ago, and now she had grown up to be everything he could have imagined, and more.

"I wonder," he said, leaning closer to her face, "if we added up everything I have given you through the years, would it be that far off?"

"Oh, Papa."

"You know, I've always wanted you to learn how to make it in the world on your own," he said proudly. "And you've succeeded marvelously. How are things at the office?"

"Couldn't be better," Tracy answered with confidence. "Things seem to be running smoothly. Oh, I did have an interesting call from a reporter today."

Jason was intrigued. It was her job to interact with reporters every day. "What made this one so interesting?"

"He's doing some research for a story he's putting together for some news magazine show."

"That's odd. Did he tell you what kind of story he was doing?"

"As a matter of fact, I asked him that exact question."

Jason smiled. "Ah, I trained you well, my dear."

"He was pretty vague though, acting like he wasn't sure yet, just doing some early research. I'm meeting him tomorrow morning."

"Well, you be careful," Jason warned her. "I don't like the idea of the press nosing around. You never know what they're really looking into."

Tracy reached over and touched her grandfather's arm. "Don't you worry. I know how to take care of myself. Are you going to be in tomorrow?"

"Probably, but I don't want to talk to your reporter friend."

Tracy giggled. "That's not what I meant. Just wondering if you'd be around."

Jason picked up his menu. "Let's order, shall we?"

HOLLYWOOD
8:12 P.M. PACIFIC

"I'm sorry, Mark, the editing took longer than I thought." Rick apologized as he slid into a booth at Pizza Hut.

"Don't apologize, Rick. I've never been invited to a proposal before. Where did you come up with the idea?"

Rick took a sip of water, then relaxed back against the cushion. "I've been trying to come up with something different. Cassie's sister was flown from Phoenix to San Diego, picked up by a limousine, and driven to the beach where her fiancé proposed to her."

Mark let out a low whistle. "Wow, I see what you mean—tough act to follow."

"Well, I'm going to try."

"She'll be blown away, I'm sure. I'm happy for you, Rick. She's a great girl."

"She hasn't said yes, yet," Rick warned. "But if she does, I'll be the luckiest man alive. Now I've delayed our discussion long enough. Where did we leave off at lunch?"

"I'm not sure. A lot's happened since then."

They were interrupted by their waitress before Mark could collect his thoughts.

"If I remember correctly," Rick finally said, after their order had been taken, "you were about to explain to me why you didn't speak up about your concern with Sam's story."

"Everything in me wanted to," Mark explained. "But as I looked around the room, I realized I was the only one with any reservations. Everybody else was salivating over the potential ratings." Mark lowered his head. "When our executive producer asked me if something was bothering me, I chickened out, as I always do. I guess I was just afraid."

"Afraid of what?"

Mark paused to think. He'd never analyzed it. What was he afraid of? "I guess being singled out, looking foolish."

"Was your objection to the story purely journalistic, or was there a moral objection as well?"

Mark looked away, unsure of how to respond. After a short moment, he looked back at Rick. "Both, actually."

"Mark, you're a Christian, right?"

Mark smiled sheepishly as he nodded. Rick realized that this was a part of Mark's life he kept to himself.

"I certainly understand your fear," Rick said. "There was a time not that long ago when I felt the same way. I remember feeling embarrassed when a friend of mine prayed over lunch. You might know him—Gary Hall?"

The name wasn't familiar to Mark as he shook his head.

"He's a great guy. I'll have to introduce you sometime. Anyway," Rick continued, "looking back on it, I'm sure fear had something to do with the embarrassment. I was afraid to look stupid or out of place. But I think I was most fearful of being labeled a right-wing fanatic in this town."

"That's it!" Mark exclaimed. "I've always felt that if I speak out about my Christian convictions, I'll be branded for life and not respected as a journalist."

"You're not alone on that, Mark," Rick explained. "That's the reason there are so many closet Christians in Hollywood."

"I know," Mark agreed. "The gays came out, and the Christians walked right in." The two chuckled.

"It was easier to talk about God in the Marines during Desert Storm than it is in this town," Mark continued. "It's starting to remind me of what it must have been like being labeled a communist during the height of the McCarthy hearings."

Rick laughed, which took Mark by surprise.

"It's not that it's funny," Rick explained. "It's just that you've made a very accurate comparison. Scary but accurate. I'm glad we're on the winning side though."

Mark smiled. "Me, too, but you'd never know it in this town."

"Oh, don't be too sure about that. Have you ever heard of CIFT?"

Mark gave Rick a questioning look as the waitress set pizza on the table. Rick placed a piece on a plate for Mark, then took one for himself.

"Well, let me pray for the dinner, and I'll explain it to you."

The two bowed their heads as Rick prayed. Then he continued, "CIFT stands for Christians in Film and Television. It's made up of people in our industry who meet in small groups once a week to encourage each other, pray, and study Scripture. It's been unbelievably helpful to me, and I've met some wonderful Christians I never knew in our field."

Mark's face brightened. Maybe he wasn't alone after all. "That sounds interesting. I wish I'd known about it before."

"I'm sorry, I should have invited you sooner, but I didn't realize that you were a Christian."

"I guess I've gotten pretty good at hiding it," Mark laughed nervously.

"I understand. I used to be the same way," Rick reassured him. "But as my relationship with the Lord has grown this past year, so has my boldness."

"How did you get over the fear of what people would say about you?"

Rick thought for a moment. "I'm not sure I ever did. I think for me it comes down to a change that happens in here." He pointed to his chest. "The closer I get to the Lord, the more I see his work in all areas of my life. It's become natural for me to talk about that, to share my faith when somebody questions me, to speak up when I feel there is a stand to take."

"So you didn't go around carrying a fifty-pound Bible and wearing a two-foot cross around your neck?" Mark asked.

"No, I never felt that was for me. People in our profession have seen it all. They don't need another example of something flashy without the substance behind it. They're starving for something real. I just want to be an example of somebody doing their best to live out the life Jesus calls us to."

Mark nodded but still struggled with the right course of action. "Then tell me how you know when to stand up and fight and when to keep quiet?"

"I think we have to listen to what God is saying at the moment," Rick answered. "There are some things that I may not approve of on our show, like John using some of his colorful language, but I don't fight it. We're a late-night show, and in this day and age, it kind of comes with the territory. But there are other times when I voice my opinion strongly.

"I remember when Madonna came out with a new video last September. As usual, it was very sensual. The writers had written me into an opening where the top of the show is all messed up. Then John walks into the control room, and I'm supposed to be there with a bunch of guys leering at Madonna's video—the reason we weren't doing our jobs. I respectfully told them that I wasn't comfortable with the bit, and with some fervent prayer and Cassie's help, we were able to kill it."

Mark nodded thoughtfully.

"There might even be times when we'll have to put our jobs on the line," Rick added. "Something so convicts us that we'd be willing to walk away from the show before we'll allow it to be produced. I thought about it once, but, fortunately, I haven't had to make that strong of a stand, yet. But I know some who have."

"Wow!" Mark sighed. "What was your story?"

"Two years ago I was directing a daytime talk show, and one show was going to be about couples having sexual problems. They booked a sexual therapist to give them advice. Our producer thought it would a great hook to have the couples sitting on the end of beds we decorated the set with as they discussed whatever problems they were having."

"Sounds like a good daytime gimmick," Mark smirked.

"Oh, it gets worse," Rick smiled as he continued. "The day before, as we were running down the format for that show, the producer was giving me the history of each couple. When he got to couple number four, he said it was going to be Bill and Tom."

Mark had been taking a sip from his Pepsi and almost choked. "What'd you do?"

"I wasn't walking as close to the Lord back then. It was just after Connie's and my divorce, but I still knew it wasn't something I wanted to help put on the air. It was ironic too. The show was produced by a company that was known for its family entertainment, so I tried to bring that point up to the producer. Did he really think that having a gay couple discuss their sexual problems while lying on a bed would be in the best interests of the company?"

"Did that work?" Mark asked.

"Not in the least. He just shrugged off my suggestion and proceeded to tell me what a great show it was going to be. I wasn't getting anywhere, so I had to let it go." Rick lowered his head. "I was new to the show, so I knew I couldn't get away with the drop-the-gay-couple-or-I-quit demand. That would have probably gotten me a quick lawsuit for breach of contract. So I did the only thing left open for me; I went home and prayed about it that night."

Rick had Mark's full attention when he glanced back up and continued.

"I showed up for work the next day fully expecting to be very frustrated, but during the first production meeting I found out that Bill and Tom were replaced by Dave and Suzy. After the meeting I asked what had changed, and the producer told me that the executives at the parent company gave him an ultimatum. He could keep the beds or keep the gay couple, but they wouldn't go with both. He was so upset about it that he canceled Bill and Tom.

"I was so relieved, but now that I think back on it, I didn't give God the credit he deserved at the time. I recognize now that he answered my prayer that night. It was a true miracle."

Mark smiled. "I would say so. That's an incredible story."

"Decisions like that and the one you're facing help make our profession that much more interesting," Rick continued. "Christians all over the world have to deal with moral issues in the workplace. Maybe they're asked to lie for the boss or do some creative billing for some project. They deal with the same struggles we do. It's all a matter of seeking God and following his direction in where we draw the battle lines."

"Well, I feel like I've come to one of those times to speak out, but I'm not quite sure how."

"I don't have a journalism background, so I'm not sure I should be the one to advise you. Have you tried to go about it with a purely journalistic argument?"

Mark nodded. "I already tried that with Russell after the pitch meeting."

"Didn't work, huh?"

"No. I got this wonderful speech from him about journalistic integrity and ratings. The bottom line was if people aren't watching the show, there's no point in worrying about integrity anyway. All in all, a pretty cynical view."

"But one I'm sure is shared by most of the executives we deal with." Rick sighed as he spoke. "You're in a tough spot."

"Yeah," Mark said meekly, "I'm sick and tired of letting things slide when I know I need to speak up for what is right."

"Then I would recommend you study Acts 4 and look at what happened to Peter and John."

Mark tried to recall the story Rick was referring to but couldn't come up with it.

"Peter and John were placed in prison in the days of the early church," Rick said. "They were warned by the high priest and those in authority not to speak or teach in the name of Jesus. But upon their release from prison, they went back to their people and praised God. Verse 29 has recently become one of my favorites. 'Now, Lord, consider their threats and enable your servants to speak your word with great boldness.'"

"That sounds like my new prayer," Mark said.

"All right, Mark, that's the spirit," Rick laughed. "And it also helps to know that you're not alone. I think you ought to seriously consider joining us at one of the CIFT meetings."

Mark didn't have to think twice. "I'll be there."

Rick grinned. "Great! Our next one is tomorrow night. You can ride over with me after the show if you want."

CHAPTER 5

The baby started crying before Vanessa pulled the bottle of formula from the pan of water on the stove. In the rush to get to her child, the bottle slipped through her fingers when she tried to screw on the top. The contents spilled all over the kitchen floor.

"Hold on, Shelby," she called out as a tear slid down her cheek. "Mommy's coming."

Vanessa ignored the mess around her feet, quickly filling another bottle and placing it into the pan of hot water. She walked into Shelby's bedroom and pulled her from the crib as she mentally calculated how long it would take for the second bottle to warm up.

"It's OK, honey, it's OK. Mommy's here now." She said as she held the baby against her chest. The closeness comforted Shelby. Her crying subsided.

She was seven months old, Vanessa's only daughter and her reason for being alive. Shelby was the one good thing to come out of Vanessa's past of prostitution, pornography, and drugs. The fact that she couldn't identify who the father was didn't dampen her love for Shelby. The pregnancy had been Vanessa's wake-up call.

Having been raised by an alcoholic mother and an abusive stepfather, Vanessa ran away at the tender age of sixteen, winding up in Hollywood looking to make it big in the movie business. The only break she received had been in pornographic movies—the life Vanessa walked away from in order to try and give little Shelby everything she had missed.

Life wasn't easy raising Shelby alone and working full time while trying to attend night classes to get her GED. Nights like this when she came home from her waitressing job, exhausted, she just wanted to plop into a hot bath. Instead, she was dealing with her fussy child.

Vanessa walked through the tiny apartment, gently bouncing Shelby and waiting for the minutes to pass. On her third trip into the kitchen, just as Shelby was gearing up for another crying fit, the bottle was warm enough. She walked over to the rocking chair; it was either that or a second-hand couch with the broken springs sitting next to it. She sat down, placed the bottle in Shelby's mouth and started rocking. The baby let out a happy coo as she began sucking in the formula.

Vanessa leaned back with a sigh as her head hit the back of the rocker. Calculating her tips added to the minimum wage the restaurant paid her, she took in roughly fifty-five dollars for her six hours of labor. Subtracting the cost for Shelby's day care, that left her with only twenty-eight dollars for the night's work.

Frustration rose up within her again. She could have made twenty times as much working the street.

Before the despair could take hold, Vanessa reached for the Bible sitting on the table beside the chair. She opened it to Psalm 34 and read her favorite passage:

> *Turn from evil and do good;*
> *seek peace and pursue it.*
> *The eyes of the Lord are on the righteous*
> *and his ears are attentive to their cry;*
> *the face of the Lord is against those who do evil,*
> *to cut off the memory of them from the earth.*
> *The righteous cry out, and the Lord hears them;*
> *he delivers them from all their troubles.*

She hugged Shelby a little closer as her eyes watered. The words brought a sense of peace in the midst of her despondency. God, deliver me, she began to pray before she was interrupted by the phone.

"Vanessa, it's me Jill. How's it going?"

"It's been one of those days, but I just read an encouraging psalm," Vanessa answered. Jill and her husband, Gary, had taken Vanessa into their home when she'd made the decision to keep Shelby. Jill had been the counselor when she'd walked into a crisis pregnancy center. Vanessa had been in the apartment and on her own for only a couple of weeks.

"I'm glad Scripture is helping. How's Shelby? We miss you two around here."

"She's doing fine. Just giving her a bottle."

"I miss being able to do that. Actually, that's why I'm calling. Can you come over for dinner Friday? Gary was just saying how the house seems empty without you two."

Vanessa smiled. Being on her own seemed like the right thing to do, but she missed Jill and Gary too. "I'd love to. But I have a class until six, so I can't get there until about six-thirty. Is that OK?"

"That's fine with us. Why don't you just stay the night? That way you won't have to worry about getting Shelby home early."

"That sounds wonderful, Jill. I'll see you then."

"Great, Vanessa. Hang in there. We'll be praying."

"I will. And thanks for calling."

She hung up as Shelby finished the bottle. She placed it aside and turned Shelby over her shoulder and started lightly patting her back. Thank you, Lord, for Jill, she thought, continuing her prayer.

NEW YORK CITY
11:42 P.M. EASTERN

Luis Thorton stood at the bar, his body moving rhythmically to the throbbing bass overpowering the room. He was making progress with the blonde sitting on the stool next to him.

"So what kind of work do you do?" She yelled to him over the loud music in the popular night spot.

Luis leaned in closer so she could hear him. "I'm a security consultant." He could see the puzzled look cross her face. "I work with Fortune 500 companies, making sure they have safeguards in place to prevent corporate espionage, protecting their executives, that kind of thing."

The young woman smiled at the phrase "Fortune 500." It was one of Luis's favorite pickup occupations—close enough to the truth that he didn't have to concentrate when questions were asked and impressive enough to get the response he just witnessed.

"That sounds like interesting work. You must travel a lot." Her hand reached over and lightly rested on his arm.

Luis broke into a grin. He wouldn't be alone tonight. Before he could respond, the cell phone in his pocket vibrated. He pulled it out, apologizing for the interruption.

"Luis, we've got a breach into one of the programs at ARI." He strained to hear the voice on the other end.

"Do you know who?" he asked, anger instantly flaring in his eyes. The woman next to him took notice of the instant mood change. She reached for her wine glass with a grin. She loved the passionate type, even with the risks involved.

"Not yet, but someone's been looking back through the gay poll."

Luis swore. He thought his problems had ended with Dawkins's death. "I'll catch a morning flight. See what else you can find out before I get there." He punched off the line.

"Sounds like you're traveling again, doesn't it?" the blonde asked tentatively.

"Yes, but there are plenty of hours left to fill. Let's say we go find ourselves someplace a little more private," Luis suggested, placing a couple of twenties on the counter to cover their drinks.

The blonde responded by gulping down the rest of her wine, then she slipped her coat over her shoulders and grabbed her purse. Luis's anger quickly faded, forgotten until morning. He had something more important to do.

STUDIO CITY
10:32 P.M. PACIFIC

"Welcome home, girl," Amy called out to Cassie as she stepped through their apartment door. "Did you have a good time?"

Cassie dropped her purse on the table and slouched into a chair, kicking her shoes off quickly. "I can't tell you how much I hate sponsor dinners."

Amy grabbed a mug. "Would you like some coffee?"

Cassie ran her fingers through her hair. "That'd be great if it's decaf. I need to get some sleep."

Amy grabbed a second mug and filled the two cups. Walking over to the table, she asked, "Was Rick with you?"

"I wish," she answered dejectedly. "He had a good excuse. A friend of his stopped by after the show, and they needed to talk. But I don't think he wanted to go anyway."

Amy sipped her coffee. "Don't let it get you down. Rick's never been the type to enjoy those kinds of things."

Cassie stretched back in her chair. "It's not just tonight. He's become distant. He's been too busy the past several days to spend any time together, and when I ask him why, he just shrugs."

"It's probably just a phase, Cassie."

"No, I think there's something else. He's been talking a lot lately about his past marriage. Does it make a difference in how I feel? Would it be right for him to remarry?"

Amy realized how serious this was to Cassie. She set her cup down and reached her hand out. "How did you leave it?"

"I told him how I felt." Cassie lowered her head. "I believe marriage is sacred and God intends it to be for a lifetime, at least that's what I used to think. When we first started dating, it did bother me. I never imagined myself with a divorced man. But as I've grown to love him, those concerns have slipped into the background." She looked back up to Amy, her eyes watering. "I'm afraid he's decided we shouldn't get married and he's pulling away."

Amy put an arm around Cassie. "I don't think that's it. You two are perfect for each other. I've never seen a couple click like you guys do."

Cassie nodded, smiling through her tears. "I think so, too, but maybe Rick isn't so sure."

"Come on now, don't think negatively. You two have a lot of stress on your relationship working together every day. There's got to be another reason he's pulling back. Just give it some time and some prayer; I'm sure it'll all work out."

Rick settled into his bed, pulling his Bible out of the top drawer of the night stand. He opened it to where he had been reading the night before, and his thoughts drifted back to the engagement video. Cassie had no idea what he was planning. He loved being mischievous, keeping her in the dark. His mind flashed to the first year of his marriage when he'd planned a big surprise party for Connie. The thought brought a smile to his face. Funny, he hadn't had a happy thought about his failed marriage in a very long time.

Would things have been different if he'd been as close to the Lord then as he was now? He couldn't say. No one could.

His job had taken control over his life, leaving Connie and the kids in distant second place. He couldn't even recall what position God held in his life back then.

Sure, he had been doing the church thing, religiously. But looking back on it now, he knew he hadn't had a true relationship with Jesus.

He looked down at the Bible in his lap.

> *Therefore, if anyone is in Christ, he is a new creation; the old has gone, the new has come! All this is from God, who reconciled us to himself through Christ and gave us the ministry of reconciliation.*

He scribbled 2 Corinthians 5:17–18 onto the tablet he kept with his Bible. Rick had been doing a topical study on divorce. He'd closely read the accounts of Matthew 19 and Mark 10 in which the Pharisees had questioned Jesus about the subject. He had written Matthew 19:9 on the pad and circled it the night before: "I tell you that anyone who divorces his wife, except for marital unfaithfulness, and marries another woman commits adultery."

He knew from his study that the Word of God was very clear about the issue. God hated divorce. "Therefore what God has joined together, let man not separate," Matthew had written earlier in the chapter. But what could he do? He couldn't turn back now, even if he wanted to. Connie had left him for someone else. She was remarried, living out her new life. There was no way to put their lives back together again.

Rick held onto verse 19 like a lifeline; marital unfaithfulness certainly described Connie's behavior. He read 2 Corinthians again: "If anyone is in Christ, he is a new creation." Another thread of hope. Did his new life in following Jesus mean that he had a clean slate before God? Did that include divorce? He wasn't sure of the answer, but he wanted it to be true. The old Rick was gone, that was for sure. "Now the new has come." Rick so desperately wanted that to include Cassie.

He laid his notepad down, closed his eyes, and leaned his head back as he prayed.

BURBANK
11:15 P.M. PACIFIC

Across the Valley Mark sat alone in his living room and flipped through the channels. It took him three times through, glancing at all 112 cable channels before he realized there was nothing worth watching. Besides, his mind was elsewhere. He kept going over his conversation with Rick, and how weak his witness had been at work. He turned off the television and picked up his Bible. What was that Scripture Rick had referred to with Peter and John? Somewhere in Acts.

He flipped through the New Testament until he found Acts chapter 3 in which Peter and John healed the lame man outside the temple. The reaction brought a crowd around them, and they proclaimed boldly the message of Jesus. In chapter 4, the high priest and the leaders of that day didn't like it much and had them placed in jail for the night.

Mark shook his head. Here Peter and John are placed in prison for speaking out. What was he worried about? The people at work not liking him? Being labeled a right-wing fanatic? The worst that could happen might be a personal rejection, but life would go on. Not a very favorable comparison to what the disciples faced.

Mark continued reading, marveling at the way Peter and John worshiped God after just being released from prison. They didn't shy away from the warnings and threats from the high priest, but they asked for an even greater boldness. "Now, Lord, consider their threats and enable your servants to speak your word with great boldness. Stretch out your hand to heal and perform miraculous signs and wonders through the name of your holy servant Jesus."

He looked up at the ceiling of his small apartment, contemplating what he'd read. His thoughts wavered between conviction and condemnation as he analyzed his own life. Condemnation seemed to be winning as Mark's depression deepened. After a moment, he prayed.

Lord, I need this boldness. Please forgive me for the times I've stayed quiet, even running from situations that would reveal to others that I'm a Christian. I'm embarrassed to compare my life with that of Peter and John.

As Mark prayed, he recalled that not long before that moment Peter had denied Jesus, not once but three times, the night Jesus had been crucified. The condemnation vanished as Mark realized that Peter wasn't perfect either. The Lord used imperfect vessels, just like Peter and just like Mark Taylor. The conviction remained, pressing Mark forward in his prayer.

But Peter denied knowing you three times, Lord. You forgave him and he received this wonderful boldness to proclaim your gospel. Please give me that same boldness. Mark looked down at verses 29 and 30. Lord, consider whatever repercussions there would be in my situation and enable me to speak your word with boldness through the name of your holy son, Jesus. Amen.

He closed the Bible with a smile, wondering how God would answer that prayer in the coming days.

CHAPTER 6

THURSDAY, FEBRUARY 8
NATIONAL STUDIOS
9:40 A.M. PACIFIC

"In the fifth segment, Chris Rock will come out and do four and a half minutes of stand-up." Rick spoke to the production staff gathered in the conference room as he glanced down at the rundown for the day's show. "Hopefully, we won't have to bleep anything after the show. Chris will cross to the couch and interview for three minutes. It's doubtful Tom Cruise will hang around that long, so we imagine it'll just be John and Chris. The final segment is good nights and credits."

"OK, everyone," Cassie said. "We'll go over the monologue material at eleven when John gets here. Let's get to it."

The staff members quickly dispersed, heading for their desks to begin their assigned tasks for the day.

"How was the dinner last night?" Rick asked Cassie as they made their way through the doorway.

"You didn't miss much," she answered a little more sharply than intended. "I can't think of a more boring way to spend the evening."

Rick smiled as they walked, happy to have had other things to attend to. "Hollywood, pretty glamorous, huh?" he teased.

"I should assign you the rerun editing this summer for not coming with me," she shot back with a laugh.

Cassie stopped as they reached her office. "Hey, you've got a light day without having any music. What do you say we get away for a nice lunch for a change?"

Rick tensed. He'd looked ahead at their schedule and saw that there wasn't a musical guest on the show. That meant he didn't have any afternoon rehearsal, so he'd scheduled a remote crew to go with him to Griffith Park during lunch to videotape his part of the proposal.

"Ahhh," Rick stammered, trying to think up a plausible excuse. But nothing came to mind. "I can't, Cassie. I've . . . already got plans."

In a flash her expression said it all—anger, frustration, and especially hurt.

"Look, I promise I'll make it up to you. Tomorrow night after the show. Just you and me."

"Don't bother, Rick. You're obviously too busy." Then without another word she stepped into her office and closed the door.

It happened so fast that Rick didn't have time to respond. She'd never been like this with him before. Now what was he going to do? He'd planned everything for Friday night.

He turned and headed for his own office, glancing around the room to see if anybody had noticed their conversation. Tina, Cassie's assistant, glanced up from her computer with her eyebrows raised. Rick smiled nonchalantly, then made a beeline for his door. Office secrets were hard to keep. He decided to continue with his plans and hope that she'd calm down before tomorrow night.

On the other side of her door, Cassie leaned against it nearly in tears. *Please, knock on the door,* she pleaded to Rick with her thoughts. *Come after me. Don't leave it like this.*

After a few moments, she knew he had walked away. Then the tears released, sliding down her cheeks. She walked to her desk and took her seat, wiping her eyes with a tissue. Then her fear and anger turned inward. *Why did I respond that way? If I haven't lost him already, that will definitely do it.*

"Cassie," the intercom interrupted her despondency, "John is on line one."

She fought back the tears as she picked up the phone, cleared her throat, and answered with her best professional voice. "Yes, John."

LOS ANGELES
10:00 A.M. PACIFIC

Mark took a moment as he looked up to the top of the magnificent skyscraper, one of the tallest and newest to grace the Los Angeles skyline. He was impressed. It even had valet parking, which was a bit embarrassing when he turned over the keys to his 1987 Honda Civic.

He walked into the marble-tiled lobby and stepped up to the guard station set in front of one of the largest atriums he'd ever seen. He had no idea a polling company would be in such lavish surroundings.

"I'm Mark Taylor. I have an appointment with Ms. Reynolds," he said to the guard sitting behind the counter.

The guard typed the name on his computer terminal, then smiled reassuringly as the screen confirmed Mark's statement.

"If you'll just sign in, Mr. Taylor," the man said as he turned a clipboard toward Mark and handed him a visitor's pass. "Ms. Reynolds is on the sixty-fourth floor."

Mark did as he was instructed, then made his way to the elevator with his visitor badge hanging from his jacket pocket. Expecting to step in alone, he was surprised to see an elevator attendant.

"Floor?" he was asked.

"Sixty-four please." He wondered what other kind of businesses operated from this building. It definitely had more class than any he'd been in before. There must be more to Reynolds Industries than just ARI, he decided. He thought back to the computer expert he'd called for help. He hoped he'd have some information on Reynolds as well.

The elevator dropped him off at a reception area. The woman behind the desk asked him to take a seat while she called Ms. Reynolds.

He was glancing through the latest edition of *Time*. When he looked up, one of the most beautiful women he'd ever laid eyes on was walking toward him.

"Mr. Taylor?" she asked.

He quickly stood. "Mark, please," he responded as they shook hands.

"Then call me Tracy."

He slowly took in the sight before him. She was about four inches shorter than he, sharply dressed in a black business suit, one that accented her trim figure. Her dark hair picked up several reddish shades from the light around the office as it curled around her shoulders. Her stunning face was balanced on either side by sparkling diamond earrings, but the true intensity before him came from her beautiful almond-shaped, hazel eyes.

He unconsciously ran his fingers through his hair, trying to do whatever he could to improve his own appearance.

"I appreciate your taking the time, Tracy," he managed to get out.

"It's my pleasure. Please follow me." She led him down a hallway and into her office.

"What a beautiful view," Mark remarked as she took her seat on the other side of the desk.

"It is on a clear day like this. When the smog builds up, it can be depressing. Now how can I help you?"

Mark took the seat facing her desk. "As I said on the phone, I'm looking into the influence polling is having on the country."

Tracy looked puzzled. "Influence? You might have the cart before the horse there, Mark. We don't influence; we study. Our results are like a barometer of where the country stands."

Mark leaned forward, pulling out his notepad. "Can you explain to me how you get your results?"

Tracy leaned back. "Sure, it's all scientific."

She took Mark step-by-step through the polling process, from planning the survey and deciding on the sample audience and size to the questioning and data analysis. He took copious notes, making sure he didn't miss anything.

"What sample size gives you the best percentage?"

"Obviously the more people sampled the better the percentages. Two hundred people give you plus or minus 8 percent, four hundred, plus or minus 6. For budgetary reasons a lot of polls stay around the six hundred number, which gives you a sampling error of plus or minus 4 percent. We prefer to try and get a full one thousand responses to a poll. That gives a sampling error of plus or minus 3 percent. After that, you have to really increase your number to get any significant changes in the percentages and it becomes pretty much cost prohibitive."

"So you're telling me," Mark asked as his gaze lifted off the notepad and locked onto Tracy's eyes, "that most surveys question around six hundred people, and with those results you're able to get within four percentage points of what 250 million Americans think?"

Tracy smiled and let out a chuckle. "No, that's not really the case, although you're not alone in that misconception."

"Then what does sampling error mean?" Mark asked, confused.

"Let me explain," Tracy said. "It's a statistical projection. It means that if you did an infinite number of surveys in the same way with the same questions, to a sample of six hundred people found the same random way, your result would be within four percentage points of the original survey."

Mark's eyebrows raised. "Wow, I've never heard it described that way before. That's not the way it's presented by the media. I'd say most people look at that sampling error and think that if you asked every person in the country the same question, you'd get the same result, within four percentage points."

"That may be so," Tracy admitted coyly, "but they'd be wrong."

Mark scribbled on his notepad, "deceptive advertising." Then he looked back at Tracy. "You mentioned sampling over a thousand people becomes cost prohibitive. How much does a normal survey run?"

"It varies greatly. In politics, a good accurate poll can cost between fifteen and twenty thousand dollars. But most of our clients want to spend a lot less. That's when you are forced to limit your sample size to get within the budget parameters."

"What kind of polling does ARI primarily do?"

"Oh, you name it, we'll poll it. We range from corporate product testing to political opinion polls and everything in between. We use focus groups, mail-out questionnaires, all sorts of different techniques. But in this day and age of immediacy, we predominately use phone polling."

"Do you have a phone bank on site, or do you farm that out?"

"We do most of our own phone polling here. Although at times we simply are too busy and have to hire outside."

"Can I look at one of your surveys?"

Tracy thought for a second. "I'll have to look back through some of our older questionnaires to find you something. All of the polls are conducted confidentially for our clients."

Mark scribbled another note. Her comment sounded more like language he would expect to hear from a lawyer. "I understand. An older survey would be just fine. I just want to get an idea of what kinds of questions go into one of these. It seems like you never see the actual survey questions reported with the results."

Tracy surprised Mark by agreeing with him. "I've always felt they should be included. I think it's just that the media doesn't want to give up the print space or take the extra time in a televised report to give all the details."

"Then how do we know the questions in the survey weren't misleading or biased toward a certain position?"

"Good question, and the answer is you don't. But that's why at ARI we have poll managers who work with our clients to provide surveys that are as scientifically accurate as possible."

Mark nodded his head.

"How about a tour of the facility?" Tracy asked as she stood from behind her desk. "Maybe it will answer more of your questions."

Mark stood with her. "I'd love that."

HOLLYWOOD
10:20 A.M. PACIFIC

Samantha prided herself on being comfortable with her body and having a contemporary attitude about sexuality, but when the moment came for her to disrobe in front of the photographer, she froze.

Which made her mad.

Where did this sudden sense of shame about nudity come from? She fought off her emotions.

"Wow! This is going to be fabulous!" the photographer exclaimed as she finally disrobed and stepped in front of the lights. The man's admiration boosted Samantha's confidence, making it easier to continue. Sam had talked Russell into hiring one of the leading magazine photographers to do her shoot. He sensed her brief moment of conflict, not uncommon for first-time models, and he was prepared. He walked over to his CD player and hit the play button.

It didn't take long for Sam to get caught up with the music as he began to direct her actions. Any lingering sense of doing something immoral vanished as the shutter began to click one picture after another.

AMERICAN RESEARCH INSTITUTE
10:36 A.M. PACIFIC

Tracy led Mark past the second phone bank. It wasn't quite as large as the first, but it could still hold two hundred operators.

"Wow, this is impressive," Mark said over the noise emanating from the room. He tried to catch some of the questions being asked as Tracy explained how many calls ARI could originate per hour. He'd been surprised by how large the company was. It never occurred to him how many people it would take to conduct a poll.

She led him across the hallway and into a dimly lighted room. A window Mark deducted was a one-way mirror stretched across the entire wall. He could see a group of about a dozen people sitting around a large-screen TV. They each had a small electronic device in their hands as they watched a program.

"A focus group?"

"Yes. They're watching a speech given by one of the candidates for a Senate seat next election. The small box in their hands allows us to record the responses throughout each second of the speech, whether favorable or unfavorable."

"I've sat on the other end of the reports from focus groups like this at the network. It's not a pretty sight. We usually sit back and say you all are nuts as soon as the researcher leaves the room."

"You might be right," Tracy laughed. She guided Mark back through the door.

"What else is in this complex?" he asked as they continued their tour.

"My grandfather owns a lot of different companies," Tracy answered. "Some of them are located in here. The rest of the building is leased office space."

Mark stopped. "With all the opportunities within your grandfather's companies, what made you choose ARI?"

"I've been fascinated with statistics and research ever since I took a sociology class in college. I started working here right out of college."

"You seem to enjoy it," Mark commented. "It's always nice to see someone who thrives on the work they do."

"Thank you. I do, as it seems you enjoy being a reporter."

"It's something I've wanted to do for a long time."

"What got you started?"

"You'll laugh if I tell you," he answered.

"No, I won't," she promised. "Try me."

"Well, I used to watch Geraldo."

True to her word, she didn't laugh. But that didn't prevent her huge grin.

"Hey!"

"I'm not laughing," she explained, lowering her head.

"I'm talking about the days back before his talk show or joining CNBC, back when he was the rebel kid reporter for *20/20*. Now I'm a bit embarrassed about it."

"But it's what got you interested, and you found a career that suits you. We're lucky people."

"I think we are," he replied. "What exactly are your duties around here?"

"Taking people like you on tours," she replied with a laugh. Mark chuckled as well; her mood was infectious. "But there's a lot more to it than that. My official duties mainly lie in communicating with the various media outlets on poll data and analysis."

"Now there's a frustrating job—trying to communicate with the media," he joked.

"They're not all morons," she said. "Some are actually quite nice."

Mark wasn't sure how to respond to that line, but before he thought of something to say, they were interrupted by another employee walking down the same hallway.

"Mark, I'd like you to meet one of our top researchers—Kevin Spencer. He's one of those poll managers I was telling you about. Kevin, Mark Taylor with *Across the Nation*."

Kevin extended his hand. "Nice to meet you, Mark. Are you doing a story on us?"

Mark shook the man's hand. "No, not really. I was doing some research about polling, and Tracy's been kind enough to show me around."

"What's your story angle?" Kevin asked.

"I'm not sure. Still developing it. Something about how important public opinion has become."

Kevin nodded. "I hope the tour has been informative."

"It has. I've learned a lot."

"Well, Tracy's a good teacher. I've learned a lot from her since coming on board."

Tracy blushed behind her smile.

"I won't bother you any longer," Kevin added. "Nice to meet you, Mark."

"Same here," Mark returned as Kevin continued his way down the hall.

"What else can I show you?" Tracy asked.

Mark looked at his watch. He'd have to leave soon to connect with his crew to get to the interview by one o'clock. "I've taken enough of your time already. I really appreciate it."

"It was my pleasure. Let me show you to the elevator."

Tracy led Mark through the maze of corridors until they were back at the reception desk near the elevator.

"Well, if there is anything else you need or any more questions you want to ask, you know my number."

"Thanks so much, Tracy. I'll be in touch," Mark said, already trying to think of a reason to contact her again.

Tracy watched him enter the elevator before turning back toward her office. She smiled as she walked down the carpeted hallway. There was something refreshing about him.

GRIFFITH PARK
12:15 P.M. PACIFIC

The National Studios van turned off Los Feliz Boulevard onto Vermont Avenue and into Griffith Park. Teresa sat in the passenger seat with a video camera on her lap. She and Rick had unpacked the camera at the studio and already had a wireless microphone on Rick so they would be ready to shoot when they found the right spot.

"Where do you want to do this?" she asked Rick.

"I'm not sure yet," he answered. He took the road on the right, circling around the Roosevelt Golf Course.

"I really appreciate you helping me out with this, Teresa."

"I'm glad you asked. I think this is so cool. It's been hard to keep it a secret."

"Hard for you? Cassie's about ready to disown me. I keep making excuses why we can't be together. Like today, she wanted to get off the lot and have a nice lunch."

"What did you tell her?"

"I ran out of excuses. I just told her I already had plans."

Teresa laughed. "That's original."

"Yeah, I know. It went over with her just as well. I hope she's still willing to see me tomorrow so I can play the tape for her."

"You're asking her tomorrow night?"

"Hopefully, if I can get it finished after the show tonight. I just have to add what we're taping here to what we did last night. I'll have to come up with another excuse not to be with her, which could be dangerous. She's ready to kill me already."

Teresa giggled. "Yeah, but once she understands what you've been doing, I think she'll forgive you."

Rick joined in the laugh. "I hope you're right." Then his eyes caught a small pond with a family of ducks paddling by a picnic area. "That looks perfect. Let's go over there."

HOLLYWOOD/BURBANK
12:48 P.M. PACIFIC

Mark pulled off the Hollywood Freeway, turned right on Barham, and headed into Burbank. He'd taken longer at ARI than intended, so he'd called the studio and sent the remote crew ahead. He found it difficult to break away from Tracy. He would have loved to have spent the whole day with her, which surprised him. Usually he was so focused that he didn't often notice the women around him. But something about Tracy broke through that barrier. He shook his head at the thought. She was so far above him—both in looks and economic status—he knew there was no chance for him. But a boy could dream, couldn't he? He laughed.

His cell phone chirped beside him. "Mark here."

"Mark, it's Jennifer. The jury's in."

"What's the verdict?"

"Thirty million!" She exclaimed. "They nailed the creeps. Isn't that great?"

"Wow! I can't believe it. Thanks, Jenn. This will help with the interview."

"Do you want me to meet you?"

"No, I'm almost there. We've got it covered. You keep working on the promo piece."

"OK, but get some good quotes. I'll bet we get the lead story."

Mark punched off the line as he passed Warner Brothers' Studio, then veered right onto Olive Drive. Thirty million dollars for running an Internet site that promoted violence toward abortion providers. He had mixed emotions about it. Although pro-life, Mark didn't condone violence of any kind in expressing his distaste for abortion. But a thirty-million-dollar award for just words on the Internet—that was unbelievable!

LOS ANGELES INTERNATIONAL AIRPORT
12:53 P.M. PACIFIC

The United L1011 touched down with a thump as the pilot hit the runway hard. Luis jerked awake. He'd slept for most of the four-and-a-half-hour flight from La Guardia. He'd never made it back to his own apartment after leaving the bar the night before. The blonde turned out to be quite a catch, one he'd like to hook up with again when he returned.

He stretched in his seat, groaning. Even with the comforts of first class, trying to sleep on a plane left him stiff. He'd have to get to a gym later and work the kinks out of his muscles. But right now he had work to do.

Once they reached the gate, he made his way out of the plane and walked the long tunnel underneath the runway to get to the main terminal. Exiting through the sliding glass door, he was greeted by a pleasant Southern California breeze, a nice change from the icy conditions he'd left in New York. He slipped on his sunglasses and made his way over to Griff, who was waiting for him beside a limousine at the curb.

"I hope you had a good flight," he said as Luis stepped into the back.

"I couldn't tell you," Luis responded coldly. As soon as the driver pulled away from the curb, he got down to business.

"What have you learned so far?"

"Someone is definitely checking the gay poll data. Our technician says it came from terminal 4276—Kevin Spencer's computer."

Underneath the dark lenses, a smile appeared. "I'm glad we put that extra security tap in the computer system." Luis looked out the window at the passing traffic as they made their way down Century Boulevard. "It was Bob's survey right?"

"That's right."

"Do you know why Spencer's looking into it?"

"Not yet. I figured you'd want to find out firsthand. Oh, and there's one more thing." Griff waited until Luis looked back toward him. "We've tracked down one phone call made from Dawkin's office to ARI last week. It went directly to extension 4276."

Griff sat in silence for Luis to react to the number, Kevin Spencer's extension. No reaction was visible from the outside, but inside Luis was fuming. The problem should have been solved when they got rid of Dawkins. Number One wouldn't be pleased.

BURBANK
1:15 P.M. PACIFIC

Mark sat just to the left of the camera and faced Sara Medford. She sat at her modest desk, nervously awaiting his first question. She had never done a TV interview before and wasn't sure how it would go.

"Can we move that picture? I'm getting a glare," the cameraman asked Sara. She looked behind her at the picture on her shelf. It was an artist's conception of a two-month-old fetus—or baby, Sara would call it.

"I'd love for it to be in the background actually," she answered.

Mark looked compassionately at her. "I wish we could, but the glare will affect the picture quality."

Sara moved the frame out of the way. Mark wished she could use it behind her as well; it would definitely make a statement—one Russell probably wouldn't allow. He hadn't thought about it before Donnie had brought it up, but he probably would have caught a lot of flak if it had stayed in the background.

"Don't be nervous, Sara. I just want to get a few comments from you to use in our report. That way we'll have your group's side of the story. Feel free to answer the questions right to me. Try not to worry about the camera at all." Then Mark turned. "Go ahead and roll, Donnie."

After a few seconds, Donnie tapped Mark on the shoulder, letting him know the tape was rolling.

"OK, Sara, what is your group called?"

"The Right to Life Advocacy Group," she answered proudly. "We're just every-day people joined together by a common cause to save the life of the unborn. I head the Southern California chapter. Took over this January."

Mark smiled pleasantly at her. She seemed nervous, and he wanted to put her at ease.

"What position does the pro-life community take on the outcome of this lawsuit?" Mark asked.

"First, let me say that our group doesn't condone violence of any kind when it comes to protesting abortion. Any person who would kill and still call himself pro-life . . . Well, I'm certain that no member of ours would be involved in any way."

Mark nodded. She was already making some good comments.

"Do you agree with the thirty-million-dollar award?"

"Heavens no! That's outlandish. First of all, how are they going to collect that kind of money from these people? And what about free speech in this country? Last time I looked, it was still covered by the First Amendment."

"Do you condone what's on the Web site?"

"Personally, no, I don't. I believe in praying for those involved with the killing of babies, not in harming them or threatening violence."

"How far would you go to stop an abortion?"

Sara thought for a moment. "That's a tough one. We have to answer to a higher law—God's law. It might be necessary to break an immoral law in order to save the life of an unborn baby. But bombings, murder, or violence of any kind are definitely not allowed, by our laws or God's. There are better ways to champion innocent babies than resorting to those things." Then she smiled, "I'll admit I've been arrested for blocking clinics, so there are areas of civil disobedience that I would support in order to save lives."

Mark smiled. That comment would be enough, but she was getting more relaxed so he thought he'd try one more question.

"What would you say to a doctor who practices abortion?"

She surprised him by taking her eyes off him and looking directly into the lens. "Think about what you're doing, ripping the life away from something so young, so helpless, so precious. Please, give them a chance to live. If you repent, God will forgive you. I'm sure of it. But if you don't and continue with your killing, you won't get away with it. God will judge you, not me."

Mark was astonished by the intensity from this woman. Her passion touched him. And she had just given him a great sound bite.

"Thanks, Sara, you've been very helpful," Mark said, breaking the moment. "You can stop tape, Donnie."

Sara blinked, taking her eyes off the camera, bringing her attention back to Mark. "That's all? I'm done?"

"That's it. You did wonderfully."

Sara smiled. "That wasn't so hard." Then her soft eyes took on a look of concern. "I've heard some terrible stories about people doing interviews like this, and then when it shows up on the air, the words are used to mean something totally different. You won't let that happen to me, will you?"

"No, Sara. I promise we'll use the comments you made today just the way you said them. You speak for your cause very well." Then he leaned in and whispered to her so the cameraman couldn't hear. "One I happen to agree with, by the way."

Sara brightened at the comment. "That's wonderful. Then I'm done?"

"In just a second. Donnie needs to get some different angles of you and me talking, so just continue to chat with me."

Mark enjoyed the next few minutes getting to know Sara on a different level as Donnie moved his camera behind her to record the reverse angle as a cutaway for editing. Then Mark asked each question again, this time with his face recorded. That would give them everything needed to piece the segment together.

CHAPTER 7

Samantha arrived at the office shortly after lunch. She'd kept her morning clear to be able to accommodate the photo shoot. It turned out to be a good decision.

The struggle she'd had with her emotions at the studio came back like a flood when she got to her car. She felt dirty, which shocked her; nudity had never bothered her before. From her earliest sexual experiences in high school on into adulthood, she'd always been cavalier about her body. But this had bothered her, and she couldn't figure out why. Instead of heading back to the office, on impulse she'd dropped by her apartment and taken a quick shower. But no amount of scrubbing had removed the dirty feeling.

"How did the shoot go?" Jeff asked as she passed his cubicle.

Sam forced her best smile. "It went great." Then she went into one of her poses. "The photographer thought I was a natural."

"I'll bet he did. When do we get the proofs back?"

"By this time tomorrow."

Tad Forrest overheard as he was walking by. "Did you bare all, Samantha?" he asked.

Samantha felt a quick flush come across her face as she turned and saw Tad behind her. "What would you care? I'm not your type, remember?"

"Funny, Sam. Hey, while I've got you both here, have you decided about using my pictures?" he asked.

Sam and Jeff looked to each other; they hadn't talked about it. "We haven't decided yet, Tad," Jeff responded.

"You might be missing the perfect opportunity."

Sam shrugged.

"Seriously, think about it," Tad continued. "You want to make a big splash with this story. So the more hits your little Internet site gets, the better it'll look, right? Why not enlarge your audience possibilities?"

"Boy, are you full of yourself, or what!" Sam giggled.

"It's not that. I can help bring in two different audiences. First, there's the young female demographic. We all know that's why they hired me around here. Those viewers won't be interested in checking out your body, except maybe to compare." He laughed. "Then there's the gay crowd. We are big into the Internet stuff. That could add a lot of interest, you know."

Sam couldn't argue with him. "What do you think, Jeff?"

Jeff was shaking his head. "As much as I really don't want to see Tad sans clothing, he does make a point. The more people who hit our site, the more impact the story will have."

"Great, then it's settled," Tad said.

"You OK with it, Sam?" Jeff asked.

"I guess." Sam was still trying to figure out Tad's angle. "We'll have to get him set up with the photographer quickly."

"No need," Tad replied as he dropped a manila envelope he'd been holding on Sam's desk.

"You're kidding," she gasped, as she picked it up.

"In journalism, you must always be prepared," he smirked as he walked away.

Sam opened the envelope. An assortment of glossy color photographs dropped in front of her with Tad in all sorts of poses and modes of undress. She looked up to Jeff, who had turned a couple of shades redder.

"I'm out of here," he said. "Pick a couple that you like."

She laughed, then turned back to the pictures with a raised eyebrow. *What a waste,* she thought.

REYNOLDS INDUSTRIES
1:48 P.M. PACIFIC

At his desk high atop the Reynolds Industries building, Jason was rummaging through the latest ARI polling data. He smiled, pleased with the results. The latest numbers were right on target.

"Mr. Reynolds," his personal assistant buzzed in on the intercom, "Mr. Robertson is on line one."

Jason set his papers down and grabbed the phone. "Jack, how are things at the White House?"

Jack Robertson was President McNeil's pollster, the man in charge of keeping the administration in tune with the mood of the American people.

"Fine, Jason, fine. I'm sorry I missed you when you were out here the other day. That was quite a gift."

"It will go to a good cause."

"Yes, it will, and it didn't hurt your image either. We did an overnight on you." Jason's mood quickly darkened. "You're up to a 64 percent recognition factor, with an amazingly high approval rating from those who recognize your name."

"Jack, if I ever hear of my name being on one of your polls again—"

"Oh, don't get your dander up, Jason. It was just something I threw in for fun. The figures will never be released, so calm down. Besides, that's not why I'm calling."

"I didn't think it was."

"We've come up with a great question on this antiabortion lawsuit from our poll last night. We're getting over 70 percent in favor of wanting the Internet site held accountable, and that was before the verdict was reached. With the way we've been sliding in the polls with this issue, the president wants to jump on this."

That was a very high number. Jason knew that the legitimate national average usually split right at 50 percent on abortion issues, and recently, in some polls close to 60 percent were against abortions, except in the extreme circumstances of rape or incest. Of course, those results were never released. The president was right to want to jump on this one, Jason thought.

"How do you have the question worded?"

"Do you think a violently charged Internet site that encourages murder should be held accountable when its propaganda is acted upon?"

Jason let out a low whistle. "That's a good one, Jack. Not even a mention of abortion in it. You say 70 percent, huh?"

"Actually, 74. It's perfect. It plays right into the president's plan on getting back federal funding for abortions, and it should support the language in the UN appropriation bill. This could be big. He wants to get this into the press polls right away."

"I understand, but we've got to be careful," Jason cautioned. "We've been saying for years that entertainment doesn't influence behavior. From TV violence to song lyrics, the standard line has been that those producing it aren't responsible for other people's actions. This kind of poll could come back to haunt us."

"Not with 74 percent on our side." The president's man was confident.

Jason shook his head. It always went this way. Robertson pushed as if McNeil wielded the power while Jason played him for the fool he was. It was always Jason's agenda, not the president's that controlled the polling.

"May I tell the president you're on board with this one, Jason?"

Jason let him sweat a bit longer before answering. "Yeah, I'll spread the word. I'm sure we can have some overnight numbers out by tomorrow."

"Thanks, Jason. You're the best."

"Talk to you soon, Jack. Give my best to the president."

Upon ending the conversation, Jason turned to his computer and typed an E-mail. Within minutes, the approved question generated from within the bowels of the White House would be in the hands of all the major press and television outlets. The hand of democracy at work.

Jason's solitude was once again interrupted by his intercom. "Mr. Reynolds, Luis Thorton is here to see you."

I thought he was in New York. "Send him in."

The door opened, and Luis stepped inside. "Mr. Reynolds," he kept the appearance of formality until the door was closed behind him.

"What are you doing here? I thought you were taking care of the New York problem."

"I think we have another one right here, Number One."

"Don't call me that here," Jason scolded. "You know better than that."

"Sorry."

"Now what's the problem?"

Luis relayed the events of the past twenty-four hours.

Jason swore. "Dawkins talked to Spencer?"

"It would appear so."

"When?"

"The call was made last Thursday. We should have questioned Dawkins before . . ." Luis let the sentence hang.

Jason glanced up at him with a wicked smile. "And miss that touching moment when we all toasted the Circle? Never! Hindsight might always be twenty-twenty, but seeing the expression on their faces when Dawkins collapsed was priceless. Talk about making a point on loyalty!" He leaned his head back and laughed.

"But now it's time again to take care of business," Jason continued without a trace of pleasure left in his voice. "Get Bob Carpenter in here, now!"

Five floors lower, Kevin Spencer stared into his computer screen. He hadn't been able to concentrate since hearing about Leeland Dawkins's death. He'd spent much of the night wondering if Leeland had been his mysterious caller. Kevin called Research International again that morning to make sure there wasn't another Lee or any variation of the name that he had missed earlier. There wasn't. Even if Leeland had made the calls, what did that mean? He died because of a heart attack. Nothing devious about that. But there was something deep down in Kevin's gut that made him think there was.

The voice on the phone had been right. The phone records didn't match the computer on the gay survey. How many other polls could have the same conflict? Could any of the ones he supervised?

He had been up with his wife until early that morning discussing the situation. They both knew that he was way over his head.

Then an idea struck him. That reporter he'd met—what was his name, Mark something from *Across the Nation*. He's looking for a story on polling, and this would be a whopper. If he got hold of this, he'd know what to do. Kevin knew he couldn't be loyal to a company that would falsify data or rig a survey, but he'd have to be careful.

He broke out of his trance, getting up quickly and heading out of the office.

"Where you going?" Cindy asked as he passed her desk.

"I need to clear my head. I'm going for a quick walk. I'll be back in about fifteen minutes."

He walked down the hallway toward the elevator. He had to get to a pay phone. He knew any contact he'd make with Mark would have to be outside the office.

He didn't notice Griff Newton, the head of security for ARI, at the other end of the hall, tracking his every movement.

"So how much does Kevin know?" Jason asked Bob Carpenter as soon as he walked into his office.

"There's no way to be sure." Bob's voice trembled as he answered. "He won't be able to break the program code. He doesn't have the technical skill. But he'll know right away the survey was flawed. He's always on my case about being unbiased—like he's the only one around here with a college degree."

Bob didn't mask his hatred for Kevin.

"Is he checking into any of the other surveys?" Reynolds asked.

"Not that we know of," Luis answered.

"I shouldn't have pushed the numbers up so high on the gay poll. If he starts looking into any of the other stuff . . ." Jason said under his breath, then looked over to Luis. "So what's your plan now?"

"We've got a tap on his phones—home, office, and cell—plus Griff's watching him," Luis answered. "Other than that, it's up to you. Do you want to question him?"

Jason paused. He didn't know Kevin at all. Just one of a thousand employees. Would he try to do something about Bob's survey? What could Leeland have passed on to him last week? If he did question Kevin, would the gain be worth the risk? Reynolds decided he didn't have enough information for a confrontation, yet.

"No. But I want somebody on him twenty-four hours a day. I want to know what he plans to do with this, who he talks to, and where he goes. I want to know when he sneezes. And between the two of you, make sure this never happens again, do you understand? Whatever it takes, I want these surveys kept totally confidential. No one outside of our group sees them."

NATIONAL STUDIOS
1:54 P.M. PACIFIC

After getting back to the office from Griffith Park, Rick checked on any changes that might have come up while he was away. There wasn't much to do on days when the show didn't have any musical guests. The only scheduled rehearsal was at three when John Harold would walk through the monologue for that night. Rick had the monologue in front of him now, and it was fairly straightforward. There were only a couple of pictures to grab from the *USA Today* newspaper.

"Chad," Rick spoke to his associate director sitting with him in the office as he handed over the paper, "would you mind getting these pictures on the still store for me? I'm going to grab Dan and finish my proposal tape."

Chad smirked, "I'd be happy to, but you better make sure Cassie doesn't end up walking back there and find out what you're doing."

"You're right," Rick thought carefully. "I'll have Tina call us if she leaves the office. I'd love to get this done before the show. She won't be too happy if I have one more excuse tonight."

"Well, good luck, partner. I hope this will all be worth it."

"If I get the answer I'm hoping for," Rick answered with a smile, "it'll be worth it."

A few minutes later, Rick walked into the tape room where Dan was reading in a chair.

"Something to do?" Dan asked, getting up as Rick walked over to him. "Wonderful, I hate slow days."

Rick handed him the tape from the park.

"I just need to add this to the video we made last night."

"Oh, personal business," Dan teased.

He popped the cassette into the A machine. Within moments, the machine's heads began scanning the tape, and the image of color bars filled the monitor. Dan quickly tweaked the hue and video level controls to ensure the machine played back the video correctly.

As Rick and Dan worked on the final edit of the videotape, Rick found himself praying silently for Cassie as he watched his performance. *Please, Lord, let her say yes. Let her be as excited about our life together as I am.*

In a moment it was all done. Dan laughed and patted Rick on the back as he asked Milton to fade the tape to black.

"You son of a gun. She's going to eat this up," Dan said.

"I just hope she says yes."

"Cassie's on her way over," Chad said through the speaker.

Rick started to panic. "I hope this didn't get out somehow."

"Don't worry, Rick. It couldn't have."

"Well, I'm getting out of here. I'll need a VHS copy of this when it's safe, Dan. And thanks for your help. I really appreciate it."

"My pleasure. It's the first time I've ever done tape on a proposal video."

Rick quickly exited the tape room and walked up the hall to the control room. He just took his seat as Cassie walked in the room.

"There're some changes that just came up," she said, handing Rick a new run-down. "I didn't expect you to be over here so early. I looked for you in your office."

"Oh," Rick stammered, scrambling to not look guilty. His attempt wasn't lost on Cassie. "I was just trying some new switcher effects we might use on some teases."

Cassie looked over at Milton, who nodded quickly, trying to back Rick up. Something was up, but she couldn't determine what these two were hiding.

"Here's the deal. We just got word that Nicole's going to be here with Tom. We're going to add her to the couch in segment two, everything else moves down, and we're bringing Chris Rock back tomorrow."

Rick glanced at the new rundown. Not that big a change for her to make her way down to the stage early. "Not a problem," he responded. "Do you want to do a tease on her coming out of segment one?"

"No, John wants to make it look unplanned."

"OK, you got it."

Cassie looked around the room once again, trying to figure out why things were out of sort. "You want to show me one of those tease effects you've been playing with?"

She nearly laughed at the look of fear that passed between Milton and Rick. "No, ahhh—we haven't come up with anything we really like yet," Milton finally answered.

Cassie scrunched up her lips as wrinkles appeared above her eyebrows. "OK, well, let me know when you do," she said as she turned to leave.

"Wait," Rick called after her, "let me walk with you for a minute."

He caught up with her, and the two walked quietly the short distance until they stepped outside the studio door.

"Look, honey, I know you think I've been acting strange," Rick said.

"You are acting strange," she responded, her voice nearly breaking.

"You're right, but I want you to know that there's nothing wrong. You have to trust me. I can't explain now, but I will soon. OK?"

Cassie didn't know how to respond. This wasn't like Rick to be secretive. Her heart wanted to trust him, but she was thinking of too many possibilities.

He could sense her internal conflict and gently placed his hand against her cheek. She leaned into it, comforted by his touch.

"Please have faith in me, Cassie. I won't do anything to hurt you."

A single tear broke free as she looked into his eyes. "You'd better not!" Searching for the right words and finding none, she chose to change the mood. "If you do, you'll be looking for a new job."

She leaned into him and kissed him lightly on the lips. She held his gaze with a thin smile before turning and heading down the path toward the office.

Two stages down, Mark and Jennifer were viewing the interview with Sara Medford. As soon as the tape ended, Jennifer looked over at Mark.

"How could you call her group 'pro-life'?" she snapped.

"That's what they are," he answered defensively.

"It's National policy to refer to them as antiabortion."

Mark frowned. He'd never heard that before, but this was his first report on the subject. Jennifer had been around TV news a lot longer than he.

"I'm sorry, I didn't know," he said, not really being sorry.

"That's OK. We can edit that part out. I'll have to watch this a few times, but I think you got what we needed."

"Of course we did," he argued. "Her comment directly to the doctor alone is gold."

"Uh-huh." Jennifer responded without really hearing as she scribbled in her notebook.

Mark let the matter drop, still thinking of the "rule" to refer to pro-life groups as antiabortion. Did the press do that with anyone else? Would an ethnic group take kindly to not being identified by its chosen name? Why would pro-life groups be any different? Then he thought further; evangelical organizations were always referred to as right-wing conservatives or the radical Christian right, yet he couldn't recall ever hearing the phrase "radical left" or "left-wing liberal." The double standard was getting too close to home. What should he do to fight it as a reporter? As a Christian?

Mark laughed in spite of the frustration. These were questions he wouldn't have even asked himself before his talk with Rick.

CHAPTER 8

Vince Sinclair sat with the rest of the Research International staff around the conference table in the president's office. This was the first meeting with the new executive, Mike Palmer, who was gloating in his new position over his former peers and giving out orders as if he were General Eisenhower on D-Day.

Vince didn't care. He wasn't there for the speech. He had a different agenda.

"So we want this poll out now. Get the quick reaction from this huge lawsuit." Palmer was completing his marching orders. "Tim," he said as he slid a folder across the table to one of his research managers, "I want you to run with this one. Get me a quick overnight. You'll find the survey questions already completed in there. Follow them to the letter."

Tim flipped the folder open, nodding his acceptance of the assignment. Vince sat next to him where he got a good look at the top page. He could see a list of questions pertaining to the thirty-million-dollar award slapped on the providers of the anti-abortion Web site. Toward the bottom he noticed one question marked in bold type: "Do you think a violently charged Internet site that encourages murder should be held accountable when its propaganda is acted upon?"

Vince made a mental note. Why would that one question garner such attention? He tried to look further, but Tim closed the folder as the meeting ended. Several executives took the opportunity to gather around the new president, wishing him their best as they positioned themselves for the top assignments.

Vince instead stepped back casually toward Palmer's desk. He glanced around, looking for anything of interest. His attention immediately went to the computer screen glowing softly in the corner. He touched a key on the keyboard, bringing the screen back to life and allowing him a glimpse of what had been there. It was an E-mail, and a quick scan revealed the exact same question that had been typed in bold on Tim's survey. Vince quickly looked at the sending party: CoSN1@csi.com. Topic: Immediate survey.

How careless, Vince thought as he mingled with the rest of the staff to make his best wishes known.

NATIONAL STUDIOS
2:10 P.M. PACIFIC

With the abortion story all but completed, Mark was back on the Internet, researching polling. It was incredible how much importance society placed on the opinion polls. Mark kept mulling over Tracy's definition of sample error. He didn't like what he thought was a blatant deception by the research industry to imply that within the error researchers reported, the survey would stand for the country's entire population when, in fact, it just stood for how accurately they could reproduce the same results. But was that enough for a story? Not yet.

His phone rang.

"Mark Taylor," he answered.

"Mark, hi, this is Kevin Spencer. We met this morning when you were at ARI."

Mark heard cars driving by in the background.

"Yes, I remember. How can I help you?"

"I think I can help you," Kevin replied. "But I've got to have your promise that if I do, I'll be protected. You'll keep my name out of it."

"Not a problem, Kevin. I protect my sources. What do you have?"

"No, not over the phone. We need to meet."

"You name the place, and I'll be there."

"Tonight. There's a driving range on Whitset in Sherman Oaks, just south of the Ventura Freeway. Meet me there at nine. Bring a set of clubs and set up next to me. We'll talk as we hit."

Mark wasn't a golfer. "But—"

"Just be there," Kevin interrupted. "It'll be worth your time." The phone went dead in Mark's hand.

I don't even have a set of golf clubs, Mark thought. Then he remembered Rick was a golfer. He looked up the booth extension for the *Harold Show* and punched in the number.

"Control room," he heard a female voice answer.

"Is Rick Treadway available?" he asked.

In a few seconds, Rick came on the line.

"Rick, hi, it's Mark. You got a second?"

"I sure do. We're just waiting for John to start his rehearsal. Are you still up for tonight?"

"I'm looking forward to it, but I need a favor. You're a golfer, right?"

"Yeah, why?"

"Would it be possible to borrow your golf clubs? I've got a meeting with somebody tonight at a driving range. It would look pretty conspicuous if I didn't have some clubs."

"Sure, they're in my car so you grab them when we drive over to the meeting. What time are you supposed to be at the driving range?"

"Nine o'clock. I figured that would still work out. I'll head there after the meeting."

"You can make an early exit if you need to. I'm just glad you're coming."

"Me too," Mark responded.

"We'll see you after the show then. You'll need your car so just follow me."

"I will, Rick, and thanks."

AMERICAN RESEARCH INSTITUTE
2:45 P.M. PACIFIC

"I followed him out of the office. He went down to the street, found a pay phone, and made a call. Then he stopped at Starbucks and bought a cup of coffee." Griff made the report to Luis, who had taken over his office on the sixty-second floor.

"You didn't get close enough to hear what the phone call was about?"

"He was too far ahead of me. I had to wait for the next elevator, or he would have known I was following him," Griff explained. "I was lucky to actually see him on the phone; he was so quick."

"He must know he's being watched or at least be suspicious. This isn't looking good." Luis thought through the information. In his opinion, it was time to bring Kevin in and find out what he knew, but he had his instructions.

"I'm going to stop by his office," Luis decided. "Maybe I can get something out of his secretary."

A minute later and a floor lower, Luis stepped into Kevin's outer office where Cindy sat behind her desk. Although he was head over security for all of Reynolds's companies, he wasn't a recognizable fixture around ARI.

"May I help you?" Cindy asked as she looked up at the imposing figure.

"Yes, I'm not sure we've met before," Luis answered with an air of authority. "My name's Luis Thorton, head of security for Reynolds International."

Cindy flinched. "How can I help you?"

"Just a routine check, Miss . . ." He looked down at the nameplate resting on the desk. "Gardner."

At the mention of routine, Cindy relaxed.

"There was a request for some information . . ." Luis was fishing, seeing if Cindy would respond as he paused.

"Oh, the phone records," she offered.

"Yes, the phone records," Luis confirmed with a smile.

On the other side of the door, Kevin was listening. The minute he heard voices in the outer office, he'd walked around his desk to eavesdrop.

"Well, Kevin was—"

Cindy stopped as Kevin walked out of his office. He handed her a memo that she'd just placed on his desk moments before. She glanced at it, confused, but Kevin ignored her reaction and turned to address the man whose voice had alerted him.

"Hello, I don't believe we've met. Kevin Spencer."

Luis reached his hand out to accept the greeting. "Luis Thorton, head of security for Reynolds Industries."

Looking into the cold, dark eyes, Kevin nearly crumbled. "It's nice to meet you," he finally said with much greater confidence than he felt. "Is there something I can help you with?"

Luis appraised the enemy before him as he released the handshake. He saw through the fake bravado and knew he could crush him, learning everything in minutes. But this wasn't the time.

"I was just talking with Ms. Gardner here about the phone records . . ." Luis attempted to lead Kevin into his trap.

"Oh yes. What about them?" Kevin replied nervously.

Luis thought for a second. "May I see them?"

"No, they've been returned," Kevin lied. The accounting department had made copies for him. He studied Luis's expression. It didn't appear that he really knew what he was asking about. Kevin certainly wasn't going to help him.

"Fine." Luis couldn't press any further. He'd have to go to accounting himself and find out what records they were talking about. "Sorry to bother you then. Just a routine check."

"Not a problem," Kevin answered, holding back his relief.

Luis turned and walked out of the office, heading down the hallway.

"Kevin, what's going on?" Cindy asked. He turned quickly toward her with his finger over his mouth until he reached out and closed the door.

"I'm not sure, Cindy," he confessed. "But I've touched a nerve somehow." How did the company know he was checking into the gay survey already? He was glad he'd been smart enough to contact the reporter from the pay phone. Then it hit him like a sledgehammer: this was no office spy game.

He was seriously jeopardizing his career, and now having come face-to-face with Luis, he was wondering if he could be jeopardizing his life as well. What if he went to them with what he's found? He might possibly be viewed as the loyal employee finding bias in their surveys. But it wasn't his assignment, so what excuse could he use for being nosy? He shivered as he remembered the darkness he'd seen behind Luis's eyes.

"I'm sorry I've gotten you into this," he said to Cindy. "But the less you know, the better. Just forget about the phone records, OK?"

Cindy nodded, hoping she wouldn't see that man again. Kevin started to walk back toward his office. "Kevin."

He turned back toward her as she handed him back the memo.

He smiled in spite of the tension. "Thanks. I, uh, needed an excuse to come out."

Cindy laughed. "I figured that out eventually. I hope my face didn't give us away."

Kevin chuckled with her. "I guess our little performance won't win any academy awards."

NATIONAL STUDIOS
4:55 P.M. PACIFIC

Mark counted down the minutes until he could get out of the office. He couldn't get the phone call from Kevin off his mind. He nervously rearranged the papers around his desk for the second time.

He hoped Rick's group would calm him down while he waited for the meeting. He looked at his watch again. Wow! Two whole minutes had passed. The phone beside him rang.

"Mark Taylor," he answered.

"Hi, Mark, it's Peter Lovil."

Mark was blank for a second, then he remembered—Samantha's computer expert.

"Yes, Peter, what have you got?" Mark asked, grabbing his notepad.

"Well, not as much as I'd like, unfortunately. Two of the companies were easy to get information on. ARI is run by Jason Reynolds, who owns a wide assortment of enterprises under Reynolds Industries. He's the guy who just gave away fifty million bucks to the UN."

"Yeah, I heard about that." Mark smiled at the memory of his first contact with Tracy.

"Research International is owned by Richard Adler of the Adler Broadcast Group."

Mark jotted the name down on the notepad.

"What's got my interest though," Peter continued, "is that third company, Nationwide Polling. It's ownership is well hidden. So far I've tracked it through three dummy corporations. Someone's hiding something there."

"That's weird. Why would somebody want to hide that they own a research company?" Mark asked.

"You got me. But I don't usually quit searching until I find out. That OK with you?"

Mark wondered how much it would cost, but it wasn't his money after all. If something interesting popped up, Russell would approve it. If not, he'd find a way to explain the expense later.

"Please, keep digging."

"All right, chief," Peter said. "I'll get back to you tomorrow."

AMERICAN RESEARCH INSTITUTE
5:12 P.M. PACIFIC

Luis sat in Griff's office with Bob Carpenter. Jason had flown back to his Malibu house in one of the Reynolds Industries's helicopters.

Just before the accounting office had closed, Luis got a copy of the phone records Kevin had requested. Bob was livid; he took it as a personal affront that Kevin was questioning his poll.

"I don't see how he knew to even look up the phone records," Bob said.

"Are you sure he hasn't figured out the computer program?" Griff asked.

"I'm not sure of anything now, but he couldn't have without outside help. Kevin's a numbers cruncher, not a computer programmer."

"Unless he was tipped off," Luis added, looking at the list of phone numbers in front of him. "What if Leeland got through to him and told him to check the phone records?"

Bob stopped pacing. "Then he may not know about the program."

"Not yet anyway, but it won't take him long," Griff said. "Now that he's seen the discrepancy, all he has to do is have it analyzed."

"I've got a bad feeling about this one," Luis said. "I'll report to Reynolds. Griff, make sure you have an eye on Mr. Spencer through the night. As long as he keeps to himself, he can live until tomorrow."

HOLLYWOOD HILLS
7:10 P.M. PACIFIC

By the time Rick was able to leave the studio and drive up to the Hollywood Hills, he and Mark were a bit late for the CIFT meeting. Mark pulled up and parked behind Rick's jeep. Rick walked around the back and opened his liftgate.

"Let's put these in your car now, in case you have to leave early," he said as he pulled out his golf clubs.

"Thanks, Rick," Mark said as he walked around and opened his trunk. "Doesn't Cassie come with you to these meetings?"

"Sometimes she does, but she mainly goes to a Wednesday night group that she was already involved with when we met." Rick placed the clubs down and closed Mark's trunk. "She left in a hurry tonight. We hardly talked after the show."

"What's going on?"

Rick leaned against the back of the car. "It's this stupid proposal tape.

Sometimes I think it wasn't such a good idea. I've been so secretive about it that I'm sure she's having second thoughts about us."

"All you have to do is get through tomorrow night, and it'll all be worth it."

"I hope so," Rick sighed, then started up the sidewalk. "Let's get inside."

As they got closer, Mark could hear voices singing from within the house. Rick smiled as he reached for the door. "You're going to love this."

MALIBU
7:29 P.M. PACIFIC

Jason Reynolds entered his plush office at his Malibu estate. His attention was drawn to the video monitors on the wall in front of him as he scanned for the day's topics on the cable news channels. His secure phone line interrupted his concentration. The digital display identified the call emanated from the White House.

"Reynolds here."

"Hi, Jason, it's Albert." Albert Fisher was the chief of staff to President McNeil and a longtime friend of Reynolds. He was also Number Seven in the Circle.

"You're working late," Reynolds laughed, thinking about the three-hour time difference.

"Give me a night when that isn't the case," Fisher sighed. "I'm beginning to miss the quiet life."

"Don't do that. You're right where we need you."

"Speaking of that, I have a request from the big guy."

"And that would be . . ."

"Are you scrambled?" Fisher asked.

Reynolds assured him this line was always on scrambler.

"He's hoping we can get the numbers higher on his economic package," Fisher explained.

Reynolds shook his head. "He's not happy with 70-plus percent? What's his problem?"

"McNeil feels like he's going to have a problem selling the UN appropriation to the Senate."

With the Republicans holding a majority in Congress in the later part of the 1990s, they were able to deny the nearly one billion dollars in funds the United States owed the United Nations from going to any international organization that performed abortions or promoted abortion rights. Although staunchly pro-choice, President Clinton was forced to go along with it for fear that if the past dues weren't paid by the end of 1999, the United States was in danger of losing its vote in the UN General Assembly. President McNeil was attempting to reverse that precedent while at the same time greatly increasing UN funding. Raising public awareness was the reason Reynolds had gone to the White House to make his donation.

"He's probably right about that, but the polling numbers won't hold any higher. He should know that." Reynolds swore, thinking about the problem with the gay-poll numbers, thanks to Kevin Spencer.

"He does, or at least I told him, but several conservative senators won't go for the new language on population control. If we don't get their votes, billions could be in jeopardy. We've got all our assets positioned for a huge UN military buildup—"

"I know, I know," Reynolds muttered as he thought. "We'll just have to add the right pressure so that even the conservatives will push this through."

Fisher smiled from nearly three thousand miles away, hearing the tone in Number One's voice that meant something devious was in the works.

SHERMAN OAKS
7:34 P.M. PACIFIC

"Where have you been?" Vickie asked her husband as he walked into the house.

"I've been driving around."

"Couldn't you have called?" She stood over the sink, finishing the dishes from her solo meal.

"I'm sorry," he said, walking over and placing his arms around her. She continued working, ignoring his touch.

"I had some thinking to do and ended up just driving around." She reached for a plate. He pulled the hair away from her neck, reaching down and kissing her lightly. She tried to continue working, but he persisted.

"Stop it!" she finally said. "I'm mad at you."

He kept nuzzling until she relented, turned around, and kissed him.

After a moment she pulled away. "I was worried about you."

"I know. I should have called." He grabbed her hands and shut off the water. "Come here. We've got to talk."

He led her to the kitchen table. "You know that survey I was concerned with last night?"

Vickie nodded, and the fear she'd felt about his coming home late returned.

"It looks like they're onto me. Cindy received a visit from somebody who's in charge of security for Reynolds Industries."

"What did he want?"

"He was asking about the phone records, but I don't think he knew anything. He was fishing. Anyway, I interrupted them before she could give him any information about what I was doing with them."

"Kevin, this is too dangerous. I told you not to get involved."

"I know, honey, but it's too late now."

"What are you going to do?"

"It's funny. I ran into a reporter today, talking with Tracy—Mark Taylor from *Across the Nation*. When I got back to my office, I realized how over my head this whole thing is, so I called him."

"You what?" she shrieked.

"It's perfect," Kevin explained. "I don't know what I'm doing with this. If there is a connection between that survey and this guy Leeland's death, maybe this reporter can dig it up."

"But they'll have to know who talked with him."

"I'm being careful. We're meeting tonight at the driving range, and then I'm out of it."

Vickie dropped her head. She wasn't so certain, but she knew once Kevin started something, he finished it. He placed his hand over hers. "Just this one meeting. Nothing will happen. I'll turn over the phone records and the program and be done with it."

"I hope so," she said, unconvinced. "Just be careful."

CHAPTER 9

HOLLYWOOD HILLS
7:52 P.M. PACIFIC

"You are the salt of the earth. But if the salt loses its saltiness, how can it be made salty again? It is no longer good for anything, except to be thrown out and trampled by men. You are the light of the world. A city on a hill cannot be hidden. Neither do people light a lamp and put it under a bowl. Instead they put it on its stand, and it gives light to everyone in the house. In the same way, let your light shine before men, that they may see your good deeds and praise your Father in heaven."

The man across the room was reading from Matthew chapter 5 as Mark and Rick listened from the floor of the living room.

"These verses encouraged me this week," the man continued. His name was Vic Caplan, a programming executive for ABC Television. "Lately, I've been struggling at work with speaking out on the content of some of our shows."

Mark felt a nudge in his side. He looked at Rick, who had a big smile across his face.

"I've been keeping a pretty low profile about my Christian walk at the network," Vic explained. "But last night I came across these verses in my devotional

86

time. I felt convicted that I haven't been the salt and light that Jesus is talking about."

Several around the room agreed for themselves as well.

"So today I went to work looking for an opportunity to be salt and light. It was amazing. One of our producers came into the office to ask my advice on an episode with a negative portrayal of a Christian character. It opened up a wonderful discussion where I was able to eventually share my faith with the man."

Mark was soaking in every word. Then the woman to Mark's left spoke. "Sometimes God presents an obvious situation like that for us to be the light."

Rick had a notepad in front of him and quickly wrote where Mark could see— Stacey Williams, Fox News. Mark's eyebrows went up as he read the name.

Stacey continued. "Other times it's difficult knowing when to speak up. When I was at CBS, I always felt this pressure to report a story the way I knew my producer would accept. That way, there was less hassle and things went a lot smoother. Unfortunately, I wasn't as strong a Christian then, and I think I let a lot of things slide I shouldn't have."

A man on the other side of the room raised his hand, eager to speak but not sure of the format yet. "It's been an interesting week for me."

Rick wrote down his name—Richard Browning, new to the group and to Jesus.

"I haven't had a problem being vocal at all," Richard said. "The change in me has been so dramatic that people are asking what the difference is. I tell them about my encounter with the living God and get quite a reaction.

"Here's the sad part. When I was doing a gram of coke a day, nobody in the industry gave it a second thought or suggested I needed help. When I mention to people now that the God of the universe has saved me . . . Well, this week I've had three people tell me I need rehab."

Chuckles were heard around the room. Mark laughed along. Richard's newness in the Lord was refreshing.

"That struggle of how and when to be salt and light in the workplace is something all Christians have." The man sitting next to Richard spoke. Mark looked down at Rick's paper—Rob Stevenson, CIFT leader.

"It's part of what Jesus mentioned in John chapter 15: '"If you belonged to the world, it would love you as its own. As it is, you do not belong to the world, but I have chosen you out of the world. That is why the world hates you."' We are not of this world, just living in it."

Mark could hear a couple of amens around the room as his attention was riveted on Rob's words.

"A friend of mine who works in the insurance industry was once told to lie for his boss and was getting a lot of pressure about it. But he stood his ground and walked up to him and said, 'I won't lie for you, Mr. Wadkins, but think about this, I won't lie to you either.' That made such an impact on his boss, that not only did my friend keep his job and prosper within the company, but not too long after that, Mr. Wadkins became a Christian.

"What complicates the decision process for us is that where we decide to draw the line often influences the entire nation, which amazingly enough, leads me to what I wanted to share tonight." Several laughed throughout the room.

"Look at Daniel chapter 6. There are two prime examples of God's people prospering in leadership positions within ungodly governments and having a dramatic impact on their cultures. Joseph, who became the number-two man in all of Pharaoh's court to protect God's people during a terrible famine. And Daniel, who served in Nebuchadnezzar's powerful Babylonian Empire. But don't forget, before these two attained their exalted positions, they'd gone through some difficult times. Joseph had been beaten, sold into slavery, and falsely accused and imprisoned, and Daniel had been thrown into a lions' den. And you thought you had it bad?"

Laughter echoed through the room as Rob continued, recounting the story of Daniel to the group. Mark listened as Rob drew parallels from Daniel's life to those in the entertainment industry making a stand for righteousness.

"Let me give you an example of how an established celebrity can make a difference, given enough courage. I remember something Charlton Heston did when Time Warner was in the middle of the controversy with Ice-T's CD, *Cop Killer*. Being a stockholder in the company, he decided to visit the annual stockholders' meeting. At one point, he asked for the floor, then proceeded to read the lyrics of the offending songs—from killing cops to sodomizing two twelve-year-old nieces of Tipper and Al Gore—all uncensored. Needless to say, there were some shocked people in that room, especially on the platform where the Time Warner executives squirmed in their chairs. Two months after that meeting, Ice-T's contract was terminated. Mr. Heston jokes today that he'll probably never be offered another film by the company or receive a favorable review from *Time* magazine.

"Now you might argue that someone of Charlton Heston's stature can speak out like that and get away with it. But I ask you, what if the Christians within Time Warner had spoken out earlier? Could that vile CD have been stopped from being released at all if God's people within that company had shown the light of Jesus Christ? We'll probably never know the answer to that, and some may have tried, but keep that in the back of your mind when the Holy Spirit prompts you about something at work."

All around the room people were nodding their heads in agreement, Mark as well. "Let's pray." Rob instructed as they bowed their heads. "Lord, we lift up those in this room, coming face-to-face with their own Babylons and Egypts daily in this city. Give them your heart, Jesus. Let them know when it's your will to speak out. Give them boldness with your Holy Spirit. Let them stand for you, both in their job situations and also in sharing their personal faith with those around them. And, Lord, protect them. Keep your angels about them as they look to make an eternal difference for your kingdom. In Jesus' name. Amen."

Rob smiled at Mark after the prayer. Mark beamed back, feeling a surge of boldness he'd never felt before.

"I take it you're glad you came?" Rick asked.

"You bet. Thanks," Mark answered. Then he looked around the room as people were starting to get up and move about. "Is that it?"

"Pretty much. There's always some time of fellowship and snacks at the end. How long do you have before your meeting?"

Mark hadn't given the meeting with Kevin a second thought since they'd walked into the house. He quickly looked at his watch. "I've got a few minutes," he said.

"Then let's get something to eat."

As they made their way to the kitchen, Rick walked over to Gary Hall, pouring himself a glass of iced tea.

"Gary, I want you to meet a friend of mine. This is Mark Taylor."

Gary set his drink down to shake Mark's hand. "Mark, good to meet you. Welcome to the group."

"Thanks. I really enjoyed it."

"This group means the world to me," Gary said. "It took quite a bit to convince Rick to come and check it out though."

Rick smiled. "Yep, that's true. It's funny though—the first night I came, the group talked about the very issue Gary and I were discussing at the time."

"That's what happened tonight," Mark exclaimed to Gary. "I've been asking Rick questions at the studio about when to speak out if things bother me, and tonight everything centered on that point. It's amazing."

"No," Gary answered. "It's God, but then he is amazing."

The three laughed.

"What's been going on at work, Mark?" Gary asked.

Mark took a couple of moments to fill Gary in on happenings at *Across the Nation,* including Samantha's Internet idea.

"I can see that you'd be struggling," Gary said.

"But I'm no Charlton Heston, so what can I do?" Mark asked.

"That's the exciting thing about following Jesus," Gary answered. "There are no pat answers. We all need to be so in tune with him that we'll know when and how he'll want us to respond."

"You sound just like Rick did over pizza last night."

"I taught him well," Gary laughed, glancing at Rick. "But seriously, he's right. Christians can't try to change this industry with the zeal of the crusades. It just wouldn't work. While not compromising our faith, we need to have God's wisdom about when we attempt to make a difference."

"I see what you're saying," Mark grinned. "If I threatened to walk unless they drop Samantha's Internet story, all I'd accomplish would be to lose my job."

"I think you're getting it," Rick laughed.

"You know who would be perfect to talk with Samantha?" Gary asked.

Rick answered in unison with Gary, "Vanessa!"

"Who's Vanessa?" Mark asked.

"She's a wonderful woman," Gary said. "She took the dramatic step to come out of the pornography business last year when she found out she was pregnant. My wife and I have stayed close to her since then. She'd have an insight into that business that would blow Samantha away. It'd be awesome."

"I'll talk with Sam." Mark was intrigued. Maybe something worthwhile could come out of the story after all. Then his attention was diverted when Stacey Williams walked into the kitchen. "Rick, I'd like to meet Stacey. It sounds as if she's been through some of the stuff I'm dealing with."

"Sure," Rick agreed. "Hey, Stacey, come over here for a minute, would ya? I'd like to introduce you to—"

"Mark Taylor." Stacey finished for him as she walked up. "What a pleasure meeting you."

"It's my pleasure, Stacey," Mark said, shaking her hand.

"I love what you're doing on *Across the Nation.* I wish we had the budget at Fox News to do some of the in-depth stuff you guys get to do."

Mark laughed. "Yeah, and we wish we had the budget *60 Minutes* has. I guess it's all relative."

"There's never enough money, is there?"

"I really appreciated what you said tonight. I'm new to the group, and I'm trying to come to grips with how all this fits into journalism. I'd love to bend your ear sometime."

"I'd be happy to, Mark. After coming to these meetings for a while, I've come to think it's a toss-up which job is more difficult for a Christian—the entertainment side of our business or the newsroom. Each one is a unique challenge."

Rick and Gary agreed.

"What's on your mind, Mark?" Stacey asked.

Mark looked at his watch. "I'd love to get into it with you, but I've got a meeting in a few minutes. Could I call you and set up something for another time?"

She reached into her purse and pulled out her card. "Call me when it's convenient. Finding another Christian journalist is rare. We need to stick together."

"I'm just beginning to understand that. Thanks, Stacey. I'll be in touch." Mark turned to Rick and Gary. "Thanks, Rick, and nice to meet you, Gary. I've got to get going."

"Be careful, Mark. I hope it's a good meeting," Rick said as Mark hurried to the door.

STUDIO CITY
9:03 P.M. PACIFIC

Mark drove into the parking lot at the Whitset driving range a few minutes after nine. He was shocked at the number of cars this late at night. He never understood the attraction of walking around a golf course, trying to get a little white ball into a hole, much less hitting ball after ball out to an empty field.

He unlocked the trunk and pulled out Rick's golf bag, slung it over his shoulder, and made his way to the entrance. He walked through the clubhouse and out toward the practice area. He looked down the row of golfers, each deep in concentration and spotted Kevin at the end of the line. There was an open space next to him.

Mark set the clubs down in the holder alongside the tee pad. Kevin continued hitting away, ignoring Mark as he worked with one of his irons. Mark pulled an iron out of the bag, then realized he didn't have any golf balls.

Kevin looked up at him for the first time, smiling. "You get the balls at the front."

"Oh, thank you." Mark left the clubs there as he made his way back to the clubhouse and purchased a bucket of balls.

"Just hit a few," Kevin whispered when he returned. "I want to make sure nobody's watching us."

Mark tried to oblige, but the first few swings netted nothing but air. How frustrating! Mark fancied himself fairly athletic. He was determined to connect with the ball. He put all his might into his next swing, finally connecting but sending the ball screaming right at Kevin. It ricocheted off the small metal divider between them with a loud twang and shot right back at Mark.

He dodged it with a yelp as several golfers down the line stopped their swings to have a good laugh.

Kevin joined in with them. *So much for the clandestine meeting,* he thought. But maybe this was to their advantage.

He stepped over to Mark. "Would you like some help?"

Mark took the hint. "Yeah, I guess I could use some. I got these clubs for my birthday."

"Here, let's start with the proper grip."

In the parking lot on the other side of the fence, Griff sat in his black Mercedes, calmly keeping his eye on the situation. He'd followed Kevin when he left the office, expertly staying with him through aimless wandering around town. He was about to call in his replacement for the night, when Kevin had pulled out of his driveway and driven to the driving range. Griff wished he'd had his clubs with him; he could use the practice.

From his car he could just make out the top of the golfers' heads as they smacked ball after ball. His cell phone rang inside his jacket.

"It's Luis. Anything happening?"

"He's been pretty restless. Drove around town some, then went home. Right now, he's at some driving range hitting away. But he's kept to himself."

"All right, keep at it. I want to make sure he doesn't meet with anybody tonight. You got that?"

"I'm on it, man!" Griff replied coldly as he punched off the line. He settled back into his seat, hoping Kevin would finish up quickly and head back home so he could call in one of his men to replace him. What a waste of time.

"Now take your hands back like this." Kevin stood behind Mark, leading him through the proper swing technique. "Just let the weight of the club bring your hands around to the striking position and then naturally follow through to this position."

"You make it look easy," Mark said. "I didn't realize how difficult this sport is."

"Now try one."

"OK, but you better stand back."

Mark tried to take everything into account Kevin had showed him as he brought the club back and swung. The ball went flying off toward the right side of the range, sailing about a hundred yards before it was stopped by the net at the boundary of the par three course.

"Wow, that helped a lot!" he exclaimed.

"You're starting to get the hang of it. Just keep hitting, and I'll fill you in on why I wanted to meet," Kevin instructed.

Mark bent over and placed another ball on the tee as Kevin continued. "I've been with ARI for a couple of years and have generally been pretty happy. But recently, some polling results have troubled me."

Kevin gave Mark a quick overview on how the poll on homosexuality had caught his interest, then on the subsequent phone calls with Lee. It was hard for Mark to concentrate on his new golf swing as he began to absorb the information Kevin was feeding him.

Mark stopped, looking at Kevin. "You mean the poll was rigged?"

"Yes, I believe so. There's no other explanation for it."

"But how would the other company come up with the same percentages?"

"I don't know. But this Lee person was onto something. When I checked the computer program with the telephone records, they didn't match. Don't you see? If there's a tie-in between ARI and this other company, it's got to be some kind of conspiracy."

The second he used the word, Kevin wished he could take it back. He saw Mark's expression change from total interest to skepticism.

"Maybe conspiracy isn't the right word," Kevin said, "but I haven't told you about who I think Lee was."

Mark didn't respond, but set another golf ball on the mat waiting for Kevin to continue.

"A couple of days ago, I heard that the president of Research International died of an apparent heart attack. His name was Leeland Dawkins."

Mark looked up from the ball and stared directly at him, trying to read Kevin's expression. "You think this was the same Lee who contacted you?"

"Yes, I do. There are only two others with similar names in the company—one a female and the other one a janitor. If it is the same man who was calling me, what if it wasn't a heart attack? What if he was murdered?"

Mark's expression gave his thoughts away.

"You must think my imagination is running wild, but I tell you something isn't right here," Kevin pleaded. "And I'm not sure what to do about it."

"I understand, Kevin. Don't worry, I'm still with you," Mark reassured him. "It's just that when you hear people start to claim conspiracies and murder, well—"

"Yeah, I know. It sounds wacky." Kevin turned around and reached into his bag, pulling out a manila envelope.

"Here are the phone records and a copy of the computer program. I've also written out what I've told you in greater detail. The head of security is suspicious of what I know, so leave my name out of any investigation you make. But have these checked out and let me know what you think."

Mark quickly slipped the envelope into Rick's bag. "I will. If I find out anything, I'll leave you a message as if I'm your . . . cousin, visiting from New York—Mark Foster. And if you have anything else to tell me, call when you think it's safe."

"I will, and thanks for hearing me out about this."

"No thanks needed. I'm glad you called. This is what I've been looking for."

"I'm going to stay and hit a few more balls," Kevin said as he reached for one of his clubs. "That way we won't be seen leaving together."

Mark understood as he picked up Rick's clubs and stepped behind Kevin. "I'll be in touch. Just be careful, Kevin."

Kevin smacked a perfect eight-iron, sending the ball straight out and landing just shy of the 150-yard marker. "I will, Mark. I hope this leads to something."

STUDIO CITY
9:42 P.M. PACIFIC

Rick pulled into his garage, tired yet invigorated. He loved the Thursday night meeting, especially when he saw the Holy Spirit at work.

He wished Cassie had been there with him, but it would be fun to call her and fill her in on what she missed. He set his wallet and keys down on the counter, grabbed the phone, and kicked off his shoes as he sat down at the kitchen table.

After a couple of rings, Rick smiled as he heard Cassie's voice.

"Hi, Cassie, it's Rick. You sure missed a good one tonight."

"Oh, hi, Rick," she responded dryly.

"Where did you go after the show? I thought you might have come to the group with us."

There was a slight pause. Rick knew she was still bothered by how the week had gone between them, but he was determined to ignore it so he could just make it through until tomorrow night.

"I just didn't feel like being out tonight," she finally answered.

Rick plunged ahead. "Well, you know it was Mark's first time there, and it was amazing. God orchestrated the whole evening to center on how Christians should act in the workplace."

"Really?" Cassie finally responded with interest. "Who taught?"

"Rob did. He talked about the ways Joseph and Daniel worked within ungodly cultures and drew parallels for us today. It really touched Mark. He was all fired up at the end."

"That's great, Rick. I know he needed some encouragement."

"Well, he definitely got it. He also hooked up with Stacey Williams from Fox News. I think it will be helpful for him."

"It sounds like I missed a lot. Is Mark still with you?"

"No, he had to run to a meeting. I'm not sure with who, but he was pretty excited about finding something to help him with his story."

"I guess I should have gone with you," Cassie said unconvincingly.

"I wish you had. It would have been nice to have you by my side."

The air was heavy for a few moments as Cassie chose not to respond.

"Are we still on for tomorrow night?" Rick broke the silence.

"I don't know, Rick. It's been a long week—"

"Cassie, please," Rick interrupted, "I want us to have some time together, just a quiet evening, here at my place."

Cassie couldn't think of anything she would like more, but her heart was guarded. "Let's just see how tomorrow goes, OK?"

Rick nearly panicked. He had to show her the tape tomorrow, but he couldn't push too hard, or she'd know something was up. He had an idea. "OK, honey, but please think about it. I really want to see you."

"I will. Thanks for calling."

"I love you," Rick replied.

Cassie paused before responding, "Yeah, me too. I'll see you tomorrow."

Rick waited for the sound of her hanging up before he punched off. He quickly ran upstairs to his computer. He'd decided the perfect thing to do would be to send her some flowers in the morning and invite her to a romantic dinner at his place that night. How could she turn that down?

BURBANK
11:13 P.M. PACIFIC

Mark walked into his apartment clutching the envelope he'd received from Kevin. He couldn't wait to analyze the information for himself. All through the drive home he kept repeating in his head what Kevin had said. Could the polls be rigged? Who would benefit? What if it did lead to a conspiracy?

He opened the envelope as he sat at his desk. He let the computer disk and the phone printout drop on the desktop as he picked out the letter Kevin had written. He slowly read through it, making notes on a legal pad beside him, grateful for all the detail Kevin had supplied in recounting his story.

It sounded convincing, but how could he check it out? He'd have to make a trip back to ARI, which would mean another meeting with Tracy. Mark grinned. That would be pleasant enough. He wondered what she would say and how he would protect Kevin's identity. He also needed to look into the mysterious phone call from Lee. Could it really have been Leeland Dawkins? He jotted down the name and wrote next to it, "Call the widow." Maybe she'd have some information.

Then he picked up the phone records. He didn't know how to compare them to the disk sitting beside them. That would take a person with some serious computer knowledge—like Peter Lovil. He jotted down, "Computer program—call Peter."

Mark yawned, feeling the late hour catch up with him. He tore off the top sheet of his legal pad and stuffed it along with the contents of Kevin's envelope into his briefcase. Tomorrow was going to be an interesting day.

CHAPTER 10

Frank Russell was in mid-sentence when Mark sneaked into the room and quietly took his seat at the conference table. Russell hated to be interrupted and glared at him.

It wasn't like Mark to show up late for a meeting. On Friday mornings they talked about the final segments for the Sunday night show. Usually, he arrived much earlier to catch up on his own work before the meeting started. But after turning his lights out last night, his mind kept churning through all the possibilities Kevin had presented. He didn't fall asleep until sometime after three.

"Now that we're all assembled . . ." Russell said sarcastically.

"I'm sorry I'm late," Mark replied, feeling about two inches tall as everyone looked at him.

"Please continue, Stan." Russell spoke to Stan Jeffries, another of the show's reporters, without acknowledging Mark.

"The India piece is going to be strong. We've got some great footage—real tear-jerker stuff," Stan reported. "There are still thousands without food, water, or shelter, but the relief agencies are in place now, and the situation seems to be improving."

"Good." Frank turned his attention to Mark. "Our lead story is going to be yours, Mark. The abortion issue is hot again with that huge award the jury stuck to those Internet clowns."

Mark smiled at the news. He hadn't had the lead in months. He hadn't given it much thought since delving into the polling research, but having Mrs. Medford's comments on his segment would be wonderful. Just the kind of thing that group of Rick's would love to see on the air.

"Mark?" he heard Russell ask.

"I'm sorry. What did you say?" Mark said, being pulled back to the meeting.

The irritation in Russell's voice increased. "I was asking if you and Jennifer had everything ready for your piece?"

"Yes, yes sir, we do." Mark answered. "I finished the last interview yesterday. All we have left is the final edit."

"Good. We need to reset the stage for the audience about the lawsuit. Tad, you take that. Pull some of the news clips with stuff we've run on the show—whatever it takes to retell the story in about a minute and a half. Then you'll turn it over to Mark who will introduce his tape."

"You got it," Tad responded.

"That means we'll bump everybody else down a segment and finish with Sam's interview with Mel Gibson." Russell looked at Samantha across the table from him. "By the way, how goes your Internet site? Are we going to get sued for thirty million dollars as well?"

Chuckles filled the room.

"We go online this weekend, and we've taken every precaution to protect the network," she said proudly, reaching into her notebook and pulling out a folder. "Anybody want to see the pictures?"

They were quickly passed around the table, accompanied by several whistles and some lewd comments from the staff. Samantha smiled coyly, feeding on the attention.

"I didn't know you were posing, Tad," Jennifer said as she glanced through his pictures, then smiled at him.

Tad returned the smile while Samantha laughed in her chair, thoroughly enjoying the moment.

Mark tensed as Jennifer passed the set of pictures toward him. What should he do? Everyone would think him a prude if he didn't look, yet he felt he'd be condoning the story he'd been so against by taking a peek. He also knew as a Christian he shouldn't fill his mind with images of Samantha's nude body, yet there was a part of him that really wanted to see the pictures. He also remembered the talk from last night's meeting about taking a stand—being bold. All this went through his mind in a fraction of a second as his hand reached toward the pictures.

Mark passed the folder along to Winston Smith on his right. He inadvertently caught a glimpse of the top picture—Tad's. That was all Mark needed to underscore the fact that he'd done the right thing.

"Aren't you even going to look?" Samantha asked provocatively.

"No, thank you, I'd rather not," Mark responded without further comment.

Russell smiled. *At least the kid's sticking to his principles,* he thought.

Samantha was enraged. "Well, you've got some nerve!"

Mark didn't quite know how to respond, but he wanted Samantha to understand his position. "Sam, I—"

"Let's not make a big deal out of this, all right?" Russell cut in. "The network wants your story next Sunday, Sam, so that gives you only a week to process whatever data you get. Jennifer, we need that piece on *The Single Life* ready next week as well. Are you and Mark all set?"

"We're going out to their studio tonight," Jennifer answered. "So next Sunday won't be a problem at all."

"Great," Russell said. "Then that wraps up—"

"Wait," Mark interrupted. "I need to tell you about some of the leads I've found on the polling story."

"Not now, Mark," Russell stopped him with a wave of his hand. "See me in my office later. We'll have to find a show after sweeps for it. We're booked up for now. Well, that's it then. Let's get to work."

Mark, irritated at being cut off, snapped his notebook closed. The room cleared fast, and he caught site of Samantha waiting by the door for him.

He walked past her, heading to his desk when she stepped forward and matched strides with him.

"So what's the big deal about looking at my pictures?" she asked sharply.

Mark stopped, searching for the right words. He sighed, trying to clear the frustration he felt toward Russell before he looked at Samantha. "Look, Sam," he said gently, "I'm sorry if I offended you. You are a very beautiful woman, and most men would love to see those pictures—"

"Then what's the problem?" Her voice took on a softer tone.

Lord, help me say the right thing, Mark prayed before he continued. "It's partly because I've been against this story from the beginning, partly because I'm against pornography—"

"This isn't porno, Mark. It's just nudity," she protested more loudly than intended.

"But, Sam, to me it is pornography. You may not realize the effect these kinds of images can have on a man, but just because it isn't something our society refers to as hard-core anymore doesn't mean it isn't harmful."

Sam's eyes hardened as she turned to walk away. His comment had brought back the same dirty feeling she'd experienced when she'd left the studio. She fought to suppress it.

"Wait, Sam," Mark said, grabbing her shoulder gently and turning her around. "I'm trying very hard not to upset you. Please hear me out. I know our society, and especially our industry, has come a long way in the past few years legitimizing nudity. Shows like *Entertainment Tonight* promote the latest centerfold, Leno and Letterman have on the hottest new *Playboy* model, actresses are able to jump-start their careers by being featured in one of those magazines."

Sam fought to hide the shock that hit her at Mark's mention of career boosts.

"But that doesn't make it right, nor does it make it good for our culture. It's so easy today for young impressionable boys—and grown men, for that matter—to jump on the Internet and view any kind of pornographic filth they choose with a simple click of the mouse. Think about how that affects them. The beautiful, God-created act of making love is reduced to an animalistic sexual drive that makes the woman an object instead of a soul mate."

He paused, wondering if his words were getting to Samantha or if he was preaching. She didn't walk away, so he decided to continue. He was shaking inside, as if he felt a deep, bone-chilling cold. He was about to break a barrier he'd never crossed before.

"The third reason I didn't look was because of my own walk with God." Mark surprised himself as he heard his own words. "I know in his Word I'm taught to dwell on things that are good and wholesome and upright. Looking at your pictures could lead me into temptation."

Sam smiled nervously. *At least he would be tempted,* she thought. *He is human.* "Now you sound like somebody else I know. We lasted all of one date."

"Sam, I wish you could understand, there are consequences to pornography. I know you don't feel this is porno." Mark quickly went on as she started to protest, "But I have an idea I'd like you to try, if you're willing."

She was curious now. "What do you have in mind?"

"There's someone I'd like you to meet."

Sam answered with a questioning tilt of her head.

"Her name's Vanessa. She's a friend of a friend, but she's come out of the skin business. She came here as a runaway, then got into prostitution, pornography, drugs, the whole bit. Please consider spending some time getting to know how her life was affected before you complete your story, OK?"

Sam looked into Mark's eyes. All she saw was his deep concern, no trace of an ulterior motive.

"I'll think about it, Mark," she finally said. "I'll think about it."

NEW YORK CITY
12:35 P.M. EASTERN

Vince Sinclair walked through the revolving door to the lobby of Research International and out onto 41st Street. A brisk New York wind cut through his light jacket as he paused to see if anyone stepped out of the building after him. After walking a couple of blocks uptown, pausing occasionally to see if he was followed, he ducked into a subway entrance. He pulled out his cell phone and punched in a number. After two rings, he heard the line connect, but no one answered.

"RI check incomplete," he said quietly and looked up the steps at the street level. "Do know that Palmer carelessly left E-mail from Number One on his computer. Will need to go in on Saturday when office is empty and search deeper, then head west sometime next week."

NATIONAL STUDIOS
10:12 A.M. PACIFIC

Rick sat anxiously at his desk. Through the open door he could keep his eye on the area around Cassie's office. He paged through his scriptbook, only half concentrating on the words before him. Cassie had been ice-cold during the morning production meeting. Now he sat like a kid waiting under a Christmas tree while the grown-ups finished cleaning up the dishes in the kitchen.

Then he saw a huge bouquet of roses—two dozen long-stem red ones—walking across the office. They were so big that all he could see of the deliveryman was his legs. The office filled with "ooohs" and "aaahs."

Rick could hear Tina giggling as she signed for the flowers and thanked the deliveryman. He silently prayed for Cassie as he watched the man walk back through the room and out the front door. He was tempted to step out to see if he could get a glimpse of Cassie's reaction, but, no, he needed to stay in his office and act busy.

Tina picked up the large bouquet and walked into Cassie's office. "Delivery for a Ms. Petterson."

Cassie looked up from her computer screen. "What are those?"

"I'd say they are roses," Tina laughed.

"I know that, but what for? It's not my birthday or any anniversary that I can remember."

Tina set them on the desk in front of her. Cassie stood in awe, placed her face close to one of the beautiful rosebuds, and took a deep breath. "I love that smell," she sighed, reached out, and took the card.

Cassie,
Roses are red, violets are blue
Never doubt that I love you.

You are cordially invited to an evening
of dining and romance at Chez Rick's.
Tonight, 7:00 P.M. Dress casual.
Please come. I need to be with you.
Love, Rick.

Cassie wiped away a tear as she smiled.
"From Rick?" Tina asked.
"Yeah," Cassie beamed. "They're from Rick."

MALIBU
10:15 A.M. PACIFIC

Jason Reynolds wore a smug grin. CNBC, MSNBC, and all the network morning shows had run stories on the latest overnight polls on abortion. With the aid of the White House question and a bit of Jason's magic, the numbers were staggeringly in favor of the verdict against the antiabortion Internet site. CNN had just reported its overnight poll showed 76 percent in favor of the verdict, followed by 63 percent in favor of abortion on demand.

"Yes!" Reynolds slammed his fist against the desk as he saw the number. He smiled. Nice touch by CNN adding the abortion-on-demand percentage. It was time to start working on his idea.

Reynolds had stayed up half the night researching and preparing the details needed to push McNeil's UN appropriation bill through the ranks of public opinion and then inevitably through Congress.

At his computer, he composed a communiqué to the other members of the Circle of Seven. Ordinary instructions to those he controlled in the polling and media companies went out by coded E-mail, but orders directly to the Circle bypassed the Internet. The encrypted messages were sent through a millisecond burst of high-band energy that bounced off a satellite in orbit above the earth. They were then picked up by the high-tech receivers of the other members of the Circle. The CIA was the only government agency—or any group, for that matter—that had the ability to intercept the messages. After all, the technology had come from the agency. But Luis had taken every precaution to ensure that wouldn't happen, and if it ever did, he had people still in the CIA on the Circle's payroll.

He completed his final instruction and hit the send button. Within twenty-four hours, President McNeil would begin to see the Circle's plan unfold.

Reynolds's reverie was interrupted by the ringing of his private line.

"Number One," he answered.

"It's Luis. I've just been alerted that someone hacked into our computers last night."

Jason's exuberance immediately changed to a boiling rage. "Which computers?"

"Several, among them Nationwide Polling and Reynolds Industries."

Reynolds let loose with a string of curses. "Were you able to trace who was doing it?"

"No, they got out clean."

"Well, what were they looking for?" Reynolds asked impatiently.

"The owners," Luis answered dryly.

"Who would care who owns ..." Then Reynolds understood. "Has Kevin talked with anyone?"

"Not to our knowledge, but that doesn't mean he got to somebody before we were onto him."

"Get him. I want to know what he knows and who he's talked to. Now!" Reynolds slammed the phone down. He glanced out the windows to the Pacific Ocean. The view did nothing to calm him. He hated not being in control. Kevin Spencer would pay.

NATIONAL STUDIOS
10:22 A.M. PACIFIC

At his desk Rick shot rubber bands across the room. The flowers had been delivered ten minutes ago. What was Cassie doing? Was the card wrong? Is she too mad for the flowers to work?

Finally, the intercom buzzed.

"Rick, it's Tina. Cassie would like to see you in her office please."

"Be right there," he called back. *Boy, she just isn't going to forgive me, is she? Calling me to her office instead of coming to mine,* he thought.

He walked through the center of the room. All eyes were on him as he knocked once and stepped inside.

No one was there, just the huge bouquet sitting on her desk. Suddenly, the door closed behind him as Cassie reached around his back and hugged him.

"They're the most beautiful flowers I've ever seen," she said as more tears slid down her cheeks. She'd waited a few minutes to try to compose herself before calling Rick, but it hadn't worked.

Without a word, he grabbed her face in his hands and leaned toward her. Their lips touched, lightly at first, almost reminiscent of their first kiss. Then he pulled her tighter, pressing their bodies together as the moment intensified.

After a moment, Rick pulled back. "But nothing is as beautiful as you are to me right now."

"Oh, Rick, I'm sorry I was so mad at you," she said, laying her head against his shoulder. "But it just seemed like you've had no time for me lately. I thought you'd changed your mind about me, about us."

"I know, and there's a reason why you've felt that way. But I can't explain until tonight. Promise me you'll be there."

Cassie was disappointed; she was tired of the mystery. He could see the joy start to leave her face.

"Just a few more hours, then you'll understand, I promise. Have dinner with me tonight," he pleaded.

The passion in his eyes was all the assurance she needed. "I'll be there, but you definitely have some explaining to do."

At his desk Mark caught CNN's report on the results of the latest abortion poll: 63 percent were in favor of abortion on demand, the drone behind the desk announced. Mark no longer trusted the numbers, and in fact, the report infuriated him. He looked through Kevin's letter and tried to decide what his next step should be.

"You got a second, Mark?" Russell poked his head over the cubicle wall.

"Sure, Frank. Step on in." Mark waved to the chair next to his desk.

"So," Russell began as he sat down, "what do you have going with your polling story?"

Mark was surprised. He thought Russell wasn't interested by the way he commented in the meeting. He set Kevin's letter aside and spun his chair toward Russell.

"Let me fill you in on what happened over at American Research Institute yesterday." Mark quickly brought Russell up to speed on his research but left out any reference to a conspiracy as he explained Kevin's information.

Russell studied Mark's face as he spoke. "I see that fire in your eyes, Mark. This story means a lot to you, doesn't it?"

"I think it means a lot to all of us. Do you realize how much this country is swayed by these polls? How often we plug their numbers into our stories, validating their importance and championing their almighty infallibility? What if they're inaccurate? Or even worse, what if they've been corrupted? Look at the numbers about abortion that just came out today: 76 percent in favor of the thirty-million-dollar award, and 64 percent in favor of abortion on demand? Those numbers seem awfully high to me. What if they were rigged? How big do you think this story is?"

Russell smiled at his young reporter, thinking back to the days when he would follow an exciting lead, expecting to find the Pulitzer Prize waiting at the end. But the result never quite matched his expectations. Oh, how he longed for those days to return.

"Listen, Mark, don't get your hopes up. What seems like a great story on the surface often leads to a deadend. Do you realize what it would take to rig the outcome of one of these surveys? How could you guarantee that CNN, *Time*, Gallup, *Newsweek, USA Today*, NBC, ABC, and CBS all came up with the same numbers? That would be impossible."

"I've thought about that, but what if my source's story is true? Then there'd have to be some collusion going on between the companies. A man could be dead because of it."

Russell thought for a second. "Or you might have some disgruntled employee trying to get back at the company in some way through you. He doesn't have a shred of evidence that the man in New York didn't die of a heart attack, does he? He could have fabricated everything."

Mark lowered his head. He hadn't thought of that, but he was generally a good judge of character, and Kevin sure seemed sincere.

"I understand what you're saying, Frank, and I know I've got a lot more groundwork to do before any conclusions can be made." Mark looked back into Russell's eyes. "But I really believe there's something to this."

"You might be right, Mark. I don't want to dampen your excitement. I just want to make sure you're asking the hard questions, that's all."

Mark understood. He'd have to make sure he analyzed this objectively and not allow his bias to make up a story if there wasn't one.

"Keep digging, and when you get to the truth, if there's falsified data being pushed through as legitimate, I'll give you the lead story—maybe even a special hour."

Mark's eyebrows raised at the prospect. His own special? Incredible!

"I'll keep at it." Russell stood to leave. "I know there's a story here, a big one."

Mark spun around to his desk again as Russell walked back toward his office. What should be his next step? He'd have to confirm Kevin's story, but how?

He grabbed the phone and punched in the number for ARI.

"Yes, Tracy Reynolds please," he said as the receptionist answered. A few seconds later he heard Tracy's pleasant voice.

"Mark, I'm surprised to hear from you so soon. How are you?"

"I'm fine, Tracy. Thanks for asking. And you?"

"Couldn't be better, just busy as usual. What can I do for you?"

"Well, I'm probably bothering you too much, but after the tour yesterday, more questions came up, and I was wondering if you'd have any more time I could steal?"

Tracy smiled. She liked the idea of seeing Mark again, even if it was professional on his part. Or was it, she wondered?

"I'm in the middle of a couple of projects right now," she told a momentarily disappointed Mark. "But are you free for a late lunch?"

"Lunch, you bet." Mark answered before giving a thought to his schedule. Then he looked at his planner and saw "*The Single Life*—tape backstage, three o'clock." "Oh, wait a minute, how late are you talking about?"

"I could get out of here by 1:30 if you could meet me downtown."

Mark mentally calculated his afternoon schedule. He could just make it if they kept lunch to an hour. "That'll work. Where can I meet you?"

"There's a wonderful Italian restaurant on the ground floor of our building, it's called Fellini's. Does that sound OK?"

"Sounds great. I'll see you then."

He hung up the phone, more excited about spending time alone with Tracy than continuing his investigation. He looked at Kevin's note one more time and analyzed his dilemma. How was he going to get any information out of Tracy while protecting Kevin?

The phone interrupted his thoughts.

"Mark, it's Rick. I just had to share the good news with someone."

The excitement in Rick's voice made Mark smile. "What good news?"

"Well, I had the idea late last night to have roses delivered to Cassie, and she just got them."

"That was brilliant, Rick, and I take it your plans are all set for tonight?"

"You bet they are. I think it was just what she needed to calm her fears. Now all I need is the courage to pop the question."

Mark laughed. "What courage? All you have to do is press play on the VCR."

Rick chuckled along with him. "You know what I mean. There's still that fear she'll say no."

"Rick, relax. You have nothing to worry about. She adores you."

"Thanks for the encouragement. Hey, that reminds me."

"What?"

"The Lord brought you to my mind this morning during my prayer time. I wanted to share a Scripture with you. Hold on."

Mark could hear rustling as Rick pulled his Bible out. This was a new experience for Mark. He wasn't sure what to expect.

"Here it is," Rick finally said. "It's in Second Thessalonians 3:3: 'But the Lord is faithful, and he will strengthen and protect you from the evil one.'"

Mark sat silent for a moment, not sure how to respond. "I appreciate that Rick, thanks."

"Wait, that's not all. When you came to mind, I saw this image of you on a plane. Are you traveling anywhere this week?"

Mark couldn't figure out where Rick was going with his question. "No, I've got a story to do right here. Why?"

"Well, maybe you will be, I don't know. But I definitely got the feeling you were flying to another city, somewhere back East. That's what I felt the Scripture was referring to, the Lord strengthening you and protecting you."

"That's eerie, Rick." Mark was snickering, "What did you have to eat last night?"

"I know this sounds bizarre, but remember the Lord works in strange ways. I've seen some wild things he's done through other people in prayer and words from him. Just keep this in mind if you end up traveling somewhere, and keep the Scripture close to your heart. God's got his hand on you."

"Thanks, Rick," Mark said humbly as he wrote the Scripture reference down on his notepad. "I'll remember."

AMERICAN RESEARCH INSTITUTE
12:11 P.M. PACIFIC

Kevin relaxed in his chair for the first time that day. He had stayed up talking with Vickie well into the early morning. She was worried and finally convinced him that he should be as well. He thought he saw a car following him from his house into work earlier, but he wasn't sure.

He'd been jumpy as he settled into work. Each phone call made him think about the security chief who had visited the day before. Was the next call going to be from him? But as the morning passed, Kevin had come to the conclusion his imagination was working overtime. Nobody was following him; he was being paranoid. Maybe it was time to step out and get a little lunch.

Then he looked up from his desk. Luis stared at him through the doorway. His heart felt like it dropped to the floor by his feet. He spoke through an instantly dry mouth. "May I help you?"

Luis's eyes bore right through him. "I was wondering if you'd please come down with me to Griff's office. We'd like to ask you a couple of questions."

Kevin analyzed his options. There didn't seem to be any. He followed Luis down the hallway.

CHAPTER 11

Mark was surfing the Internet. His eyes kept glancing to the clock at the corner of the computer screen to see when he could leave for lunch. He was interrupted by the phone.

"Mark, it's Peter."

"Hi, Peter. I meant to call you today but forgot. Have you had any luck?"

"Yeah, I found some interesting stuff."

Mark rolled away from his computer terminal and reached for his notepad. "Let's have it."

"It was a challenge. As I said yesterday, ARI is openly owned by Jason Reynolds. But when it came to Nationwide Polling, it took quite a bit of digging and a little bit of hacking."

Mark tensed. He hadn't intended for Peter to do anything illegal.

"Well, after I searched through about six different corporations, some legitimate but most of them dummies, the trail led me back to Mr. Reynolds."

"Are you sure? Isn't that strange for him to own two of the leading research companies?" Mark asked.

"It's not just two. I asked the same question last night myself, so I kept digging. Reynolds, in one way or another, is connected to eight of the ten polling companies I checked out."

Mark wrote down the names of the companies as Peter read them off. "That's incredible," Mark exclaimed.

"And let me tell you, nobody would know about his connection. It was so well hidden, I had to—"

"No," Mark interrupted him. "I don't want to know how you did it."

Peter was disappointed. He was proud of the way he'd hacked into Reynolds's computers. "OK, but you might be interested to know that he also owns National Studios."

Mark was skeptical. "There must be some mistake, Peter. Jared Winter runs this place with an iron hand." Jared was the president of National Studios and had a reputation in the industry for ruling it like a dictator.

"That's what the public thinks, but I'm telling you the power behind Winter is Reynolds. It's hidden very well, but Reynolds owns National, some major radio networks and even has a publishing arm that owns several newspapers throughout the country."

Mark tried to jot down everything Peter was saying. "Can you get me documentation on this?"

"Sure, I can print out the paper trail, but be careful with it," Peter warned. "Mr. Reynolds has gone through a lot of trouble and expense to stay behind the scenes of these ventures. I'm sure he'd be very upset if he knew this information was out, if you know what I mean."

"I understand, but I'm going to need some proof of this."

"OK, it's your neck. There won't be any ties to me though, and I'll deny everything if you ever say I was involved."

"Don't worry. I protect my sources," Mark assured him.

"Oh, and don't count out Richard Adler, the owner of Research International."

"Why, what do you mean?"

"Remember I said that eight of the ten companies I checked out were owned by Reynolds?"

"Yes." Mark wondered where Peter was going with this.

"The other two are owned by Adler."

That seemed odd, Mark thought. "It's beginning to sound like a monopoly in the research business, isn't it?"

"If you can tie Reynolds and Adler together in some way, yes, it is. I'll keep digging." Peter answered excitedly.

"Oh, Peter, one more thing." Mark reached over, touching the envelope Kevin had given him. "I wondered if you'd be able to analyze a computer disk for me."

NATIONAL STUDIOS-EXECUTIVE OFFICES
12:21 P.M. PACIFIC

Frank Russell wondered what he was doing there, sitting opposite the desk of Jared Winter, the president of National Studios, as he studied the rundown for Sunday night's show. Winter had never taken interest in a particular show before. Was it because of the low ratings? Frank didn't know, but he felt uncomfortable.

"About this story on India," Winter questioned, "what's the angle going to be on it?"

"Mainly human interest," Frank answered. "Stan's got some powerful footage of families left homeless by the earthquake, kids starving in the streets. It's pretty bad over there."

"I know." Winter leaned back in his executive chair as he set the rundown on his desk. "I want him to take a different approach."

"Excuse me?" Frank asked cautiously.

"I want him to expand the piece," he explained. "India's not just dealing with the earthquake; the drought has left millions of people trying to share inadequate resources. You add Pakistan right across the border ready to pounce at any sign of weakness—two nations with nuclear capabilities—and you've got an international incident. Now that's a story!"

Frank was taken aback. This was the first time Winter had ever instructed him on how to cover a story—and he was right.

"That's a good angle," Frank admitted. "Do you want to bump it to the lead story?"

"No!" Winter answered quickly. "Keep the abortion ruling where it is."

"OK. I'll talk to Stan."

"Better yet," Winter continued, "have him come in and see me. We've got a tense situation over there—Pakistan could amass troops on that border at the drop of a hat. The UN is going to have to step in and do something. I want to make sure he understands that."

"I'll have him over this afternoon." Frank responded.

NATIONAL STUDIOS
12:30 P.M. PACIFIC

Each step led to more questions. Mark decided it was time to get information from a different source. He picked up the phone and dialed a number from the top of his notepad.

A weak voice answered.

"Mrs. Dawkins?"

"Yes, this is she."

"My name is Mark Taylor. I'm a reporter with *Across the Nation*."

"Oh my," she responded. "How can I help you?"

"First, let me offer my condolences on the loss of your husband. I'm very sorry."

"Thank you, but why are you calling?" A tone of suspicion rose in her voice.

"I've been researching a story and wondered if you would be willing to talk with me about your husband."

She didn't answer right away. Mark thought she was going to hang up. "What type of story are you doing, Mr. . . ."

"Taylor, ma'am, but you can call me Mark if you like. I'm researching the effect public opinion polls are having on national policy."

"How could I be of help? I had nothing to do with Leeland's work."

Mark wasn't sure how much he should say. He wanted to gently ask if she ever suspected that her husband's death wasn't by natural causes, but he wasn't even sure he believed Kevin's theory himself.

"What was your reaction to his cause of death?" he finally asked.

There was a long pause. "Look, Mr. Taylor, I'm willing to answer whatever questions you might have, but not over the phone. Could you find your way out here?"

Mark hadn't mentioned he was calling from Los Angeles. He tried to figure out how quickly he could get to the East Coast and back before Sunday night's show, then he remembered the Scripture and vision Rick had shared with him earlier.

"How about tomorrow, late morning?"

"That would be fine. Let's say eleven o'clock." She gave Mark the directions to her estate in Franklin Lakes, New Jersey.

He disconnected the line, then called the studio travel department and asked for red-eye connections between LA and New York for that night, returning as early as possible on Sunday morning.

While he was waiting for the information, he had another idea.

When Mark heard the cost of the ticket, he hesitated. He knew he would have a lot of explaining to do. He wrote down his flight information, United Airlines leaving LAX at 10:00, arriving in Newark at 6 A.M. Then he checked his notes and quickly dialed another number.

"Research International."

"Hi, my name is Mark Tay ... back," he finally spit out. "Could I speak with Mr. Palmer please?"

"Hold one moment, Mr. Tayback."

A few seconds later he heard, "Executive offices. This is Norma. How may I help you?"

"Hi, Norma, this is Mark Tayback with the National Gay-Lesbian Alliance. I wonder if I could speak with Mr. Palmer please."

His name wasn't familiar to Norma, but she recognized the organization Mark had mentioned. He'd discovered in Kevin's notes that the gay opinion poll ARI had conducted was commissioned by the National Gay-Lesbian Alliance. He hoped it would open the door with Research International.

"Hold on, Mr. Tayback. I'll see if he's in."

After a second, he heard a man's voice. "Mr. Tayback, how are you doing today?"

"Fine, Mr. Palmer, but please call me Mark."

"OK, Mark it is," Palmer agreed, preferring to keep things less formal. "We've normally been communicating with Bryan. Is everything all right?"

"Yes, everything is fine. It's just that I'm going to be in New York on business this weekend, and Bryan thought it might be good if I stopped by in person while I'm in the city. Would you have time for a chat?"

Mark held his breath as the president of Research International contemplated his proposal. "I guess that would be possible. It's kind of irregular on a weekend, but I suppose your group has spent enough money with our firm that we can accommodate a request like that. What time did you have in mind?"

Mark breathed a sigh of relief under his breath. "Well, I have another appointment in the morning. How about midafternoon, say around three?"

"Three it is then, Mark. May I ask exactly what you want to discuss? You've received the results, haven't you?"

"Oh yes, and we're very pleased." Mark prayed silently as he continued, hoping he wouldn't slip up as he created this cover story on the fly. "As a matter of fact, we've had an idea to sanction another poll to build on the success of the last one. It could mean a considerable increase in our contract."

Mark could nearly see the smile on Palmer's face. "Well, that's certainly good news. I'll be looking forward to our time together."

Mark hung up the phone. His hands were shaking. He'd never attempted doing undercover reporting in any of his stories since joining *Across the Nation*, but he'd created Mark Tayback on the spot as he made the call. *Interesting*, he thought, *I just lied, repeatedly.* He wondered how that would stack up with being a bold Christian in the workplace, something he'd have to think about, later.

Right now he needed to be able to back up his cover story. He dialed the graphics department.

"Allan, I wonder if you could come up with some business cards for me."

"Sure, Mark, I could do that. How soon do you need them?"

"This afternoon."

"Wow, that doesn't give me much time. But I have a set of those laser-printed ones that come ten to a page. They're not quite as thick as the real thing, but usually pass muster pretty well. Will that do?"

"I guess it will have to."

"OK, how do you want them to read? Mark Taylor—"

"No, actually, I need to be Mark Tayback from a group called the National Gay-Lesbian Alliance."

He could hear Allan laughing. "Wow, that's quite a lifestyle change for you, isn't it? Is Tad aware of this?"

"Very funny, but it's for a story I'm researching. I'll need to pick them up before I head over to stage 29, sometime before three this afternoon."

"No problem Mark. I'll have them ready for you. Oh, and don't worry, your little secret is safe with me."

AMERICAN RESEARCH INSTITUTE
12:38 P.M. PACIFIC

Kevin was seated directly in front of Luis, who stood over him. Griff sat close by on his left. They had somehow managed to dim the lights in the room, yet Kevin felt as if there was a spotlight pointed directly at his chair.

"Now, Mr. Spencer," Luis began, "it's time you let us in on what's been going on around here."

Kevin looked up, but in the darkness he couldn't read Luis's eyes. "I don't know what you're talking about. I've just been doing my job." He tried to sound confident, but his voice quivered.

"Let me refresh your memory," Luis paced in front of him as he talked. "We know that your computer terminal has been checking into a certain poll that you were not assigned to. We know that you requested the phone records that coincided with when that poll was conducted. We also know that you still have those records, along with a computer disk copy of the program and data from that poll. Does that refresh your memory?"

With each detail that Luis mentioned, Kevin sank deeper and deeper into despair. He should never have started playing amateur detective.

"Look, this has all been a misunderstanding. I was curious, that's all. So I did some checking, all right? I've learned my lesson. I'll stay out of other people's business, and their programs, OK?"

Luis stopped directly in front of Kevin's chair and lowered his face inches away from Kevin's. "It's a little late for that now, Kevin. Who have you talked to? Who else knows about this?"

"Nobody. I've been doing this all on my own." Kevin involuntarily began to shake as he talked. "I haven't even let my secretary in on any of this."

"Then who's been hacking into our computer systems?" Luis yelled inches from his face. "Who are you working with?"

"Nobody, I swear," Kevin said as he thought of Mark Taylor. Could Mark be hacking into the computer network for information? Kevin didn't think so. He decided to keep that information to himself for his own safety. If they knew he'd already talked with the press, he wasn't sure what would happen to him. He still hoped he could walk out of this and get everything back to normal.

"Mr. Spencer," Luis began again, backing away and calming his voice. "We take corporate security around here very seriously. When one of our own starts dabbling in areas he's not supposed to, well, it makes us distrust him. Do you know what I mean?"

Kevin nodded.

"Good, now maybe we can all walk away from this and get back to our jobs, but that's only if there is some way you can help us trust you again." Luis brought up a chair and placed it in front of Kevin's before he sat down. "Do you know how you can do that?"

"How?"

"By telling us the truth now."

The silence echoed in Kevin's ears as they waited for his response. He thought of Mark, of Cindy, of his wife. What should he say? Would they let him go if he told them everything? He'd never been so afraid and so unsure of what to do in his life.

"Look, I'm telling you the truth. I haven't talked with anybody."

"Oh?" Luis chided, "then who did you talk with from Research International."

Kevin looked up, unable to keep the stunned expression from his face. "How did you know?" he said before he could stop himself.

"You see, Kevin, we know much more than you think. We just want to hear it from you, then we can decide how to handle the situation."

"OK, I understand." Kevin sighed, having made his decision. "I had called them when I saw that their research had produced pretty much the same results on the gay poll that ours had, and I knew how biased our questions had been. But I couldn't get through to anybody. All I got was the standard line about the poll being confidential. So I was just going to drop the whole thing. Then I get this call out of the blue from someone claiming to be with RI. He called himself Lee, but I never could connect that name with any employee at the company."

Luis leaned back in his chair, grinning. Finally, they were getting somewhere. "What day was that?"

Kevin tried to think back. "That was over a week ago, sometime late last week."

Luis nodded, that matched the records he had of Leeland calling Kevin's office last Thursday. "And what did this mysterious Lee tell you?"

"Not much, believe me. At first he just wanted to know why I was asking questions. Then he hung up on me, told me he'd get back to me later."

"Did he?"

"Yes, early this week. I believe it was Monday."

Luis listened intently. He didn't know about a second call between the two. Leeland must have done that from outside his office and on the very day he'd been eliminated.

"Go on, what was said then?"

"That's when he told me to look up the phone records, to compare the actual calls made with what the computer program had recorded. That's when I requested the phone logs."

Silence again.

"Oh, and one more thing," Kevin volunteered. "He also read off one of the questions from their poll, a rather intricate one. It matched one of our questions exactly, so I knew there was something weird going on."

"So you decided to investigate?" Griff asked.

"I've always taken this job very seriously. I couldn't believe we'd be involved with any kind of unscientific polling. I had to check it out."

"Without going to your superior?" Luis asked.

Kevin shrugged.

Luis again brought himself nose to nose with Kevin. "Now think very carefully this time, Kevin. Have you told anybody else about this?"

Kevin swallowed and looked down at his feet. "No," he finally said.

"Then," Luis asked, "you won't mind if we take a trip with you to wherever you've hidden the phone records and the disk, right?"

NATIONAL STUDIOS
SAME TIME

Rick was just about to walk out the door when the phone rang.

"Rick Treadway."

"Rick, you're not going to believe what happened," Mark said.

"You want to tell me over lunch? I was just heading over to the commissary."

"No, I've got lunch plans already. Sorry."

"OK, then tell me the unbelievable."

"I'm flying to New York tonight."

Rick laughed. "Wow, I guess that vision or whatever it was did come from God. Why so sudden?"

Mark filled him in on the events of the morning.

"Be careful," Rick warned. "If there's the possibility that guy was murdered, it could happen again, you know."

"I know, but then remember that verse: God will strengthen and protect me from the evil one."

"I hear you. How are you going to get there and back before Sunday's show?"

"With a couple of red-eyes. I guess that's where the strengthening part comes from."

They both laughed.

"Rick, what do you think about a Christian doing undercover stuff?" Mark asked.

Rick was taken aback. "What do you mean, like a cop or federal agent, something like that?"

"Somewhat, but to be more specific, let's say an investigative reporter researching a story by using an assumed name."

"I get the feeling this has something to do with your New York trip."

"Yeah, it does. When I called Research International, I just couldn't use my real name. Without thinking, I said I was Mark Tayback."

"That's interesting. To tell you the truth, I've never really thought about it. I guess you're wondering if it would be lying?"

"Yeah. I didn't really think about it until it was already out."

Rick smiled. "Sounds like the old 'it's easier to ask forgiveness than to ask permission.'"

"Exactly, and I'm not so sure God didn't lead me into it, you know, for my protection," Mark said.

"It sounds like you're committed either way. Off the top of my head the only story that comes to mind is Rahab the harlot. She lied about the spies Joshua had sent into Jericho and helped them escape. That deception saved her and her entire household when God gave the city to the Israelites."

"You're right." Mark felt a little better.

"I'll do some digging when I get a chance and see what else I can come up with," Rick assured him.

"I'd appreciate it, and I'll do the same. If it's wrong, I guess I'll have to figure out a way to deal with it as a journalist. It's a pretty common investigative technique."

"I would imagine there have to be Christian undercover police officers and federal agents, not to mention Christian spies in wartime. It's an interesting quandary. Is there ever a time when lying is justified?"

"Oh, Rick, one more thing. Do you have Vanessa's phone number? I had a talk with Samantha. She might actually want to speak to her."

"Wow, that was quick. How did that work out?"

"I took a step of boldness. Last night's meeting has really helped, thanks."

"Don't thank me, thank God. Here's the phone number. I hope you find what you're looking for in New York. I'll be praying for you."

"As I will be for you and Cassie. But let me be the first to congratulate you two."

"I like your faith, Mark," Rick said with a smile.

CHAPTER 12

AMERICAN RESEARCH INSTITUTE
SAME TIME

"I don't have them," Kevin finally answered.

"Then who does?" Luis asked.

"It's not what you think. I was afraid to keep them after you came into my office yesterday. So I mailed them off, to my cousin. I'll be able to get them for you in a couple of days."

Luis wasn't buying it, but he didn't want to do anything rash until they had the computer program and the phone logs back in their possession.

"Keep an eye on him, Griff. I've got a call to make."

Luis made his way down the hallway and into the stairway before pulling out his cell phone. He hit speed dial for Reynolds's private line.

"It's Luis. I've just finished questioning Kevin."

"And?"

"Well, it took awhile to get some truth out of him. He confessed to the talks with Leeland."

"Talks? You mean there was more than one?"

"Yeah, the second one on Monday. He must have made that one out of the office. Leeland was the one to point him in the direction of the phone logs."

Reynolds swore. "We should have never used that old technique. What was Bob thinking?"

"You'll have to ask him that, sir," Luis replied. "Evidently, Lee confirmed that one of RI's questions matched one of ARI's on the gay poll, which added to Kevin's suspicions."

"Anything else?"

"Not really. He's scared, big time, so I think he's been fairly truthful with what he's said so far."

"But you still think there's more."

"Yeah, I do. He can't offer up the disk and phone logs for a couple of days. Says he mailed them to his cousin."

"You don't believe him?"

"Not sure. He's holding something back, but I can't put my finger on it. He's got to be working with somebody to explain the computer hacking. I thought I'd see what you wanted to do before we finished with him."

"I don't want him out of our sight until that stuff's been recovered and we find out who he's talked to." Reynolds thought for a second. "Bring him out here. I want to have a talk with him."

AMERICAN RESEARCH INSTITUTE
1:30 P.M. PACIFIC

Mark made it downtown on time. The entrance to Fellini's was on the other side of the lobby from the elevators so he didn't have to deal with the security guards. He stepped into the restaurant looking for Tracy. She waved to him from a table beside the window overlooking Grant Street.

Mark made his way to her table. He admired how pretty she looked and noticed the slight dimple in her left cheek when she smiled as she stood and took his hand in greeting.

"Nice to see you again, Mark."

"It's great to see you, Tracy. Thanks so much for fitting me into your schedule. Some other things came up in my research that sparked my curiosity."

He took the menu in his hands. "So what's good here?"

"Everything," Tracy answered, picking up her own menu. "I love the antipasta salad, and they have a wonderful fettuccini Michelangelo."

"What's in that?" he asked.

"Chicken, mushrooms, and onions in a wonderful cream sauce."

"That sounds good to me."

"So tell me how I can help," Tracy offered after they had ordered.

Mark sat back and sipped his water, "First, tell me more about Tracy Reynolds."

Her face flushed. She was embarrassed by his personal attention. "What would you like to know?"

"Oh, I don't know, like where you went to college?"

"UCLA."

"Major was sociology, right?"

"Correct, but I double-majored in computer sciences."

"Good combination. How long have you lived in LA?"

"All my life, with a couple of summers in Europe—France and Switzerland."

Mark was firing questions at her faster with each answer. Tracy followed right along.

"How long have you been with ARI?"

"Five years, started right out of college."

"Favorite movie?"

"Um, *Gone with the Wind.*"

"Favorite food?"

"Italian."

"Favorite color?"

"Pink, no green." She laughed at her own mistake, which brought a warmth within Mark he couldn't have imagined. He laughed with her as he took another drink.

"OK, my turn," she said. "Where did you go to school?"

"Went through night school at University of California at Northridge while working my way up the ranks at National. Started as an intern. It took me seven years to get the journalism degree, eight years to get the chance to be a reporter."

"Where were you before that?"

"Kuwait. Desert Storm."

"Wow, what branch of the service?"

"Marines. I was with a special ops-extraction force."

Tracy's head tilted slightly, "What is that exactly?"

"I'm sorry. Special operations. We were the guys sent into Iraqi territory if any of our boys got shot down."

"Wow, that must have been exciting. Why did you leave the service?"

"When the war was over and my time was up, I headed to Los Angeles. The main reason I went into the Marines was to get government support for my education. My family couldn't afford to send me to college, and I wanted to be a journalist, ever since high school."

"Oh yeah." Tracy smiled, "the Geraldo factor."

Mark laughed.

"Where did you grow up?"

"Smyrna, Tennessee. Just outside of Nashville."

"That's amazing. You don't have an accent."

"I worked hard to get rid of it," he answered, then slid into an overemphasized Southern drawl. "You cain't get them there folks in television to give you a job by talkin' like this."

He pronounced the final word with two syllables.

Mark loved the sparkle in Tracy's eyes as she laughed. The two sat in silence for a moment.

"I'm glad you suggested lunch, Tracy." Mark smiled warmly. "Even though we come from opposite worlds, I really enjoy being with you."

Tracy responded with a flush and a beautiful smile.

Luis had decided to keep Kevin in Griff's office until after the lunch crowd had returned. He didn't want anybody from the company catching a glimpse of him in the parking garage. They'd taken the stairway down a couple of floors just to be safe. From there they took the elevator to the parking garage, second level.

Kevin stepped out of the elevator after Griff gave him a heavy shove. He looked around for anybody who could help. He noticed two Reynolds Building security guards approach the trio.

"This floor is clear," the first one reported, shattering any hope Kevin harbored of rescue.

A white van pulled up right beside them, and the side door opened.

"Get in," Griff ordered.

"You can't do this to me," Kevin argued. "This is kidnapping."

"Think of it this way," Luis said as he pushed Kevin inside. "You're going to see the boss. You play your cards right, and this might mean a promotion for you."

Griff laughed as he climbed in next to Kevin. Luis took the front passenger seat as he ordered the driver to move out. Kevin racked his brain for any ideas on how to get out of his predicament.

The salad had been wonderful, the fettuccini Michelangelo superb, but Mark hardly noticed as he continued gazing at Tracy across the table. The conversation had quieted when they'd been served their entrees.

"So tell me, Mark, what questions prompted you to call me again?"

Mark fought back a flash of panic. He'd gotten so caught up in the joy of the moment, he wasn't prepared to pry her for information, nor was he sure he still wanted to. He paused to think as he swallowed the bite in his mouth, then reached for his glass of water.

"Let's say I wanted to conduct a poll, but I wanted a certain outcome, a guaranteed result. Could it be done?"

Tracy hesitated. "This is what you were trying to get at yesterday—"

"I know, and you pointed out, very astutely I might add, how ARI works hard to avoid that. But say, hypothetically, a company—one not as scrupulous as yours, of course—wanted to rig a poll. How could they make that happen?"

Mark analyzed her face as Tracy thought for a minute. There seemed to be no anxiety or attempt to deceive. Instead she concentrated, trying to come up with a scenario Mark had described as if it were the first time she'd ever thought about it.

"Well, I guess," she finally answered, "there would be several ways somebody could go about it. The easiest would be to just lie. Put together a survey and then publish whatever results you want, but there wouldn't be any data to back it up."

"What else?"

"Another way would be to write some leading, very biased questions so that whoever answered the survey would lean toward the intended results."

"Give me an example."

"Let's say your poll was on gun control, and you wanted the results to be in favor of it. You could word one of the questions something like this, and this is off the top of my head now."

"I understand," Mark assured her.

"OK. In light of the recent shootings and deaths in high schools across the country, would you be in favor of a ban on assault weapons so that kids wouldn't have access to high-powered automatic rifles?"

Mark laughed. "I could see how that would get you a pretty high percentage of positive responses."

"Especially if you surveyed right after a tragedy like that occurred."

"OK, I've got that one. What else do you think could be done?"

"Another way would be to corrupt your sample, the people you're polling."

"Please explain." Mark took out his notebook and pen.

"In other words, rather than get an accurate random sampling of your target audience, you intentionally question a higher percentage of those who will respond favorably. For instance, that same poll on gun control, you could pollute the sample by asking twice as many Democrats who tend to favor gun control."

Mark made a note, then looked at her intently as he added, "Or maybe you could call a higher percentage of cities known for their liberal leanings than a true random sampling of phone numbers."

Tracy looked at him with her head slightly cocked. "That's interesting, complicated, but very good. I never would have thought of that."

She seemed sincere, but could he believe her?

"The only problem with that scenario though," she added, "is that the telephone numbers for phone polling come directly out of our computers, from a random sampling program that picks the numbers automatically."

"Couldn't the program be changed?"

Tracy thought a second longer. "Well, yes, I guess it could. But I can't imagine somebody actually doing it. We're all in this for the most accurate results we can find, plus any false data testing like that would stick out drastically when any other company did a similar poll."

"Unless those companies were doing the same thing," Mark interjected.

Tracy looked at him with a puzzled expression. "Now that's far-fetched. Who have you been talking to, some screenwriters at the studio?"

"No," Mark shrugged. "Maybe I'm just searching for the plot of a good novel."

Tracy smiled again. "Well, you had me going there for a second. It sure makes you think of the possibilities, doesn't it?"

He nodded, returning her smile. Mark had intended to drill Tracy for some answers but now found himself confronted with two nearly insurmountable obstacles. First, he desperately wanted to believe she had nothing to do with the rigging of the gay poll, and second, during the course of their lunch together, the journalistic wolf inside him had lapsed into a playful puppy. He needed to awaken the wolf.

"Do you think I could get an appointment with your grandfather?"

Tracy looked up surprised. "I doubt it. He never gives interviews. Why do you want to see him?"

Mark watched her intently as he spoke. "I've been doing some research on your company and a few others, and there are a few questions I'd love to ask him."

"Like what?"

In spite of the friendly rapport that had developed, Mark knew he had to be careful. He was in danger of losing the connection to Reynolds and probably his relationship with Tracy as well.

After a quick request to God for wisdom, Mark continued. "Did you know that your grandfather owns or has a controlling interest in at least eight research companies?"

Tracy's eyes darkened. Mark could see she was surprised. "My grandfather owns or has a controlling interest in a lot of different companies. I couldn't begin to name them."

"But isn't it a bit odd to own companies in competition with each other? Why would he need to have ARI, Nationwide Polling, Chicago Institute of Research, North American Statistical Analysis, the Billings Institute?"

With each name, Tracy's eyes widened farther. Her head began to shake back and forth. "I'm finding this very hard to accept, Mark. I would know if he owned those companies."

"Would you, Tracy?" he responded gently. "It took a lot of digging to find this out. Some of the connections are very well hidden. I also found out he owns a number of media outlets, including my own network."

"Where are you going with this?" she asked sharply. "Are you saying my grandfather fits into your fictitious scenario of false polls and grand conspiracy? Is your story now centered on the evil Reynolds Industries empire?"

"No, Tracy, I'm just trying—"

"Our company painstakingly attempts to provide our clients with the most accurate data possible," Tracy cut him off. Her voice started to quiver. "I can't conceive that any of our surveys would be compromised in any way. I'm too close to the process. I would know."

Mark reached across the table and placed his hand over hers. "Tracy, please forgive me."

Tracy pulled in a breath. Mark's hand on her skin and his abrupt apology softened her rage.

"I'm not accusing you of anything," he said as she looked up into his eyes. "Or your grandfather, for that matter. OK?"

She smiled weakly. "It sure sounded like it."

"I'm sorry, really." His hand lingered on top of hers; their eyes remained fixed on each other. The connection was returning. "My story isn't worth upsetting you," he confessed more to himself than to her.

"What is your story, Mark?"

"I'm not sure yet, Tracy. But I'm sure glad it brought me to you."

Her cheeks flushed, the smile returned. "Boy, go in for the kill, then turn on the charm. Is that what they taught you at broadcast school, or did you learn that in the Marines?"

"Neither. I just got so caught up with—with you. I apologize for my lack of professionalism."

"Apology accepted." She eyed him with a fiendish grin. "I'll make you a deal. I'll try to set up a meeting with my grandfather so he can put your wild imagination to rest. No promises, because he'll probably say no. But whether he agrees to meet or not, you have to take me out to dinner this weekend."

A soft summer breeze could have knocked Mark over. "You've got a deal. How about Sunday night? Maybe you could join me in the studio during the show, and we'll have a wonderful dinner after we're off the air."

"That sounds exciting. I'd love to."

NATIONAL STUDIOS
2:37 P.M. PACIFIC

Samantha returned to her desk after being out most of the day since the morning production meeting. Everything seemed to be in place for her edited interview with Mel Gibson on Sunday night. All she needed to do was write her copy introducing the tape. The Internet site would be up and running Sunday so the network would be able to promote the site heavily on the show.

The red message light blinked at her from the telephone as she picked up the receiver to check her voice mail. The third message was from Mark.

"Samantha, just wanted to follow up on our conversation this morning. Here is the phone number of the woman I mentioned. Her name is Vanessa Roberts."

Samantha scribbled down the name and number in irritation, then leaned back in her chair. What was it about Mark that was getting to her? She had been upset when he responded negatively to her story, then furious when he wouldn't even look at her pictures. He reminded her of Rick Treadway and that evening when . . . now why did she think of that?

She rubbed at her temples, replaying the embarrassing evening in her mind. They'd enjoyed a nice dinner after meeting during the production of an infomercial she had hosted and Rick had directed. The evening went well enough, a lot of fun and laughs, then she had to return to the ABC affiliate to do a report for the eleven o'clock news on the murder she'd been covering. On a whim, Sam had decided to drop by Rick's place after work, having added several drinks to the wine she'd consumed at dinner. In Rick's living room and uninhibited from the effect of the alcohol, Samantha had pressed hard to seduce him. She'd nearly succeeded before Rick pulled away. She'd tried to recapture the passion of the moment, but Rick remained adamant. She remembered storming out of his house, vowing for revenge.

Vanessa Roberts. The name flashed through her mind, bringing Sam back to the present. What was there to lose anyway? Besides, she could always ignore whatever this woman had to say and do the report however she liked.

She picked up the phone and dialed.

Vanessa was running late. She was supposed to be at the restaurant by three, and she still had a fifteen-minute drive to get her daughter to day care. With little Shelby in her arms and grabbing the diaper bag, she reached for her keys as the phone rang. On impulse her hand grabbed the receiver instead.

"Is this Vanessa Roberts?" she heard on the other end.

Oh, great! A sales call! she thought. "Look, I'm running late, and I don't have any money to buy anything."

"I'm not selling." Samantha chuckled at the thought. "This is Samantha Steel from *Across the Nation*."

Vanessa nearly dropped the diaper bag.

"I'm working on a story that I'd love to spend a few minutes talking with you about," Sam continued. "Is there a chance we could meet?"

"What's the story about?" Vanessa asked.

"It's based on Internet porn. A friend of mine, Mark Taylor, here at the show gave me your name."

"I don't think I know him," Vanessa answered skeptically.

"Well, he said a friend of his gave him your number. I'm not even sure who it was. He said you've come out of the pornography business and would have some insight I should consider before I complete my story. Are you up for it?"

Lord, is this your will? Vanessa prayed. She remembered the way Samantha Steel had handled her reporting last year and didn't trust her one bit. But if God wanted her to talk with Sam, she wouldn't say no.

"I guess it would be all right," she finally responded.

"How about tomorrow afternoon? I could come by your apartment."

Vanessa reluctantly agreed and gave her directions before hanging up. As she rushed out the front door, she continued her prayer. *Please give me the right words to say, God.*

MALIBU
2:57 P.M. PACIFIC

The van pulled around to the side of the Reynolds estate where a six-car garage had been chiseled into the surrounding rock. Luis stepped out and opened the side door for Griff. The two quickly led Kevin inside the lower levels of the huge mansion to a room that had been prepared for him.

"You keep him here," Luis instructed. "I'll go get Reynolds."

"I don't see how you expect to get away with this," Kevin tried to argue as Luis closed the door on them.

Griff glanced up at him, then looked around the room. "I don't see anybody stopping us."

Kevin lowered his head. He didn't see anybody stopping them either.

CHAPTER 13

Mark looked at his watch as he walked up to stage 29. Fifteen minutes late, not good. He'd run into more traffic than expected coming out of downtown, and stopping at the graphics department to get his "business cards" for New York delayed him even further.

He showed the guard his *Across the Nation* press ID and was allowed to enter the studio. He quietly walked along the front of the audience bleachers. The cast of the sit-com was in the middle of rehearsing a scene for that night's taping. Jennifer was already set up across the studio with the camera crew. She rushed over to Mark, anger flaring in her eyes.

"Where have you been? We had Cynthia Packer lined up to do the first interview. When you didn't show, the director called her back into rehearsal."

Cynthia was one of the female leads in the show, and one of the hardest actresses to get any kind of comments from. Jennifer was afraid they'd lost their shot at getting her altogether.

"I'm sorry, Jenn. I was following up a lead on the polling story." He noticed her eyes roll. "I thought I left in plenty of time, but traffic—"

129

"Right, just drop it. Hopefully, we'll have another chance after this scene. Let's go over the questions I want you to ask."

Jennifer prepped Mark on the schedule and her questions for each cast member. Mark found it difficult to concentrate; his mind kept drifting back to Tracy. Jennifer completed her instruction, and Mark saw that the cast was still involved with rehearsal, so he stepped over to the audio mixer.

"Hey, Steve," he asked, "I wonder if you could help me."

"Sure, Mark, what do you need?"

"I've got an undercover thing going this weekend and wondered if you could hook me up with some kind of secret recording device?"

Steve looked at him in surprise. "I'm not aware of anything scheduled this weekend."

"I know. It just came up. I'll be going out solo, but it would be great to get a meeting I've set up on tape. Do we have anything I could borrow?"

Steve smiled. "I have just the right thing, but it's not National's. Come back with me after our shoot tonight, and I'll get you hooked up."

"Thanks. I appreciate it."

"Mark!" He could hear Jennifer calling him in an exaggerated whisper. "They're wrapping it up. Get ready."

Oh, boy, Mark thought, *here we go.*

MALIBU
3:22 P.M. PACIFIC

"I don't care what it takes," Jason said as he and Luis stepped into the elevator. "We've got to retrieve the disk and the phone records before he's terminated."

Luis turned to face the elevator doors as they closed. "If he did mail them to his cousin, then he's bought himself a few days until we can recover them."

"And if he didn't mail them?" Jason asked.

"We'll know that soon enough," Luis said coldly.

"I don't care how you do it, Luis. I want this leak plugged."

The doors opened as they reached the basement level. Luis led the way down the hallway toward the room where Kevin was being held.

"So, Kevin," Jason said with a smile as he entered, "I'm sorry for the inconvenience of bringing you here, but I thought we should talk."

Kevin was taken aback by Reynolds's demeanor. "You have a strange way of making an appointment, Mr. Reynolds," he responded.

Reynolds laughed, then turned to Luis. "Leave us alone for a minute."

Luis started to argue.

"Now!" Jason cut him off sternly. Luis nodded toward Griff, and they left the room.

Jason took a seat next to Kevin, then paused a moment before speaking. "From what I understand Kevin, you've been an excellent employee. It's unfortunate that circumstances dictated meeting this way for the first time."

Kevin remained silent, wondering what was coming next.

"You've been with the company how long now?" Jason asked.

Kevin swallowed hard. "About two years, sir."

"And in that time, you've been loyal to ARI. I'm curious Kevin, what caused you to start this inquiry of yours?"

Kevin didn't know if anything he said right then would help him regain his freedom or not. Reynolds had the upper hand. Perhaps he could plead his way out.

"Look, Mr. Reynolds. I didn't mean anything by it. There's always been a little . . . let's say professional rivalry between Bob and myself. When I saw the results of his survey, I just couldn't believe it was accurate."

Droplets of perspiration began to form on Kevin's forehead as he continued. "I guess I didn't think it through, but something in me had to see what he did with the survey."

"So you took it upon yourself to investigate, even calling up another research firm, something expressly forbidden," Jason stood up and faced Kevin, his voice rising along with his irritation, "rather than going to your manager about the conflict, is that right?"

Kevin looked up at the commanding presence over him, "Yes, but I had to have some proof before I could go to my supervisor, or I would be written off as someone with a grudge. Once I found out what Bob had done, I was going to report it. I knew ARI wouldn't want inaccurate data being published."

"No, I wouldn't tolerate that within my company, Kevin, almost as much as I won't tolerate spying."

Kevin looked up into his eyes, hoping to see some sign of mercy.

"Well, let's see if we can get this all behind us, shall we?" Jason brought his voice level back down, vacillating between the role of interrogator and friend.

Jason once again took the seat next to him. "Now tell me, Kevin, who else knows about all this?"

"I've already told your security chief everything there is to tell. I kept the research to myself. Not even my secretary knew what I was doing."

"What about your wife, the cousin you apparently sent the information to?"

"My wife doesn't know anything; neither does my cousin," Kevin tried to think. The reporter had mentioned a name he'd use as his cousin to contact him, but what was it?

Jason noticed the hesitation, "Your cousin, Kevin, what is his name?"

"Mark," Kevin finally remembered. "Mark Foster. He lives in Pasadena."

Jason's eyes darkened skeptically. "Is there anything else you want to tell me?"

Kevin knew he was on thin ice but didn't know what else to say. "No, sir, I swear. That's the truth. Look, I'm sorry, I didn't think about what I was doing. Let's just get me back to the office where I can get to work, OK?"

"All right, Kevin," Jason responded. "We'll get you back to the office." He got up and walked over to the door. Kevin stood up, overwhelmed with relief.

"Oh, Kevin, one more thing." Jason knocked once on the door, then turned back toward him. The door opened, revealing Luis standing in the hallway holding a syringe and a medical vial.

"Luis here is going to go over your story with you one last time," Jason said. "When he's finished, I'm sure we'll know whether you've been telling the truth or not."

NATIONAL STUDIOS
4:08 P.M. PACIFIC

Rick sat alone in the control room. During this hour before the show started, he would go over his script and make any notes he'd need to give to the crew at the 4:30 meeting. It was like the calm before the storm, and Rick always enjoyed the peacefulness of it. As he looked over the musical director's rundown, the phone beside him rang.

"Control room," he answered automatically.

"Rick Treadway, please."

"Speaking."

"Rick, hi. This is Frank Russell, the executive producer for *Across the Nation*. Is this a bad time to reach you?"

"No, Frank, we're a good hour away from rolling tape. Everyone else is at lunch. What can I do for you?"

"I was wondering if you might be available to direct our show next Sunday night?" Russell said. "Terri has some family emergency that just came up and is going to need to leave town right after the show. The National execs suggested I give you a call. Are you interested?"

"Wow, I'm sorry to hear about Terri's problem. I hope it's not too serious."

"Thanks, Rick, we do too. But she also thought you'd be a good fill-in. So what do you say?"

"I'm flattered and would love to help if I can."

"That's great. I'll give your agent a call and work everything out. We'd like you to observe this weekend with us, if you're available."

"I think I'd better," Rick laughed. "I wouldn't want to embarrass myself next week. What time should I be there?"

"Terri thinks you can drop in early afternoon, say around three, and she'll get you up to speed. We go live at six o'clock."

"Sounds good, and thanks, Frank, for thinking of me."

"You're welcome. I'll see you Sunday."

Rick paused before getting back to his script. An opportunity to direct Mark's show, just as they were connecting spiritually. What a coincidence. Then he laughed. *Divine coincidence,* he thought.

"OK, people, that's a break," the first assistant director called out to the cast and crew of *The Single Life.* "The audience loads in at seven. Be in position by fifteen after."

Mark turned toward the camera crew. "Let's get ready to roll, guys. When Jennifer gets back, she's going to want to go."

He took his place in front of the camera with microphone in hand. He and Jennifer were doing this piece informally, making it look as if Mark was just walking around backstage, catching the actors behind the scenes.

A few moments later, Jennifer came walking up with Cynthia.

"Cynthia, I'd like you to meet our reporter, Mark Taylor."

Mark extended his hand to greet her, "It's a plea—"

"Yeah, yeah, let's just get this thing going. I've got to get into wardrobe."

Mark turned toward the camera operator with a grimace Cynthia couldn't see. "Let's roll tape, shall we?"

"Speed," the operator called out after a few seconds.

"Cynthia," Mark began, "you've got a runaway hit on your hands with *The Single Life,* and it's electrified your career. You're starring in your first feature this summer. How does it feel?"

What a lame question! Mark hated it the minute it came out of his mouth. How could Russell expect him to take this report seriously?

The irritated starlet disappeared immediately, replaced by a near duplicate of the bubbly, slightly ditzy, yet beautiful character Cynthia played on the show.

"It's been so-o-o amazing," she giggled. "We've had such a wonderful year together. This cast is terrific. And to think I have the opportunity to star in my first feature this summer . . ."

It was all Mark could do to keep an interested look on his face and not look at his watch.

WESTWOOD
6:38 P.M. PACIFIC

When Jill saw Vanessa's car pull into the driveway, she quickly rushed outside and ran up to the back door where little Shelby was sitting in her car seat.

"Hi there, Shelby," she cooed as she gently pulled her out of the car.

"Hi, Vanessa," Gary called as he stepped out of the house, helping her get the diaper bag. "As you can see, Jill's really missed having Shelby around."

Vanessa saw the big smile spread across Shelby's face. "And I think Shelby's missed being here."

"Hi, Vanessa," Jill said as she slid her free arm around her.

"It's great to see you both," Vanessa said. "It's like coming home, something I never thought I'd say again."

They made their way into the house and sat around the kitchen table where Jill could check on the roast chicken. Vanessa sat at what had been her normal seat for so many months while she'd been pregnant. Jill held onto Shelby as she took the seat beside Vanessa.

"It smells delicious," Vanessa remarked.

"I remembered it was one of your favorites," Jill smiled.

"It'll be nice to sit and relax during a meal instead of serving somebody else," Vanessa said with a grin.

"How's it going at the restaurant?" Gary asked.

Vanessa sighed. "It seems like it gets harder and harder to leave Shelby at day care and go to work. I thought it would get easier."

"I can imagine," Jill remarked, looking into Shelby's perfect little face. "Every time I see her, I wish you hadn't moved out on your own."

"Sometimes I wonder if it was the right thing to do. I really miss you two. When you called the other night, I was feeling pretty low. Just hearing your voice helped."

Jill smiled at her.

"Oh, you'll never guess who called me today." Vanessa sat up excitedly.

"Who?" Gary asked.

"Samantha Steel."

The silence hung over the room for a brief moment as Jill and Gary sat stunned.

"Wow, it worked," Gary finally said.

"What do you mean 'it worked'?" Vanessa asked.

"Yeah!" Jill looked at her husband in surprise.

"Oh, I forgot to tell you," Gary apologized. "Rick and I were at home group the other night."

Gary explained the conversation they'd had with Mark about adding Vanessa to the Internet story.

"Do you think she realizes the connection with Rick?" Jill asked.

"She didn't mention anything, and obviously neither did I," Vanessa replied. "I had no idea when she mentioned a friend of a friend had given her my number, she was talking about Rick and Gary."

Gary chuckled, "I doubt she realized it either, or she wouldn't have called."

Jill and Vanessa laughed with him.

"When are you meeting with her?" Jill asked.

"Tomorrow afternoon."

"Wow!" Gary and Jill responded in unison.

"We'll have to pray for you to have the right words for her," Jill suggested.

Vanessa sighed. "I'll take all the prayer I can get."

"You'll have it," Gary promised.

Jill gave Shelby a quick hug, then handed her back to Vanessa. "Here, I'd better get dinner on the table."

"I'll help you, honey," Gary said. "We do need to get started so we won't be late."

Vanessa looked up at the two perplexed. "Late for what?"

"It's a surprise," Jill giggled, "but you're going to love it."

SHERMAN OAKS
6:52 P.M. PACIFIC

Vickie Spencer sat at the dinner table, picking at what was left of the Chinese food. Two dinners in a row ruined by Kevin not even calling to say he'd be late. After last night, she couldn't believe he would do it again. Something must be wrong. She knew he wasn't working late. She'd tried to call him a dozen times. Did he have an accident? Could he have gotten into trouble with that survey he was investigating? The knot at the bottom of her stomach was growing; she couldn't sit there any longer. She had to call somebody.

The reporter. Did Kevin mention his name? She dug deep, but couldn't come up with it. There had to be a way to get the name.

She went to the kitchen phone and pulled out their address book. Under the *R*'s . . . yes, Tracy Reynolds. She quickly dialed the number. After two rings, Tracy came on the line.

"Tracy, hi. This is Vickie Spencer. Would you happen to know if Kevin is working late on a project?"

"No, Vickie, I don't think so. Is he not home yet?"

"No, he's not, and I'm worried. I couldn't reach him all afternoon either."

"That's odd, but you know, now that you mention it, I didn't see him after lunch myself. I don't think he'd be at the office. We don't have anything going on this weekend that I know of."

"It's not like him to not call if he's going to be late."

"Have you tried the highway patrol or checked with the hospitals?"

"No, not yet. I'm afraid to."

"I understand. Hopefully he'll be there soon. If I hear from him, I'll let you know, and please let me know when he gets home, OK?"

"I will, and, Tracy, one more thing. Kevin mentioned you had a television reporter there yesterday. What was his name?"

"Mark Taylor, from *Across the Nation*. Why do you ask?"

"That's right," she said as she wrote the name down. "From *Across the Nation*. I just wondered which reporter it was. Thanks again, Tracy. I'm sorry to have bothered you."

"Oh, it was no bother." Tracy was concerned. "Maybe he just stopped off for a drink or something, and everything is fine."

"I hope you're right."

Vickie set the phone down, then called information.

"The production offices for *Across the Nation* are presently closed. If you would like a listing of our staff, please press 1."

Vickie went through the process of punching in the correct numbers until she was able to ring Mark's extension.

"This is Mark Taylor. I'm not available right now, but please leave a message. If this is an emergency, you can page me at 800-555-4899."

Vickie waited for the beep. "Mark, this is Vickie Spencer, Kevin's wife. It's Friday night, and he's not made it home yet. I was wondering if you two might have had a second meeting. I'll try and page you but please call me."

She left him her number, then quickly dialed his pager. The only option it gave her was to punch in her phone number. Now all she could do was wait. She let out a heavy sigh as she fought back the growing tears. If he didn't call back soon, she'd start calling the hospitals.

CHAPTER 14

"You're killing me with this," Cassie said as she took her final bite of filet mignon. "When are you going to tell me what's been going on?"

Rick laughed. "Aren't you enjoying your meal?" He'd kept the conversation light, trying to steer her away from any serious talk until dinner was out of the way and he could play the video for her. He was running out of time as her patience waned.

"Yes, dinner was wonderful. But I thought this night was for you to explain why you've been acting so strange. When do I get to hear your explanation?"

Rick got up and reached for her hand. "Come with me."

Cassie looked up into his eyes and smiled as she took his hand. It was sweaty. She laughed inwardly, hoping she was reading him right. He'd been so nervous through dinner, trying to keep the conversation flowing without talking about anything serious. But his attempt with the flowers and the romantic dinner made her wonder if he was preparing to pop the question. Now as she felt his clammy hand, she thought she had it figured out.

He walked her to the couch. Expecting him to sit next to her, she was shocked as he turned away and walked over to the entertainment unit, turning on the television.

"What are you doing?" she asked, not hiding her irritation. "We're going to watch TV?"

"You asked me a question," he answered calmly. "Let me answer it in my way and in my time. There's a movie on TV that I wanted to watch with you tonight."

Cassie was stunned. How could she have guessed so wrong! A movie! He wanted to watch a movie? She was seconds away from getting up and walking out of the house until Rick turned back toward her and she caught sight of his mischievous grin. It was just enough to keep her on the couch.

She held his gaze, trying to keep her disappointment hidden as Rick came back and sat next to her. With a huge sigh Cassie reluctantly turned her attention to the television. The exhaustion from a long week and the frustration of her relationship with Rick didn't excite her about watching a stupid movie.

Rick nervously tried to watch her out of the corner of his eye as the videotape played.

"This movie has been rated PG by the Motion Picture Association." Then the music began. Celine Dion softly sang the opening verse to "My Heart Will Go On." The first visual faded up on the screen: a picture of Cassie as a baby, laying naked on a rug and smiling at the camera.

Cassie gasped. She wondered how her picture got on TV. Then she glanced at Rick and saw the foolish grin spread across his face. She deducted that this was Rick's doing, not any network's. She continued to see pictures of herself growing up as image after image went by—running through the sprinkler in her diapers, sitting on a clown's lap at her third birthday party, playing kickball in sixth grade, cheerleading in high school, her sixteenth birthday—braces and all, high school graduation. Her mom must have been in on this, she realized. The shots continued through her college years until she saw backstage pictures of her on *The John Harold Show*.

The final picture of Rick and Cassie together at last year's Emmy Awards faded away slowly as the words "you are safe in my heart and my heart will go on" filled the room. Then the scene faded to Rick, kneeling beside a pond with ducks swimming in the background.

"Cassie," Rick on the screen spoke right to her, "I've known you nearly a year now, and it's become painfully obvious to me how much my life wouldn't be complete without you in it."

Cassie glanced at Rick beside her, her eyes watering. He pointed her back to the television, not wanting her to miss any part of the video.

"So, as I've prayed and prayed about us and searched God's heart along with my own. I feel that it is God's will to join our lives together as one. Cassie, I love you, more than I could have ever believed possible. I'm asking . . ."

Rick couldn't take his eyes off her as she watched. A tear slid down her cheek. Cassie couldn't believe what she was hearing and watching.

The Rick on TV reached his hand out toward her, revealing a jewelry box sitting in his palm.

". . . will you marry me?"

Rick had left a moment of silence on the tape as he knelt before her and held his hand out with the engagement ring sitting in it. This was the moment he'd hoped she'd answer a resounding yes before the music kicked back in with a flourish of celebration. But as he looked into Cassie's face, no answer came. She couldn't speak, she could only cry as she reached her arms around him and hugged with all her might.

After a few moments, Rick finally pulled away.

"Well, what's your answer?"

She wiped her arm across her eyes. Mascara left black streaks above her cheeks. She didn't give it a second thought.

"Yes! Of course I'll marry you. I love you, Rick."

She took the ring and admired the cluster of small diamonds arranged around a two-carat marquis. He reclaimed the ring and slowly slid it onto her finger.

He took her face gently into his hands. "I love you, Cassie Petterson."

They inched toward each other until their lips met in a soft, deeply passionate kiss to seal their promise of marriage.

They held each other for several minutes: Neither spoke. Then Rick suddenly went to the front door.

"What are you doing?"

"I forgot to turn on the porch light," Rick answered.

"So? Get back over here."

Rick flipped on the switch, then stepped lightly back to the living room, jumping over the couch and landing beside her.

"You're crazy, you know that?" Cassie laughed.

"Just crazy about you." He responded with a quick kiss.

"How did you put this whole thing together without my knowing about it?"

"It wasn't easy. Remember yesterday when you came into the control room? We'd just finished the tape."

"I knew something was up. You and Milton looked like a couple of kids caught smoking behind the schoolhouse."

"I know," Rick laughed. "That excuse about trying new effects for teases was pretty lame, but it was all that came to mind."

Cassie joined in laughing. "You should have seen Milton's face when he tried to go along with the cover-up. It was priceless."

They were interrupted by Rick's doorbell chime.

"Are you expecting anyone?" Cassie asked, analyzing Rick's expression.

"No. It's probably a salesman or maybe a kid selling candy."

"Then why are you smiling?"

He opened the door to the sound of a dozen people yelling, "Surprise!"

Cassie shrieked and ducked behind the couch. She was going to kill Rick. With all the crying she'd done, her face must look a wreck. Cassie's roommate Amy was the first to reach her as the two hugged.

"Oh, Cassie, congratulations. I told you not to worry."

Tears started flowing again. "Did you know about this?"

"Well, maybe. But I couldn't tell you."

Looking over Amy's shoulder, Cassie noticed the rest of the gang Rick had secretly invited to their proposal. She saw several members of her home group, a few of the show's staff members, Gary and Jill Hall, Vanessa Roberts with her little baby, and Rob Stevenson, the CIFT leader.

"So did you say yes?" Jill asked.

Cassie blushed as Rick came back to her side and put his arm around her waist.

"I said yes," Cassie answered, then looked at her fiancé with a grim expression. "You were pretty sure of yourself, weren't you?"

Rick looked back at her innocently. "Why? What do you mean?"

"What if I had said no? What kind of party do you think this would be then?"

Rick thought for a second then smiled. "I guess we'll never know."

NATIONAL STUDIOS
9:17 P.M. PACIFIC

Mark glanced at his watch for the fifth time in the past twelve minutes. The studio audience had been thoroughly enamored with the performance from the cast, laughing at all the right spots, even screaming wildly the first time Cynthia made her entrance. But Mark didn't get it. The humor was debased. In the half-hour episode, four of the members of the cast had been in bed with somebody—one of them twice and, one had been a homosexual encounter. If this was what his generation thought of *The Single Life,* he was glad to be living under a different banner. He thought back to a *TV Guide* article he'd read a few months back about the increase in positive gay characters on prime-time television. It concluded that it was a natural step because many writers in Hollywood were gay. Mark thought it was time to see an influx of Christian writers. Then it would be natural to see positive Christian characters on some of these shows. *Lord, make it so,* he prayed.

Looking at his watch one more time, Mark calculated he had about an hour left before he'd have to be on his way to the airport to catch his flight. The show was finished and the cast returned for its bows. The end of a sit-com looked like a Broadway curtain call. Each actor was brought back out to the stage for a final bow, much to the delight of the audience. Cynthia was the last cast member to retake the stage. She made her final appearance still scantily clad in the nightgown her last scene had called for. She bowed with no hint of modesty as she received the audience's adoration. As a man, Mark had to admit she looked enticing, but as a Christian, his heart broke for the path she and her devoted fans blindly walked.

And his job tonight was to put together a segment for his show that would make people want to watch this drivel. Mark lowered his head as the crowd continued cheering wildly. Maybe Russell had been right: he wasn't a journalist, just a salesman.

"We'll just get one more shot with the whole cast," Jennifer said excitedly. "Then we'll be done."

"Fine by me," Mark replied. He reached into his pocket and pulled out his pager. He'd turned it off once they started tapping the interviews and left it off during the performance. Turning it back on, a number flashed on the readout. He knew it was from somebody in the Valley by the area code, but he didn't recognize the number. He left it in the memory, planning to call the number when he got out of the studio.

Mark helped the crew get the equipment back outside the stage to the van.

"You didn't have to do that," Steve mentioned as Mark slid the camera case into the van.

"Oh, I don't mind. Besides I've got to go back with you to get the extra equipment I need."

"I'm glad you mentioned that. I almost forgot," Steve said. "Jump in. I wouldn't want you to miss your flight."

"Your flight! Where are you off to?" Jennifer asked, stepping up beside Mark.

He hadn't seen her follow them outside the studio. He didn't want anybody to know where he was headed this weekend. He turned toward her, trying to quickly think of an answer.

"We have to finish the edit on the abortion lawsuit story tomorrow." Jennifer had run out of patience with Mark. She'd put up with his lack of enthusiasm for her story long enough. Her stored up anger came out as she drilled into him. "You can't possibly be planning to fly somewhere, especially without telling me!"

"Look, Jennifer, calm down," he shot back at her. "I hadn't had a chance to talk to you about it, but something came up late this afternoon with the other story. I have to go somewhere just for the day. I'll be back Sunday, in plenty of time for the broadcast."

Jennifer crossed her arms over her chest. "What about the editing?"

"You can take care of that without me."

She held her pose, challenging him.

"Please, could you handle the editing? This is really important to me, and all you have to do is pull a couple of sound bites from that lady with the pro-life"— her eyes narrowed—"I know, antiabortion group. It won't take any time at all. There are a couple of great quotes you can use in context."

Jennifer ran a hand through her hair. "Fine, Mark! Go on your wild goose chase. I'll handle it all here."

Mark gave her a quick hug. "Thanks, Jenn. I owe you one, big time. I won't forget it either."

He climbed into the van before she could change her mind. "I'll see you Sunday."

Once the van was unloaded, Steve took Mark to his car and unlocked the trunk.

"This is exactly what you need," he said.

Mark accepted what Steve held in his hand. "A pen? I said I needed something to record conversations with."

"It's not just a pen. It's called a micro-pen recorder, the MPR-1."

Mark looked it over carefully. It looked just like a pen. It was perfect. In his shirt pocket, nobody would think twice about it actually recording a conversation.

"Where's the tape?"

"It records on eight megabites of what they call flash memory. You can record up to seventy minutes' worth. Will that be enough?"

"It's perfect. How much does one of these cost?"

"Not that much. I got this baby for under three hundred bucks."

"That's incredible." Mark whistled as he turned it around in his hand. "Does it write?"

MALIBU
9:42 P.M. PACIFIC

Kevin lay unconscious in the chair, held in place by ropes across his torso and legs. His head hung over his chest. Blood from his face collected on the floor between his legs. Luis had enjoyed using some of his old interrogation techniques before injecting the sodium pentothal. He was certain now he had the full story, one he knew they should have forced out of Number Four before Reynolds's ceremonial toast.

"Let me know when he comes to," Luis instructed Griff. "I'll be up with Reynolds." He headed toward the elevator.

Luis could hear Jason on the phone, so he stepped quietly through the door and waited.

"Look, Richard, this is critical. The situation over there could escalate quickly. Every other network is on board. You're going to be seeing the story everywhere this weekend. I just don't want you to be left behind."

Jason noticed Luis for the first time and waved him over to the desk. Jason listened for a moment, uttering a few grunts in acknowledgment. "Good, you're doing the right thing. Let me know if you need anything." He hung up the phone, looking expectantly up to Luis.

"We know everything now," Luis appraised him. "Most of what Kevin had said was the truth. He just left out one thing."

Jason sat still, waiting for the news.

"He passed the computer program and phone records on to a reporter. Mark Taylor at *Across the Nation*."

Luis waited for the reaction. After a second it came ... the sound of shattering glass as the wine goblet that had been in Reynolds's hand crashed against the door Luis had just closed.

SOMEWHERE OVER CALIFORNIA
10:20 P.M. PACIFIC

Mark Taylor looked out the plane window at the lights of Southern California fading into the distance. He knew he should get some sleep, but he was too restless.

Thoughts kept churning through his mind; questions about the polling story, frustration over the disgusting sit-com he was helping promote, fear of how Samantha would respond to their discussion. But most prominent were thoughts of Tracy Reynolds.

He pulled out his laptop computer, hoping to make notes and maybe some sense out of the facts he'd learned so far. He reached into his pocket and pulled out his notepad. Mark liked to make quick notes in the pad throughout the day, then he transferred everything to his computer.

He thumbed through the pages until his eye caught one note he'd written while chatting with Rick on the phone: 2 Thessalonians 3. He couldn't exactly remember the verse Rick had mentioned, except that it had something to do with safety and protection.

Mark reached for the computer and opened his Bible program. In seconds he was reading from the start of chapter 3:

Finally, brothers, pray for us that the message of the Lord may spread rapidly and be honored, just as it was with you. And pray that we may be delivered from wicked and evil men, for not everyone has faith. But the Lord is faithful, and he will strengthen and protect you from the evil one.

There it was, verse 3: "The Lord is faithful, and he will strengthen and protect you from the evil one." Mark closed his eyes. He didn't know what he faced back East; he wasn't even sure the questions he should ask. But he was sure the events that had led him on this trip had come from God, and he was willing to follow his lead. It still amazed him that Rick had seen that vision, or whatever it was, and here he was sitting on this plane.

He glanced through the rest of the chapter, and his eyes fell on verse 13: "And as for you, brothers, never tire of doing what is right." Mark smiled. He was exhausted and tired of trying to fit into a world where he didn't belong, tired of keeping the cry of righteousness bottled up within him, tired of accepting the tyranny of darkness. No more! It was time to change.

He closed his notepad and computer, forgetting about organizing his notes of the day. He laid his head back against the seat and closed his eyes.

Lord, I'm tired of playing the role of the closet Christian. I'm sorry, Jesus. Forgive me. Fill me with your Spirit as you did your disciples, just like John and Peter in Acts 4. I pray you'd instill in me the boldness to proclaim your truth, to not be ashamed to speak out for you. Help me be the light and salt of the earth as I learned in Rick's group the other night. You've placed me in the position I have, Lord. Help me be like Daniel and do what is right in your eyes.

He sat quietly for a few moments. A sense of peace filled him as the plane continued along. He thought back to his conversation with Samantha, how he'd spoken up for what he believed. He hadn't thought about it at the time; he'd just reacted. But he felt a sense that this new boldness wouldn't be as difficult as he imagined, but it would be in steps just like the one he took with Samantha, as God led him.

He opened his eyes and looked out the window. A full moon cast a beautiful blue light across the clouds in the distance. Still in a prayerful spirit, Mark's thoughts drifted to Tracy, and without thinking he began to pray for her—that God would reveal himself to her through their relationship. And if things turned out the way he expected about her grandfather, that she would be protected and not involved in any way.

After a few moments, Mark drifted off to sleep.

CHAPTER 15

Mark pulled a brush out of his briefcase and tried to spruce up his appearance as much as possible while he looked into the rearview mirror of his rented car. *Boy, I could have packed in the bags under my eyes,* he thought with a laugh.

He stepped out of the car and walked through the snow-covered sidewalk to the front door of the spacious two-story colonial house. He had no idea there were such luxurious neighborhoods in New Jersey, this close to New York City. The drive had been refreshing as he had made his way twisting and turning over the hills along Highway 208. The countryside was so different from what he was used to in Los Angeles and so beautiful.

He uttered a quick prayer before touching the doorbell. He still didn't know what he was looking for or what he was going to say.

The door was opened by a little boy Mark guessed to be around six or seven years old.

"Hi there. Is your mother home?" Mark asked.

"Nope, my nana's watching me." The boy turned and ran off down the hallway.

"Freddy, I told you I'd get the door," Mark heard as a short, frail woman with silver hair approached the doorway. "I'm sorry. Freddy's always two steps ahead of me. He's my grandson. I've got him for the day."

"Hello, Mrs. Dawkins, I'm Mark Taylor. We talked on the phone yesterday."

"Yes, yes. Come in. I've been expecting you."

"Thank you," Mark said as he followed her into the house.

"Let's talk in the parlor. I don't get much of a chance to use that anymore. Would you like anything, coffee or iced tea?"

"Coffee would be wonderful."

After sending Freddy to the office to play one of his grandfather's computer games, she went to the kitchen, grabbed a couple of mugs, and filled them from a fresh pot of coffee. Mark added two spoonfuls of sugar to his before they made their way into the parlor.

"First, I'm sorry about your husband's death," Mark said as he took his seat.

"Thank you; it was quite a shock," she answered sadly.

"Did he have any history of heart trouble?"

"No, he was the picture of perfect health, and he was only sixty-four. But I guess when the heart decides to give out, there's not much one can do."

"I understand that he was found at the office the next morning. You didn't notice his absence before that?" Mark asked gently.

"No. I should've been suspicious about his not coming home that night, but we must have gotten our wires crossed somehow. I thought he was going out of town."

"Really? Why was that?"

"I thought he'd said something about having some kind of meeting in Chicago."

"What made you think he was traveling?" Mark pressed.

"Well, I know sometimes I get things mixed up, but I remembered him saying something about going to the Drake Hotel, one of our favorite places to stay when we visit there. So needless to say, I was shocked when I was called the next morning and told he'd been found in his office."

"Interesting." Mark thought out loud. *Why would he say he was leaving town?* "Were any airline tickets found on him or in his briefcase at the office?"

"No, they said he'd just been working late and his heart gave out. It was quick, thank God. But I really miss him."

"I'm sure you do, Mrs. Dawkins. Did they do an autopsy?"

"No, our personal physician told me all that they did during an autopsy, and I couldn't permit that. His will called for cremation which I didn't even know, so . . ." Her sentence trailed off as she looked out into the backyard. A moment later, she continued as if she hadn't paused. "Our doctor signed the death certificate as a heart attack and that was that. Why are you so interested, Mr. Taylor?"

"I've come across a person who might have been in contact with your husband a few days before he passed away, Mrs. Dawkins. We're not sure if it was him or not, but he called himself Lee."

"And what makes you think it was my Leeland?"

"We know the call came from your husband's company, and as far as we can tell, there isn't another Lee that works there except for a janitor. It was somebody who knew the inside details concerning a specific poll. The last call my friend received was on Monday, Mrs. Dawkins."

The timing of the last contact wasn't lost on her. "So you think that since you haven't heard from your mysterious Lee, and my husband died that same night, there is a connection?"

"I'm just here to check out the possibility. Was he acting strange in any way prior to that night?"

She paused to take a sip of coffee, either reflecting on the last week with her husband or deciding how much to tell Mark.

"Well, actually, he'd been acting strange for a couple of months. Something was weighing heavy on him, but he wouldn't confide in me. I think it was related to his work somehow. He was jumpy, you know, kind of fidgety. Usually he'd love to talk about his work: what politician looked good in the next election, everybody's approval rating, that kind of thing. But recently, he wouldn't talk about it—"

A loud wail came from the other room. Mrs. Dawkins sprang up from her chair and dashed into the other room. Mark followed.

Sitting in front of a glowing computer monitor, Freddy was throwing a tantrum.

"What's wrong?" Mrs. Dawkins asked.

"The words are all wrong," Freddy said, pointing to the screen.

"Oh my!" Mrs. Dawkins gasped. "You scared me to death, Freddy. Don't scream like that!"

Mark chuckled behind them as he realized that everything was all right.

"I don't know a thing about computers, Freddy, I'm sorry."

"But I can't spell those words!" Freddy complained.

"Could I help, Mrs. Dawkins?" Mark offered.

"Be my guest."

"Let's see if we can figure this out."

Mark reached over Freddy's shoulder to see what game he was playing. It was an educational spelling program.

Freddy pointed to the "see word" box. "When you press that," he explained, "it shows you the word you have to spell. But all the words are too hard. Something's wrong."

"OK, let's try it out," Mark reached for the mouse and clicked on "see word."

The box immediately changed to the word "Dawkins" over a blue background for a few seconds, then the letters disappeared and a dash was left where each letter had been.

"That one I know! That's my last name," Freddy screeched and quickly typed in the letters as Mrs. Dawkins and Mark looked at each other. Then he clicked on the "check word" box. The sliding box moved to the right, then slid back over to the left where a cartoon character appeared. Freddy hit the "see word" button again, and the screen displayed "Reynolds."

Mark stared at the screen in surprise.

"See!" Freddy cried. "That's not a word." He jumped out of the chair and ran crying into the other room, with Mrs. Dawkins following. Mark settled into the chair in front of the computer.

He nervously typed "r-e-y-n-o-l-d-s." The computer once again slid the box to the right, then back to the left. Mark clicked on "see word." Highlighted for just a moment on the screen was "Adler." He thought for a second. That was the name of the owner of the other two research companies Peter had checked out—Richard Adler.

Mark dragged the mouse up to the file menu, wondering if there was another way to look at whatever list Freddy had been trying to spell. Navigating to the main program menu, he noticed a section titled "Criss/Cross Game" that was shaped like a crossword puzzle. He clicked on it.

On a grid pattern on the left side of the screen, squares were left vacant to create the crossword. On the right side of the screen was a column of words, the ones little Freddy hadn't been able to spell.

```
Reynolds
Capshaw
Davidson
Dawkins
Adler
Winter
Fisher
```

Not a list of words but names—seven of them. Mark pulled the pen out of his pocket and tried to write down the list. Unfortunately, it was the MPR-1 and it didn't work. He pulled a pencil from a mug on the desk and wrote the list in his notepad. He just finished when Mrs. Dawkins reentered the room.

"Do these names look familiar to you, Mrs. Dawkins?"

She scanned the list. "Not all of them, but some of them do. Obviously our name and Reynolds. I think that would be Jason Reynolds, a friend of my late husband's. Adler, would be Richard Adler, the CEO over my husband's company, I guess. I'm not sure about any of the other ones."

"I think your husband was keeping this list in your grandson's spelling game for some reason."

"That's odd. Why would he do that?"

"Perhaps to keep it from being discovered. Did anybody from the company come and look through your husband's office after his death?"

"Yes, a couple of people. They said they were from the research company making sure there were no business files left at the house. Our lawyer was with them so I assumed it was all right."

"That's probably precisely why your husband added this list to Freddy's spelling game, so they wouldn't find it. Would you mind if I kept the CD? It could be very useful."

"No, I guess not," Mrs. Dawkins replied, trembling. "Do you think there is something there that was worth my husband's life?"

"I'm not sure, Mrs. Dawkins. That's what I plan to find out."

BURBANK

8:32 A.M. PACIFIC

Officer Ben Williams spotted the crowd gawking over the fence of the Los Angeles River as he reached the corner of Mariposa and Valleyheart Drive. He turned on the patrol lights as he pulled up behind the people in his police car.

"Here come the police," someone shouted, as a pathway suddenly opened for him to get a look below. Officer Williams was now able to see a burned-out shell of an automobile smoldering thirty feet below. It was obvious from the smashed roof that the car had rolled over at least once before it had settled at its final resting place. He could tell by the tracks in the dirt path under his feet that the car had driven off Mariposa, knocking down the small fence.

Why wasn't this discovered last night? he wondered as he surveyed the scene. He realized the car had already burned itself out. It had to have been there several hours already.

He had to walk several hundred yards down the path to find access to the river basin. As his luck would have it, the usually dry concrete bed had a half an inch of water gently running down it. He sloshed his way back toward the car, cursing as he felt the moisture seeping through his boots.

"All right, step back please," he yelled at the kids who were a little too close to the still smoking car. *I hope there's nobody inside.*

He took the last few steps toward the driver's door slowly, knowing what he'd see if whoever had been driving the car hadn't gotten out. Laying across the driver's seat was a charred, disfigured corpse.

The officer turned away, gagging slightly as he coughed several times, then took some deep breaths. After a moment, he walked around to the back of the vehicle. The license plate hung at an angle held on by one remaining bolt. Through the blackened soot he was able to read the letters and numbers. He called the information about the car and body back to his precinct on his portable radio.

A few moments later, he heard the name of the registered owner called back to him—Kevin Spencer of Sherman Oaks.

New Jersey
12:41 P.M. Eastern

Mark drove south along New Jersey's Garden State Parkway. He didn't want to drive into the city and worry about parking or the New York City traffic, so he headed back toward Newark airport. He decided there was plenty of time to return the rental car and grab a cab into the city.

He'd spent the last hour with Mrs. Dawkins, going over every detail she could remember about her husband. She was so gracious, even allowing him to look through Dawkins's office. But nothing indicated he was the one who'd called Kevin. All he had was the list of names sitting beside him on his notepad.

His pager beeped. He looked at the digital display—Russell's office extension. Great! The last person he wanted to talk to. He noticed the memory blinking at him as well. Oh yeah, he'd forgotten to return that page from last night.

He pulled out his cell phone and punched in the numbers to reach Russell at the office.

"Russell here."

"Yeah, Frank, it's Mark. You paged me?"

"I did. I was wondering why I just saw Jennifer in the edit bay without you. What's going on?"

Mark thought quickly. Did Jennifer mention where he was? His first impulse was to lie, but that wouldn't be right, and even if she had covered for him, he'd have to explain the cost of the plane tickets on his expense report later. He might as well face up to it now.

"I'm in New York," he confessed. "I had some important leads on the polling story that I needed to check out."

"At least you didn't try and hide it. Jennifer told me," Russell replied roughly. "I didn't authorize any trip, much less on the day before a show. You know the rules. What's gotten into you?"

"It all came up last minute, Frank. I'm sorry I didn't check with you, but you were out yesterday afternoon, and it was an impulse decision. Jennifer agreed to cover the edit session. We've got it all worked out."

"I hope you do," Russell said, unconvinced. "But we're still having a chat when you return, and that's what I'm ordering you to do right now. Get back here because, I swear, if you jeopardize the show Sunday night, you'll wish you stayed in New York and interviewed for another job."

"I'm on a red-eye tonight. I'll be back in plenty of time—" But Russell had disconnected. *I hope this trip is worth it.*

He looked at his notepad. The seven names were important; he could feel it. If he could just put the pieces together, Mark was sure he could figure out why Dawkins had been murdered. Murdered—the thought had taken root without Mark realizing it. For the first time, Mark was beginning to believe that Kevin's suspicions were true.

He reached for his pager, calling up the number from the night before. He wondered who he was calling.

"Hello?" He heard a frantic woman answer.

"Hi. Did you page me yesterday? This is Mark Taylor."

"Yes, yes, I did. My husband is missing. Has he been with you?"

"I'm sorry, ma'am, but who is this?"

"Oh yes, of course. I'm Kevin Spencer's wife, Vickie. He didn't come home last night, and I was hoping he's been with you."

"No, I'm sorry, Vickie. I haven't seen him since Thursday night. Has he still not come home?"

"No, he hasn't. I've been checking all the hospitals, but I can't find out anything. I'm so worried."

"I'm sure there's an explanation," Mark tried to comfort her, but as he glanced at the list again, his mind wandered. If there was enough there to get Dawkins killed, could Kevin had been targeted as well?

"I know he's in trouble, all because of that stuff he gave you. He's never stayed out all night!" Her voice rose. Mark could tell her fears were giving way to anger, and she was directing it toward him.

"Vickie, try not to worry." Mark attempted to extinguish his own growing fear as much as hers. "I'll give Tracy a call—see if he was sent—"

"I talked with her last night. He wasn't working."

Mark was at a loss for words. "Well, give him a little more time. I'm sure he'll turn up." He hoped it was said with a little more conviction than he felt. "I'm in New York, but I'll be back first thing in the morning. I'll call you then."

SHERMAN OAKS

10:19 A.M. PACIFIC

Vickie couldn't sit still. She paced between the kitchen and the family room. She'd been struggling to keep her hopes up, but the conversation with Mark had defeated her. He'd been her last hope that there was some explanation for Kevin's disappearance. Now she didn't know what to do—who to call—where to go. *Oh, Kevin, come home to me please,* she thought before placing her face into her hands, finally allowing the tears she'd kept bottled up to pour out.

She didn't see the patrol car pull up to the front of the house. She didn't hear the door close as the officer got out of the car and made his way to the front door. The doorbell went unnoticed as she wept. It was the persistent knocking that finally caught her attention.

She wiped at her eyes with the sleeve of her robe as her head popped up. She rushed to the door.

"Mrs. Spencer?" the uniformed patrol officer asked as she faced him.

She saw it in his eyes—sorrow, compassion.

"Yes," she finally responded.

"I'm sorry to inform you, Mrs. Spencer, but your husband was killed in an accident last night."

She backed against the door just before her legs quit supporting her. She slid slowly down until she was sitting on the entryway tile.

STUDIO CITY
11:00 A.M. PACIFIC

Rick stood in the third-base coach's box, cupping his hands over his mouth. "Level swing, Justin, level swing."

Rick's son was stepping up to the plate. He paused, taking the bat and tapping each of his feet. He adjusted the helmet that dwarfed his six-year-old head. Rick laughed, watching Justin imitate the motions of his favorite big-league player.

"C'mon, Justin, kill the ball!" Cassie yelled from behind him as she relaxed on a blanket with Jennifer, Rick's ten-year-old daughter.

Justin glanced in their direction. A little smile creased his lips. Then he turned toward the T-stand as he shut out the world and concentrated only on the white ball in front of him. He placed the bat next to the ball, then brought it back over his shoulder and swung with all his might. The ball rocketed off the tee and flew over all three shortstops' heads before it rolled between the two left fielders. Justin took off running, the helmet spinning on his head, blocking part of his vision. He made it around second base before the other team caught up with the ball in the outfield.

"Run! Run!" Rick screamed and pointed home as Justin came churning toward third base. The opposing team had finally managed to get the ball back to the infield as Justin headed for the plate. It was now a contest between Justin's legs and the arm of one of the seven-year-old shortstops. Justin poured on all the speed he could muster as he barreled toward home. The ball was thrown perfectly into the catcher's mitt, which surprised the kid so much it bounced out and rolled toward the pitcher as Justin crossed the plate.

"All right! Home run!" Rick shouted as he ran up to Justin and twirled him around into a hug.

"Dad!" he laughed. "Not during the game!"

Rick put him down and allowed him to be swarmed by his teammates.

"Pretty impressive," Cassie called from behind Rick.

"He takes after his father," Rick shot back as he made his way back to the coach's box.

He was having a great time with the kids. But as he contemplated the end of the game, nervousness began to build. How were they going to take the news about him and Cassie?

CHAPTER 16

MALIBU
11:24 A.M. PACIFIC

Tracy stepped on the accelerator as she came out of the turn along Highway 1. Her auburn hair blew straight back as the Miata hit sixty in the thirty-five-mile-per-hour zone. She slowed quickly as she spotted her grandfather's driveway. The sight of the mansion atop the hill with the dark blue of the Pacific Ocean stretching beyond always lifted her spirits.

She had been raised by her grandmother and grandfather after the death of her parents when she was nine years old. That tragedy turned out to be Tracy's lifeline. Her father, the only son of Jason Reynolds, had traveled well down the path of self-destruction. In spite of the opportunities available because of Jason's powerful influence, he couldn't stay away from alcohol and cocaine. Tracy's mother did her best, but being the daughter of a famous surgeon and having lived a spoiled life herself, she didn't have the fortitude to handle him or her own alcohol dependency, much less the needs of a growing little girl.

Tracy's life had changed forever the night her parents were killed instantly in a crash along Highway 1. Jason had vowed not to make the same mistakes with Tracy he'd made with her dad. He refused to spoil her and made her work for everything she'd attained in life.

She entered the front door without knocking and walked down the hallway to her bedroom so she could drop off her bag and change into a bathing suit before hitting the beach. She didn't know if her grandfather would be home or not. It seemed as if more and more weekends spent here were times spent alone.

"Tracy, is that you, honey?"

Tracy heard his voice calling from behind her.

"Yes, Papa," she yelled back. "I'm in my room."

She set her bag on top of the canopied bed, then reached into the middle drawer of the antique dresser and pulled out a one-piece swimsuit.

"There's my little pumpkin," Jason said affectionately as he walked up behind her and placed his arms around her.

"You haven't called me that since I was ten," she protested with a laugh. "Grab your suit. Let's hit the beach."

Jason loosened his embrace to glance at his watch. "OK, but I've only got about forty-five minutes or so."

"Then hurry up. I hate sharing my weekends with all of your business distractions."

Minutes later, they met at the other end of the house where the elevator would take them down to the beach level. Tracy was amazed at how good Jason still looked in a swimsuit. He kept in shape, using the weight and exercise room in the house frequently. She was happy to see that he still had a drive to live life to its fullest and the desire to succeed in whatever he touched—including personal fitness.

She stepped in front of him into the elevator when the doors opened for them. He pressed the B button. At the Reynolds mansion, B stood for beach.

"How was the rest of your week?" she asked.

"It's been busy. A lot of calls on that UN gift."

"I can imagine."

"I'm beginning to think I should have made the donation anonymously."

Tracy laughed. "And lose the spotlight? I'm sure you're enjoying it, probably more than you should."

The doors opened, revealing a large glass enclosed atrium looking out through the cliffs to the small beach. There was a small kitchen set in one corner of the room and a comfortable lounging area with couches and a large-screen television on the other side.

They headed out onto the beach, the sun shining brightly. It was cool when the breeze hit Tracy's skin, but she knew it would only take a few moments of basking in the sunlight to warm up. She laid a towel across a lounge chair, put her sunglasses on, then lay down with a long sigh. Jason took a chair next to her.

They sat in silence for a moment, listening to the sound of the waves crashing against the rocks on either side of the cliffs.

"It's so relaxing down here." Tracy smiled as the stress from the week began to dissipate.

"Kind of cool for me still," Jason said. "I don't know why I even changed into this suit. There's no way I'm touching that water."

"It's to get a tan silly, not for swimming."

"And do you think there's anybody who would really care whether these legs take on a bronze tan?"

She looked at them through her sunglasses. "Your tennis partner in your next doubles match comes to mind. You could blind him with those things."

"How do you think we beat the other team?"

They both laughed.

"Have you thought about dating again, Papa?"

It had been two years since Jason's wife had lost her battle with breast cancer. Two lonely years. They had been soul mates. Nothing could replace her. Not that he'd remained faithful to her. A man of his power didn't even consider that to be part of the agreement. But through forty-five years of marriage, they'd established a partnership that was special. The closest thing he had in his life to the companionship that he'd had with Rose was lying right next to him.

"I don't know how I'd even begin again," he said. "Life is so busy as it is. There's no time to cultivate a relationship with anybody."

One of the ways Jason had dealt with the loss was to pour his every waking hour into his work. It was the most natural thing to do since he had lived that way when Rose was alive anyway. She had been the kind of woman who knew how to live within Jason's expectations. She was there when he needed her and happily existed in her own private life when he did not. Tracy never saw that side of their relationship. She always understood that her grandfather was just a very busy man and had a lot of important things to take care of.

"I know how that can be," Tracy said, her mind drifting back to her lunch with Mark.

Jason looked away from the ocean and at his granddaughter. "I sense there's some new romantic interest in your life?"

Tracy scowled. She hated to be so transparent in front of him. "Oh, Papa! Just forget I said anything."

"Oh no you don't. I heard that reflective tone in your voice, no backing out of it now. Who is he, somebody you met this week?"

"It's nothing," Tracy sat up and looked at her grandfather. "Really!" she tried to convince him as he broke into a wide grin.

"It was all business, but in a refreshing sort of way. He just seemed so . . . real compared to the guys I've been around lately."

"And does this mystery person have a name?"

"He's that reporter I told you called the other day."

"The one doing the research without a story."

"Right. We had lunch together yesterday, and I really enjoyed myself. But there's nothing romantic going on. He's just interesting."

"I see." Jason let it rest.

"He wants to meet you."

Jason looked up at her, tilting his head slightly. "Me? You know I don't give interviews."

"I know, Papa, but please."

"Are you sure he's not just using you to get to me?" Jason asked skeptically.

"Now that hurts!" she shot back, not wanting to even entertain the possibility. Then it hit him.

"I'm sorry, honey. I didn't mean that." Jason tried to keep his voice calm as his mind raced. "So what's this reporter's name?"

"Mark Taylor. He's on *Across the Nation*," she answered brightly.

He glanced out over the waves making their way up the cove, desperate to suppress his seething rage. In a few seconds he had it under control as he turned back toward Tracy.

"I'll meet with him," he said to her utter shock. "But first you have to tell me everything you can remember about what you two have talked about."

RESEARCH INTERNATIONAL
3:00 P.M. EASTERN

The cab pulled up in front of a massive skyscraper. Mark snuggled down into his coat as a bitter wind cut against his face. He paid the driver and quickly made his way into the building.

It took him a minute to spot Research International on the information board in the lobby. He stepped into an empty elevator and punched in the sixty-seventh floor. He pulled the MPR-1 pen from his jacket pocket and hit the record function. He kept saying his new name in his mind. *I'm Mark Tayback. I'm Mark Tayback.* He hoped the deception was justified.

After yawning to get his ears to pop a second time, the elevator doors opened up before him. He stepped out looking for a sign that would alert him to RI's offices, but the company had the whole floor.

"My name is Mark Tayback," he told the receptionist. "I have an appointment with Mr. Palmer."

"Yes, Mr. Tayback, he's expecting you. Mr. Palmer's assistant isn't in today, so I'll take you to the executive offices."

She led the way down a wide hallway. Between the luxuriance of this complex and the offices of ARI, Mark decided the field of research must be very lucrative. Either that, or image was a high priority.

"Mr. Tayback, nice to have you with us," Mike Palmer announced as the receptionist stopped in front of his office. Palmer was dressed casually, having interrupted his day off to be in the office.

"Please call me Mark." He handed one of his phony business cards across their handshake.

"Then call me Mike. I trust you had a good flight?"

"It was pleasant enough, thank you. I wanted to start by letting you know how happy everyone at the alliance is with the results of your firm's poll."

"It was our pleasure. It's good to see the country coming around and dropping some of its prejudice. I think these results are long overdue," Palmer said with pride as he held up the report.

"Well, that's one thing we wanted to talk to you about. Bryan and I were wondering what you thought about the possibility of designing a poll that could put the numbers right through the roof?"

Mark was baiting him, seeing if Palmer would concede to any irregularities in the research process.

"Well, Mark, I don't know if you realize how close we've already come to that. These results you already have are phenomenal. How much did Bryan fill you in on the process?"

"Oh, I'm well aware of, shall we say, the extraordinary steps your firm has already taken—"

Palmer smiled from behind his desk, feeling more comfortable that Mark was in-the-know.

"Then let me be frank with you, Mark," Palmer said. Mark leaned in close to the desk to make sure his MPR-1 would pick up every word.

Several offices down the large hallway, Vince Sinclair leaned closer to a small speaker at his desk to make sure he could pick up every word as well.

"I don't think it would be in your best interest to inflate the numbers any greater than they are." Palmer talked as if Mark was the pupil and Palmer had all the answers. "It's been our experience that moderation in our increases ensures less scrutiny by our detractors. The other side will already want to refute these percentages." He tapped the report in front of him. "If we were to sanction another poll and raise the results even higher, we could be in jeopardy of losing our credibility, which could adversely affect your cause."

Mark nodded. He wanted Palmer to talk more specifically. "OK, Mike, I understand. And I'm sure I can make Bryan see where you're coming from. But for future argument's sake, what would be the next step you could take to ensure an even better response?"

"It'll be easy when the time is right, my friend. Don't worry." He settled back in his chair, apparently finished with the topic.

Mark squirmed. He had been so close. "I forgot to congratulate you on the promotion. It must feel good to take over the top spot here. You deserve it. Bryan and I were thrilled to see your hard work pay off."

Palmer swelled up with pride. "It's a mixed blessing. I'm sure I'll be able to take this company to new heights, but at the same time, Mr. Dawkins will be missed."

"I'm not sure I know the whole story on that. How did you get the job?"

Palmer's eyes darkened, and Mark was sure he'd made a mistake in bringing the topic up. "It was a sudden heart attack. I'm sure I told Bryan this." He looked up for Mark's response.

"We were so thrilled with the poll's results, I don't think we talked about the details of how you became president."

That seemed to placate Palmer. "Well, anyway, it's been a very busy time of transition. I hope you'll understand if I need to get back to other business."

"Yes, I'm sorry for taking up so much of your time," Mark said as he stood in front of his desk. "There's just one more thing. I was wondering if you could recall an employee here named Lee."

Palmer didn't respond right away but slowly looked up into Mark's eyes. His gaze was piercing. Mark knew he had gone too far.

"Why do you ask?" Palmer finally responded.

"Oh, it's probably just a mistake. But I received a call from here early last week.

My secretary thought it was from a man named Lee, but I could never reach anybody here by that name."

"I'm sorry. I don't know of anybody who works here by that name," Palmer answered coldly.

"OK," Mark said. "Just thought I'd ask. You mentioned tweaking the questions a bit for a new survey. I didn't bring along one of the surveys. Would it be possible to take a copy with me so I could go over how that could be done on the plane trip home?"

"Sure," Palmer agreed to get rid of him. "I can let you take this copy. I'll just print another one."

"Thank you, I appreciate it." Mark took the report, then looked at Palmer with a sly grin. "You wouldn't be able to let me have any of the research material that went into making this, would you? Like the phone records or the field data? I'd love to see how this all comes together."

Palmer shook his head. "That's out of the question. All of that stays within the company. What you and Bryan received in the final report breaks a lot of that down for you, but the raw data stays in our hands."

Well, it was worth a try, Mark thought.

"You've been very kind to see me on a weekend like this," Mark said as he stood and stretched out his hand.

Palmer accepted the handshake from across his desk with a smile. "We're here to serve. We'll be in touch when the time is right for another report."

Now that was interesting, Mark thought as he took the survey. He figured it would be the Alliance that would instigate another poll.

"I'll find my way out. Thanks again."

Mark made his way out of the office and headed toward the elevator.

"Pssst! Hey you! Come here."

Mark looked up startled as a man caught his attention standing in an office doorway on his left.

"Who, me?"

"Yes!" The man whispered with intensity. "Can I talk with you a second?"

Mark felt nervous, but he stopped and walked over to him. He was quickly pushed inside the man's office and the door closed behind them.

"Look, friend," the man said in a threatening tone, "I don't know who you really are or what your game is, and I don't really care. But I do know you aren't from the National Gay-Lesbian Alliance."

Mark started to protest but was cut off.

"Quiet!" the man said. "Just listen. If you know what's good for you, you'll forget about whatever heroic mission you're on and go home."

"Who are you?" Mark asked.

"Call me Vince, your guardian angel, OK? I'm just telling you if you want to stay healthy, take my advice!" He stressed the last word with his eyes opened wide. "You're in way over your head, and you're messing with things you don't understand. You won't be warned again."

With that, he shoved Mark back out into the hallway and closed the door behind him. Mark stood there in shock. He wanted to bust through the door and give this Vince guy a Marine's lesson in manners, but then he heard footsteps coming from Palmer's office. He didn't want to be caught hanging around so he continued toward the elevator in a confused daze.

MALIBU
12:31 P.M. PACIFIC

Jason Reynolds left Tracy on the beach to enjoy the sun as he made his way back up the elevator to the top floor. He stormed into his office. He'd kept his composure as Tracy innocently recounted Mark's line of questions relating to their polling techniques. In one sense, he was proud of how his granddaughter had answered Mark's questions, but most of that was because she didn't know anything. He'd always kept her in the dark about what ARI and his other companies were doing behind the scenes.

But of all people for Tracy to have become enamored with—Mark Taylor. That made Jason wonder what had come first, Tracy's relationship with Mark or Mark's contact with Kevin. He suspected the latter and that Mark was using Tracy to get to him. *Well, it worked, young man,* Jason thought, *and you'll be sorry for it, believe me.*

Jason picked up the phone and dialed the new Number Four's cell phone. If Mark was already on the trail with ARI, his next step would be to contact Research International as well.

Mike Palmer decided he had wasted enough time in his office on a Saturday. He signed off the Internet and was grabbing his car keys when his cell phone rang.

"Yeah, Palmer here."

"It's Number One. Are you alone?"

Palmer felt a chill go through his body. He hadn't been contacted by Number One since the offer to become part of the Circle of Seven. The meeting in Chicago was more than enough for him to realize he'd better tread carefully around this man.

"Yes, I can speak freely."

Vince Sinclair had been working on an E-mail he'd been composing since he'd thrown Mark back into the hallway. He listened when Palmer's voice began coming through his little speaker again. He quickly read through his prepared E-mail and pushed send.

"I wanted to warn you about a reporter who's probably going to be paying you a visit," Reynolds said. "He's been fishing around ARI, and he's probably going to be digging into your company as well. I want to make sure he gets nothing from you, is that clear?"

"Very clear, sir. As far as I know, we haven't been contacted by any reporters recently. What was he searching for at ARI?"

"He's been tipped off about the gay survey, and he could be asking questions about Dawkins. I doubt seriously that he'd be so blatant as to show up as himself. Be on the lookout for anything out of the ordinary. The reporter's name is Mark Taylor. I'm going to get a picture of him and E-mail it as soon as I can."

"Oh no," Palmer gasped before he could stop himself. He had a strange feeling about the man who just left. It had to have been him; the names were too close to be a coincidence. He crumpled back into his chair as the support went out from his legs.

"What do you mean 'oh, no,'" Reynolds demanded. Just then his computer prompted him of an incoming E-mail.

"I just had a man leave my office, claiming to be with the National Gay-Lesbian Alliance. He called yesterday, saying he was going to be in town on business and wanted to talk about another survey. He had a business card and everything." Palmer tried to justify his actions, then quietly confessed. "He said his name was Mark Tayback."

Reynolds' obscenities caused Palmer to wince and hold the phone away from his ear. It took a few seconds before Reynolds calmed down enough to demand Palmer tell him everything about the meeting.

Alone in his office down the hall, Vince made notes of everything he heard. He would have loved to have been able to hear both sides of the conversation, but half was better than none.

Reynolds slammed the phone back into its cradle, telling no one in particular what he thought of the new president of RI, as well as of Mark Taylor. The pressure behind his eyes was blinding as he fought to control his rage. Within a couple of minutes, he was able to function again, catching the blinking mailbox at the top of his computer screen. He clicked to his E-mail, surprised it was for his Circle of Seven account and he didn't recognize the return address.

All documents to that account were automatically encoded, so Reynolds had to turn off his security software before he could open the E-mail:

To: CoSN1@csi.com
From: Vsinclair@researchinternational.org
Topic: Confidential

Number One,

You don't know me yet, but I can be of service to you. I feel it is my duty to inform you how careless your new president at Research International has been. I've spotted your E-mails on his computer, been tracking the homosexual poll as well as the new questions for the abortion poll. You've got a loose cannon in the head chair. Not fit to serve you.

Even now, Mr. Palmer is entertaining someone claiming to be from the National Gay-Lesbian Alliance, but I know that isn't the case, and Palmer's probably spilling his guts to him.

I'm on your side and willing and able to be of use. Let me know how I can be of further assistance to you in the future.

Your loyal friend,
Vince Sinclair

Reynolds let out a long exhale, not realizing he'd been holding his breath as he read. First Taylor and now this unknown . . . friend. Things were getting out of hand. He needed to find out more about this Vince Sinclair before he responded.

CHAPTER 17

"Duck ... duck ... goose!" Justin shouted as he slammed his hand on top of Rick's head.

"Ow!" Rick reacted as he fought to get up from the blanket. By the time he made it to his feet and started running, Justin, Rick's son, was already between Jennifer and Cassie on the other side. Rick knew he had no chance of beating him around, so he leaped over Cassie and tackled Justin before he could plop down in Rick's spot.

"Hey, you're cheating!" Justin yelled as the two rolled through the grass.

"Monkey pile!" Jennifer, Rick's ten-year-old, screamed as she jumped on top of her dad and brother. Cassie, not to be left out, jumped right in with her as all four became a tangled mess of arms, legs, and laughter.

Later, the four lay on their backs looking up through a big eucalyptus tree at the clouds. They were enjoying an afternoon at the park.

"You're fun, Cassie," Justin said.

"Yeah!" Jennifer agreed. "I can't believe you monkey-piled with us."

"Why, thank you, Justin and Jennifer. I think you're both fun too," Cassie returned.

166

Rick looked at the three with a huge grin on his face. "I'm glad you feel that way kids because there's something we wanted to tell you."

"You're getting married?" Jennifer squealed in delight.

Rick looked at Cassie, then back to Jennifer, laughing. "What makes you think that?"

"Well, we've been wondering what you've been waiting for, haven't we, Justin?" She elbowed her little brother.

"Married—yuck!" Justin mimicked gagging while pointing a finger at his throat.

"Oh, it won't be that bad, little buddy." Rick reached over and gave him a hug.

Jennifer jumped up into Cassie's arms. "Then it's true, you are getting married?"

Cassie held her close, warmth flooding through her, "Yes, Jennifer, I've agreed to marry your dad."

"When? Can I be in the wedding? What will I wear?"

Rick smiled at the exchange between Cassie and Jennifer, but when he looked over and saw Justin sitting quietly with his head down, he reached over and pulled him into his lap.

"What's wrong, Justin?"

Silence.

Rick prayed as he continued. "I know you've been through a lot of changes. Life is like that sometimes."

Rick could hear Cassie behind him quietly suggest that she and Jennifer take a walk.

"Do you like Cassie?" Rick asked.

"Yes," Justin responded sheepishly.

"Then what's the problem, Justin?"

"It's just that—well—"

"Come on, spit it out. I can take it."

"Well, if you marry Cassie, then I . . ."

Rick stayed silent, hoping Justin could get the words out.

"I've always wanted you and Mommy to be back together." He got the words out as he started crying. "So we can be a family again."

Rick's eyes watered. A huge lump instantly caught in his throat. He placed his arms around his boy and gave him a long hug. It took a moment before he was able to speak. Then he pulled away and placed Justin directly in front of him.

"Listen, Justin, I know the changes have been hard on everybody, and it's probably been the hardest on you." Rick's heart was about to burst as Justin looked up into his eyes. Huge tears rolled down Justin's cheeks, and his breathing came in gasps as he fought to gain control.

"But as much as we might want to, we can't step backward. Your mom has gone on with her life; she's made a new family now, and you're part of that family. Cassie and I love each other very much, and we want to be together as a family too. And you know what?"

Justin barely whispered, "What?"

"You're going to be part of our family, with Cassie, Jennifer, and me. So you'll have two families." *Not the way God intended it,* Rick thought, but he wanted to make it sound like it was a good thing. "Don't you think it'll be fun to have Cassie around?"

"Yeah, I guess."

Rick took Justin's baseball cap off and rubbed his head. "And don't you worry. We'll still have lots of time when it'll be just you and me."

"Daddy! Daddy!" Jennifer called as she ran through the grass and jumped into his arms. "Cassie wants me to be a bridesmaid!"

"That's wonderful, sweetie!" Rick exclaimed as he gave her a big hug. "Which brings me to my next question, Mr. Justin." He turned back to his son.

Justin looked at his dad with expectation, wiping away the last tear.

"Would you be my best man?"

Justin's mouth opened into a wide grin and the life sparkled back into his eyes. "You bet, Dad! Hey, Jennifer, I'm going to be Dad's best man!"

Cassie walked back up to the threesome, smiling as if she'd just won the lottery. No, it was better than that. She'd just won her place in this wonderful family.

NEW YORK CITY
3:45 P.M. EASTERN

The cab shot through the New York streets. With the light weekend traffic, the driver was able to dart and weave among the other cars, but the excitement was lost on Mark as he replayed the confrontation with Vince.

He pulled out his plane ticket and checked the departure time. He either had to wait another seven hours before he took off, or he could try to get another flight. He looked out the window as heavy snowflakes started dropping from the sky. Getting the earlier flight would be wise, he decided.

He used his cell phone to book a flight out of Newark at 6:15 that evening. He then placed another call to Kevin's house. A female voice answered on the third ring.

"Hi, Vickie, it's Mark."

"I'm sorry. This is Rhonda, Vickie's sister."

"Oh, my apologies. Is Vickie available?"

"Well, she's kind of upset at the moment. Can I take a message?"

"I was trying to reach her to see if she's heard from Kevin yet. I'm a friend of his."

"Oh, then you haven't heard," Rhonda said matter-of-factly. "Kevin's dead."

The news hit him like a freight train. He couldn't respond.

"His car was found this morning. He ran off the road last night and crashed into the Los Angeles River."

"I can't believe it," Mark said, closing his eyes. "Please tell Vickie how sorry I am."

He disconnected the call as he fought back tears. Leeland's dead, Kevin's dead, and now he had just been threatened by that guy at RI. Whatever is happening, Mark decided, Jason Reynolds seemed to be right in the middle of it all. But why would Kevin be killed over the rigging of a stupid poll about homosexuality? *It doesn't make any sense*, he thought, staring blindly out the window as the snowfall increased.

MALIBU

12:56 P.M. PACIFIC

"I'm holding you responsible for this!" Jason Reynolds exclaimed to Luis seated on the other side of his desk. "You say it's controlled after we take care of Dawkins. Then Spencer starts sticking his nose where it doesn't belong. Now even with him out of the picture, we've got a stinking reporter picking up the hunt and some unknown employee at RI with way too much information."

"I knew we should have questioned Dawkins first," Luis interjected.

The look Reynolds shot toward Luis could have melted steel. "If I want your I-told-you-so comments, I'll ask for them. All I want to know is what will put an end to this disaster once and for all?"

Luis kept silent as his irritation grew.

"Find out where Mark Taylor lives," Reynolds demanded. "Get every kind of camera or listening device we have in there. I want to know what he knows and who he talks to. I want to know for sure that when we take care of him, this will be over for good. And get me information on Vince Sinclair. Do you understand?"

"Of course, sir," Luis said. "I'll take care of it right now."

Jason watched him leave, then turned his chair around to take in the view of the Pacific Ocean. Why was it that no matter how much money and power he had managed to achieve, there was always something that sprang up to rob him of it all? He tried to recall the number of times he'd looked out this window and just enjoyed his magnificent view with a sense of peace about him. He couldn't remember one.

"Who was that, Papa?" he heard Tracy ask behind him.

He spun around in surprise. She usually didn't venture up here. How much had she heard?

"Who do you mean?"

"That man who just walked out of here—who is he?"

"His name is Luis Thorton. He works for me."

Tracy nodded, "I thought I saw him at the office yesterday, but he's not with ARI. What's going on?"

"Nothing you need to worry about, honey. Just a little internal security problem."

Tracy could tell her grandfather would say nothing more, although she was curious. "Well, OK, if you want to keep your little secrets. I'm going home. I've got a lot to do this weekend. Don't forget about Tuesday; you promised to have lunch with Mark Taylor."

"Believe me. I won't forget."

NORTH HOLLYWOOD
1:10 P.M. PACIFIC

Vanessa slipped quietly out of Shelby's room after taking one last peek at her daughter cuddling her favorite teddy bear. The night before at Gary and Jill's house had done wonders for Vanessa. She'd really missed them. They were the closest thing she'd ever had to a real family.

Samantha would be there any second, so Vanessa quietly added to the prayers from last night, that God would be present in their talk. The doorbell rang. Vanessa jerked slightly. She was jumpier than she realized.

She opened the door, revealing Samantha Steel dressed in a short khaki skirt and a halter top. Her blond hair was pinned back behind her head, and dark sunglasses covered her eyes.

"Vanessa?"

"That's right. You must be Samantha. Please come on in."

Sam stepped into the apartment, taking off her sunglasses and putting them in her purse. Vanessa motioned her to the lumpy, second-hand couch as she took a seat next to her in the rocking chair.

"Please, call me Sam," Samantha said as she took her seat carefully. "Thanks for seeing me."

"You're welcome. I hope I can be of some help."

"Well, Mark certainly thinks you will be. He's very intent on our speaking together." She looked intently into Vanessa's face. Something about it was familiar, but she couldn't place it.

"Tell me about the story you're doing," Vanessa said.

"Well, in a nutshell, it's on adult Internet sites, part of which will be our own Web page, a celebrity nude site where myself and others from our staff will be posing," Sam said proudly.

"Are you trying to analyze the affect these sites have?"

"That among other things. Like what kind of people go online to check these things out. If we can determine their age ranges or anything else about them, it'll help the story. I understand you were involved with pornography for a while."

Vanessa nodded. "That's right. It started about five years ago when I moved here from North Dakota, looking to see my name in lights."

Sam grinned. What girl didn't have that dream?

"I didn't know what I was doing; I was sixteen years old and very naive. It wasn't long at all before I was sleeping with guys—doing whatever their perverted minds could think of—just to scrape enough money together to eat. It took a couple of years before I got what I thought was a break, a meeting with a director for a movie role. Well, to make a long story short, all the director was interested in was how I could service him. At least he was impressed enough to give me a role in his movie."

Samantha took out her notepad, feigning interest in what appeared to be another runaway-turned-prostitute story. Why had she agreed to come here anyway?

Vanessa continued, recounting her slide down the path of pornography and drugs. At times she went into stark detail to try to break through to Samantha. She eventually recounted how she'd caught the eye of the leading pornographer in town, Gabriel Flint, who set her up as his mistress. At the sound of his name, Samantha sat up, suddenly excited.

"Gabriel Flint, you used to work with him? You were at Rick Treadway's house that night he was arrested, weren't you?"

"Yes, I was."

"I thought you looked familiar, but I couldn't place you until you mentioned Flint. Why didn't you tell me before?"

"I didn't know if you would remember me. Besides, it was your idea to talk, not mine."

"True," Samantha agreed. "Wow! Gabriel Flint was the pornographer you worked for."

"Why does that surprise you?" Vanessa asked.

"I had my own . . . proposition from Mr. Flint," Samantha confessed, shrugging off the disgusting memory. The night Rick had been arrested for the murder of Wade Bennett, Samantha had been waiting outside his condominium with her camera crew to catch it all on tape for the lead story on the 11:00 news that night. "How do you think I got the tip to be at Rick's house that night?"

Vanessa nodded. "That doesn't surprise me. I'm sorry to bring up the past if it's painful for you."

"Actually, I hadn't thought about it in a long time."

Vanessa smiled warmly. "He's somebody I'd like to forget, that's for sure. Let me give you some advice. I think any story you do about pornography should warn your audience about the victims of this industry."

"Look, Vanessa," Sam responded, slightly offended by the remark, "I'm sure it's been difficult pulling your life out of that awful mess. But it was all choices you made. How can you call yourself a victim?"

Vanessa lowered her head and thought for a second, then looked back up. "Let's forget about me for a second. Let's talk about the other victims."

"Other victims?"

"Yes, like the thirteen-year-old boy who will get his first taste of sexuality by looking at your pictures on the Web. His attitude about women and how he will relate to them as he matures, the expectations he'll have for his girlfriends, his lovers, his future wife could begin with your Web page, or any of a thousand other ones not nearly as tame as yours. Are you ready for that responsibility?"

Samantha didn't answer. "Or the young man who's been married for six years, with two young kids and a lovely wife who hasn't quite got her weight back down to their honeymoon level. What do you tell her while her husband is wasting away hours of time, browsing the Internet looking at pictures of you, and other actresses, models, and porno queens? How does she compete with the cosmetically altered breasts, the air-brushed images, the visual fantasy that her husband has become addicted to? What do you tell the kids when their family eventually breaks up because of his obsession?"

"That's not my responsibility—" Samantha tried to argue as the dirty feeling she'd fought the last couple of days returned.

"What about you, Sam?" Vanessa continued, her voice softening. "How about the little piece of you that died inside while you posed for the camera?"

Samantha's eyes widened in shock. How could this woman know what she'd gone through? She blinked quickly, trying to hold back the tears.

Vanessa leaned forward. "I know how it is. I lived through it and nearly didn't make it out. You feel dirty at first; your conscience tries to get the message across that what you're doing is wrong. But you resist. You fight it, usually with the help of the cameraman and the crew as they adore you with praise, blinding you to restraint as you thrive on their attention."

"You don't know—" Samantha argued weakly.

"Oh, but I do. I know you think there's no comparison between all the stuff I've done and your little pictorial. But if you're honest with yourself, something was seared in your soul that day."

She paused, allowing the words to sink in. "The path downhill for me was easy. It started with abuse at home, so my conscience was already numb. But for a lot of the girls in the industry it's like a slow eating away of their souls. With each step, something dies within. I know you're not in the same boat the rest of us are in. You've got a career. You feel good about yourself—this Internet idea is just a story for you. But take a hard look inside and be honest with yourself. And when you're writing your observations, don't discount the many victims this industry eats up and spits out on both sides of the camera."

Samantha sat on the couch speechless. She'd given up the fight to hold her tears back.

"Do you want to know what saved me?" Vanessa asked.

Samantha nodded her head, but she really wasn't sure if she did.

"Come with me." She said as she got up from the couch and led Sam down the hallway. She quietly opened the door, and the two stepped into the darkened room. Vanessa brought Sam up to the edge of the crib, pointing to Shelby, sleeping peacefully with her arms wrapped around her bear.

"This was my wake-up call, Sam," Vanessa whispered. "When I found out I was pregnant, it was like a light broke through to my fogged-up brain. Everything I'd done up until that point in my life screamed out at me to wake up!"

Samantha looked down at the sleeping child, then up into Vanessa's face.

"I know now that it was God speaking to me. I had a choice; keep on with my selfish, destructive life and abort this child . . ." Vanessa reached out and stroked her hand over Shelby's head. ". . . or make the decision to turn it all around and give my little Shelby the chance I never had. With God's help, I chose life."

"I don't know what to say, Vanessa."

"You don't have to say anything." Vanessa placed her hand over Sam's. "I think God just wanted you to hear my story. Give it some time and open up your heart. You'll hear what he's saying to you."

STUDIO CITY

2:15 P.M. PACIFIC

"So when?" Cassie asked as she sat across Rick's dining room table from him.

Rick looked up from the stack of mail he was sifting through. "When what?"

"When are we going to do it, silly?"

He leaned in closer, watching her eyes and without a hint of a smile said, "Not until we get married."

Her right hand whacked him on the shoulder, and Rick laughed. "I wasn't talking about that. I was talking about the wedding," Cassie said, giggling in response.

"I don't know," Rick admitted. "I'd been working so hard on the video and so nervous about whether you were going to say yes or no, I haven't thought about it. I don't want to wait long though. I guess the perfect time would be when we take our hiatus at the end of June. We'll have the time off to have a great honeymoon. What do you think?"

Cassie smiled. "That sounds perfect if we can get everything together by then."

"What kind of a wedding do you want, Cassie?" Rick had been through the process once, and he didn't care how this one went as long as Cassie was happy.

She paused for a moment. "I'm not sure. Part of me wants to have what I've always dreamed of—a big wedding with all my friends and relatives, walking down an aisle where you'll be standing there waiting for me."

Rick smiled. He couldn't wait to be there for her.

"But there's also a part of me that wants to make it intimate. You know, just you and me and the people who really matter to us."

"Well, we don't have to decide today. You probably need to think about it and maybe talk with your parents."

"Oh, my parents!" Cassie suddenly remembered. "We have to tell them."

"I wondered when that was coming. How do you want to do it?"

"Could we go see them in person?" Cassie asked. Her parents lived in Bakersfield, about ninety minutes up Interstate 5 in the San Joaquin Valley.

"I think that could be arranged," Rick answered. "How about if we head up after we drop the kids off at six?"

Cassie wrapped her arms around Rick and kissed him. "You're the best."

"No, just lucky enough to have found the best. Call your mom and make sure they'll be home, but don't tell them anything yet."

"That'll be hard, but I'll try."

NEWARK AIRPORT
6:30 P.M. EASTERN

Mark waited for his flight that should have departed fifteen minutes earlier. It was delayed in Boston, because of the same snowstorm.

The television in the waiting area caught his attention as the CBS evening news began. "Tonight our lead story takes a look at the tension building between India and Pakistan," the anchor reported. "It seems the struggle India is facing with the drought combined with the massive earthquake of last week might be just the beginning of its problems. Also, evidence of Pakistan troop deployment along the border has surfaced. Our report begins in New Delhi..."

The situation seems to be heating up in Asia, Mark thought. *I wonder if Stan is looking into this for his story tomorrow.*

Glancing out the windows, he could see the flurries increasing as the snow began to build up on the concrete around the gate area. It was too dark to see much beyond that, but he was beginning to fear his flight might not get out tonight at all. If he couldn't get back and missed the show Sunday night, he'd be dead meat with Russell.

Mark walked over to the woman standing behind the counter at the gate.

"Excuse me, Tina," he said politely as he read her name tag, "Do you have an estimate of when our flight will be departing?"

Tina looked at her computer monitor, then to Mark with her pasted-on smile. "The inbound flight from Boston is on final approach and should be at the gate in just a few minutes. We'll try and turn this flight around as quickly as possible before they shut the airport down."

"Shut the airport down?" Mark asked.

"Yes, sir. The storm is getting worse, and we're estimating that all flights might be canceled within the next half-hour."

Mark returned to his seat, wondering what time he could get back to LA if he had to wait until morning. He reached into his briefcase and pulled out an airlines guide. He scanned through it until he found Newark airport to LAX and started looking at his options. A couple of flights left early enough in the morning to arrive in LA before noon. Plenty of time to get over to the studio and be ready for the show at six. He tried to relax as he set the guide back into his briefcase. He was exhausted. Relatively no sleep the night before on the flight out and now he could be stuck waiting here overnight. *You promised in that verse to strengthen and protect me, Lord. I could sure use some of that strength now,* he prayed.

Mark decided he might as well make good use of the time. He pulled out his notebook and cell phone. He punched in Peter Lovil's phone number and hit talk.

"Yeah, Peter here."

"Peter, it's Mark. How's the research going?"

"Great! Didn't you get my message?" Peter asked.

"Not yet, I'm stuck at Newark's airport in a snowstorm. I haven't checked the office lately. What's up?"

"I've been all over that program you left for me at the office yesterday. It's an amazing work of art."

"Did you compare it to the phone records?" Mark asked.

"Sure did. The basic program is designed to randomly select phone numbers throughout the nation. But there's a subprogram that's been added on this disk, so that with a simple code word the program jumps out of the random sampling mode and instigates calls to specified numbers in a subroutine. In the case of the report you're looking at, 50 percent of the calls were made to area codes within three cities, Miami, San Francisco, and New York—Greenwich Village specifically."

"Kevin had mentioned San Francisco and Miami, and when you add Greenwich Village to it, that would certainly taint a gay opinion poll, wouldn't it?"

"You bet it would, and the operators doing the questioning would be none the wiser. The computer program does a nifty job of hiding the actual numbers called by logging in false random numbers."

"I can see how calling those specific cities would influence a gay poll, but I don't see how that would be useful to manipulate other surveys, something like a Senate race or an approval rating. Can you tell if the subroutine has an assigned list of phone numbers, or does it just send a higher percentage to the selected area codes?"

"All of the information isn't on this disk. It's not big enough, but I found there are specific lists of phone numbers that the code word can instruct the computer to call."

Mark scribbled furiously as he listened to Peter.

"For instance," Peter continued, "I found several headings available for different phone lists: Democrat, Republican, ACLU, NRA, NAACP, Christian Coalition, and others. This particular program accessed the Gay and Lesbian Association Against Defamation and the National Gay-Lesbian Alliance lists, both pro-homosexual groups, which resulted in the increase in phone calls to the Miami, San Francisco, and New York areas."

"Then Kevin was onto something," Mark mumbled to himself. Kevin's accident now didn't seem like much of an accident at all.

"I'd be very careful if I were you," Peter's warning broke through his thoughts. "Whoever is behind this has gone through a lot of trouble. They'll be protecting their investment with everything they've got."

"I plan to be careful," Mark said. *But I don't plan to stop.* "I want you to do two more things for me."

"Only if they don't involve sticking my neck out in any way," Peter answered with a trace of fear.

"They shouldn't. First, I want you to print out the entire survey from the computer disk. I want to compare it to one I just received from Research International."

"OK, that one's easy. What's number two?"

"I've got a list of seven names. I want everything you can find on each one of them and see how they could be tied together."

Chapter 18

Luis casually walked through the courtyard of the Rosewood apartments looking for Mark's building. It hadn't taken Griff's team long to come up with his address while Luis got the equipment together. Dressed in his Pacific Bell coveralls and carrying his duffel bag of little bugs and cameras, Luis spotted the letter G on the tan stucco building up to his left. Mark's apartment would be upstairs, unit 7. He walked around the ground floor until he saw the telephone junction box. Glancing around to see if anybody would take notice of his actions, he set his bag down and got to work.

Within minutes, Luis was upstairs at Mark's unit picking the lock. The lock finally gave, and he was in the door.

Luis made a mental note of where everything was placed as he put his bag on top of the table. If there had been more time to plan, he would have had twice as much equipment, but for the limited amount of time he would be tracking Mark, what he had would be enough.

He started by placing bugs inside the three phones. For good measure he placed listening devices in the two bedrooms as well. He unscrewed the grates over the air-conditioning vents in each of the rooms and placed small, wide-angled video cameras and transmitters above them.

In less than an hour he had completed his mission and was walking out the door. Luis had even taken the time to carefully search through the apartment looking for the missing disk and telephone records but to no avail. It had been a long shot anyway.

"Is there some problem with the phones?" He heard a female voice call from behind him as he started down the steps. He turned and saw a woman he guessed to be around forty standing in the doorway of apartment 8 with her hands on her hips.

"Not anymore, ma'am," Luis said politely without lifting his head, then continued on his way. He hoped she was the type to keep to herself and not mention anything to Taylor about seeing the serviceman at his door.

He made his way back through the courtyard and to the van where Griff was waiting for him.

"Are you getting everything?" he asked as he shut the door.

"I've got video from the four cameras, and I could hear every sound you made in the room. We're all set."

"Good. Let's get round-the-clock surveillance set up starting tonight. I'm not sure when he'll get back, and I want us ready."

Newark Airport
6:58 p.m. Eastern

"We're sorry to announce that all flights in and out of Newark airport have been canceled due to the heavy snowstorm. Should you require assistance, please visit the nearest . . ." The announcement came over the public-address system as Mark stared at the plane parked at his gate. The flight had arrived from Boston fifteen minutes before, but the United ground personnel couldn't turn the flight around in time to beat the storm.

Mark decided to avoid the crowded ticket counter and dialed the 800 number for United reservations. He booked the first flight out in the morning, hoping desperately that the storm would pass.

After taking care of the reservation, he decided he'd better check in with Jennifer, someone else who wouldn't be too happy about his delay in getting home. Since it was only three on the West Coast, he figured she'd still be at the office. She answered the phone on the first ring.

"Williams."

"Hi, Jennifer, how's it going?" he asked.

"Oh, Mark, I'm glad you called. Did Russell reach you yet?"

Mark laughed. "Oh yeah, we talked."

"I'm sorry about that. When he saw that we weren't working together, he really cornered me on where you were. I tried to cover, but he persisted."

"It's all right. He made it very clear he wasn't happy about the trip. He wants me back home ASAP, which is why I'm calling."

"What's up?" she asked.

"I'm stuck out here for now, a big snowstorm."

"Oh no! When can you get out?"

"I'm booked on the first flight in the morning. If the storm clears, I'll get in before noon."

"You'd better hope it does. We've got the lead story. I don't want somebody else introducing your taped piece."

"How did the editing go?"

"Great. I finished up right around noon. You got some good stuff on that lady. I'm using her to tag the piece."

Mark smiled; that's what he'd hoped. "Good, Jenn. I told you she was gold."

"What about your story?" Jennifer asked. "Have any of your leads panned out?"

"There is some interesting stuff coming together. I'll fill you in when I get back."

"OK, you just figure out a way to get back here by showtime tomorrow."

"I will, don't worry, and thanks for covering everything today."

"No problem, Mark. Just remember you owe me."

Mark disconnected the call. He was exhausted and didn't like the idea of spending the night sitting around the gate. He grabbed his bag and headed for a cab. There had to be a hotel nearby where he could get a room for the night. It'd be worth it, or he'd look terrible on the show tomorrow.

SHERMAN OAKS
6:03 P.M. PACIFIC

Samantha stepped into her apartment mentally exhausted. The discussion with Vanessa so disturbed her that instead of coming home and getting her weekend to-do list completed, she'd driven out to the beach and sat in the sand, staring into the ocean.

Her thoughts were scattered, remembering her teenage experiences and rebelliousness and how she'd become sexually active at the age of fifteen. Then her mind skipped forward to the present, and she recalled the unclean feeling when she disrobed in front of the photographer and the piercing way that Vanessa had so accurately pinpointed those feelings. It was eerie.

She'd stopped by her neighborhood video store on the way home. It took awhile, but she finally found a video that Vanessa had appeared in called *Feisty Flight Attendants*. Samantha hoped the tape would help her complete the research on Vanessa.

The message light on her answering machine blinked as she set her purse and the videotape on the kitchen counter. She hit the play button.

"Sam, it's me, Peter. I thought you might want to look at the site. It's up and running—samsnudes.com. Let me know what you think."

She sighed—not quite the reaction she would have expected from herself just twenty-four hours ago. She decided to face her internal conflict head-on and walked toward her computer. The video could wait.

PADUCAH, KENTUCKY
8:04 P.M. CENTRAL

"Did you lock the door?" fourteen-year-old Stephen asked his younger cousin as he jumped up next to him at the desk.

"Yeah. Our parents just started a game of bridge, so they won't be worried about us for a while. Let's do it."

"OK. It's connecting now." Stephen was excited. The computer was already up and running, and he had typed in his dad's AOL member password.

"Welcome. You've got mail."

"Cool, let's check out your dad's mail." Tommy fidgeted in the chair.

"No, there's better stuff than that. Let's do some surfing, dude." Stephen laughed. Soon there was a box for Stephen to type in what he was searching for. He typed "xxx, nudes" then hit the return button.

In less than thirty seconds, the two boys were looking at the first list of ten from over 550,000 matches to their search. They were one mouse click away from having explicit sexual pictures right in front of their faces. Stephen scanned down the list in front of him.

"Hey, there's a new one—samsnudes.com. Let's try that one."

Tommy was just along for the ride. "Whatever you say, Steve."

Stephen clicked on the underlined heading that stated, "Free—Celebrity Nudes—porno, sex, xxx . . ." The screen flashed, and within a few moments they were greeted by Samantha's title page and a warning.

"What's that?" Tommy asked.

"It's telling us if we're under eighteen to take a hike." Stephen laughed as he reached for the mouse and clicked the "Yes, I'm over 18" button.

The screen flashed once again, and the boys' faces brightened as the pictures from samsnudes.com started appearing on the screen.

SHERMAN OAKS
6:08 P.M. PACIFIC

Samantha could feel the butterflies in her stomach as the disclaimer for her Web page greeted her. She quickly clicked on the "over 18" button herself as she waited for the final product to be displayed before her eyes.

The first things to load were the title page and the text. She waited nervously as the graphics and pictures started filling the screen. Within moments, the site was completed before her. Samsnudes.com was a reality. The metallic gold, three-dimensional lettering at the top of the page looked classy. Hanging with one elbow resting against the last letter was herself, wearing nothing but a smile. She clicked on the icon that would show her the pictures she'd submitted, and she was surprised to see her computer image animate and wink at her before the screen changed.

Looking at her own nude pictures that were now available for the world to see disturbed her deeply. Once again Vanessa's words echoed through her mind, and the feeling that she had somehow defiled herself returned. She fought to look at her pictures with a sense of pride and accomplishment. But she couldn't. All she could muster was a sense of loss—as if she'd let a part of herself die to allow these images to be spread across the Web.

Samantha spent the next twenty minutes scanning the different areas of the site—the survey, Tad's pictorial, and about twenty other celebrities that Peter had included. Eventually the flashing mailbox at the top of her screen caught her attention.

She clicked over to her E-mail area and was shocked to see that over fifty responses had been left for her from the site's survey. That was incredible! The network hadn't even publicized it yet.

She opened the most recent one, anxious to see what kind of data she would receive for her story. She glanced through the response; it was from Stephen, a fourteen-year-old in Kentucky.

WESTWOOD
6:31 P.M. PACIFIC

Tracy returned to her condominium, refreshed by the time spent in Malibu. Getting back into the city always refocused her mind on her job. Her first thought was wondering if Kevin had returned from his mysterious absence. She picked up the phone to call his house. It was answered after the third ring.

"Hi, is Kevin home please?" Tracy asked.

"Who's calling?" The voice sounded as though the woman had been crying. Tracy decided she'd better sit down.

"It's Tracy Reynolds. Is this Vickie?"

"Yes," Vickie's voice broke as she tried to talk. "He's dead, Tracy."

Tracy nearly collapsed into a chair, her legs giving out as she heard the news. "Vickie, no! How?"

Through the tears, Vickie recounted the patrolman's story. Tracy's heart seized, breaking for her lost friend and for the poor young wife left alone. "I'm so sorry, Vickie," she got out through her own tears. "If there is anything you need . . ."

RAMADA INN, NEWARK, NEW JERSEY
9:45 P.M. EASTERN

Mark lay in the queen-sized bed, trying to review Palmer's survey. But his eyes kept losing their focus, and he soon realized he was taking extremely long blinks. He set the report aside and reached up to turn out the light. Then he stopped. There was one more thing he wanted to do before he turned in for the night. He reached for his wallet and pulled out Tracy's card on which she'd scribbled her home number. He grabbed the phone and dialed, hoping she'd be home.

"Hello." Her voice brought a smile to his face.

"Hi, Tracy. It's Mark Taylor."

"Mark, it's good to hear from you."

Mark caught the edge in her voice. "Is this a bad time? You sound upset."

"I just got some bad news a few minutes ago."

"Tracy, I'm sorry. Anything I can do?"

"No, but thanks for asking. You sound far away. Where are you?"

"I'm at a lovely Ramada Inn in Newark, New Jersey."

"You're kidding. What are you doing there?"

"More research—you know the life of an investigative reporter. I was supposed to be flying back right now, but we're having this lovely snowstorm, so I'm stuck here for the night. I'm calling about tomorrow. Are you still interested in coming to the show?"

"You bet I am, and you definitely owe me dinner now."

"What do you mean?"

"I talked with my grandfather this morning, and he's agreed to have lunch with us on Tuesday."

"Wow! That was fast."

"I was kind of surprised myself. But when I mentioned your name, he agreed right away."

Mark hesitated. Why would his name mean anything to Jason Reynolds? "I'm not sure I understand. How would he know me?"

Tracy laughed. "You said yourself he owns your network. Don't be surprised if he has a good idea of who works for him. He's pretty sharp, you know."

"I'm sure of that, Tracy," Mark responded apprehensively, hoping that was the only way Reynolds had heard of him. "About tomorrow night, since I'm stuck in a snowstorm, I'm not sure exactly when I'll get back to LA. Would it be all right if you met me at the studio?"

"Sure, if you tell me where to go."

"Just drive up to the main gate at National. It's on Santa Monica, just east of Highland. The guard will have your name, and he'll give you directions to the studio."

"What time should I be there?"

"We go live at six. Can you get there about 5:30?"

"I'll be there, Mark."

"OK, see you then. Have a good night."

"You too, and good luck getting back in the morning."

He hung up the phone and turned off the light. He knew it was not good policy to mix work with romantic interest, and what was even more important, he didn't know the first thing about how she felt about the Lord. But he couldn't stop thinking about her. He'd have to watch himself. She was the type he could fall head over heals for, and there were many reasons why that was a bad idea.

CHAPTER 19

SUNDAY, FEBRUARY 11
NATIONAL STUDIOS
3:00 P.M. PACIFIC

Rick pulled into his assigned parking space on the National Studios lot. He walked quickly past *The John Harold Show* stage and made his way through the *Across the Nation* doors. The difference between the two productions amazed him.

While his show had room for a live studio audience of 350 people surrounding a lavishly decorated set, this studio was only one-quarter the size. It contained no audience seating and had three cameras pointing toward a half circular desk. Everything behind the desk was green, even the floor.

This high-tech news show relied on computerized images, what was called a virtual-reality set. The green would be electronically extracted from the camera's image, and the computer would insert furniture, paintings, even moving globes—whatever the designers could conceive would be placed electronically around the hosts of the show.

This was Rick's first show using this technology. He looked forward to learning how it all came together.

"Hi, Rick, glad you could make it," Terri Barnett, the show's director, called out.

They knew each other back in the days when she was an associate director and Rick a stage manager.

"Thanks, Terri. I hope everything's all right with your family," Rick answered.

"My dad's been having some heart trouble, and he's going in for surgery later this week. I talked to Russell, and once he found out you were able to fill in, he gave me next week off. So I thank you for helping."

"I'm looking forward to it. I've never had a chance to do a virtual show before. It should be interesting."

"Interesting, yes, but not nearly as exciting as doing the kind of show you do. I'll show you around."

Terri led Rick through the doorway to the control room. The technical director and the associate director were at their stations, building teases for that night's show. Rick hadn't met them before, so Terri made the introductions. It was the room next to the control room that held Rick's interest. Two technicians sat behind identical keyboards that operated the computers.

"So this is where your set is. Amazing," Rick said.

"Yeah, it's gotten to be old hat for us. Everybody's settled into the format we use, so I don't think you'll have any trouble next week. But the first month when we were trying to get all of this online, it wasn't a pretty sight."

"That must have been fun, doing it live."

"That's where Russell was smart. We started off doing the show by tape delay. We'd record it earlier in the day for the first several weeks until we got all the bugs out, then we went live." She looked at her watch, then back to Rick. "It's time for our final rundown meeting."

Terri led Rick back through the studio and to the production offices. Around the conference table sat the hosts and producers for the show. Rick spotted Samantha at the far end of the table. She hadn't noticed him yet.

"Welcome, Rick." Russell waved. "Come on over here, and I'll introduce you to everybody."

Rick stepped toward the table where two seats waited for him and Terri. Russell's mention of him brought Samantha's head up from her notes, and her eyebrows rose sharply. Rick couldn't read her expression.

"Gang, this is Rick Treadway, director of Harold's show. He's agreed to help us out next week and direct the show so Terri can spend time with her father." Russell explained.

He went around the table, introducing the cast and producers. When he got to Samantha, she just shrugged. "We've met," she said.

It suddenly dawned on Russell that the two had a past together. He'd forgotten that Rick had been a suspect when Samantha had scooped all the other stations by reporting from outside his house the night he'd been arrested. Russell had never found out how she'd been tipped off.

Oh, well, it's a done deal now, Russell thought. Rick would have known Samantha was on the show. If he'd had a problem with it, he would have spoken up. "It's good to have you with us, Rick," Russell concluded.

"I'm happy to be here."

"Now can somebody tell me where Mark is?" Russell snapped as he looked around the table.

Jennifer, sitting next to an empty chair, looked up as if she was at fault. "I heard from him last night. He was stuck in Newark—the snowstorm."

Confused expressions filtered through the room. Nobody else on the staff knew Mark was away on his private assignment. "He said he'd get the first flight out this morning," Jennifer added.

"Great!" Russell exclaimed. "Heather," he waved to the production assistant, "please try his cell phone, then page him if you have to. I want to know where he is."

"Right away, Frank," she answered as she left the table.

"All right, let's get down to it. If Mark manages to make it back to his job, he's still got the lead story. Tad, are you ready with the recap piece on the abortion lawsuit?"

"Yes, sir. We've got the footage all lined up and edited."

"OK, good. If for some reason he doesn't show, we'll write something for you to introduce the tape—Mark Taylor on assignment kind of thing. Jennifer, the piece is all done?"

"Yeah, the only problem we'd have is that Mark planned to tag it live. We kind of left the end of the piece at an interesting point, but it's good journalism. Somebody would need to wrap it up."

"Yeah, I remember that when you showed it to me yesterday."

"Mark just called in," Heather announced to Russell as she returned to the table. "He's on the plane, still about an hour out from LAX."

"He's cutting it awfully close." Russell swore. "Jennifer go ahead and write the opening and closing as if Tad's doing it. That way we'll be ready in case Mark doesn't get here, or he does and I decide to bench him.

"Stan, I'm bumping up your story to the number-two slot. It seemed like every-where I turned this weekend I saw a story on the crisis in India. Are you all set?"

"Yes, sir."

It took another thirty minutes for Russell to go through the rest of the show, making sure each and every segment was covered thoroughly.

"People, I've got one last important announcement to make. I just found out this weekend that the network has canceled *Galaxy Seven*."

"I'm sure that's heartbreaking for the cast and crew," Samantha snickered, "but what does that have to do with us?"

"The network wants us to take their time slot for the time being—Wednesday nights at nine. So we're doing two shows a week starting now."

The staff members were shocked. As it was, there was only one real day off the staff could count on, and that was normally followed by six ten-hour days. How could they add another show in the same production week?

"I know what you're thinking," Russell said, "and I've been thinking the same thing ever since I heard. But this is make or break time for us. We all know the ratings haven't been all they could be. With this extra time slot we have a chance to reach a whole new audience. Of course, the risk is great as well, with the added exposure, if our ratings don't take a turn upward. So with that in mind, we're pulling out all the stops for the premier show. All the plans for next week's sweeps show will be moved up to Wednesday."

A chorus of complaints rose from the table. The common thread—there wasn't enough time to have the stories ready by then. Russell held up the palm of his hand to the group.

"I know this puts a strain on everybody. So I'm calling a production meeting to discuss all the specifics of our new venture tomorrow." More grumbling came from the staff. "That's right, I'm canceling your day off, so enjoy the morning. The meeting will be here at one o'clock." He glanced out over the top of his glasses. "Don't be late!"

With his last statement, Russell calmly got up and left the conference table. For several seconds, nobody else moved. Then they all started talking at once. Lots of questions but no answers.

Rick looked at Terri. "How does this affect your time off?"

"Good question. I'll have to talk with Russell. What are you doing Wednesday night around six?"

Rick sounded apologetic. "I should be fading to black on our show."

"I'm sure we'll work out something," Terri said without much confidence. "Now let's get back into show mode. At this point I usually get together with the computer and graphics people to make sure they're ready for all the visuals we'll need."

"You head on in. I'll meet you in the computer room," Rick said as he noticed Samantha stepping away from her seat at the table and heading toward him. The two hadn't spoken in nearly a year.

"It's nice to see you again, Rick," she said holding out her hand.

Rick took it politely. "Thank you, Samantha. It's nice to see you as well. You've been doing a great job around here."

"Thank you." She smiled at him. "I spent an interesting day with your friend Vanessa yesterday."

"I heard you were going to talk with her. How did it go?"

"I'll have to say it was eye-opening. It brought back some memories when it finally dawned on me where I'd seen her before."

"I'm sure it did. She's been through a lot since then, but she's managed to really turn her life around. I hope you considered what she had to say."

"I did more than that," Samantha confessed. "Seeing little Shelby as the turning point in her life had an impact. It goes against the story I was planning. I'm still trying to decide how I should respond to it all."

"Just give it time," Rick advised. "Let it sink in a little. Maybe God will have some answers for you."

Samantha laughed. "That's what she said."

"Then it must be true."

"But time is the one thing I just lost on this story. It'll have to be ready by Wednesday now. I'm glad you're filling in next week. It'll be fun having you around as the director—just like old times."

"Thanks, Sam, that's a nice thing to hear."

MALIBU
3:12 P.M. PACIFIC

Jason Reynolds leaned back in his chair, staring off into the blue Pacific waters as he half listened to the voice of a golf commentator. The phone beside him rang.

"Reynolds here," he answered.

"Jason, it's Albert. Listen, I've got the president with me, and he's pretty upset about all this publicity—"

Jason heard a voice say, "Give me that phone," just before he heard the president's voice on the line.

"What have you done, Jason?" McNeil exclaimed. "Your little trick is about to set off a nuclear war!"

Reynolds shook his head, holding back laughter. "Calm down, Andrew. Everything's under control."

"You call it under control when every newscast last night and all the Sunday morning talking heads are making predictions about Pakistan invading India? *60 Minutes* is doing a piece on it right now!"

"And *Across the Nation* will be doing one in less than three hours. It's all part of the plan."

"What plan?" the president shouted in rage.

"You want your economic package approved, including the funding for the UN, correct?"

"Yes," McNeil answered, not hiding his irritation.

"What better way to show the need for the appropriations than showing the drastic urgency for the UN to intervene. We had a ready-made situation in Asia waiting to be exploited. I just took advantage of it."

"Your exploitation has heightened the tension over there, Jason. How is your trumped-up international crisis going to help me?"

Reynolds shook his head. "It's simple. India is struggling—not enough food to go around because of the drought, thousands homeless from the earthquake. What a wonderful opportunity to show the world the wisdom of the UN's position on family planning—too many people struggling with not enough resources. India is a perfect example of that. The members of the Senate that have you so worried about blocking your plan won't be able to vote against the tide of public opinion after this weekend of reports."

Reynolds continued as the president remained silent. "At the same time, you've got Pakistan across the border looking for the right time to instigate another war with a weakened India, a perfect reason for you to jump on the bandwagon for a strong military buildup within the UN, the reason your proposal must be passed immediately."

"You're mad, Reynolds," McNeil finally said. "Do you realize that Pakistan is actually amassing troops along the border?"

Reynolds's eyebrows rose as a smile spread across his face; he hadn't realized that. "Then everything's in place for you. Call a press conference. Share with the American people your vision for a strong UN, which, in spite of having peacekeeping forces on every continent around the globe, can still step in on a moment's notice to save the world from nuclear disaster. Wake up, Andrew, and be presidential. Speak out for the importance of international intervention, the need for UN's sanctioned family planning around the globe as we see more and more nations struggle with not enough resources for out-of-control populations. We're set up perfectly for you to combine your pro-choice forces and your UN backers to push this through. This is a gold mine!"

McNeil paused as Reynolds's plan finally sank in. "I still think you're psychotic, Jason, but I've got work to do."

"I'll have polls out within forty-eight hours showing the vast majority of Americans support your position, Mr. President," Reynolds said before the line was disconnected.

SOMEWHERE OVER ARIZONA
3:29 P.M. PACIFIC

Mark looked helplessly out the airplane's window. By now Russell knew where he was and was probably fuming.

His miserable day started with him getting up early and getting to the airport to catch his early morning flight to Los Angeles. The snow had stopped, and things were looking good as he rode in the cab. He was sitting in the plane as it taxied to the runway. The pilot began his takeoff. The plane was speeding down the runway when it suddenly braked, sending Mark and the rest of the passengers lurching forward. Then the plane turned around and headed back to the terminal.

That was over nine hours ago. An engine failure light in the cockpit had prevented the flight from leaving Newark. The airline had kept the passengers on the plane while it was checked out. There was no chance for Mark to deplane and get on another flight. He was stuck.

Now as he looked down at the desolate Arizona desert, the frustration nearly overwhelmed him. He knew he'd be in deep water with Russell. He wanted to go over his copy with Jennifer, see the final edit on the abortion tape, make sure everything was just right for his lead story. Mark looked at his watch. Maybe he'd have a chance to look through things quickly.

"Ladies and gentlemen," the pilot said, "we've just been informed that there's quite a bit of heavy traffic around Los Angeles at this time. We've been instructed to slow our airspeed a bit to give them a little breathing space between airplanes. It shouldn't delay us much. We expect to get to the gate about fifteen minutes later than expected. Our new arrival time is 4:22."

Mark clenched his teeth. His right hand squeezed into a tight fist as he reached for the airphone. Maybe he could go over his copy with Jennifer before he landed.

BURBANK
3:54 P.M. PACIFIC

The man in the white van read the latest Grisham novel. This had to be one of the most boring duties he'd ever been assigned since he'd began working with Reynolds Industries security. He was going into his ninth hour with his legs cramped in the back of the van as he watched and listened for any sign of movement in apartment G-7.

The monotony was interrupted by his cell phone chirping beside him.

"Yeah," he answered.

"It's Luis. Anything yet?"

"No. Still quiet."

"OK. We'll have somebody out there to spell you within the hour."

NATIONAL STUDIOS
5:30 P.M. PACIFIC

Thirty Minutes to Air

Rick sat in the control room as Terri did her last talk through the rundown with her crew. It was very similar to what he did each night with his staff just before the show, making sure that nothing slipped through the cracks before going live. He was hoping to see Mark come through the studio doors any second. He kept praying in the back of his mind as he tried to make notes of what Terri was doing.

"All right, that's it. Everybody in position ten minutes before the show—no later." Terri wrapped up her meeting with the final instruction.

Rick walked back out to the studio. His prayers were answered as Mark charged through the stage doors.

"Where have you been?" Rick asked as he stepped in pace with Mark rushing toward the office.

"Stuck in the great airline abyss."

"How was the trip?"

"Incredible! There's so much to tell you. But I've got to get into makeup. Could you do me a favor, Rick?"

"Sure, name it."

"A lady named Tracy Reynolds should be arriving soon—she may already be here. Could you find her for me and let her know how late I'm running? Tell her I probably won't be able to see her until after the show. Get her a chair somewhere out on the stage by a monitor. Talk to Bret, the stage manager. He'll know where to put her."

"You've got it, Mark. Just go get ready."

"Thanks, Rick." Mark shot through the door and into the office, leaving Rick in the studio.

"There you are," Jennifer called out as Mark walked up to her desk.

"I'm heading to makeup. Bring the script and we'll go over it."

"Great, go ahead. I'll let Russell know you're here."

Mark dropped his bag in his cubicle and went straight for the makeup room. Fortunately, the chair in front of Roberta, his favorite makeup artist, was open. Finally, something was going right in this awful day, and then Russell stepped into the room.

"Nice you could make it to our little show."

"Sorry," Mark apologized. "I tried to call from the plane, but I missed you."

"I heard. Do you see why we have guidelines about weekend travel?"

Mark left the question unanswered as Russell continued. "I have half a mind to keep you off the air tonight to teach you a lesson, but you have the lead story. It's too important for the show. So get your act together, Taylor, and be on that set ready to go."

Russell stormed out of the makeup room as Mark closed his eyes and Roberta quickly started applying foundation.

Twenty Minutes to Air

Rick looked outside the stage door and noticed a stunningly beautiful woman making her way toward him.

"You aren't by any chance Tracy Reynolds, are you?" Rick asked.

"Yes I am, and you are—"

"Rick Treadway. I'm a friend of Mark's. He asked me to look out for you. His plane just arrived, and he's rushing through makeup and wardrobe. He probably won't be able to see you until he comes on the set for the show."

"What happened to his flight? I thought he said he was taking the first one out this morning?"

"I'm still not sure of all the details. I just know he arrived here about ten minutes ago. Come on inside. We have a chair set up off stage for you."

Rick led her to a folding chair near the off-stage monitor. The producer's table was just in front of it, where Russell would sit with each of the segment producers during the show.

"You can sit right here. Mark will be out on the set in no time."

Tracy looked at the center of the room. "What set? Where is it?"

Rick laughed. "It's all electronically inserted where you see the green. I'll explain it after the show if you'd like. Right now I have to get back to the control room. Have a good time."

"Thanks, Rick. I appreciate your help."

Seven Minutes to Air

"Who wrote the copy for me after the tape?" Mark asked as he looked over the script in the makeup chair.

"I did," Jennifer answered. "Russell wanted it as a backup for Tad to read in case you didn't show. What do you want changed?"

"I'm not sure, but this definitely doesn't work. I'd love to see the final edit on the piece."

"I know, but there isn't time. You're still not dressed."

"OK, just leave the TelePrompTer blank after the tape rolls. I'll ad-lib my final comment."

"OK, if you're sure."

"That's probably best, unless I come up with something while I'm changing," Mark said, stepping out of the chair and walking down the hall to wardrobe.

Five Minutes to Air

"Five minutes," the associate director to Terri's left called out.

The production people were ready. Rick sat at the back bench beside the lighting director and a production assistant who timed the show.

"Everybody in place?" Terri called.

The three camera operators checked in by number as well as the two tape operators.

A female intern handed out last-minute script changes on yellow paper to everyone on the front row. Mark could see Terri's irritation.

"It's a little late for new pages," she said to no one in particular as she searched her book for the right pages to pull out.

"Lighting ready," the man to Rick's left said.

"Tape, let me see the opening once," Terri said.

The color monitor in the center of the room came to life with the *Across the Nation* graphic—images of staff reporters from locations around the country.

"OK, thanks, Ron," Terri said to the tape room. "Audio, you guys all checked out?"

"We're locked and loaded, Terri. Mark's the only one we haven't heard yet. He was still getting dressed."

Three Minutes to Air

Mark stepped out the door to the stage, weaving through a maze of technicians and production staff as they rushed through last-minute preparations. In the hurry to get himself ready, Mark had nearly forgotten about Tracy until he spotted her sitting behind the producer's table. She looked radiant.

He walked over to her chair as she stood to greet him with a warm hug. He liked that.

"Two minutes, everybody," Bret, the stage manager, called out through the studio.

"I'm glad you're here," Mark told her.

"From what I hear, you must be glad you're here too." She grinned.

"Yeah, it's been quite a day. I've got to get on the set. I'll talk to you after the show."

"Break a leg," Tracy called as he left.

Mark laughed. In the short time he'd been one of the reporters of *Across the Nation*, this was the first time anyone had told him that.

He took his seat at the news desk, where Steve helped him with the microphone.

"Cutting it kind of close tonight, aren't you?" Steve chuckled.

"Yeah, it's been one of those days." Mark reached inside his coat pocket and pulled out the MPR-1 recording pen. "Could you download what's on this thing, then give it back to me after the show? I still might need it this week."

"Sure thing," Steve said, taking the pen. "Have a good show."

Chapter 20

One Minute to Air

"One minute," the associate director called out in the booth.

"OK, everyone, let's look sharp. Have a great show," Terri said into her headset.

Rick glanced around the room. He could almost see the tension as the hour arrived. He wondered if his control room felt this way right before taping. His crew members always did their show "live-to-tape," which meant they rolled right through the show as if it was live, but in the event of a catastrophe, they could stop. Here there was no option. What was said and shot within this studio in the next fifty-eight minutes would be going out across the country instantly.

"Thirty seconds."

"Stand by, videotape," Terri called out. She sat up on the edge of her seat.

On the set, Tad shifted in his chair and cleared his throat. He leaned over to Mark. "Glad you could make it, sport."

Mark took a deep breath and did his ritual silent prayer for the Lord to be with him.

"Did you hear we're going to be adding a Wednesday night show this week?" Tad asked.

Mark's concentration was broken as he looked over to see if Tad was serious. He started to ask a question.

"In ten, nine, eight . . ." the stage manager yelled from behind the camera in sync with the associate director in the booth.

"And roll A," Terri called as the countdown hit two. "Up on A."

The center monitor lighted up a beat later as the opening tape filled the screen. The video monitors in the studio did the same. Tracy could feel the excitement in the small room.

"Welcome to *Across the Nation* . . ." the announcer's voice on the tape boomed through the studio. Mark looked up at Tracy and gave her a quick smile.

"And now, Tad Forrest." The tape ended as the center camera moved toward the desk and the stage manager pointed to its lens.

"Thanks for tuning in tonight. Thirty million dollars, that was the award a jury in . . ." Tad took his cue and started reading the TelePrompTer.

Tracy took her concentration off the set and looked at the monitor beside her. The difference was startling. She could see the live Tad sitting at the desk with just green surrounding him, but on the monitor he was surrounded by a beautiful set with colored windows, marbled walls, and classy works of art. Over Tad's shoulder, dollar bills started floating down as if they'd been dropped from the sky as the graphic "$30,000,000" appeared on the screen, yet there was nothing in the studio. Amazing, she thought.

"Ready, graphics, go!" Terri was cueing from inside the control room as she followed along in the script. Rick wrote down the words she was using to tell the crew what to do in his own script. He'd record the show when it aired in Los Angeles later that night and then compare his notes to the final product.

Mark sat next to Tad, unconsciously reading the TelePrompTer along with him. He was dazed by the last comment Tad had made just as they hit the air—a Wednesday show! What brought that on?

"So with the jury reaching this momentous decision," Tad wrapped up his opening, "we decided to have our own Mark Taylor take a look at our nation and abortion. Mark."

"Take three," Terri called as the shot on the monitor changed from Tad to shot of Tad and Mark. "Stand by to zoom on my cue. Go graphics. Zoom camera 3."

Mark turned his attention from Tad and looked straight into the camera lens. "Thanks, Tad. A cultural war is ravaging our nation. It's a war in which the members on both sides believe to the very core of their being that they are right. It's a war that if it continues on its present course, America can't possibly win."

Mark paused dramatically before he continued. "Just this past week, a jury in Washington State presented Planned Parenthood with a thirty-million-dollar award—an amount that probably will never be collected, and the verdict is sure to be appealed. The war will continue.

"For the courtroom is the frontline of this war, and that's where we, the press, focus your attention most often. But the courtroom is not where the forces of conflict in this war are inflicting the most damage to our nation. Tonight, we're going to delve deeper—beyond the courtroom—behind the demonstrations—and try to catch a glimpse of what's at the very heart of this issue. Tonight, *Across the Nation* goes behind the front lines of the Abortion War."

Mark held his expression into the camera lens until he saw the red light go off. Then the sound of his videotape piece could be heard filling the studio as footage of street marchers holding their pro-choice banners high shouted their chant: "Our bodies, our choice."

Russell leaned over to Jennifer sitting next to him at the producer's table. "Good lead-in, Jenn. I could sense the passion in Mark. Wonderful."

Jennifer smiled as she looked at Mark and gave him a thumbs-up sign. Mark knew he was clear for the next five minutes and twenty-seven seconds while the tape played, but this was his first chance to see the completed version, so he stayed transfixed on the monitor in front of him.

Rick was impressed. He hadn't had a chance to see Mark in action, and the way he introduced the story was compelling. He was a natural talent.

MALIBU
6:04 P.M. PACIFIC

Jason Reynolds sat behind his desk, watching the monitor with the National network East Coast feed on it. He had his sound system up so he could hear every word from Mark Taylor. Reynolds hadn't taken much interest in the show since it began last fall, but now that Mark was snooping around, he thought he'd better get an idea of who this kid was. *He was good,* Jason thought. There was a sincerity about him that came across well. He seemed believable, a must for an investigative journalist.

National Studios
Same Time

As the tape played, Mark smiled. Jennifer had done a wonderful job with the edit-ing. The pro-choice side was covered masterfully, even though it countered Mark's personal beliefs. He wanted the piece to be balanced, to present each side's argu-ment. Mark had done one of the interviews early last week with a sixteen-year-old girl who had touched him greatly. She'd chosen to have an abortion after being date-raped by the high school football captain. Her voice was electronically altered on the tape, and she was shown only in silhouette. Mark wished he'd met her before the abortion; maybe he would have had a chance to talk her out of it. The interview was a tear-jerker as she pleaded for understanding. She said she didn't want to risk her future by carrying this "mistake" to term. In her opinion, and, unfortunately, that of her parents too, she didn't have another option.

Without thinking, Mark scooted to the edge of his stool. The interview with Sara had to be coming up. Jennifer had saved it for last, just the way he'd wanted it. This would be great. The last thing would be Sara's eloquent defense of the pro-life position. That was why Mark wanted to ad-lib his final comments rather than read them off the TelePrompTer. He wanted his closing tag to come from his heart. He waited anxiously.

The tape showed another line of protesters carrying signs: "Stop the Killing" and "What About the Baby's Choice?" as Mark's prerecorded voice introduced Sara Medford of the Right to Life Advocacy Group.

The scene cut to Sara sitting at her desk. "We're just everyday people joined together by a common cause to save the life of the unborn."

"Do you agree with the thirty-million-dollar award?" Mark asked her.

"Heavens no! That's outlandish. First of all, how are they going to collect that kind of money from these people? And what about free speech in this country? Last time I looked, it was still covered by the First Amendment."

Her comments were broken by a shot over her shoulder, showing Mark listen-ing to her. It was an obvious edit.

"We have to answer to a higher law—God's law. It might be necessary to break an immoral law in order to save the life of an unborn baby. . . ."

Another shot was edited in—this time a close-up of Mark nodding his head. Then Sara continued, ". . . so there are areas of civil disobedience that I would sup-port in order to save lives."

Mark asked, "What would you say to a doctor who practices abortion?"

"Think about what you're doing, ripping the life away from something so young, so helpless, so precious. Please give them a chance to live."

Once again the scene changed to that of Mark listening. So many edits in just a few seconds: Mark couldn't believe it. Jennifer could have easily used an entire quote from Sara.

"If you don't . . ." Sara's voice was heard over Mark's head shot, then her face filled the screen again with her final comment. ". . . you won't get away with it."

Mark was furious. Here was this sweet woman Mark had come to adore, and Jennifer had hacked away at her comments until they meant something totally different than what she'd originally said. Her last statement sounded like a threat. How could Jennifer have done that? Mark had promised Sara that she'd be treated fairly.

The light was on again, and Bret was waving frantically to get Mark's attention. He was live! The ending of the tape had so taken Mark by surprise; he was left starring blankly at the camera.

"What's wrong with him, Jenn?" Russell whispered sharply at the producer's table. "I thought you said he wanted to ad-lib the tag. TelePrompTer, put up item four, quick." He tried to get the words they'd written for Tad up in front of the camera to give Mark something to say.

Behind them Tracy could tell that something was wrong. When Tad had turned the show over to Mark, she was at first nervous for him. But as he confidently led into the story, she began to relax, even feeling a sense of respect in how well he did his job. Then the commotion between the producers in front of her alarmed Tracy. Mark obviously was in trouble, and there seemed to be no one who could help him.

Fifteen miles away in Burbank, Sara Medford sat surrounded by a dozen of her closest friends, both from church and from the group she represented. They'd gathered at the house of one of her friend's who had Direct TV, and they could watch the live East Coast feed there. Her hands were cupped over her mouth as her eyes reddened. Tears started down her cheeks. Her closest friend, Mabel, reached out and placed her arm around her as the weeping began.

"He promised he wouldn't do this."

The rest of her friends kept their eyes glued to the television set, not believing what they'd just witnessed. It sounded so convincing—Sara in her own words threatening an abortion doctor. But they knew her; they knew she was the gentlest of creatures and couldn't harm anybody, even over an issue as sacred to her as abortion. But they were her words. How could this be?

NATIONAL STUDIOS
6:10 P.M. PACIFIC

Mark was seething. He looked down at his hands to buy himself a brief second as he prayed. He looked back into the lens, ignoring the prompted words that popped up in front of him. "What you've just witnessed is what some refer to as the magic of television." Mark spoke slowly, with conviction.

"What's he doing?" Russell hissed to Jennifer. But she had no answer.

"I interviewed Sara Medford last Thursday, but I was called out of town on assignment this weekend and wasn't able to be in on the final editing process for the piece you just saw. Sara, I apologize to you."

"Can we cut him off?" Jennifer asked Russell.

Russell held out his hand. "Let's see where this goes."

It was obvious Mark was fighting his anger. His voice was nearly breaking. "I apologize for this show, this network, but most of all I want you to know how sorry I am. You see, I promised her that her comments would not be taken out of context, and the edited piece you just saw moments ago did exactly that. She is a sweet, sweet lady, and I know that she would never condone violence in any way. It would go completely against her very nature. Please do not judge her by what you just witnessed."

"We're running long," the associate director in the booth called out.

"Shhhh!" Terri returned. "I want to hear what he's saying."

Rick sat behind them stunned. He started praying as Mark continued.

"Sara Medford spoke eloquently for the pro-life cause. I remember her final comments very well last week. After she pleaded to give babies a chance to live, she asked the doctor to repent and to ask for God's forgiveness. There was no threat in her tone—not a hint of violence intended—just concern for the doctor. Sara, you were the victim of someone's misplaced loyalty to his or her own political agenda—what some people would refer to as media bias. Yes, it exists. You've all just seen proof of that. As I said earlier, the war continues, and Sara Medford is the latest casualty. It's inexcusable. I'm sorry, Sara." Mark looked down at his hands one more time. He felt drained but good. Not knowing what else he could say, after a beat he looked back up. "We'll be back right after this."

"Stand by, commercial," Terri yelled trying to get the production back on track. "Take two on a wide shot. Roll the bumper tape on B. Track tape."

Mark kept his eye trained directly on the camera even after the light went out. His vision blurred everything into nothingness, and he wondered what would happen next.

Sara Medford continued crying, but her tears were now from relief. The small crowd around her cheered.

"I don't know what just happened, Sara," Mabel said, "but that young man's comments probably impacted the country more than anything you could have said in the interview. God had his hand in there somehow."

"I hope he knows that I do forgive him," Sara pronounced through her tears.

"We'll have to make sure he does," Mabel said.

As soon as Bret yelled, "Clear!" to signal a commercial break, the studio erupted.

Tad, sitting closest to Mark, looked over at him. "Are you nuts?"

Russell came immediately to the desk, with Jennifer trailing him. "You and I are having a long chat after this show, young man."

But Mark looked straight past him at Jennifer and asked, "How could you do that to her?"

"Do what?" Jennifer shot back defensively. "Those were her own words. Besides, if you weren't off in New York, this wouldn't have happened."

"Knock it off, both of you!" Russell shouted. "We're back in less than a minute! Taylor, I want you in my office right after the show. Now everybody back to work!"

Jason Reynolds was still starring blankly into the screen. He couldn't believe what he'd just heard Mark say. His little confession could set their cause back a dozen years. The phone buzzed in front of him.

"Yeah," he answered gruffly.

"Reynolds, it's Robertson. What just happened on *Across the Nation?* The president's going to be livid."

"Calm down, Jack, calm down." Jason tried to hide the anxiety in his own voice.

"Calm down! Do you have your TV on? Did you see what that reporter just did? We've just run the numbers over 60 percent in favor of abortion on demand—numbers the president needs to get the UN funding he's pushing for, and your reporter goes off apologizing to an antiabortion group for misquoting them!"

"I know, Jack. I'm watching the show. I'll get to the bottom of it. One crackpot comment from a reporter doesn't change anything. Give it a couple of days, and this will all be forgotten. I'll take care of it."

"You'd better, unless you want to take the next call from the man himself."

"You don't know who 'the man' is," Jason muttered to himself as he slammed his phone down. "And, Mark Taylor, you don't know who you're dealing with!" He screamed to the empty room.

CHAPTER 21

"That's a wrap, everybody!" Bret called as the final credits faded to black on the studio monitors.

"Nice show, everybody." Russell gave his customary praise. However, this one seemed a bit reserved. Without another word he headed through the doors and to the production offices.

Mark took his microphone off and got up from his spot at the desk. Was it his imagination, or was everyone on the staff and crew giving him a lot of space? Samantha started to walk the same direction off the set, then realized where Mark was headed and turned to walk the other way. It wasn't just imagination.

Tracy walked up to him. "Wow, Mark. That was quite a show. Do they all go like this?"

"With the exception of my going off script and losing it, pretty much."

"But was it true? Did the edited version of that tape misrepresent that woman?"

"I'll show you the original interview if you're interested. It didn't just misrepresent her; it butchered her. But I still can't believe I said what I did on the air—"

204

"I can't either," Rick said walking up to the two of them. "But I was certainly glad to hear it. It was great television, Mark, and wonderful to hear such a fired-up plea for integrity with such compassion. You'll probably have this whole city talking tomorrow."

Cassie joined them. "I think Rick is right. How about being a guest on our show tomorrow night and talking about it?"

"Where did you come from?" Mark wondered.

"I was over in our office catching up on some paperwork," Cassie explained, "but I was watching the in-house feed. I admire you for what you did, Mark, and I'm serious about you coming on our show. I think John would agree."

"I don't think we need to make this any bigger than it already is," Mark said. "I just want to get on with my work; that is, if I still have a job."

"Don't get down about it," Rick said. "It felt like God at work to me. You'll just have to see where he takes it."

"I don't know if it was God's idea, or an exhausted-from-flying-back-and-forth-to-New-York-in-forty-eight-hours idea." Mark realized Tracy was still next to him. "Oh, I'm sorry, I haven't introduced you two. Tracy, this is Cassie, I believe Rick's fiancé now, aren't you?"

Cassie broke into an enormous smile. "That's right. Tracy, nice to meet you."

"It's nice to meet you too. Congratulations," Tracy returned.

"Let me see that ring," Mark said.

Cassie held it up as he whistled. "That's gorgeous, Cassie." Then Mark looked at Rick. "I told you there was nothing to worry about."

"He was pretty confident," Cassie said as she snuggled under Rick's arm. "He even had several of our friends show up as a surprise."

"That's great. I'm happy for you both. So when is the magic day?" Mark asked.

"We're still thinking about it. Probably this June when the show's on hiatus," Cassie answered.

"You guys are going to be very happy together," Mark said, then remembered he had an appointment with Russell. "I better run. Would you mind keeping Tracy entertained while I go in and see if I still have a job?"

Rick smiled. "We'd be happy to. Go on. She'll be fine."

Steve walked by the group, handing the MPR-1 to Mark. "Here's your pen, Mark," he said with a wink. His thumb pointing upward let Mark know the transfer was successful.

"Thanks, Steve," Mark said with a nod, then turned back to Tracy. "OK, I guess it's time to face the music. I'll get back out as quickly as I can."

"Would you care to explain to me how that could happen on your show?"

Jarod Winter, the president of National Studios, fixed himself another scotch—this time no soda—while talking with Jason Reynolds on his wireless phone. He had spent the past forty-five minutes asking himself the same question. Now he had to answer it for Number One.

"I don't know. It was obvious that reporter went off script. Russell would have never allowed it."

"I could see that! My question still remains," Reynolds yelled, "how could that have happened?"

"I'll check into it first thing in the morning." Winter tried to appease him. "I've already called the producer in for an early meeting. Do you want him or the reporter fired?"

Jason thought for a second. Would that solve the real problem? "Let me think about that. What time is the producer coming in?"

"Ten."

"Call me before you talk with him. I'll let you know by then."

"OK, Jason, I will. Did you see the report on India though? It was perfect."

"Yeah, it was fine," Reynolds said coldly.

"Look, I'm sorry about the abortion thing, Jason," Winter continued, "but I think it'll all blow over. Nobody's been watching that show anyway."

Mark walked through the production office on his way to meet Russell. All conversation stopped as every eye rested on him. He did his best to act as if everything was normal, but inside his stomach was doing somersaults.

Mark opened the door to Russell's office and stepped inside. Russell was seated behind his desk with Jennifer sitting in front of him.

"Take a seat," Russell ordered.

He sat next to Jennifer.

"Jennifer and I have already talked somewhat, Mark," Russell began. "I plan to thoroughly check the unedited tapes to see if indeed Ms. Williams edited that lady in such a way as to subvert her comments. If she did as you suggested on the air, then I'll deal with her directly, is that understood?"

"Yes, sir."

"Good, then I don't want this to become an issue between you two. You work well together and have done some great pieces. Don't let this little mix-up interfere with that."

"Yes, sir," Jennifer said.

Russell looked over for Mark's reaction.

"I hope to be able to, Frank, but there are some things I need to clear up about it first."

"Such as . . ."

"Why she did it," Mark answered. "I don't understand why."

"Because I thought that's what you would have wanted, Mark. I was sure you were pro-choice just like everyone else around here," Jennifer responded.

"I don't think it matters whether I'm pro-choice, pro-life, or pro-cottage cheese. As journalists, we're responsible for what we put out, to be fair to both sides of an issue. I don't think Mrs. Medford was treated fairly at all, and I personally promised her she would be."

"I just used her words to convey what all antiabortionists think."

"How dare you!" Mark spun to face her. "You didn't convey what she thought or what most of that movement thinks. You certainly didn't convey my thoughts."

"All right," Russell interjected. "I think we're at an impasse on this for the moment. Let's hold off on any more judgments until I can view the tapes and you two can calm down."

Jennifer and Mark reluctantly broke eye contact and looked back at Russell.

"Jennifer, I want to talk with Mark alone. We'll deal with this later."

"Fine. I'll see you tomorrow," Jennifer said coldly and left.

Russell waited for her to close the door and then waited some more. The silence was deafening. Mark fidgeted, waiting for the hammer to drop.

"Do you know what you've done?" Russell kept his voice low.

"Yes, I know. I overreacted. I'm sorry—"

"You've created controversy," Russell interrupted, his voice rising with emotion, "live, on the air, you confessed to this show's editing somebody's words out of context and changing their meaning. Then you apologized for it. This will hit all the radio talk shows tomorrow, we'll probably get calls from *Nightline*, CNN, CNBC, Fox News." Russell smiled. Mark couldn't tell if Frank was furious or delirious. "We're going to be the talk of the nation. Just what I've been looking for to give this show a chance."

"But I thought you'd be furious—"

"Oh, don't get me wrong, son, I am. You had no right to do that on the air. You should have cleared it with me first."

"If I had been able to view the tape, I would have come straight to you."

"And you have no one to blame for that except yourself—running off to New York—again I might add—without my approval."

"I know, Frank, and I'm sorry. But when I saw what that tape did to Sara, I just reacted. I wasn't even thinking."

"That's the first intelligent thing you've said all night. Do you think she'll sue?" Russell asked.

"Sue?" Mark asked surprised. He hadn't even thought of that possibility. "You mean Sara? No, at least, I don't think so."

"I want you to give her a call, tonight. Smooth the waters. Make sure she knows you did your best, that sort of thing, but no more confessions of guilt. That's the only downside I can see to all this. If she does want to sue, you've already confessed for the network."

"Sorry."

"Look, Mark, I've got to tell you. During the show, I was boiling. But as I sat there, I realized what kind of press we're going to get out of this. You may have inadvertently given this show a chance. I wish we could have planned it, but sometimes you've got to go with what's handed you."

Mark was relieved. He sighed and sat back.

"Oh, don't get too comfortable over there. We're headed for turbulent waters. I would imagine the network is going to want to have your hide, and rightfully so. I already got a call from Winter, and we're meeting early tomorrow. You had no right to do what you did, bad editing or not. But if we can take the publicity about all this and use it to our benefit—especially with our Wednesday night show debuting this week—our ratings could go through the roof."

"How do you want me to handle it then?" Mark asked.

"Truthfully! That you're in trouble. I'm placing you on probation as of this minute. That means any little screwup, and I'll have grounds to fire you on the spot. Do you understand?"

"Yes, sir."

"Good. Now in the event that this thing takes legs, I want any request for an interview to go through my office. We'll see what comes up and work out a plan together, understood?"

"Yes, sir, but I've already got one."

Russell's eyebrows went up. "You do?"

"Yeah, *The John Harold Show* tomorrow night."

"You're kidding. Wow, that's right. Rick is here."

"Along with the producer, Cassie Petterson. I think she might have been kidding, but she did ask."

"Tell her it's a possibility. I'll have to run this by the network brass in the morning. This could be good . . ." Russell drifted off thinking of all the possibilities. Then he looked back at Mark. "But don't get the idea that you're off the hook. I'm serious about the probation. You weren't at the meeting before the show. I announced we'll be doing two shows a week for at least the next month. We need everybody right now, or I'd make an example out of you and force you to take some time off—without pay. So let's get into the game here and make a difference. And while I'm at it, drop that stupid political story you're working on. It's taking too much of your time and going nowhere."

"But, Frank, you haven't heard what I found—"

"And I don't want to. I'm ordering you to drop it, Mark!" Russell dropped a fist on his desktop. "Now!"

After being excused, Mark made his way to the common area. It looked as if nearly everyone had left for the night. He pulled Sara's card out of his wallet and grabbed the phone.

"Mrs. Medford?" Mark asked as she answered.

"Yes, this is she."

"Hi, it's Mark Taylor."

"Oh, Mark, thanks for calling. I was hoping I could talk with you."

"Then I take it you saw the show?"

"Oh yes. We met at a friend's house that has satellite TV to watch it."

"Well, I wanted to call and apologize personally for what happened."

"That's sweet of you. And I want you to know that I do forgive you."

Mark breathed a sigh of relief. "Thank you, Sara. I'm glad you feel that way."

"You know, some of our friends from church think that the way this has all worked out could be the hand of the Lord."

Mark was dumbfounded. "How do you mean?"

"Well, if you had used my interview correctly—I'm sorry, a bad choice of words. I know you had nothing to do with it from what you said on TV. If my interview hadn't been altered somewhat, your story would have been just another their-side-says-this-our-side-says-that."

Mark understood. Even though he'd wanted to get into the psychological underpinnings of both sides of the abortion debate, when it came right down to it, it would have been just another story in which each side tried to defend its beliefs.

"But the way it happened, and with your reaction," Sara continued, "I can see God using this in a much greater way. I've already had a couple of reporters contact me about doing interviews with them. I've also had one lawyer already call."

Mark gulped. "Are you thinking about retaining a lawyer?"

"Oh, heavens no. Don't worry about that, Mark. I'm going to use whatever means God opens up to get our message across and to say what a charming and wonderful reporter you are."

"You don't have to do that, Sara. I just wanted to make sure you knew how sorry I was about what happened."

"But don't be. It's all in God's hands."

"Thank you, Sara, I needed to hear that."

"You're welcome. Now you go on fighting for what you believe in, and I'll do the same."

"I will. Good night, Sara."

"Good night, Mark, and God be with you."

Mark hung up the phone thinking, *Wow! What a wonderfully gracious lady.*

Tracy, Rick, and Cassie were waiting for him in the darkened studio.

"So are you still employed?" Rick asked.

"For the time being," Mark smiled in reply. "Let's get out of here, and I'll explain everything."

The foursome made their way outside the studio and walked toward the parking area to make sure they wouldn't be overheard before Mark explained more.

"Russell put me on probation, which basically means he can fire me for pretty much just about anything right now."

"Wow, that must be hard to take," Tracy said.

"Actually, he was great about it. I think he's just doing that for the appearance. He was pretty excited about what happened?"

"Excited?" Cassie laughed. "How?"

"Funny you should ask, Cassie. He wants me to keep your invitation open to be on the show tomorrow if you're still interested."

"You bet I am."

"Well, Russell's idea now is to jump on the controversy and use it in every way we can to promote the show."

"That's incredible," Rick said. "Not the exact reaction I would have expected."

"I know. I was shocked too," Mark said.

"Then this whole thing could work out to your advantage?" Tracy asked.

"In some ways, maybe." Mark thought as he answered. "But I'm still in a lot of trouble. Some of the executives may want to have my hide in the morning, and there'd be nothing Frank could do about it."

"Like my grandfather," Tracy said.

"Exactly. It'll be interesting to see how he and the rest of the National brass react."

"Do you want me to talk with him?" Tracy asked.

"No, I think it would be better if you don't. But thank you, anyway. I guess this could make the Tuesday lunch even more interesting?"

"What are you two talking about?" Rick asked.

"Mark wanted to talk with my grandfather, Jason Reynolds, about some of his questions on that polling story he's working on. I set him up with a lunch date for Tuesday."

"*The* Jason Reynolds is your grandfather?" Rick asked.

"Yes, he is."

"And he's also the one at the top of the corporate ladder when it comes to National Studios," Mark explained.

Rick and Tracy looked at each other, then Rick responded. "I thought Jared Winter was."

"Through some of my research," Mark answered. "I found out that although Winter is the president, the real power behind us and a lot of other media outlets is Tracy's grandfather."

"Wow, I never knew," Rick said.

"I'm still not too sure," Tracy admitted. "I know he owns a lot, but I would have known about some of the companies Mark has mentioned."

"Did you ask him about any of them yesterday?" Mark asked.

"What, and miss the two of you discussing it in front of me? Not on your life." Tracy laughed.

Mark smiled at her choice of words. "But I'm not sure about the interview now."

"What do you mean?" Tracy asked.

"Russell ordered me to drop the polling story."

"Does that mean I won't get to see you anymore?" she teased.

"Something tells me that Mark won't drop it that easily," Rick pointed out.

"I've got to think about it," Mark said as they reached the parking area. "Maybe if I can put together a quick report of what I learned over the weekend and show it to Russell, he might reconsider. Don't cancel our lunch date yet."

"Good. I think watching you and Papa sparring with each other could make for great sport." Tracy giggled.

Mark laughed along with her, allowing the tension to release from his body. He hadn't realized how he'd kept it all in until that moment.

"Well, you did good tonight, Mark," Rick said. "I'm sorry if it's gotten you into trouble, but I'm glad you were bold and spoke your convictions. God's been at work. Looks like a new Mark Taylor to me."

"Me too," Cassie agreed.

"Thanks, both of you," Mark said with a smile. "Tomorrow should prove to be an interesting day."

"Give me a call as early as you can about being a guest," Cassie said. "I'll run it by John first thing, if he's interested, which I'm sure he will be. We'd love to have you."

"I will, Cassie. Thanks for coming by tonight."

"I'm glad I didn't miss it." Cassie turned to Tracy. "It was great meeting you."

"Same here, and, Rick, thanks for taking care of me earlier."

"My pleasure. If you want to come by tomorrow when Mark's on the show, here's my card. Just give me a call, and I'll get you into the show."

"Thanks, I may just do that."

"I hope you do. Good-bye."

Rick and Cassie walked away toward their car.

"So, you ready for that dinner?" Mark asked Tracy.

"If you're still up for it. You've had quite a night," she answered.

"And spending it with you seems like the perfect way to cap it off. How about if we just leave our cars here? I'm really not up for a big dinner, but there's a quaint little coffee bar with great sandwiches just down the street."

"That sounds perfect to me," Tracy said as she slipped her arm under Mark's elbow and they strolled off toward National's front gate.

HOLLYWOOD
7:36 P.M. PACIFIC

Mark and Tracy found a quiet table along a window that overlooked Santa Monica Boulevard. Although not a fancy restaurant by any stretch of the imagination, it had a comfortable atmosphere, and they sat at a small circular table with a candle flickering between them.

"Do you think that woman will be upset about how her interview turned out and sue the network?" Tracy asked after she sipped her coffee.

"That was one of Russell's main concerns, but I called her before I came out of the office. She was—how do I put this—actually pretty happy about it."

Tracy looked up surprised. "How do you mean?"

"Well, at first she was devastated by the way it was edited, just like I was. But as she saw how the segment ended, she felt the final result will actually benefit her cause. She's already received a couple of invitations to be interviewed."

"Wow! That was fast."

"That's what I thought. Don't get me wrong. She felt betrayed by our show for doing that to her in the first place, but like Russell wanting to make this a positive event to promote our show, she sees it as a positive way for her to have more opportunities to voice the pro-life cause."

"What's your position?"

Mark tilted his head. "On abortion?"

"Yes. You seemed very . . . passionate about it when you did your report, but you never stated which side you're on."

"That's because I've always felt that a good journalist should keep his personal beliefs separated from his work. Let the story tell itself." Mark thought about the past hour of his life. "But it was reinforced to me tonight that on certain issues like abortion some in the media, like my producer for one, think it's perfectly acceptable to push their agenda."

"So I take it you're anti-abortion then?" Tracy asked.

"Pro-life, yes." Mark corrected her gently.

"What's the difference?"

"Pro-life is the position I hold. Antiabortion is the media's label for us."

"I see." Tracy said. "I never thought of it that way."

"It's something our industry does without even thinking. Pro-life is too positive a term to give to a group most disagree with, kind of like labeling the conservative movement with the term radical right wing. When was the last time you heard somebody labeled a left-wing radical?"

"So you're saying the media is liberally biased?"

"In a lot of ways, I believe they are, yes. Maybe what I did tonight will open up some eyes to that fact."

"What did Rick mean when he referred to what you did as God's doing?"

Mark paused, not expecting the question. He smiled, realizing he wasn't going to stay a closet Christian with her much longer. *Continue to give me that boldness,* he prayed. "Rick just felt that God had his hand in the whole thing. When I reacted on the air the way I did, I was actually doing what God wanted me to."

"Do you agree with that?"

"To be honest with you, right now I'm not sure. I was angry, that's for sure. But it wasn't just the anger coming out. I felt something deeper. I don't really know how to explain it. I guess time will tell."

Tracy glanced out the window as a police car rushed by with its lights flashing. It gave her a moment to think, then she looked back at Mark. "You guys talk about God like he's right there with you or something."

Mark met her gaze directly. "He is. As I saw how that tape ended and what Jennifer had done to that sweet lady, I started praying right there at the desk. I felt God's presence. Then when I realized I was back on the air and I started speaking, it felt like the words were coming directly from God." Mark stopped as he contemplated what had happened. "Maybe it was God at work."

Tracy's head lowered; she wasn't sure how to respond. Mark reached over and gently placed his hand under her chin and pulled her head up.

"What about you, Tracy? Does all this talk about God make you uncomfortable?"

Tracy nodded. "I've never been much on religion. My parents never went to church, that I can remember. I think my grandfather was raised Catholic, but something turned him off to the whole concept. He always says it's the weak who need the crutch of religion." She saw the reaction in Mark's eyes. "I'm sorry, I didn't mean to offend you."

"Oh, you didn't offend me, Tracy." Mark shook his head. "Do you know what makes a person a Christian?"

"No, not really. I guess going to church, right?"

Mark grinned. "Well, that might make a person religious, but there's a big difference in being religious and being a Christian."

"How so?"

"Being religious is following a system of do's and don'ts. The do's—go to church, read your Bible, pray, help others. The don'ts—don't drink, don't smoke, don't swear, don't kill people, that kind of thing. In my opinion, the trouble with religion is that it traps people into a false sense of security that if they follow the rules, then they will somehow be acceptable to God."

"You just defined what I've always thought Christians were all about." Tracy smiled. "So tell me what being a Christian is then."

"Are you sure I'm not boring you with all of this?" Mark asked.

"Boring? No, I'm fascinated. Please go on."

"OK, you asked for it." Mark laughed softly. "The one thing that sets Christianity apart from being a religious system like what I just described is this: Christians believe that no matter what you do, no matter how perfect you may try to be, you still aren't good enough to be accepted by God."

"Wow, that's pretty depressing."

"It is, until you understand God's plan. He sent his son Jesus to earth, born of a virgin. He led a sinless life, only to be killed on a cross and died for our sins. Then he rose from the grave, defeating death." Studying Tracy's face, Mark tried to gauge her reaction. She seemed to understand, so he continued. "You see, the Bible teaches that we have all sinned. That's what separates us from the love of God. It's only through what Jesus did—taking the punishment of death for the sins that we commit—that we're able to be reunited with our heavenly Father. It's only through the righteousness of his Son."

"So how does this differ, say, from Buddhists or Muslims?" Tracy asked.

"From what I understand about most other religions, you have to work—achieve some level of perfection within yourself by adhering to their guidelines. There's always something you have to do to achieve nirvana, heaven, whatever it is that religion is striving for. With Christianity it's all about grace. It's not about what you can do; it's about what Jesus did.

"When you accept Christ as your Lord and Savior—believing that he paid the price for your sins—then you are born again, meaning you are born spiritually. God places his Holy Spirit within you, and you are alive spiritually for the first time in your life. Now instead of doing everything in your power to be good on the outside, God's spirit is working within you to change you from the inside. I like to think of it as a walking-talking-daily relationship with God, as his Holy Spirit lives within you. Jesus himself didn't follow the religious rules of his day. He said he went about doing what he saw his Father doing. Being a Christian is not a boring, rules-following, fun-killing religion. It's an exciting daily walk, doing our best to follow what we see God is doing."

"I've never heard it put that way before," Tracy sighed. "The way my grandfather talks about it, you'd think religion was the worst thing that had ever happened to us."

"Well, the organized church has done a lot of things in our culture to turn people off. But if you find out what a relationship with Jesus Christ is really all about, it's a wonderful, gracious thing. One I happen to highly recommend."

"I can tell. You sound as passionate as you did on the air tonight. So people like you and Rick live your lives as if God's Spirit is with you always."

"Yes, we do, because he is. He's with us right now." Mark paused, sensing he should allow his words to sink in.

The two sat quietly, sipping from their mugs.

"You're an interesting man, Mark Taylor."

"And you," Mark raised his mug in a toast, "are an intriguing and very beautiful woman. I'm glad my research brought us together."

"Me too."

"Then you don't think I'm too weird?" Mark laughed.

"I wouldn't say that." Tracy laughed along with him. "But weird isn't necessarily bad."

BURBANK
10:15 P.M. PACIFIC

The man in the white van was hungry. He'd taken his position over three hours ago and as yet hadn't seen so much as a mouse make any movement in that apartment. He had the feeling he was in for a long night.

Then he saw movement out of the corner of his eye. On the fourth monitor he saw the front door swing open. The target was finally coming home. He quickly reached over and started recording on all his video and audiotape machines. Now things would get interesting. He picked up the phone and reported that the subject was under surveillance.

The man walked into the kitchen, setting what appeared to be a clump of mail on the table, then stepped over to the countertop and hit the play button of his message machine.

"Message one, 2:27, Sunday," a computerized voice rang out. "Mark, it's Peter. I've got some info for you. It's getting more interesting all the time. Give me a call when you get a chance."

The man in the van made a notation on his pad of the time on the tape and the name, Peter.

"Message two, 3:10, Sunday—Mark, hi, it's Heather at the show. We're trying to track you down. I'll try your cell."

The man started to make another note on his pad, but he noticed above the page the same notations had been made by the guy he replaced. He put his pencil down and relaxed while he watched the screens.

"Message three, 6:15, Sunday—Mark, it's your mom. I just saw your show and wanted to make sure everything is OK. It was a wonderful piece, but what happened with the editing that you were so upset over? Give us a call. Don't worry about the time difference; we'll be up late."

"End of messages."

The man in the van tracked his eyes across the monitors as the subject went from the kitchen into his bedroom, making an uneventful phone call to his parents. Everything was recorded as Mark went into the bathroom, stripped off his clothes, threw them into his closet, then stepped into the shower. Not too long after that, Mark was climbing into bed and reading something he kept on the night stand. The man watching was irritated. He always hoped on assignments like this there'd be a woman in the apartment, to add a little excitement to a boring shift. He sighed and tried to find a comfortable position in the cramped compartment. It was going to be a long night.

CHAPTER 22

MONDAY, FEBRUARY 12
BURBANK
9:00 A.M. PACIFIC

Mark opened his eyes and looked at the clock radio on his night stand. He couldn't believe he'd slept until nine, but after the past couple of days, he needed it. He sat up in bed and stretched, grimacing from a couple of sore muscles, probably from trying to sleep on the plane Friday night.

His mind immediately flashed back to his report on *Across the Nation*. Should he have done anything different? Would it have been better for all concerned if he had tagged the story as if nothing were wrong? But he couldn't have. He was so fed up with how his industry treated people like Sara Medford. If Rick was right and this really was God's doing, Mark wished he would have picked somebody else to do it.

The phone beside the night stand rang, and he answered it with half a voice.

"I'm looking for a Mark Taylor," a man said.

"You're speaking to him."

"Mark, this is David Lester. I'm a producer with CNBC—*Hardball with Chris Matthews*. We caught wind of what happened on your show last night and wondered if you'd consent to doing a segment with Chris tonight."

218

Mark snapped wide awake. It was happening as Russell had predicted. "I'm interested, Mr. Lester, but all interviews are going to have to be cleared by National Studios. Contact Frank Russell." Mark gave him the production office phone number, then disconnected the call.

Mark laughed; suddenly, the journalist is the news. The phone rang again. This time it was from a local radio talk show. Mark gave the woman at the other end the same information, but when he hung up, he left the phone off the hook. He changed his answering machine message to give the production office phone number and told anybody seeking an interview to call Russell.

He slipped his feet out of the bed, stretching one more time as he thought about the upcoming day. Although he didn't have to be at the office until the one o'clock meeting, he decided to go in early so he could put together a detailed report on what he'd learned over the weekend. He'd return Peter's call from there.

At that same moment, a different employee of Reynolds Industries occupied the white van parked outside Mark's building. He reached for the phone and punched in the number to Luis's cell phone.

"He's up and at 'em," the man reported.

"Anything of interest?" Luis asked.

"His phone's been very busy—a couple of calls from people wanting to interview him."

Luis cursed on the other end.

"It looks like he's getting ready to leave the unit soon, so you better have the tails ready to go."

"They're in place. Just stay put in case he comes back."

"Roger that," the man said. The bathroom monitor showed the back of Mark's head as he brushed his teeth.

Within twenty minutes, Mark was in his car and on the way to Hollywood. He turned the radio to KFI, one of the local talk stations. Rush Limbaugh's booming baritone filled the car.

"I know a lot of you out there are concerned about this Pakistan-India thing, and we'll get back to that, but did you hear the reporter on *Across the Nation* last night?" Mark nearly hit the car in front of him.

"It's not a show I normally watch, but my crack staff was on top of it. This reporter—Mark Taylor's his name—was doing a piece on the ridiculous lawsuit

Planned Parenthood won against the Internet pro-lifers as we call them. Well, evidently, without his knowledge—and that's the one thing about this story I don't quite understand—how the tape could have aired without him seeing it first. But nevertheless it did, and some comments from a pro-life activist were edited in such a way as to twist her words completely—as if that's never been done before in the media—but this reporter went ballistic. He apologized to the lady, ah-h-h, I don't have her name here, sorry, but, anyway, the reporter went on and on about how sorry he was that the network would do such a thing to her, how sweet she was, and how she would never threaten anybody as the tape seemed to imply. It's incredible. I saw the tape this morning; it was classic, ladies and gentlemen."

Mark felt as if he were on *The Twilight Zone*. This couldn't be happening to him. After being timid for so long, then he made one stand for what he believed in, and suddenly he was today's hottest headline.

MALIBU
9:28 A.M. PACIFIC

"Thirty-eight, thirty-nine, forty." Jason Reynolds's veins bulged on his biceps as he completed his fourth set of ten repetitions, bench-pressing two hundred pounds. His workout room rivaled any health club in Beverly Hills—all state-of-the-art equipment with everything from cycling machines and treadmills to the best in weight training.

A hard workout cleared his mind whenever he was stressed. It seemed to be working until he sat up and looked at the large-screen television in front of him. CNBC was doing a story on what had happened on *Across the Nation* the night before.

Jason wiped his brow with a towel, then flung it at the screen in disgust. The last thing he wanted to see was Mark Taylor spewing out his drivel.

He noticed Luis standing in the doorway.

"Yeah."

"It's about Sinclair."

"What do we know?"

"He seems above-board, new employee, started six months ago, clean history, recent graduate of New York University, raised in upstate New York, pretty much keeps to himself—a model employee."

"Any connection between him and Dawkins?"

"Only that they worked together. We can't establish any other specific relationship. What else do you want me to do?"

"Nothing at this point. I'll play his little game and respond to his E-mail. If he knows too much, you might have to take care of him later."

Jason moved to his stationary bicycle, then shot Luis a frozen stare, silently asking why he was still there.

"It's Taylor. He's on the move—looks like he's heading into the office."

"Do you have any idea what he knows?"

"Not yet, he's been very quiet since getting in last night. He only talked with his parents. We're still trying to find out who this Peter was who left a message over the weekend. But there's a lot of interest in him this morning. He's already received a couple of calls to be interviewed."

"I was afraid of that. The story's been all over the morning shows—overshadowing reports on the Indian crisis," Reynolds spat out.

"It's going to be very difficult to take care of somebody so ..." Luis searched to find the correct words, "high profile. There will be a lot of questions."

"I've been thinking the same thing. I'm meeting with him tomorrow. By then I want to know everything he knows. Maybe there's a way to get to him, bring him into our confidence. Otherwise ..."

Number One didn't need to elaborate. Luis smiled at the thought as he stepped back out of the room and headed down the hallway.

NATIONAL STUDIOS
9:32 A.M. PACIFIC

"OK, everybody," Cassie yelled over the noisy conference room. "Let's get started please."

Her colleagues quieted and took their seats for the morning production meeting.

"Before we begin, Rick has an announcement to make." She smirked as he gave her a questioning look. Then he nodded and returned the smile.

He stood up and cleared his throat. "After the show Friday night," he began in a somber tone, attempting to trick them into thinking he had some problem to deal with from last week, "a special project that I had been working on—with some help from a few of you in this room—was completed."

The few staff members who had been in on helping Rick with the proposal tape started clapping and laughing. The rest were totally in the dark.

Rick smiled at the response, then continued. "Anyway, to make a long story short, that project was a proposal video. I asked Cassie if she would marry me Friday night."

Many of the women responded with a drawn-out "ohh."

The guys were more vocal. "All right!"

Rick turned toward Cassie. "And I'll let her tell you how she answered."

Cassie stood up next to him with the biggest smile the staff had ever seen and held up her left hand.

Across the lot in another production office, Mark entered the darkened room. He hadn't set foot in there on a Monday since he had been hired, always relishing his one day off.

Alone was good. The rest of the staff wouldn't be piling in for another three hours. That should give him ample time to have something in writing to change Frank's mind.

He made it to his cubicle and turned on his computer. The message light on his phone blinked. He had twenty-four messages waiting for him. He decided to deal with them later.

The first thing he needed to do was talk with Peter and see what he dug up over the weekend. He dialed the number.

"Peter, it's Mark."

"Mark, it's about time. I've been wondering about you. Everything all right?"

"Yeah, fine. I was just so exhausted last night. I thought it would be better if we talked today."

"OK, I understand. But what gives with the press? You're all over the place, man."

"What do you mean?" Mark asked.

"You haven't been watching the tube? They mentioned what you did last night on practically every morning show. I know Diane Sawyer did a quick thing about it. I heard Matt Lauer mention it as well. As a matter of fact, Regis is talking about you right now."

"You've got to be kidding. I heard Rush mention it this morning, but I thought it was just a fluke."

"No fluke, Mark. You've wrestled some trees."

Mark laughed. "My boss is either going to be ecstatic, or I'll be in even more trouble when the executives get through with him."

"I'd be more worried about the list of names you gave me."

"OK, tell me what you found out."

"Let's go through them one at a time. Top of the list, Reynolds, who you already know, owns at least eight research polling companies, your network, several radio stations, and very heavy into newspaper publication."

"Right, what about the others?"

"Capshaw I'm assuming is Stephen Capshaw when you put all the names together and see how they're related."

"I'm not familiar with him."

"He is Capshaw Brokerage House in New York, one of the top, if not the largest, Wall Street brokerage firms."

"Pretty heavy hitter then, right?"

"There aren't any bigger, but it gets better. Richard Adler of Dallas, who is number three on the list, not only owned two of the polling companies I checked out earlier, but after digging a little deeper, I found out he runs at least six more plus a lot of controlling interest in media outlets as well. He's got a line of independent television and radio stations, some holdings in several major newspapers, plus a publishing arm of books, magazines, and journals—almost an identical portfolio to Reynolds."

"That's interesting."

"Number four, Dawkins, the now deceased Leeland Dawkins. We're both aware he used to be president of Research International, owned by Adler."

Mark saddened, thinking about Mrs. Dawkins.

"Then we have Winter," Peter continued, "who, I'm assuming, is current president of National Studios, domestic and international, Jared Winter, one of your bosses."

"I figured out that one. Who does that leave?"

"Number six is Davidson, as in Bob Davidson, American Press International."

"Wow!"

"And to round out our list of names, number seven, I believe, is Albert Fisher, chief of staff to President McNeil."

A cold chill settled over Mark's body. "How did you come up with that connection?"

"Searching through past associations," Peter answered. "Reynolds and Fisher have crossed paths frequently over the years. It's the only Fisher I can come up with that fits."

Mark looked down at the list of names and notations he'd made. "That's a powerful group of people."

"That list of seven names controls an incredible amount of television, film studios, newspapers, books, magazines, a major percentage of the top polling companies, and the White House."

"And if they were so inclined, could very well manipulate the public opinion polling that their own companies are conducting and then have nearly complete control over the disseminating of that data."

"I think you're beginning to see the picture, Mark. Keep in mind you're also talking about your boss," Peter warned. "I hope you have a good idea what to do with this information."

"Right now, Peter, I have no idea what to do with it. Officially I'm not supposed to be looking into this story at all."

"Well, I'll E-mail you this stuff, through a blind account that can't be traced back to me. Remember, you promised to keep my name out of this."

"And I will, Peter," Mark promised, wishing he could have protected Kevin in some way.

"Oh, there's one more thing I couldn't figure out," Peter added. "I dissected the computer disk you gave me. Not only was there the homosexual poll's data, but there was also data from another survey—an approval rating for the president. I spent some time looking through the computer language line by line on that one. Something came up I can't explain."

"What is it?"

"It's weird, but there seem to be two extra lines of instructions that are written into the program before any data is analyzed, but they completely disappear after the program is run. I can't figure out why the discrepancy or what it's doing. The instructions have something to do with a weigh-factor. I need to do some more research and get back with you."

"OK, keep digging. I could use all the information you can get."

"Hey, by the way, what do you think of the Web site?" Peter asked.

"What Web site?"

"Sam's Web site. What'd you think about it?"

It had totally skipped Mark's mind that he'd first run into Peter because of Samantha's Web site.

"I'm sorry, Peter, I haven't seen it yet. Is it getting lots of hits?"

"Last time I checked we had over fifty thousand, most of them right after the show Sunday night. Pretty cool, huh?"

"Yeah." Mark tried not to deflate Peter's excitement. "Samantha's going to be thrilled. You do great work, Peter. Thanks for all your help."

"You're welcome. If there's anything else I can do for you, let me know."

"I will," Mark said. "Oh, one more thing, Peter. I need to get the disk back and the survey printout you did."

"I understand," Peter answered. "I'll make a copy so I can keep analyzing it and get these back to you this afternoon."

SHERMAN OAKS
SAME TIME

Thrilled was not the word Samantha would have used to describe what she was feeling; overwhelmed was more accurate. With the number of hits continuing to climb on samsnudes.com, a proportionate number of surveys and E-mails were added to her mailbox. She couldn't keep up with them. What had started as a great idea to perk up her career and get some ratings suddenly was turning into a real pain. How could she get through all this information, formulate it into some kind of report and come up with a real story by Wednesday night? She didn't think it was possible.

She pulled her blond hair back and tucked it behind her right ear as she opened up the next survey.

Another teenager responding from somewhere in Kansas. Samantha was shocked at the number of kids answering the survey. She knew there'd be some underage hits but assumed they'd either lie about their ages or not respond at all. But these kids were bold. Nearly half of what she'd read so far identified the respondents as under eighteen.

Vanessa's words rang loudly in her head: *like the thirteen-year-old boy, who will get his first taste of sexuality by looking at your pictures on the Web. His attitude about women and how he will relate to them as he matures, the expectations he'll have for his girlfriends, his lovers, his future wife could begin with your Web page, or any of a thousand other ones not nearly as tame as yours. Are you ready for that responsibility?*

Samantha sighed as she looked at the next survey; at least this person was older, claiming to be twenty-seven and married with two children. She wondered if this man fit the scenario Vanessa described of the married man getting hooked on Internet pornography.

Samantha swore as she pulled away from her computer. She couldn't let Vanessa get to her; she had a job to do. But all she could think about were her comments, and every time she did, the dirty feeling came back like a bad dream. She couldn't continue like this.

She picked up the phone in the kitchen and called her producer.

"Jeff, it's Sam."

"Hi, Sam. How goes the research?" he asked brightly.

"Not great. I need your help," Samantha responded coldly. "There are so many responses, I can't keep up with them. There's got to be a better way than just me reading through each one."

"I thought Peter had set it up so that the survey results could all be tabulated on one report. How many have responded?"

"Over fifteen hundred."

"Wow, no wonder you sound like you're going bonkers. I'll call Peter and find out how to get the total results. Then after the meeting, you and I can go through it all at the office."

Samantha breathed a sigh of relief. "That sounds wonderful."

"Good," Jeff responded. "Take a break. You don't need to go into the meeting all worked up like this."

"Thanks, Jeff." Samantha hung up and looked at the clock on the microwave. She had a couple of hours before she'd have to be at the office.

Now what can I do to get my mind clear of Vanessa? she thought with aggravation, but underneath wondered if it was really Vanessa she was running from, or something far greater.

MALIBU
10:03 A.M. PACIFIC

For the first time since Jason had moved into the mansion, the monitors across his wall were shut off. Earlier several of the networks covered the Indian-Pakistan crisis, which had pleased him to no end. Then one of the others did a piece on Mark's outburst on *Across the Nation*. Jason couldn't take any more of it and had finally turned the whole monitor wall off.

He needed to focus. ARI had promised the National Gay-Lesbian Alliance that it would release the polling data today. But with Taylor sniffing around, Jason was sure that when he saw the media attention they were planning, he'd jump all over the story. He had to be neutralized first.

"Mr. Reynolds, Jared Winter on line one." His personal assistant's voice broke through the quiet. Even though she was in his building downtown, Jason had installed a system that allowed her to send important calls to his home and a radio system to act as an intercom between them.

Jason picked up the phone. "Hi, Jared."

"Hi, Jason. I guess thinking this whole thing was just going to blow over was kind of naive, huh?" Winter started off.

"Maybe just wishful thinking. Have you talked with the producer yet?"

"He's waiting outside my office right now."

"What's your line of thinking on this?" he asked.

"Well, the publicity has been incredible. I've never heard so many people talking about *Across the Nation*. We're getting an enormous number of requests for Taylor to do interviews—all the cable shows, including Larry King. *Nightline* is even interested."

"Great, just what I needed," Reynolds griped.

"Well, from strictly a ratings standpoint, it's a gold mine, especially with Wednesday night's debut this week. We couldn't buy this kind of publicity. But I'll do whatever you want, Jason, you know that."

"Yeah, I know you will. But there's more to it than one reporter bowing to the radical right," Jason paused, reluctant to bring Winter up to speed, but he had to. "We've got a security problem that I haven't told you about yet, Jared. Give me a call on the secure line, and I'll explain it to you."

The two disconnected the call, and a few moments later Reynolds's private line rang at his desk. In Hollywood, Winter leaned back in his chair listening intently as Jason brought him up-to-date.

"So it all started with Dawkins in New York." Winter sighed, as the reason for the Chicago meeting the week before became clear in his mind. "I was afraid to ask, but what was he doing?"

"Dawkins was compiling information about all the members of the Circle," Jason informed him. "We think he was going to go to the FBI."

"Why?"

"He never seemed to get on board with the military buildup plan, even through the UN, although we stand to make billions." He explained. Jason had led the Circle into either buying controlling interest or orchestrating corporate takeovers of many of the weakened companies that held defense contracts during the downsizing of the 1990s under President Clinton. With massive restructuring and company consolidation, the Circle members were now in prime position to reap a huge return by funneling the next military buildup through the United Nations and into companies the Circle controlled.

"I guess his conscience got the best of him," Reynolds sneered.

"But I can't believe he would jeopardize everything like that."

"Neither could we, but that's why he was let go. We thought it was contained, but every time we plug a hole, another leak opens up someplace else. Listen, I want you to make it very clear to the producer that this story Taylor is working on goes nowhere. I want him off of it now!" Jason pounded his fist on the desk.

"It's done, but what do we do with him?"

Jason thought for a second before responding. "I think we manipulate this publicity for all it's worth. It's good for the show and great for the network. But we definitely have to control the spin on this." Jason's mind began to race now that he'd made the decision which way to go. "Integrity, honesty, the hard-hitting truth—that's what you'll get from *Across the Nation*."

"Now you're talking, Jason."

"Book Taylor on every show you can get him on. I'll start calling in some favors myself. I want him so busy that he won't have time to brush his hair much less look into what he's got on us. Then when his ego catches up to our press releases, he'll be right where I want him." Reynolds finished with a sadistic smile.

Jason stood after he hung up the phone, walked to a control box in the corner closet, and flipped the breaker for his monitor wall. Now that he had a plan for Taylor, his distaste for all the publicity turned to a thriving hunger.

As he got back to his desk, he hit the button that would send his voice directly to his assistant at his corporate headquarters.

"Carla, get Mike Palmer in New York for me, please."

As he waited, he scanned the monitors in front of him.

Fox News was replaying the moment from the night before where Mark had apologized. Jason watched with heightened interest. Last night, his anger had overshadowed any rational thought, but watching it again, Reynolds was amazed. It was good television. The raw emotion pouring out of Taylor was captivating. No wonder the other networks were pulling clips from it.

Fox News switched at the end of Mark's comment to a split screen between the host of the program and Jerry Falwell, one of Reynolds's least favorite people.

"Your reaction, Mr. Falwell," Shephard Smith said.

"It's incredible to see someone this genuine come from the press corps." Falwell spoke slowly. "You see, Shephard, there was a point several years ago when I stopped granting taped interviews for that very same reason. I never could be sure that my comments wouldn't be taken out of context or twisted in some way. It's amazing how reporters can make someone look by pulling one sentence out of a three-minute answer, depending on how it's been set up. That's why with the addition of your network and others, I'm happy to be back on the air with my opinions, but live, when there's no chance for somebody to do what happened to poor Mrs. Medford."

You pompous hypocrite, Jason thought as the monitor switched back to the host.

"Mr. Reynolds," his assistant's voice cut through, "Mr. Palmer, line one."

Jason killed the audio in the room as he picked up the phone. "Mike, I've decided to hold off on any release on the gay data until we get a handle on this reporter."

"But we're all set to release this afternoon."

"I understand, but there's no other option. We can't release any data on this while Taylor's onto this story. I want everything stopped. This whole gay poll has caused us more trouble than it's worth anyway. Kill it!" Reynolds said forcefully. "Do you understand?"

"Yes, sir, I understand. But will the Gay Alliance?" Palmer asked.

"I don't care if they do. The UN stuff is a million times more important. Tell them there'll be a delay. Make up some excuse. But take care of it. You'll be getting some new survey questions we need to get out ASAP. They're the priority now."

"Yes, sir." Palmer knew that Number One's orders were to be obeyed without question.

CHAPTER 23

Mark pounded furiously at his computer keyboard. He was nearly finished with his detailed report for Russell and was completing the section on the list of seven names, when it hit him. He couldn't include the names. Winter was their boss. At worst, Russell could be involved himself; at the least he'd laugh him out of the office for thinking Winter was part of a conspiracy. He deleted the list of names. His thoughts were interrupted by someone clearing his throat behind him.

Mark jumped. He had been concentrating so hard, he hadn't heard Frank Russell enter the office.

"Sorry, didn't mean to startle you," Frank said laughing.

"Oh, that's OK. I didn't hear you come in. How was the meeting this morning?"

"Better than I thought. I was surprised. Come to my office, and I'll fill you in."

"Just let me print this out for you, and I'll be right there." Mark turned back to his report. He quickly typed a closing sentence then sent his pages to the printer. He wanted to present this to Russell before the production meeting began. He left his computer and headed for the copy room.

230

"So do I still have a job?" Mark tried to make light of his situation as he stepped into Russell's office, report in hand.

"For the time being, yes. Please sit down, Mark."

Mark took the chair in front of the desk. Frank's smile reassured him; maybe this would all work out after all.

"I had a long talk with Winter and our vice-president in charge of promotions, Eugene Diamond," Frank reported. "I have to tell you Mark, if the rest of the press hadn't picked up on this story, you'd probably be in big trouble."

"Really?"

"Really. Legally and professionally you stepped into areas where you have no business. Did you talk with your antiabortion friend?"

"Yes, I did. She has no intention of suing. As a matter of fact, she was pleased with the way it all turned out. She said she was getting requests to be interviewed and felt like it would work out for her to get her story out to more people."

"You're lucky she feels that way," Frank growled.

Mark fidgeted. "What do you mean I'm lucky? What about Jennifer? She's the one who edited the piece."

"I told you not to worry about that last night. I'm going to watch the raw footage this afternoon, then we'll deal with what happened. Right now we're dealing with how you reacted."

"I understand."

"Fine, now let's get back to what the executives want to do. They agreed with my decision to put you on probation so you'd better toe the line from now on. We've got an extra show to produce each week for at least the next month. We need the whole team pulling together."

"I'll be there," Mark assured him.

"Good. I told them you would." Russell smiled. "Now about *you*."

It sounded ominous. Mark swallowed hard and waited.

"They want us to take this publicity and run with it," Frank smiled. "Book you on anything and everything we can. You're going to be the poster boy for truth and integrity on the National network."

Mark was speechless. He wasn't ready for anything like this.

"All of your requests are going directly to the promotions department. Lori Larson will be heading up your schedule."

"Wow!" Mark gasped.

"Wow is right. Make every effort to be available, Mark. As far as this show is concerned, this is the most important assignment you've ever had. You and

Jennifer are pretty far along with the report on *The Single Life,* so make every press contact you can."

"I will, but what do I say when they ask me questions about the editing?"

Russell looked away from him, thinking. "We're putting you out there as a reporter with integrity—just be yourself—be totally honest about it."

"What about any ramifications with Jennifer about the piece?" Mark asked.

"I'll handle that. There are many people who believe the myth about the press being biased. Let's show them how wrong they are."

Mark was tempted to laugh, then he realized Frank was serious.

"OK, Frank, I'll give Lori a call right away. But there's one more thing."

Frank raised his eyebrows.

"I want you to read this," Mark said as he handed over his seven-page report.

"What is it?"

"It's a detailed analysis on what I've learned so far about the polling companies I've been looking into, including everything from the New York trip."

"Mark," Frank looked at him from above his glasses, "you've been told to drop this story."

"I know, Frank. But please. It's more than just a polling story. We're looking at possibly two murders here."

"Two murders? You only mentioned one last week."

"My source at the research institute," Mark answered grimly, "was found dead Saturday morning."

"Murdered?"

"Unclear. He was killed when his car crashed into the Los Angeles River."

Russell dropped his head, weighing what he'd just heard.

"Please read it," Mark pleaded. "If you still want to order me off the story afterward, then there's nothing I can do."

Frank looked at the pages in front of him, "There's nothing that you can do now, Mark. You're assigned to do every interview that you can—mentioning the name of this show and this network at every opportunity."

He paused and looked directly into Mark's eyes. "You could be the key to keeping this show on the air. This is the chance of a lifetime, for us and for your career. Are you willing to let this one story get in the way of that?"

Mark held his gaze. "Please, just look it over."

"I can't believe a man was killed over rigging an opinion poll about gays, Mark," Russell stated flatly. "It just doesn't add up."

The two men looked at each other. Finally, Frank nodded. "I'll read it. But I don't want you spending one more second on this until we talk again. Understood?"

"Yes. Thank you, Frank."

"Don't thank me yet."

When he stepped out of Russell's office, Mark noticed several of the staff were beginning to arrive. He caught sight of Jennifer, walking away from where their cubicles were. He wasn't ready to face her yet, but he had to call the publicist quickly. She ducked into the copy room, where the fax machine, printer, and copy machine for the staff were located. He hoped whatever she was doing would take a couple of minutes.

Mark stepped back into his cubicle. His thoughts whirled. Everything was happening so fast; he didn't know how to deal with it. He was surprised to see that his computer's screen-saver program wasn't running; the screen displayed the report he'd written for Russell. That was weird. He closed the file as he reached for his phone.

He punched 0 to reach the studio operator and asked for Lori Larson. She came on the line moments later.

"Hi, Mark, I've been trying to call you." Lori said

"So I understand. We need to talk."

"Yes, we do. Let me tell you what we've got going so far and see if you have any problems, OK?"

Mark picked up a pen and his notepad. "Go."

"First up, *The John Harold Show,* our own network no less. You need to be over at the studio by 4:15 for makeup."

"No problem," Mark said, hiding his nervousness. He'd become comfortable reporting on television, but he'd never had to be himself on the air. This would be different.

"We're trying to work out an interview with Larry King, but they want you tonight, which would air before the *Harold Show*. National wants you on Harold first. So we're trying to get Larry King tomorrow night. *Nightline* is interested, too, but same story. They'll be in direct conflict with Harold, so we're holding them off as well. We've got all the cable shows interested, but they come after we finalize *Nightline* and King."

"It sounds like I'm going to be busy."

"As busy as we can keep you up until the debut Wednesday night. We couldn't ask for better publicity. Be prepared for something early tomorrow morning. All the network morning shows are interested. I'm sure at least one of them will come through. By the way, you've got two different radio interviews this afternoon. One at two for a New York station and the other one at three with KABC here in town."

"How does that work?" Mark asked.

"They're both done by phone patch. You just give me an extension of a quiet room where you won't be interrupted, and they'll call you just before you go on the air."

"Oh, OK. I'll check with Russell, see if he can give me the small conference room."

"That'd be great. Give me a call back as soon as you know. The producers are waiting for me to get the phone number to them."

Mark checked with Russell and got permission to use the conference room. After calling Lori back with the extension, he decided he'd better have some statistics with him so he wouldn't look foolish on the radio interviews. He dialed up his connection to the Internet and started a search on media bias. He quickly spotted a Web site that sounded interesting: mediaresearch.org. It turned out to be just what Mark needed. He found several things that fit and sent them to the printer.

He decided he'd better eat before the production meeting, and he lost the rest of the afternoon. Besides, he was fortunate that Jennifer hadn't come back to her cubicle; he didn't mind delaying their confrontation. He grabbed his wallet and keys and headed for the door.

NATIONAL STUDIOS
12:22 P.M. PACIFIC

Rick and Cassie worked their way through the twelve o'clock lunch rush at the commissary. Rick was looking for a table when he spotted Mark sitting by himself. He waited for Cassie, then the two made their way over to his table.

"Mind if we join you?" Rick asked.

"Of course not." Mark stood. "Please, have a seat."

"We were just talking about you," Cassie said. "I'm so glad you're going to do the show."

"I just hope I don't make a fool of myself."

Cassie tried to reassure him. "Just be yourself. Rick had a great idea walking over here."

Mark looked to Rick. "What was it?"

"To have Mrs. Medford come on the show with you. That way the two of you can talk about how the interview misrepresented her views."

"That's a good idea. I think she'll be thrilled to come on," Mark responded.

"Do you think Russell will let us have a copy of the original interview?" Rick asked. "I think it would be great to show what she really said and how the edited piece made her sound."

Mark thought for a second. "Well, Russell told me to go out and be honest about the whole thing, but releasing that kind of damaging evidence could be a problem."

"I'm going to ask him right after lunch," Rick said. "I can't believe the show isn't worried about covering this whole thing up instead of promoting you."

"That's what I would have thought too," Mark answered. "But evidently they think the controversy will get us ratings, and there's nothing more important than ratings."

"What about your relationship with your producer?" Cassie asked. "Isn't all this publicity going to make her look bad?"

Mark nodded. "That's what I'm most worried about. As mad as I am with her for doing what she did, she's still a friend. I don't know how to be honest about the whole thing without making her look bad."

"Maybe you should talk to her before you start doing the interviews," Rick suggested.

"Yeah, I will. We have a production meeting at one. I'll try to let her know what's going on. She didn't seem to think she'd done anything wrong last night."

"They never do," Cassie said.

"You're right," Mark agreed. "Even Russell told me to go out and show people we're not biased. He doesn't even see it."

"Well, thanks to you, Mark," Rick laughed, "it's definitely something the media is talking about now."

NEW YORK CITY
3:48 P.M. EASTERN

Vince Sinclair was sending E-mails and making phone calls, frantically trying to pull back the information that was about to be released from the homosexual poll. A flash in the corner of the computer screen caught his eye—incoming E-mail. It was from Number One.

To: Vsinclair@researchinternational.org
From: CoSN1@csi.com
Topic: Confidential Response

To say I don't have any idea what you're talking about would probably be
an insult to both you and me. You seem to have a knack for getting information that shouldn't be available to you. What else could you possibly
know about me?

I'm curious, but not sure what to do with you.

Number One

Vince smiled. He typed a reply and sent it. He was getting close. It was nearly
time to head out West.

NATIONAL STUDIOS
1:00 P.M. PACIFIC

Mark arrived at the office just as everyone was congregating for the meeting. The
short time with Rick and Cassie had revived his spirits, but seeing the staff, and
especially Jennifer, he wasn't sure how to respond. Evidently, Jennifer wasn't sure
either as she took her seat next to him without saying a word.

Russell called the meeting to order. "Sorry about the shortened day off, but
we've got an exciting week ahead of us, so here we go.

"First, great show last night, everybody. Stan, your piece on India was great,
better than anything else I saw on it this weekend. Good job."

Stan smiled from across the table.

"I understand the president is doing a press conference on the crisis tonight.
Let's follow up on that with something for Wednesday night's show on where
McNeil stands."

"You've got it, Frank," Stan responded.

Russell outlined the Wednesday show and discussed how it could provide a
whole new audience.

"We've got a tremendous opportunity with our first show, thanks to Mark's outburst last night," Russell said. "We're getting so much press about this whole thing
that our audience should be enormous Wednesday. So with that in mind, we need
to do the best show we've ever done."

Russell turned toward Samantha. "How's your story coming, Samantha?"

"The site is doing better than we thought possible," she responded. "At last count, we'd had nearly seventy-five thousand hits and over three thousand responses to our survey."

"Will you be ready by Wednesday?"

"I don't see why not. We've just got to analyze what we're getting," Samantha answered.

"Good. That will be our lead," Russell continued. He reviewed the show segment by segment. Mark and Jennifer's story on *The Single Life* would air last, where most of the fluff pieces were placed. Mark would have preferred it not to air. With all the publicity surrounding what had happened, the biggest audience of the show's history was going to see him do a report on National's new sit-com. Not exactly the follow-up story he would have picked after the abortion controversy.

As the meeting wrapped up, Mark looked at his watch. He had about fifteen minutes before the first radio interview. He looked at Jennifer. "Let's talk. We can use the small conference room. I've got it reserved anyway."

Jennifer turned to him and smiled as they entered the room. "Look, Mark, I'm sorry for the way that tape ended up. I really thought you would have done the same thing."

"Well, I hope now you know I wouldn't have. I had promised Sara that we wouldn't use her words out of context," Mark said. "When I saw the edited version, I just snapped. I couldn't stop myself from apologizing to her. Do you understand that?"

"I understand that this publicity is going to make you the conservative hero, and me the evil, biased producer," Jennifer said coldly.

"You've talked with Russell?"

Jennifer nodded. "He said you've been instructed to speak the truth. And I put words in her mouth."

"And you didn't?"

"I used her words to say what she really felt," Jennifer explained. "Those hypocrite antiabortionists say all the right things in front of the camera, then go out and encourage people to shoot doctors down in cold blood. You call that pro-life?"

Mark could see that she was as emotional about her beliefs as he was about his.

"Do you really believe that?" When she didn't respond, he continued. "I'm pro-life. I despise the thought of killing innocent babies as a matter of 'choice'. But I, like every other pro-life person that I know, would never condone, encourage, or be involved in any kind of violence to promote my position."

The two locked eyes for several moments. Finally, Mark said, "I have to get ready for an interview, but I wanted to talk to you first. I've been ordered by Russell to promote the show any way I can while the door is open for us. I want you to know that it is not personal at all, but I'm planning to be honest during these interviews."

"So you're going to crucify me in the press," Jennifer said with dark eyes.

"No, Jennifer, I'm going to keep your name out of it as best I can, but I'm going to be honest about how I feel the press has been biased. The way you edited that piece is a perfect example."

"What I did was honest reporting." She crossed her arms defiantly.

"The sad part is, I think you really believe that."

Jennifer stormed out of the room and slammed the door. Mark was jolted by her anger. He wondered how they were going to be able to continue to work together with the chasm growing between them. He needed a moment to get his thoughts in order, but before he could, the phone on the table rang.

"Mr. Taylor?"

"Yes."

"This is Brandy, the producer in New York. We're just about to go on the air. Are you ready?"

Mark let out a long breath, praying for God's Spirit to give him wisdom. "I guess so."

"Jennifer," Frank Russell called as Jennifer angrily walked back to her desk. "Could I see you in my office for a moment?"

Jennifer rolled her eyes as she made a quick U-turn. She entered the office with a forced smile.

Frank sighed, taking his seat. "I looked at the field tapes of the interview with Sara Medford. Mark was right. You crossed the line, big time."

Jennifer shook her head almost imperceptibly. "Look, I admit I edited her comments. What interview doesn't get chopped up? But Mark wanted to end with her comments, and you saw them, Frank. It would have left the piece flat, boring."

"That doesn't give you the right—"

"The issue wasn't about forgiveness or her little speech to the abortion doctor," Jennifer interrupted. "It was about liability when groups like hers promote their hate and it turns into violence. Her comments taken at face value would have been the lie. I edited her so that the truth would be told, and it would have been great television if Mark hadn't screwed it up."

Frank had had enough, "No, Jennifer, Mark saved you. We would probably have been sued if he hadn't spoken out."

Jennifer started to protest, but Frank continued. "No, you listen to me. What you did was inexcusable. You're on probation as of right now. I expect a written apology sent to this lady today, and I'm debating whether to have some kind of on-air apology prepared for Wednesday's show."

She stood, looking into Frank's reddened face. "Is that all?"

"For now, I want to see that letter within the hour."

Jennifer quickly left the office.

CHAPTER 24

"Tracy!" Brenda called out from outside Tracy's office.

"What?" Tracy yelled back irritated. It had been a hectic day, and the void without Kevin further upset her. She stepped out of her office.

"Listen." Brenda turned up the radio she kept by her desk.

"It really came down to what was right for me," Tracy could hear Mark's voice coming through the speaker.

"He's on with Larry Elder," Brenda responded, referring to the KABC radio host.

"I had promised Sara Medford that her words would not be edited out of context ..." Mark was explaining.

Tracy and Brenda listened for the rest of the hour as Mark answered the host's questions and took phone calls from the listening audience. Tracy had Brenda screen all of her calls so she wouldn't be disturbed. She was getting to know Mark on a much deeper level as he talked, and although they had their differences politically, she was drawn to what she was hearing.

Forty miles away from the smog and traffic of downtown Los Angeles, Jason Reynolds sat with his pool speaker system tuned to the same radio station, listening intently as he tried to enjoy the sunshine. Jared Winter had faxed him a copy of Mark's interview schedule.

Jason wondered how much damage Mark could do to his cause. Mark was good; Jason had to give him that. Jason kept a mental count of how many callers agreed with Mark's position and how many disagreed. He was happy to see that they were running two-to-one against Mark's belief in a biased media. Much of Jason's success depended on the nation's belief that the media was fair and the polling data was accurate.

Jason laughed as a caller opposed Mark's opinion and recounted the horrible press coverage Clinton had received during the eight years of his administration. How was Mark going to answer that one?

"Let's talk about the Clinton administration," Mark responded calmly over the radio. "A lot's been said about how negative his press was during his presidency, but if you look objectively at it, the mainstream press, and by that I mean the big three networks, often deliberately chose not to report the news when it came to Clinton. Any Republican president with the number and the scope of the scandals surrounding the Clinton White House would have been buried alive by the press. But not Bill Clinton.

"Let me give you just one example. The Whitewater scandal first broke in an article in the *New York Times*, March eighth of 1992, during the primaries. Of the thousands of stories reported on the evening news between March 8 through election day in November, how many stories were done on Whitewater?"

"I wouldn't have a clue," the host commented.

"Five," Mark answered, "and three of them dismissed it. It took *Nightline* an unbelievable 668 days before it felt the story was newsworthy. This is a great example of news media bias when it comes to somebody in office they want to keep in power—bias by omission."

"Yeah, but—" the caller tried to interrupt, but Mark was on a roll.

"And what about the election lies in 1996 that were propagated by the media for Clinton? Just to name one, it was accepted and reported as true that the Republicans wanted to cut Medicare funding in the budget debate. Every station you turned to propagated this misinformation, when the truth was they were calling for a reduction in the growth of spending. The fact was their budget still allowed for more money in Medicare than any previous budget ever had. But the media continued to hammer away that the Republicans were going to cut Medicare, which simply wasn't true. When you've got 89 percent of the nation's reporters and editors saying they voted for Clinton in 1992, how can we sit here and say there isn't a media bias?"

The smile on Jason's face quickly faded. Mark was handling himself too well. Something was going to have to be done—and soon.

NATIONAL STUDIOS
3:15 P.M. PACIFIC

"So, Rick, I'm going to need that last graphic to come up just a hair later. I don't want you to upstage me with the visual," John Harold said, looking up to the ceiling as he talked to Rick in the control room.

Rick pressed the button that would send his voice over the speakers into the studio. "I understand, John. I'll wait for you."

"OK, then that's about it," John said as he finished his rehearsal.

"Then that's lunch, everybody," Rick announced.

"John and Cassie are on their way in to see you, Rick," Debbie warned over Rick's headset.

A moment later, as the booth cleared, Cassie and John stepped in.

"You know, one of you is going to have to find a new job," John joked as he reached for Rick's hand. "I can't have my director married to my producer."

"Thanks, I hope you're kidding," Rick responded.

"Yeah, I am. Congratulations. I think you two are going to make a great couple."

"We already do," Cassie laughed.

"Oh, we should tell Rick about Wednesday," John said.

"John has a conflict with taping Wednesday night," Cassie explained. "It seems he's been invited to the White House to host a gala for the first couple."

"You must be excited; that's a great opportunity."

"That's how the network brass saw it," John explained. "Actually, they called it wonderful exposure for the show."

"So anyway," Cassie continued, "we'll air a rerun to give John a chance to hop on a plane and get back here by Thursday. So let the crew know after lunch, will you?"

"I will . . ."

"What are you thinking?" Cassie felt Rick's hesitation.

"About taking *Across the Nation*. Terri was looking for some time off for family reasons. Maybe I can still help her out by taking their show that night."

"Give them a call. You'll be free," Cassie said.

"Now about having Mark on the show tonight—" John changed the subject.

Cassie picked up the conversation. "John's concerned that if we have Sara on with Mark, the pro-life side is going to be overrepresented."

"I take it you're pro-choice?" Rick asked.

"Of course. Aren't you?" John responded.

"No, I'm not actually. I'm very much pro-life," Rick returned.

"What about you, Cassie?"

"I'm pro-life as well, John."

John looked from one to another, then shook his head. "I should have known. You just assume in this town that everyone is pro-choice."

"What are you concerned about with Sara?" Rick asked.

"That we'll have this sweet old lady give her opinions about the issue, and there'll be no way I can argue against her without looking like a jerk."

"Good point."

"But I think you're missing the point of the interview if you go there," Cassie argued. "Her position on abortion is not the issue. It's the fact that her words were twisted by a biased producer. Stay with that story, and you won't have to appear mean—you'll be sympathetic to her plight."

John thought for a moment.

"Cassie's right, John," Rick said. "The controversy isn't about pro-life or pro-choice. It's about whether the media has treated the issue with a bias. Look at us three right here. You assumed that Cassie and I would be pro-choice even though you know we are both Christians—just because we work in Hollywood with you."

John nodded. "I see your point."

"I've talked with Sara," Cassie continued, "and you saw her on Mark's report. Our audience will love her. You'll come out the hero for letting her tell her story."

"You're right. Let's do it," John said. "However it goes, it'll be good TV."

"That it will, John," Rick agreed.

Once Cassie and John left the booth, Rick picked up the phone and called *Across the Nation*'s production office.

"This is Terri," Rick heard a few moments later.

"Terri, it's Rick Treadway. Has the show found a director to replace you for Wednesday night yet?"

"No, they haven't," Terri said dejectedly. "Frank feels real bad about it, but they're not releasing me until after the show."

"How's your father doing?"

"He's holding his own. The surgery is scheduled for Wednesday. So it looks like I'll miss it but get to be with him the day after."

"What if I told you I just found out we're airing a rerun on Wednesday?" Rick offered.

"I'd run over there and kiss you! Are you serious?"

"Yes, John's been invited to some White House function. So if you can talk Russell into using me on Wednesday, you could go be with your dad."

"Oh, thanks, Rick. I'll go in and talk to him right now. He should go for it. Everybody felt comfortable with you being around on Sunday. I'll call you back."

NATIONAL STUDIOS
4:00 P.M. PACIFIC

Mark hung up the phone in the conference room and laid his head down on the table. He was exhausted. He let out a long, slow breath, trying to release the tension he'd felt for the past few hours. He'd never dreamed it would be so difficult to be a guest on a radio talk show, but every question—every comment—required his full attention. He often found he was trying to think ahead to what his next argument should be while he was still speaking about the last point. He felt wrung out.

He looked at his watch. In fifteen minutes he had to be in makeup. He made his way to the outer office. Everyone was hard at work and didn't notice him as he walked back to his desk. He recalled Kevin Spencer's number from his pager, hoping Vickie would answer.

"Hello," the female voice said.

"Vickie?"

"Yes. Who's this?"

"It's Mark Taylor. I'm back in town and wanted to let you know how sorry I am about Kevin. If there's anything I can do for you ..."

"No, there's nothing you can do," she said dejectedly.

"Is there any more information about the accident?" Mark asked.

"No, the police just found his car Saturday morning. He evidently ran off the road and into the river basin. They believe the car rolled over as it went down the hill and caught on fire." Mark could hear her voice breaking as she recounted the story. "They found his body in the car—burned beyond recognition."

"I'm so sorry, Vickie." Mark tried to comfort her, but what could he say? He wanted to press further to see if there were any clues that would point to it not being an accident. "Did the police have any idea what time the accident happened?"

"Why do you ask?"

He had to be careful; he didn't want to add to her misery. "Well, you were so upset that he hadn't come home from work the night before, I wondered if they knew what time the accident had happened—if there was any clue as to where he'd gone that night."

"I didn't even think to ask," Vickie said. "I just assumed that it'd happened after work and that it wasn't discovered until Saturday morning."

"If you don't mind, maybe I'll give the police a call and check on it for you. It might help you in understanding what happened the night before."

"Why? Do you think this is somehow tied into the company thing?"

"I'm not saying that, Vickie," Mark cautioned. "It's just that there's still some question in my mind why the car wasn't discovered the evening before if the accident had happened when he was on his way home."

"I hadn't thought of that."

Mark looked at his watch. It was time to get over to the other studio. "If I find out anything at all, I'll call you, Vickie. But right now I'm running late."

"Well, thanks for your call."

"You're welcome. I just wish it was under different circumstances."

Mark hung up and made a note to call the police about the accident—although with his schedule, he didn't know when that would be. Then he hurried out of the office and headed across the lot.

NATIONAL STUDIOS
4:30 P.M. PACIFIC

The second stage manager led Mark into the makeup room. He was happy to see Sara Medford sitting in one of the chairs.

"Sara, so they got you to come down too?" Mark asked.

"Hi, Mark. Isn't it wonderful?" She beamed. "I'm going to be on the show with you."

Mark returned the smile. "That's great. I knew they were thinking about it."

She leaned into him as he reached over to give her a hug and whispered, "I told you this was all working out according to God's plan."

"After what has happened the last twenty-four hours, I'd have to say you're right," Mark laughed as he sat in the chair next to her.

"There's the star of the show now," Rick called out as he entered the room.

"Rick, good to see you. Any tips from the director before the show?"

"Just go out there in the power of the Lord."

"Rick, this is Sara Medford, the woman from the pro-life group."

Rick took her hand gently. "Nice to meet you. It's a pleasure having you on our show."

"You're a Christian?" Sara asked.

"Yes, ma'am, I am," Rick answered.

"I never would have thought there were so many Christians in this profession," Sara said in bewilderment.

"We're here, all right, Sara. But we could use a lot more," Rick said. He noticed the makeup artists trading looks. Two women and a gay man tried to act oblivious to the continual mention of Christianity.

Chad, Rick's associate director, stuck his head in the room. "Rick, there's a call for you in the control room."

"Thanks, Chad. I've got some last-minute things to take care of anyway," Rick said. "I'll meet you in the greenroom in a couple of minutes. Maybe we could share a quick prayer together before the show."

Mark nodded.

"That'd be wonderful." Sarah grinned at him.

Rick walked down the hallway and into the booth. He picked up the flashing line. "Treadway here."

"Rick, this is Frank Russell."

"Yes, Frank. Did you talk with Terri?"

"Yeah, she's sitting right here. I just wanted to confirm with you that you're available Wednesday night. If so, I'm going to let her head up north to her dad's house."

"I'm all yours, and from what I saw Sunday, I don't see any problem jumping in Wednesday night."

"That's great, Rick. We appreciate your help."

"My pleasure. Tell Terri to go be with her family, and I'll be praying for her."

"OK." Rick heard hesitation in Russell's voice. "I'll tell her."

Sitting in the greenroom with twenty minutes to go before the show started, Mark was growing nervous. It was one thing to be on the radio and talk about these issues, but to be on television where every expression will get caught by the cameras was something else altogether.

"Mr. Taylor."

"Yes, over here." He gestured to a stage manager holding a phone at the other end of the room.

"Phone call."

Mark picked it up, wondering who could be calling.

"Break a leg," Mark heard after he answered.

"Tracy!" Mark laughed. "What a nice surprise. How did you find me?"

"It wasn't easy. You're suddenly the most protected man in Hollywood. But one of my jobs is to know my way around you television people. I've left messages at your office, but I'm sure you've had a hectic day."

"That's for sure. Last time I checked there were over thirty messages, and I still haven't had time to retrieve them. Sorry I missed yours."

"I was just trying to reach you to confirm our lunch tomorrow. Are you still interested?"

Mark thought about Russell's orders, but he could always say it was just a lunch with the network CEO. "Sure, I'm interested. What time and where?"

"Well, Papa will be at the office down here tomorrow, so it'll be easiest to meet at Fellini's again, say around 12:30?"

"That sounds good to me. I'll be there, and thanks, Tracy."

"I hope it will be helpful for you."

"I'm sure it will be interesting in either case." Mark joked.

"I wanted to come and see the show, but I'm swamped over here. We lost one of our managers this weekend—he was killed in a car crash."

"Yes—Kevin Spencer—I know."

"How did you know that?" Tracy asked perplexed.

"Oh—" Mark realized his mistake. Tracy didn't know about his meeting with Kevin or that Mark knew about his accident. He tried to recover. "I met him the day I was doing the tour with you and heard about it on the news. I'm sorry, Tracy, it must be quite a shock for everybody at ARI."

"Yes, Kevin was a great guy. It's been hard getting into things around here. I really miss him."

"I'm sure you do," Mark said, thinking the same thing. "I'm sorry for your loss."

"Thank you." Tracy didn't pursue the topic any further. "Well, like I said, break a leg. Have a great show, Mark."

"I'll try. See you tomorrow, 12:30."

Mark was relieved. He was so tired with all the attention and the interviews, he couldn't believe he'd slipped up. But then what did it matter? He didn't have to hide

Kevin's identity anymore. Maybe he should tell Tracy what Kevin told him, but could he trust her? Something about her made him want to, but after all, Reynolds was her grandfather.

Mark sat on the couch next to Sara. They were the only two in the room. Mark knew that Sandra Bullock was also booked on the show, but he hadn't seen her yet. She must be in her dressing room.

The door opened, and Rick peeked around the corner. "You two ready?"

"As ready as we'll ever be," Mark answered.

Rick stepped into the room with Cassie right behind him.

"Sara, I'm Cassie Petterson," Cassie said extending her hand. "We talked earlier on the phone."

"Yes, Cassie," Sara accepted the handshake warmly, "it's so nice to meet you."

"I'm glad you're alone in here," Rick said. "We wanted to pray with both of you before the show."

"I'm all for that," Sara returned.

"Just remember to go out there and be yourselves," Cassie advised. "John's going to mainly talk about the press issues, but I'm sure there'll be a chance for you to get your message across, Sara."

Sara smiled confidently. "God will open the door."

"Let's pray," Rick said. The four formed a small circle and joined hands right there in the greenroom of *The John Harold Show.*

"God, we come to you in the mighty name of Jesus Christ and pray that your hand would be on these two," Rick began. "We thank you for how you've opened up the doors in the last twenty-four hours for Sara's important message about the precious value of unborn babies and for Mark's opportunity to open the eyes of our society to the media's bias. I pray for boldness for both of them. May your Holy Spirit anoint them now as they go out. Let them speak your words, Lord, and have a clear head and your wisdom about them."

"I also pray, Lord," Cassie followed up, "that you would take away any nervousness. As your Scripture says, to be anxious about nothing, but by prayer and supplication make our requests known to you. I pray that your peace would surround them. Let them feel your presence as they step out on that stage. In the name of Jesus. Amen."

Sara and Mark looked up and thanked them.

"You're welcome," Rick said. "I've got to go. Have a great show."

Cassie looked down at her rundown for the show. "You're going to be segment three, Mark. I don't think Sandra is going to stay on the couch while you're out there. John wants to deal directly with you." She turned to Sara. "After Mark's segment, we'll add you to the discussion, Sara."

"Did Russell give you a copy of the original footage?" Mark asked.

"No, we tried, but the lawyers wouldn't release it," Rick answered.

"That's too bad, but I understand their position," Mark commented. "If they let that tape out, there'd be no question of biased editing."

"Well, we've got a show to do. Have a good time, you two." Cassie stepped out the door and headed for the stage.

MALIBU
4:45 P.M. PACIFIC

Jason sat in his office, contemplating flying over to the studio and seeing the taping of *The John Harold Show*. He could chopper over there in under twenty minutes and be over to the stage before Mark was introduced.

No, he decided. The first meeting between him and Mark Taylor would be at lunch tomorrow afternoon as planned. He would stay home and watch the show on his microwave link from the studio. Something he didn't use too often, but today it would be worth the thirty thousand dollars it had cost to install.

He turned his attention toward the computer screen, deciding to check his E-mail. Among the normal amount of business-oriented messages, one caught his eye. A response from Vsinclair.

> To: CoSN1@csi.com
> From: Vsinclair@researchinternational.org
> Topic: Confidential
>
> Number One,
>
> I'm glad I've sparked your curiosity. As I said earlier, I'm on your team, or at least would like to be. I plan to be in LA later this week and would love to chat with you about what value I could be to your organization. I hope the information I supplied from here has been helpful. There's more where that came from.
>
> Vince

Reynolds shook his head. The last thing he needed was one more mystery. He was tempted to send Luis to New York and take care of this one, but something about Vince's boldness captured his attention. He found to his surprise that he wanted to meet this man—to see what he was made of—maybe he could fit into the group. *We'll see if you have what it takes, young man,* Jason thought. *We'll see.*

"Mr. Reynolds," his assistant's voice cut through the silence, "the president is on the line."

"Thanks, Carla." He muttered, reaching for the phone.

"This is Jason Reynolds." He knew that in White House protocol, the executive secretary made sure the correct person was on the line before transferring him into the Oval Office.

A moment later, Jason was greeted with the president's voice.

"Jason."

"Hello, Mr. President," Reynolds responded. "Don't you have a press conference to attend?" The networks were planning to break into the prime-time East Coast broadcast at eight o'clock to air McNeil's press conference on what was now called the crisis in India.

"Yes, in a few minutes. I wanted to talk to you first. What's with your newest National celebrity?"

"You must be referring to Mark Taylor," Jason laughed lightly.

"You bet I am," the president answered angrily. "Why don't you fire the right-winger and get him off the air instead of giving him all this press?"

"If I fired him right now, it would be like adding gasoline to the fire, and this thing would blow up even bigger," Jason tried to explain. "Give it a couple of days, and it'll run its course and allow the publicity to give my start-up network a nice boost."

"So you're willing to jeopardize everything including the UN appropriation just for some free publicity?" the president asked.

You don't understand the scope of what you're referring to, Jason thought. "Nothing will be jeopardized by giving the antiabortion side a brief moment in the sun, McNeil."

"Is it true you're going to have him as a guest on *The John Harold Show* tonight?"

"Yes. It was either my show, *Nightline,* King—somebody was going to grab him tonight."

"Oh yeah, go for the ratings, while our polling results are nearing 70 percent in our favor on the whole abortion debate." Jason could hear McNeil's anger. "It's too risky, Jason. We need to enlarge the pro-choice base. You brought this whole India thing up before the public, and now I'm about to stick my neck out with this press conference. We've got to keep the UN's family planning objectives and the economic package the focus. It's too much of a distraction to get caught up in a national frenzy about media bias."

"Don't worry. Those numbers will hold," Reynolds replied. "You haven't seen the results we'll be able to publish tomorrow since the India situation hit the networks. I'll tell you what. I'll keep my eye on the *Harold Show*. If anything comes out that will really damage you, I'll kill it and send up a rerun."

"You do that!" the president ordered. "Or I'll hold you personally responsible."

It took all of Jason's control to respond cordially to the overinflated windbag who held the office of the president. After every election there was always a learning curve to discover who was "really" in power. Jason was getting impatient with how long it was taking this one to come to grips with reality.

He fought the desire for revenge as he turned to his computer. He typed a memo, preparing it for all the channels he controlled. As he clicked on the send button, a wicked smile spread across his lips. Within forty-eight hours, the Senate leadership opposed to McNeil's plan would see a drop of 7 percentage points in its approval ratings. Jason wanted to do the same to the ever-arrogant President McNeil, but that would jeopardize everything he'd put into motion. But there would come a day . . .

CHAPTER 25

"We're back," John Harold said to camera 2 as the applause in the studio died down. "Sandra Bullock was great—wasn't she—but she had to get back to the set of her new picture. The guest coming out now has been the talk of the town for the past twenty-four hours—and not just this town, but of New York and our nation's capital as well. It all started last night on this network, on *Across the Nation*."

"Ready B," Rick cued in the booth as John paused. "Roll B."

"Here's how it went," John said.

"Dissolve to B and track it," Rick said to Milton, the technical director, as he moved the fader bar, the lever that dissolved the videotape online.

The program monitor switched to the replay of Mark's reaction after the interview with Sara Medford had played.

"Stand by on camera 2; we're coming back to John," Rick called out as the associate director to his left counted out of the taped piece.

John watched the playback from his monitor just to the left of camera 2, then turned his eyes into the lens when the stage manager cued him. "Wow! That was quite a moment for our network, and it's captured the attention of the rest of the

252

country. We're happy to say we've got him here for his first television interview since last night. Please welcome Mark Taylor."

The house band kicked into the theme of *Across the Nation* as Mark nervously stepped out from behind the wall that separated John's home base from the center-stage performance area. The spotlights nearly blinded him as he carefully stepped up on the small stage where John greeted him. They shook hands before John motioned him to take his place on the couch.

"So, Mark," John said, "I've been a big fan of yours over at *Across the Nation*. But last night, you really outdid yourself."

"Ready three, take three," Rick snapped in the control room as Mark's close-up went on the air.

"Thanks, John, it was an interesting evening," Mark responded.

"As we just saw," John smiled. "We're going to bring out Sara Medford in just a couple of minutes, so before we get into her exact story, let's talk about the media bias that's been on everybody's mind today, thanks to you. Do you really think there is one?"

"Let me give you a few of the statistics I found doing a little research, then you tell me." Mark pulled a piece of paper out of his pocket. He didn't want to misquote any of the information he'd found in his search. "Going back to 1981, Dr. Robert Lichter published a survey of the media. The numbers were staggering: at least 81 percent of the news media had voted for the Democratic nominee for president in every election going back to 1964. He also discovered that 90 percent favored abortion."

"But that was back in 1981," John protested. "That's twenty years ago."

"And it's gotten worse," Mark responded. "In 1994, the Gannett Foundation did a similar study. They found that 89 percent admitted to voting for Bill Clinton while only 7 percent for George Bush. In 2000, a whopping 93 percent voted for President McNeil."

Mark paused, letting the numbers sink in. "But it's not just about political affiliation, it's how the media uses its influence. Since the immediate controversy on our show was about abortion, let's talk about that."

John nodded slightly, allowing Mark to continue.

"Analyzing 1,050 news stories about abortion between the years 1995 and 1996, the pro-life side was given some form of conservative label in 178 out of 378 stories or 47 percent of the time. The pro-choice side were labeled liberal just 19 out of 682 stories, or 2.8 percent of the time. Planned Parenthood, the nation's largest abortion provider, in sixty-four stories in *USA Today* was not given a liberal label once.

"In another debate, a study by MediaWatch reviewed 411 national newspaper stories from 1995 to mid-1998 on five leftist gay groups and found only five 'liberal' labels or 1.2 percent in the entire sample. By contrast, several groups were consistently marked with conservative warning labels: the Family Research Council, 63 percent; Concerned Women for America, 71 percent; and Phyllis Schlafly's Eagle Forum in 75 percent of the stories.

"That's a pretty blatant way the media suggests to the American people that these groups are radical while the militant gay movement is mainstream—the pro-life movement is termed the radical right wing while the pro-choice side is portrayed as centrist."

"Well, just the other day," John broke in, "a CNN poll said that 64 percent of Americans agree with abortion. That would seem fairly centrist to me."

"And tell me what else you know about that survey, John?" Mark asked.

"What do you mean?" John looked confused.

"We cite these survey percentages like they're some kind of Holy Grail in our society. We never question them. I want to know what questions were asked. How many people did they sample? How did they sample them? Were the questions biased in any way?"

"I don't know," John admitted.

"Exactly my point," Mark responded. "We don't know. The language used can make a world of difference in a survey's results. For example, if the question was worded something like, 'Do you believe that when a woman's life is at risk, abortion should be permitted' would get a much higher percentage of positive responses than one worded, 'Do you believe that a woman has the right to an abortion during the third trimester?' I would bet you that the last question wouldn't get you a 64 percent approval. In fact, I've seen polls that put the approval for third-trimester abortions below 20 percent. But the point is if the consumer is not informed about all the poll's pertinent information, how can we know the interpretation by the media is accurate?"

John nodded at Mark's conclusion despite his political leanings. "I'd have to agree with you on that, but what's the difference between this poll that you're criticizing and the statistics you've been throwing out?"

"Good question," Mark replied. "The percentages I've been quoting have come from analyzing newspaper stories, studying recorded news programs, and taking factual surveys—questions like 'Who did you vote for? Are you a Democrat or a Republican?' Those are not opinion surveys that can be open to interpretation or manipulated by biased questions."

"OK, I see your point," John conceded. "But how in your opinion does this bias of the press play itself out?"

"Let's stay with the abortion debate. Look at how the media refers to pro-life groups as antiabortion or sometimes even antichoice. They take all the positive connotations of *pro* and discard them with the underlying negativity of *anti*. That's a decision by those in the media. The pro-life people don't want to be called antiabortion. I can't think of one pro-life person who refers to himself or herself as antiabortion. Yet that is the label they're stuck with. How would the pro-choice crowd react to being labeled antilife, or even a less inflammatory title, pro-abortion. They would be outraged and rightfully so. But where's the outrage when a group of committed people who believe in the sanctity of life and desire to be called pro-life are labeled antichoice?"

"I never thought of it that way," John admitted.

"To be honest with you, I hadn't either until we did that story. I was chastised for referring to Sara's group as pro-life, not knowing there was an unwritten rule at our network that we call them antiabortion."

"Your network and mine—the National Studios?"

"That's right."

"We'll have to change the intro to Sara after the commercial. I didn't know I was supposed to say she's antiabortion."

The audience laughed. John had a unique gift of finding the right spot to insert a joke.

"You have to at least admit there's a perception of media bias out there." Mark spoke after the audience quieted down. "Just look at some of the Fox News promos they're running—'Fox is unbiased, fair, and honest'—'we report, you decide.' They wouldn't be out there trying to fill that void in the media if it wasn't perceived that the mainstream press is biased."

"Now, Mark," John decided to change the subject, "explain to us what happened with Sara's interview. Was it intended by somebody on your staff to use her comments to mislead the audience?"

Mark paused, choosing his words carefully. "I had a wonderful interview with Sara. She personified the pro-life stance with grace and candor, without a hint of condoning violence in any way. But you saw the finished product. What would be your opinion of her after viewing the tape?"

"I guess it would be that she agreed with the radical Internet group and that the doctor who was murdered deserved what he got."

"Exactly what most people in the country would think after seeing that. Those were all her words, just scrambled around in the magical world of editing—sentences clipped and moved so that you'd have that impression. That's why I did what I did last night. It wasn't right. It shouldn't have happened. Was it maliciously done? Honestly, I don't believe so."

John's eyebrows went up, surprised by the comment. "What do you mean?"

"I happen to believe that in this case—and maybe in other cases of media bias—the person editing the piece fell victim to his or her own misplaced preconceptions of the pro-life position. That person wasn't at the interview and didn't get the same firsthand view that I got of Sara's sincere belief of the right of the unborn—of her distaste and condemnation for violence in any way. In the editing room, Sara was portrayed the way that our producer felt all antiabortion people must believe, or at least the way the media wants them to believe. I'm sure she thought she was doing the 'right' thing. Certainly not fair to Sara, but it's something that happens in the editing room of our industry and the print media every day."

"Wow!" John exclaimed. "A powerful statement. And we'll give you a chance to meet Sara Medford, right after this."

While the commercial was running, Cassie walked up to the couch, smiled at Mark, and gave him a wink. "You're doing great, Mark. Keep it up."

Mark took a deep breath and let it out slowly.

Cassie handed John the blue card with the interview questions on it for Sara's segment. He scanned it quickly, nodding.

"How do you think it's going, John?" she asked.

"Real good. Mark's certainly done his homework. I wonder how this will be perceived by the press?"

"We'll just have to see, but I'm glad we got him first." Cassie nearly had to yell to be heard over the band playing loudly during the commercial break. "Now with Sara, don't try to go head-to-head with her about the abortion issue. You won't be able to win, trust me."

John smiled; he'd had the same impression. "Don't worry, I'm not stupid."

"I'll go give her a pep talk. We've got a great show going. Keep it up."

Cassie launched one last encouraging smile toward Mark, then walked upstage where Sara was waiting to come on.

"Are you ready to go?" Cassie asked her.

"I guess as ready as I'll ever be," Sara responded nervously. "Mark's done a good job out there."

"He's laid the groundwork for you, Sara. Now just go out there and be yourself. The audience will love you."

Sara bit her lip, trying to hide the tension she felt.

Cassie gave her a quick smile. Sara bowed her head and uttered a quick prayer.

MALIBU
SAME TIME

During the commercial, Jason Reynolds contemplated everything he'd heard Mark say. It wasn't anything new. He'd heard all the arguments before about media bias and had always laughed them off as coming from the radical right wing, even though he knew it was true—or more accurately—had spent millions of dollars and years of his life making sure that it was true.

As Jason watched, Mark was sounding more and more like Jerry Falwell or Pat Robertson, which in his mind would make it easier to discount his opinion as radical thinking. Still, it was controversy, and would be great for the debut of *Across the Nation-Wednesday Edition*. So far Jason couldn't see any reason for yanking the show off the air in spite of the president's worries. Besides, John Harold had done a good job of bringing up the new abortion numbers from the recent polls. Jason had felt the stirrings of panic begin as Mark started asking questions about how the poll was conducted. But he quickly relaxed as the topic sputtered and John moved on. Mark still didn't have the full story on his polling, or he would have gone further.

Jason sat back in his leather chair, waiting for the show to return. He was beginning to look forward to his lunch tomorrow with Taylor. Would he be able to keep Mark distracted, possibly recruit him to their cause, or would he have to be taken care of? Jason laughed. The situation was like watching the spinning wheels on a slot machine, although in this case, wherever it landed, he would still be the winner.

SAME TIME
NATIONAL STUDIOS

"Our next guest," John Harold began as Debbie cued him, "heads up the Southern California chapter of the Right to Life Advocacy Group. We're happy to have her here to be able to tell her side of this story, live. We promise there will be no editing from the time she steps out here on this stage. Please welcome, the very anti-abortion—Sara Medford."

The band kicked in with a generic upbeat tune as Sara rounded the corner and made her way to greet John. She smiled nervously, embarrassed by the applause, then made her way on the couch as Mark slid over and gave her the seat next to John.

"Sara, glad you could be here with us," John said.

"Oh, it's my pleasure."

"Do you watch the show often?" John asked.

"No," Sara answered honestly. "We don't watch a lot of television at our house."

The audience chuckled as John gave the camera a wry look at being one-upped by his guest.

"Now I have to tell our audience, we tried to get the tape from the original interview between Sara and Mark, but the studio wouldn't release it for some reason." John snickered. "Lawyers. Now, Sara, tell us how you felt after watching the interview the way it aired on *Across the Nation* last night."

Sara answered quietly, and the audio man had to quickly increase the volume on her microphone. "At first I was upset, in tears actually."

It seemed as if all the lights in the studio lowered and a bright spotlight centered on Sara, but the lights hadn't changed. Her countenance silenced the studio audience; all eyes and ears were on her.

Sara patted Mark's arm. "This fine young man had come to my house and spent an hour with me going over how I felt about the jury's verdict, about abortion—that murderous, evil procedure this culture chooses to call freedom of choice."

"Wow, Sara," John interrupted. "Don't hold back on us now."

"I'm sorry." Sara smiled at him apologetically. "I get a little worked up over the issue. Anyway, I thought the interview with Mark had gone very well; I even had a group of my church friends gather last night to watch the show with me. Then when I saw the way my words had been twisted, to infer that I would threaten an abortion doctor, I was devastated."

"So the way that interview was edited did not reflect what you really said?" John prompted.

"Oh, heavens no," Sara answered with a shake of her head and a frown that conveyed more than words. Then her face brightened. "But when the camera came back on this young man, well, I believe he said more in his reaction to what had happened than what my words could ever have."

"What do you mean?" John asked.

"Well, Mark was able to convey to his audience not just what I said but how I felt. He was right: I would never condone any act of violence against an abortion doctor or against anyone. Our whole movement is that way. Pro-life means pro-life. When I mentioned we might have to break an immoral law in order to answer to a higher law—that of God—I was referring to peaceful demonstrations like praying outside abortion clinics. I was definitely not suggesting in any way to harm, or God forbid, kill a doctor."

"I see," John intoned. "So how do you feel about that thirty-million-dollar verdict?"

Sara pursed her lips as she thought. "I have mixed emotions actually. I don't like what that group on the Internet was doing. Anyone who promotes violence, like I said, would have a hard time convincing me they were pro-life. But there's also the First Amendment issue. They have a right to free speech as much as any other group should have."

John looked from Sara to Mark. "What's your feeling, Mark?"

Mark laughed. "Being a journalist, I've never expressed my own beliefs publicly. I've always felt that when a reporter expresses his opinion, it makes him less credible. But when you stop and think about a network news anchor speaking before the American people night after night where 75 to 80 percent of what he's saying is factual—how are we to know when he slips into something editorial, something that is slanted toward his personal beliefs? More and more, I'm seeing the deception of journalists as they try to appear neutral yet pull the tricks we talked about earlier. If the public knows where a reporter stands on a controversial social issue like abortion, then listeners can make a more intelligent decision on whatever bias may be present."

John nodded. "An interesting point. I wonder how many of your colleagues would agree with you?"

"Probably not many."

"But you still haven't answered the question," John pushed.

"I like to say that I'm pro-choice." Mark smiled at the shocked reactions from John and Sara. "But the choice happens prior to conception. Women have the right to choose up until a life is created, then I'm all pro-life. Now the woman has to consider the rights of the life within her, which doesn't have a voice." Mark reached over and took Sara's hand gently. "I think Sara gave a very eloquent defense of the pro-life argument, both here on this show and when I interviewed her last week."

The interview continued, quickly filling up the six and a half minutes Cassie had slated for the segment. As John was getting his cue to wrap it up, he asked one more question.

"So where do you two go from here?"

Sara smiled. "The publicity that we've received from what Mark did has increased the interest in our cause a thousandfold. I've been asked to do more interviews today than I have the entire year of heading up the Right to Life Advocacy Group. I think Mark did a wonderful thing, and we praise God for him."

Mark blushed.

"What about you, Mark?" John asked, ignoring Sara's reference to God.

"Well, our show, *Across the Nation,* debuts its Wednesday night edition right here on this network at nine o'clock. So I'm sure I'll be pretty busy with that added to our schedule. I hope your audience will tune in and see what we've got in store. Remember, it's live; anything can happen."

"Nice plug, Mark." John laughed. "I thank you both for being here. It's sure made me rethink how I view the press."

Thank you, God, Cassie thought to herself as she watched from her position just off stage. She thought both segments had been fantastic. It had been nearly a year since she'd started producing the show, and she couldn't remember another time that she'd felt this excited about its message to the nation. Rick waited until he directed the crew into the commercial break before he sat back in his chair with a huge smile across his face.

NATIONAL STUDIOS
6:00 P.M. PACIFIC

Mark smiled faintly at the audience as he stepped off the platform. He hadn't felt this tired since a mission in Iraq when his team had spent forty straight hours behind enemy lines without sleep, searching through the desert for a downed Navy pilot. The mental stress of the past hour added to that of the two radio interviews had taken their toll. He was exhausted.

"Great job, Mark!" Cassie walked toward him, grinning. "Your boldness was a great testimony. I'm so proud of you."

"Thanks, Cassie," was all Mark could manage. Cassie made her way up to the stage to talk with John as a woman approached Mark.

"Mark Taylor," she said. "Lori Larson, your new publicist."

"Hi, Lori, it's nice to finally meet you," Mark said. "How have I done so far?"

"Unbelievable. We couldn't pay for this kind of exposure. Good job at the end plugging the show." Lori couldn't care less about the issues, just the number of shows she could book Mark on while he was "hot" and how many times they could get the network and *Across the Nation* mentioned. "I wanted to make sure you had your schedule for the next twenty-four hours—"

"You mean there's more?" Mark asked.

"Oh yeah. We're doing everything we can to keep this issue and you before the public through Wednesday. You've got to be at your studio by 3:45 tomorrow morning for makeup. We're doing a couple of feeds into the morning shows, *Good Morning America* and *The Today Show*. For some reason, *The Early Show* passed. You're first on-camera hits at 4:10 A.M."

Mark lowered his head and closed his eyes. How could he drag himself out of bed that early? And when was he going to have time to continue his investigation? He could feel the muscles in his shoulders tighten again; everything was moving too fast. His mind numbed as Lori continued reading out his schedule.

"Here's a printout of everything." She handed him a piece of paper. "Don't be late."

Mark glanced at it, looking for what was scheduled around noon. He was scheduled for another radio interview at 11 and a television feed from the studio again at 1:30. That would be too tight to make it downtown and back. He didn't see how he was going to make the lunch appointment with Tracy and Jason Reynolds.

"I've already got a lunch meeting scheduled—" Mark tried to explain.

"Cancel it," Lori shot back. "That schedule has been cleared through Mr. Winter himself. You don't want to miss any of the appointments on that piece of paper. I'll be in touch with what we'll have for you on Wednesday some time tomorrow."

Lori headed back into the darkness of the studio. Mark wanted to stop her, but he had no idea what he could say to change the situation.

"Wow, Mark!" Rick laughed as he found him staring off in the direction Lori had walked. "You were awesome."

Mark smiled at the sight of his friend. "Thanks, Rick. I'm not really sure what I said—I just tried to follow my gut."

"More like follow the Lord," Rick returned. "It was great."

"I hope so. You should see the schedule they've got for me." Mark held out the piece of paper.

Rick scanned it. "Man, they're not giving you time to breathe. I can't believe the networks are giving you a chance to air your opinion like this. That's a miracle in itself."

"It's scary!"

"Don't forget the Scripture. God will protect you and strengthen you. It looks like you could use some of that strength right now."

"I know. I'm exhausted. But I need to talk to you about some stuff. Do you think you and Cassie could join me for a cup of coffee?"

"Sure. She'll need a few minutes back at the office though. Where do you want to meet?"

"I've got to pick up my stuff too," Mark said. "How about the Coffee Click?"

"Sounds good. We'll meet you there."

The walk across the lot did little to refresh Mark. It took tremendous effort just to place one foot in front of the other. By the time he made it to the production office, he had walked through a myriad of halfhearted congratulations and "you were great" comments from the staff. He reached his cubicle and collapsed into the chair, thanking God for the opportunity of speaking out but at the same time feeling overwhelmed by all that was happening.

"Nice performance," he heard over his shoulder. He swiveled and opened his eyes to see Frank Russell standing at the entrance to his cubicle.

"Thanks, Frank—I think," Mark responded, not sure what he'd meant by "performance."

"No, really, I thought you did a great job. I'm not sure I agree with your politics," Frank smiled, "but I sure know I liked the number of times I heard *Across the Nation* mentioned."

"Good, because I lost count."

"I also looked at the raw footage of your interview."

Mark raised his eyebrows, wondering what Frank's conclusion would be.

"You were right to be upset. It was one of the worst hatchet jobs I've ever seen. I've had a little talk with Jennifer. It won't happen again on this show."

"Thanks, Frank. I appreciate your taking the time to do that."

"Now for the bad news. I looked over your report."

Mark sat up, anxious for his response.

"I don't see the connection between a heart attack, a car accident, and rigging the results of one gay poll."

Mark's hope evaporated. He sank back into the chair.

"I'm sorry, Mark. I think you're reaching at straws here. If you really think there's something to these two deaths, I think you need to turn this over to the authorities. But the order stands, and not just from me but Winter as well. You're off the story for good."

It was more than Mark could take under the exhaustion. "You're wrong, Frank. This is big. You gave me the speech a few days ago about playing the game until 'the story' came along. Well, for me this is it. I can feel it, and I know that Jas—" Mark stopped himself before mentioning Reynolds's name. He'd nearly forgotten he'd left the list of names off Russell's report. "Just that there's something drastically wrong at ARI. You give me a few more days to dig under some more rocks, and I'll prove it."

Russell looked down at his young reporter, weighing the pros and cons of allowing him to continue. With a hardened look in his eyes, he decided. "It's over, Mark. Drop it. You're already on probation, so don't cross me on this. Enjoy the spotlight while it's shining on you. Very few reporters get this kind of opportunity; I don't think you're fully aware of what strings are being pulled. Don't buck the system!"

Russell left the comment hanging as he turned and walked away.

Mark kicked the cubicle wall, sending a dull thud throughout the office and vibrating his desk. How could he stop now? He was close—he knew it.

"I heard that, Taylor," Russell called out as he walked into his office.

Mark turned back toward his desk and picked up his report. Underneath it lay a manila envelope with his name on the front. There was no return address. In it he found the computer disk and phone records he'd turned over to Peter Lovil. Along with it he spotted the printout of ARI's gay questionnaire and the background information Peter had dug up on the seven names. He glanced around to see if anybody was still watching him; it appeared that everybody was back to their business.

From his briefcase he pulled the questionnaire Mike Palmer had given him at Research International. He placed the two questionnaires side by side on his desk. It didn't surprise him to find that they were identical. He had it right in front of him—two surveys sanctioned by two distinct polling companies, only one of which was owned by Jason Reynolds, yet the questions matched. What were the odds? Within a margin of error of plus or minus 3 percent, he figured zero.

He stuffed the reports and disks back into the envelope and put them in his briefcase. He'd deal with it all later. He didn't have the energy, and besides, he didn't think it would be wise to get caught looking over the material in the office.

He did want to make one last phone call—for personal reasons if for none other. When he needed information, he had a contact in the Los Angeles Police Department—a fellow Marine who had been in his unit during Desert Storm. It didn't take long for Mark to get the name and phone number of the patrolman who had found Kevin Spencer's body—Ben Williams.

"Officer Williams, this is Mark Taylor with the National Network's *Across the Nation*." Mark identified himself once he got the patrolman on the phone.

"I'm not supposed to talk with any reporters. You'll have to talk with my sergeant," Williams answered.

"I'm not calling in any official capacity, Mr. Williams. It's of a personal nature, and I won't quote you on the record. Would that be all right?"

"It depends on what you're asking."

"You were the officer of record in discovering the body of a friend of mine Saturday morning. The one that was burned in the Los Angeles River?"

"Yes, Mr. Taylor. I remember it all too well."

"One of the things I was wondering was what time did the accident occur?" Mark asked.

"Well, I was called to the scene right after my shift started, around 8:30 or so. But the car was just smoldering by that time. It would have had to have happened several hours before."

"But no one reported it before then?"

"No, which now that you mention it, surprised me as well. When I saw the burned-out car, I remember wishing it'd been called in earlier so I wouldn't have had to deal with it."

"Is there an estimate of the time of the accident?"

"From what the firemen figured, the car had probably crashed and burned sometime around 3:30 to 4:00 in the morning."

"But no one saw the accident?"

"Well, that time of morning there's not much traffic in that part of town, and the basin at that point is way below the 134 Freeway on one side and blocked to a neighborhood by a row of trees on the other. Why are you so interested?"

"Well, my friend had been missing since early afternoon. I'm trying to come up with what he could have been doing between then and 4:00 in the morning."

"We guessed he'd been drinking," Williams offered.

"What do you mean?" Mark asked.

"There were several beer cans opened within the vehicle. We assumed the cause of the crash was DUI."

"That doesn't sound like Kevin," Mark offered. "Was there anything to suggest it might not have been an accident?"

"You mean like somebody running him off the road, something like that?"

"Yes," Mark answered excitedly.

"No. There was no sign of any other vehicle being involved. It was as if your friend's car just drove right off the street, down the horse path a few feet before crashing through the fence and into the river basin. It rolled over at least once before catching fire as it crashed to the bottom," Williams responded. "What else would explain the accident, except that he had been drinking?"

Mark tried to visualize how that could happen if Kevin indeed had been sober. "That's what I'm trying to find out, officer. Thanks for your time."

"If I can be of any more help, just give me a call."

CHAPTER 26

Jason Reynolds walked along his private beach, letting the sound of the surf and the breaking waves calm his nerves. The cold evening breeze coming off the ocean and the biting sand pierced through his cluttered thoughts. The best part of Malibu and his private beach was the solitude he could find while living in the midst of seven million people.

He'd seen the updated fax of Taylor's press schedule. Even knowing the calls he'd made and the connections Jared Winter had made, Jason was surprised. Mark Taylor was becoming a household name. *A star is born,* he thought. Reynolds just hoped he'd be able to control this one. He needed to keep the lunch appointment with Taylor, but with the interview schedule their lunch was in jeopardy. It was during times of contemplation like these that he sought solace on his beach.

Then an idea came to him—he could bring Taylor out to the mansion. What better way to impress the rising star than by showing him the rewards of power and wealth? He could chopper him out from the studio, have a wonderful lunch prepared on the gazebo overlooking the Pacific, and still get him back before the

266

next interview. What man could resist his influence when confronted by these lavish surroundings and his power? It was perfect.

Jason laughed at the possibilities. Tomorrow would prove to either be Taylor's crowning moment in his rise to fame, or he'd be forever silenced, quickly forgotten by a fickle public.

HOLLYWOOD
7:15 P.M. PACIFIC

By the time Mark made it to the Coffee Click, Rick and Cassie had already secured a booth in the back where they could talk. Mark sat opposite them.

"You look exhausted, Mark," Cassie observed. "This must be taking its toll on you."

Mark sighed. "I'm not sure I've caught up from the weekend yet—and then to be thrown into this circus, it's unbelievable."

"I thought the media would bury this story," she added. "I can't believe they're giving you all this exposure."

"I know, that's what Rick said earlier. There's something going on, but I can't figure it out."

The waitress arrived, and the three of them ordered. Instead of the coffee they'd planned after the show, they chose sandwiches and fries.

"We haven't had a chance to really talk since your trip," Rick said. "How did your undercover assignment go?"

Mark laughed. "I lived through it, but I don't think I'm cut out to be a spy."

"Any reservations about it?" Rick asked.

"Actually, I had a good time. When it came right down to it, I felt like it was part of God's plan. Did you come up with any thoughts on it?"

Rick laughed. "In between getting engaged this weekend, driving up to Bakersfield to tell Cassie's parents, and coming to your show last night—yes."

Cassie and Mark laughed.

"Well, along with Rahab, who we talked about the other day, there were a few other instances in which people used deception with God's blessing."

"Really?" Cassie and Mark said together. Rick hadn't had a chance to discuss the topic with Cassie either.

"I looked it up late last night. One example was when the Israelites were enslaved in Egypt. The king of Egypt ordered two Hebrew midwives to kill all the male children when they were born and let the female babies live, but they disobeyed him. When called before the king, their excuse was that the Hebrew women were so vigorous that they gave birth before they could get there. Exodus 1:20 says that God was kind to the midwives and their people increased."

Mark smiled. "What else did you find?"

"Jonathan lied to his dad, King Saul, when he was helping David hide, but the one that fits you the best actually came from Jesus himself."

"Jesus?"

"Yeah," Cassie responded as well, "what are you talking about?"

Rick laughed as he pulled out his pocket New Testament. "I wouldn't have believed it myself until I researched it. I found it in John, chapter 7. It came at a time in Jesus' life when his brothers who really didn't believe in him were egging him to go on to Judea to perform his miracles and show himself to the world, as they put it. Jesus said in verse 8, 'You go to the Feast. I am not yet going up to this Feast, because for me the right time has not yet come. Having said this, he stayed in Galilee. However, after his brothers had left for the Feast, he went also, not publicly, but in secret.'"

Cassie and Mark laughed in amazement.

"Jesus went undercover," Cassie said. "I never would have remembered that."

"That's incredible, Rick. Thanks," Mark said.

"So tell us what you found out," Rick said.

Mark filled them in on the events in New York—the list of seven names on Dawkins's computer, the same survey Research International and ARI did for the Gay-Lesbian Alliance, and the strong warning the strange man gave him after the meeting at RI.

"It sounds like you're heading into dangerous territory," Rick warned. "Don't you think it's time to turn this over to somebody like the FBI?"

"I don't know. I've thought about it, but I don't have enough proof yet. I gave all this to Russell, and he wasn't convinced."

"What did he say?" Cassie asked.

"The same thing Rick did: turn it over to the police. Then he ordered me to drop it." Mark shrugged his shoulders. "Threatened to fire me if I didn't."

"What are you going to do?" Rick asked.

"I'm not sure. I'm too tired to make any decisions right now. Besides, with this schedule, how am I going to do anything but interviews for the next two days? There's no time to dig any deeper."

"Maybe that's the way they want it," Cassie said more to herself than to Mark, but he caught the words.

"What do you mean?"

"I'm not sure, the thought just hit me," Cassie explained. "But if Reynolds and the rest of his group are so connected in the media, couldn't they have just as easily had this story killed as opposed to the way it keeps growing?"

Rick and Mark were stunned.

"So you're saying," Rick said, "that this whole media explosion is a diversion so Mark will let the polling story alone?"

"Think about it." Cassie straightened up. "By all logical reasons, the media should be ignoring Mark's outburst, if for no other reason than to hide all this talk about their bias. But they're not. Could Reynolds be driving the publicity?"

Mark scratched his head. "It's been good for his network, but like you said, if there is a conspiracy to manipulate the polls, wouldn't my publicity backfire on them?"

"Unless," Rick observed, "it's all designed to keep you too busy to finish the story, like Cassie said."

"Yes," Cassie agreed. "They're willing to lose a small battle if they still win the war."

Mark shook his head. "I can't believe they would have this much power to set me up like this—"

Mark's cell phone chirped in his pocket. He looked at the caller ID on the display and gave the other two a questioning look.

"I wonder who this is?" Mark said as he punched talk. "Hello."

Mark's eyes widened. "Mark Taylor, this is Jason Reynolds."

"Mr. Reynolds, I'm surprised to hear from you. How did you get this number?"

Rick's and Cassie's expressions matched Mark's as he answered.

"Oh, I have my resources, and please call me Jason," Reynolds said. "Listen, I'll be brief. I know we're scheduled to have lunch tomorrow afternoon, and with your schedule I'm sure it's going to be hard for you to get away from the studio."

"Yes," Mark answered cautiously.

"Well, I don't want to miss our appointment. I've been hearing a lot about you from Tracy. So what I was thinking is having one of my choppers pick you up at the studio and fly you out here to Malibu. We'll have a nice chat and you'll be back in plenty of time to make your afternoon interviews. What do you say?"

Mark didn't know what to say. "I guess that'd be fine."

"Great." Mark could hear the confidence in the man's voice. "Just head over to the roof of the executive office building. My pilot will be there to pick you up at 11:30. I understand you should be done by then."

"I'll be there, and thanks Mr.—uh, Jason."

"You're welcome, Mark. See you tomorrow."

Mark punched off the call and slipped the phone back into his pocket. "Wow!"

"Wow is right!" Cassie echoed. "What did he want?"

"He didn't want us to miss our lunch date tomorrow, so he's sending one of his helicopters over to National to pick me up and fly me out to Malibu to meet him."

Rick whistled. "I guess he's not intimidated by the idea of answering any of your questions."

"No, it would appear not," Mark agreed. "He knew my schedule and my cell phone number. I have a feeling he knows a lot more about me than I do about him."

"So about continuing the investigation," Cassie looked into Mark's eyes, "what are you going to do?"

The question hung over the table as the waitress approached with their meal.

"Right now, I'm going to eat." Mark said with a laugh as his sandwich was set in front of him.

Two eyes watched intently through the long lens of a camera as Mark took the first bite out of his sandwich. The man had followed him out of the studio and parked in the back of the lot where he got a clear shot at the window booth where the three sat.

He took a couple more pictures, making sure he could make out the faces of the couple with Mark. They'd be noted and identified later—for future surveillance if necessary. He set the camera down and reached for a cigarette. *We should have had a bug planted on him by now,* he thought with disgust. *I need to hear what they're saying.*

The three ate their meal, and the conversation drifted away from Jason Reynolds and the investigation.

"So how did the kids take the news?" Mark asked.

Rick chuckled, "Jennifer thinks it's great. Justin didn't like the idea at first, but he's coming around."

"I would think they'd be thrilled to add Cassie to the little family."

"It's a big adjustment," Rick responded. "It took them quite awhile to accept Connie's new husband."

"Kid's really have a rough road—living in two different worlds when there's a divorce," Cassie commented.

Mark agreed. "I know what you mean. My parents separated when I was six-teen. I remember getting the third degree for the first year or so whenever we'd come home from a visit with the other parent: Who was there? Who were they seeing? What was it like? You'd think if they'd cared that much when they were together, maybe they wouldn't have divorced."

"I knew it would be an adjustment for them," Rick offered. "But I had no idea how hard it was until I lived through it. I can see why the Bible says God hates divorce. There's nothing pretty about it."

Mark held up his coffee cup. "Here's to a lifelong marriage grounded in the Lord."

"Amen," Cassie and Rick said together.

Mark felt his eyelids growing heavier as the stress of the day and the thought of getting back to the studio before four gently nudged him. "I need to get home and get some sleep."

"You've got quite a day tomorrow," Cassie said.

"Hey, Mark," Rick said, "I've been thinking—with the schedule you've got, is there a way we could help you look into anything?"

"I'll have to give it some thought," Mark said, rubbing his chin. "I'll let you know, but in the meantime, there is one thing."

"You name it."

Mark reached into this briefcase and pulled out the manila envelope. "Here's a copy of the report I made for Russell, the stuff from ARI, and the research from my computer expert that Russell didn't see. Please hold onto it for me and look it over. Let me know if you have any ideas of what the next step should be."

Rick took the file. Neither of them noticed the man in the black sedan snapping pictures of the exchange.

"Besides," Mark continued, "if Reynolds knows all about me, including my cell phone number, I wouldn't put it past him to search my house, and I don't want to lose this stuff."

MALIBU
7:45 P.M. PACIFIC

In the warmth of his mansion, Jason smiled over the plan he'd concocted for Taylor and reveled in the success of the India media hype. President McNeil had done a masterful job linking the possible crisis between India and Pakistan with the appropriations bill needed to fund a stronger, more militarily prepared UN.

He sipped his martini while his thoughts churned trying to decide how to handle Mark if he refused to cooperate. He was sure the surveillance would turn up any problems if Mark had talked too much, but the one thing he'd need in his possession would be the phone records and the computer disk. He had to get his hands on those before he could act. But how?

His thoughts were interrupted as Griff walked into the room and dropped seven faxed pages on the coffee table in front of him.

"What's this?" Jason asked, looking at the top page's heading: "To Frank Russell, from Mark Taylor. An update on the abuse of the political polling process, ARI, and other companies."

"Luis wanted to make sure you had it—everything Taylor knows up to this point."

"From the studio?"

"Yes," Griff replied flatly.

"Good, this will give me some idea of how to handle him tomorrow. Does it identify who's doing the computer searches for him?"

Griff shook his head. "No, but I think we know who it is. The message left on his machine from Peter the other day..."

Jason looked up.

"There's a Peter Lovil working with another reporter on some Internet story. Luis thinks it's the same computer expert that Mark is using as well."

"When will we know for sure?"

Griff looked at his watch. "I'd say within the next hour. Luis is on his way there now. It's the only lead we have. He's a good hacker. We couldn't trace anything."

"Let's hope he's the guy. And Mr. Taylor..."

"...is having a quiet dinner at a coffee shop with a couple from the studio. We're not sure who they are yet. We'll have IDs sometime tomorrow."

"Do we have audio?"

"No, just visual surveillance. We haven't got a bug on him. We thought the apartment surveillance would tell us everything we needed to know."

"Well, obviously it hasn't yet, has it?" Jason was irritated.

"No, sir."

"Get me something I can give him tomorrow that's bugged—a watch or a pen, some kind of gift that he'd keep with him. I don't want a word coming out of his mouth that we aren't recording. For all we know, he could be spilling everything right now, and we wouldn't know it."

"I've got just the thing."

"Good." Jason sounded pleased for the first time. "I want this leak plugged."

Griff waited in silence.

"Leave me now," Jason ordered. "I want to call my granddaughter."

After Griff left the room, Jason dialed Tracy's number.

"Hello."

"Hi, Trace, it's me."

"Hi, Papa."

"I wanted to talk to you about the lunch tomorrow."

"You're not canceling, are you?"

Jason explained his plan for bringing Mark to the mansion instead of meeting downtown.

"That'd be great. Can the helicopter come downtown and pick me up first? That way I'd avoid all the traffic and get to spend a little extra time with him."

"Sure, honey." Jason grimaced. Tracy was getting too close to Mark. "If that's what you want."

"It'll be fun. I haven't been up in a long time. Is Ray flying?"

"No, he's on another assignment with Chopper 1," Reynolds lied. He had two helicopters, but kept only one full-time pilot. He could fly himself whenever he wanted to, and Luis had his helicopter's license from his days in the CIA. "Luis will be flying you, the man you bumped into out here at the house this weekend."

Tracy didn't like the sound of that. Something about that man bothered her.

GLENDALE
8:14 P.M. PACIFIC

Luis squinted as he tried to read the numbers on the houses while driving down the street. He was close, but not every house was identified. There it was, 1241 Sonora Avenue, the white duplex to his right. He pulled over and parked along the sidewalk just past the house.

Walking up to the front entrance, he noticed several lights were on inside. He hoped this was the right address as he touched the doorbell.

Peter Lovil opened the door. "What can I do for you?" he asked with irritation.

Luis smiled pleasantly, flashing a fake badge. "FBI. Special agent Brad Johnson. I need to speak with you."

Luis pushed the door all the way open, stepping into the house and brushing Peter aside.

"Hey," Peter protested. "You can't barge in here—"

He caught the look in Luis's eyes as he stopped in mid-sentence. A knot formed in his stomach. This was not someone to mess with.

"Look, Lovil," Luis said as he casually let his sports coat open enough to reveal the holstered gun under his left shoulder, "we can do this the easy way, here, just the two of us. Or we can take a ride downtown and waste several hours of both our lives until you tell me what I want to know."

Peter didn't like the threat. "What are you looking for?" he asked as he followed him down the hallway.

"Just some information, that's all," Luis said as he spotted the bedroom where Peter kept all of his computer equipment. He stepped into the room, catching an eyeful of Samantha's Internet site on the glowing monitor. He turned and stared Peter down. "Tell me what you know about hacking into Reynolds Industries's computer systems?"

Peter's expression gave himself away. "I don't know what you're talking about."

"Look, pal, I can keep this unofficial—you know, just between you and me— no reason for a nice kid like you to have to deal with a felony, if you catch my drift. Or I can take you into custody, confiscate all of this lovely hardware you got here, and we'll spend the next few days digging through it all. Either way, I'll get what I want."

How could they have traced me? Peter thought. They couldn't have. He's bluffing. They could tear apart his computer chip by chip and they wouldn't find anything. Unless, Mark told somebody at the office about him? Even so, if he kept his mouth shut, they couldn't prove anything.

"You can do it however you want." Peter feigned bravery. "I still don't know what you're talking about."

Luis lost his patience. "Look here, you little pencil-necked geek," he spit out as he loomed over Peter. It really didn't matter whether he cooperated or not. The moment his eyes widened in fear when Luis mentioned Reynolds Industries, Peter's fate was sealed. The only thing Luis needed to know was if anybody else had the information he'd supplied to Mark.

Peter cowered in fear as Luis reached into his coat and pulled the gun out from under his coat. "You've got about three seconds to start talking."

BURBANK
9:07 P.M. PACIFIC

Mark walked into his apartment and went straight into the bedroom. If he was lucky he could get five hours' sleep. But one thing he wanted to do first. He picked up the phone and dialed from memory.

"Hello," Tracy answered.

The sound of her voice somehow lessened his exhaustion.

"Hi, Tracy, it's Mark."

"Mark." He noticed the excitement in her voice. "How did the show go?"

"I think it went really well. It's hard to judge when you're actually doing it."

"I can't wait to see it. Are you gonna watch it?"

"No, I'm going straight to bed. I have to be back at the studio before 4:00."

"In the morning?"

"Yeah. The price of stardom. I wanted to make sure you knew about the change in plans tomorrow."

"You mean having lunch at the house?"

"Would that be in Malibu?" Mark asked.

"Yeah, it is." Tracy answered.

"Then you talked with your grandfather."

"Yes, he called me a little while ago."

"Are you still going to be there?"

"I'm planning to," Tracy said. "I've got to make sure I can clear an early afternoon appointment."

"I hope you can make it. I'm not sure I can handle your grandfather without you."

"I don't think I'll be much help. I've never seen anybody handle my grandfather."

Mark smiled; he liked her style. "He may have met his match. Well, I've got to get some sleep. Hopefully, I'll see you tomorrow."

"I'll try. Bye Mark."

"Good night."

After hanging up, he stepped into the bathroom and prepared for bed— oblivious to the surveillance equipment throughout his apartment.

The man in the white van, although sitting in a different spot in the parking lot, continued his mission of tracking everything Mark did. All calls coming in had been logged and recorded—as was this call to Tracy.

Mark set the timer on his VCR to record his appearance on *The John Harold Show*.

He lay down in bed and picked up his Bible. It was his nightly ritual to end each day with Scripture, even if only a few verses as he felt tonight was going to be. He flipped it open to the bookmark,. Matthew chapter 10.

He tried to concentrate on the words before him, but thoughts kept filling his mind about Dawkins and Kevin. Were they really murdered? What did that say about his investigation? Was he in trouble? Reynolds obviously knew a lot about him. What was he going to say to him tomorrow?

The emotion started like a ripple, vibrating through him so subtly that he couldn't identify it. But as his mind continued to wander while his eyes went through the motion of moving over the words, the ripple became a swell, the swell a wave, until there was no question of what was gripping him—fear.

Mark rubbed his eyes as he took a deep breath. He'd faced danger before— countless times as a Marine. He'd brought back a downed pilot behind the Iraqi border. The team's pilot had been wounded, which left Mark behind the controls of the chopper as the emergency pilot. He had to live with the nickname "Rocky" for the rest of his tour, to commemorate the rough landing when the team finally reached its base in Kuwait, but everyone had survived.

The fear binding him now was different, more intense than anything he'd felt before. He thought back to the Scripture Rick had given him before the trip: the Lord would strengthen and protect him from the evil one. Maybe that was part of it: he wasn't dealing with just a human enemy, but the evil one as well.

Mark prayed, quoting the verse out loud as he fought to quench the rising fear within him.

The van outside his apartment rocked as the man inside sat up startled. He couldn't figure out who Mark was talking to. He quickly scanned all the video feeds from the apartment. Nobody else was there. *This guy must be loony,* he thought.

Mark felt the tension ease. He let his gaze return to the Scripture before him, set- tling on verses 26–28.

> *So do not be afraid of them. There is nothing concealed that will not be disclosed, or hidden that will not be made known. What I tell you in the dark, speak in the daylight; what is whispered in your ear, proclaim from the roofs. Do not be afraid of those who kill the body but cannot kill the soul. Rather, be afraid of the One who can destroy both soul and body in hell.*

"So they kill me, then what else can they do?" Mark chuckled to no one in the room. He reread the verses—this time out loud as a proclamation of his newly found assurance of faith. What is concealed will be disclosed—speak in the daylight—proclaim from the roofs—do not be afraid of those who kill the body but cannot kill the soul. Mark's voice rose in strength and confidence as he read through the passage.

The man in the van shook his head, chuckling as he scribbled another note on the clipboard.

CHAPTER 27

TUESDAY, FEBRUARY 13TH
BURBANK
3:20 A.M. PACIFIC

Mark opened his eyes and tried to focus on the clock radio blaring at him from his headboard. He couldn't remember how many times he'd pressed the snooze button—obviously too many times. He needed fifteen minutes to get into Hollywood, which left him only ten minutes to get showered, dressed, and out of the apartment.

He groaned as he willed his legs out from under the covers and onto the carpeted floor. So much for the glamour of stardom. What show was he on first this morning? He couldn't remember.

Mark stumbled into the bathroom, unconsciously hitting the light switch as he entered. Outside in the parking lot, the man in the white van continued snoring as the monitor in front of him came to life.

Forty minutes later, Mark took his place on the set of *Across the Nation*. A minimal crew had been called in to man the camera, bring the lights up, put a microphone on him, and put the image up on the satellite. The stage manager rushed him to the stool in the middle of the room.

"Mark, this is New York. Can you hear us?" a voice asked through the small earpiece he'd been given.

"Yes, I can hear you."

"Good. We're coming out of commercial in twenty seconds. Katie will go right into your intro, then we're off and running." The associate director from New York gave the warning.

Mark could hear Katie Couric take her cue out of the commercial. She quickly brought the viewers up to speed on Mark's allegation that the media was biased. Mark focused his attention toward the lens of the camera in front of him, smiling as he tried to shake out the last remaining cobwebs from the lack of sleep.

The interview closely matched those he'd done on the radio the day before. Mark held his own, keeping his voice calm.

"We report the facts as we see them," Katie countered. "Are you saying there's a conspiracy to mislead the American people, Mark?"

Mark chuckled. "I never used the word *conspiracy*, Katie. Like I said on *Across the Nation,* I believe sometimes it's just reporters following their own ideology—not even consciously aware of the misinformation they're serving the public. Look at the difference in the way the mainstream media treated the Juanita Broaddrick story as compared to Anita Hill. Where were the headlines—the feminist outrage for what was allegedly done to Juanita? Here's a woman who charged a sitting president with rape, but not much was heard about it or seen in print, while Ms. Hill's charges of verbal sexual harassment toward Clarence Thomas, a nominated Supreme Court justice, were the lead story on every broadcast, the banner headline of every newspaper, proclaiming that when a woman bravely steps forward, she needs to be heard. Ms. Broaddrick wasn't heard—she was ignored."

"But you must—"

"Then there's the partial-birth abortion controversy," Mark cut in. "The three networks spent years advocating the pro-choice position even when their arguments were false. At first, it was reported that the procedure didn't even exist, then they tried to claim the fetus was already dead from the mother's anesthesia. Finally they argued that the procedure was 'rare,' or 'done only in extreme cases of birth defects'—all the while ignoring every one of the pro-life arguments.

"It took the admission of Ron Fitzsimmons of the National Coalition of Abortion Providers to finally bring some truth to the debate that it wasn't rare. Thousands were performed each year, many when baby and mother were totally healthy. Unfortunately, it was too late in the debate to stop a presidential veto from killing the bill. But even after the admission, several network anchors continue to use the term 'rare' when discussing the topic. A lot of them won't even use the term 'partial-birth abortion.' They refer to it as 'a particular kind of late-term abortion' or qualify it as something 'opponents call partial-birth abortion.' I'm not sure I'd call it a conspiracy, but there's ample evidence of ideology filtering the information the public is getting."

Katie looked into her camera. "That's very interesting, Mark. Thanks for being with us. In the next hour we'll have—"

Mark continued to smile toward the camera, relieved that this one was over. In his ear he heard the New York voice thank him for being on the show and that he was clear. Mark started to take the earpiece out, but the stage manager stopped him. The studio was setting up the audio for the next show in line.

NATIONAL STUDIOS
9:45 A.M. PACIFIC

Samantha walked into the office, feeling as if she were already behind, and the day had just begun. There was much to do before she could complete her story on the Internet site, not the least of which was deciding what her story would be. Vanessa's words were like fingernails screeching down a chalkboard. Every time she accessed her Internet site to check on the surveys, she kept hearing Vanessa's words about the victims—the young boys, the married men, or the women caught up in the pornography business.

She stopped at Mark's cubicle to see how his media blitz was going. She'd caught him on one of the network morning shows and wanted to ask him a question.

He was leaning on his desk. His head lying on top of his arms covered a section of the *Los Angeles Times*. She could see the heading of the article he'd been reading.

Polls Show Nation Alarmed Over Possible Pakistan Aggression
Against India; Broad Support Behind President McNeil's Call for
UN Action

"Mark?"

No response. He was out cold.

Samantha shook her head with a grin, then turned and walked toward her cubicle.

"Jeff, come help me for a minute," she called to her producer as she passed his desk.

She plopped down in her chair, setting the updated report on her desk from the Internet survey.

"Is that the latest version?" Jeff asked.

"Yep. We're had over a hundred thousand hits now with five thousand responses to the survey."

"Wow! I didn't expect that many."

"Neither did I," Samantha confessed. A week ago, she would have been proud of the fact, but all she could feel now was a dull numbness. "I'm amazed at these responses."

"What do you mean?"

"Look at the age range, over half admit to being under eighteen."

"So what's the big deal?"

Samantha cocked her head at him. "I don't know—it just bothers me. What time was Peter meeting us here?"

"I think he said he'd be here by ten."

"I hope he's not late. There are some notations at the end of this report I want to go over with him."

Jeff quietly made his exit as she pored over the details. Samantha's agitation was growing. Jeff knew her well enough to keep his distance.

NATIONAL STUDIOS
11:42 A.M. PACIFIC

"I really think he's got a solid case here," Rick commented. After the morning production meeting, he and Cassie had secluded themselves in her office to examine the details of Mark's investigation.

Cassie looked up from her copy of the homosexual poll. "With these kinds of results, it's no wonder we're losing the cultural war."

"You know, when you think about it, why is it we rarely see the questions in the survey when the results are reported?" Rick got up from the couch and walked over to Cassie's desk, putting the questionnaire back with the rest of Mark's material.

"Maybe it's a topic for our show to consider?" Cassie asked.

"I think we're lucky we got John to have Mark on last night. I don't think we'll see him wanting to challenge the system any more than we already have, do you?"

"I'm not so sure," Cassie said. "I think John was intrigued by what Mark said."

"I hope so. I've been praying for him ever since I took over this show."

"Me too. But how can we help Mark? If he's right and two people have been murdered to protect this group . . . he could be in danger himself."

"I know. I'm amazed at what his computer expert was able to compile on the seven names." Rick looked down at Mark's notes and whistled. "Talk about some heavy hitters—all the way to the White House. The first thing we need to do is pray. After that we'll just have to follow where God may lead us."

"Then pray it is," Cassie agreed as she stood up next to him.

Rick took Cassie's hands in his. "Lord, we come to you . . ."

"Are there any messages for me?" Samantha asked the receptionist as she passed her desk.

"I've sent all your calls through to your extension, Samantha. Have you tried your voice mail?"

"Yes, there's nothing there," Samantha responded coldly, heading back to her cubicle.

"Jeff," she yelled as she walked down the aisle, "where is Peter?" "I've tried calling him. There's no message. He was supposed to be here an hour ago."

"I know. I don't know what's happened to him. I've paged him three times myself," Jeff said.

"I've got to get this story finished for Wednesday's show."

"Take it easy, Sam," Jeff consoled. "What's eating at you anyway?"

Samantha looked up at him, a hard edge to her eyes. "I'm just mad that I'm stuck without his help. The report he designed is too confusing. Where is he?"

"Maybe if we went through the surveys together—"

"No!" Samantha snapped. "I need Peter. Find him for me." Then, grabbing her purse and pushing past Jeff, she called over her shoulder, "I'll be on my cell phone when you do."

Jeff watched her fume out of the office as did the rest of the staff. When the door slammed behind her, all eyes turned to Jeff, who just shrugged and walked back to this cubicle.

Bright sunlight hit Mark as he stepped onto the roof of the executive building. The sleek black helicopter with Reynolds Industries painted in gold letters on the side sat on the landing pad, rotors spinning. The back door was open, and he was elated to see Tracy standing next to it.

"Welcome aboard Reynolds' Chopper 2." Tracy yelled at him.

Mark embraced her, "I'm glad you could make it, Tracy."

"Me too. Jump in."

They sat in the backseat, buckled their seat belts, and put on headsets that would allow them to communicate over the engine noise in flight.

"This is Luis, my grandfather's chief of security and our pilot. Luis, this is Mark." Tracy introduced them as the whine of the turbine increased.

"Nice to meet you, Luis," Mark offered as he wondered why their pilot would need to be from Reynold's security force.

Luis responded with a wave. In seconds, he had the helicopter up to full power and slowly lifted the skids off the pad. The craft rotated until it faced northwest, then he tilted it forward and accelerated over the studio.

This was the first time Mark had flown in a civilian helicopter. He looked out the window, taking in the view of his stage from the air, then turned to Tracy who was smiling at him. He reached out and took her hand.

"Thanks again for setting this up," he said. "How long will it take to get there?"

"About fifteen minutes." Mark was surprised when Luis answered over the headset from the front. He'd forgotten they weren't alone.

"How's your day been?" Tracy asked.

"One interview after another. It's not even noon, and I'm exhausted," Mark replied, resting his head against the back of the seat.

"Well, sit back and relax. It's a wonderful ride. Wait until we get over Malibu. It's breathtaking."

She was right. Luis brought the chopper up the coastline, flying low over the water before making a dramatic sweep up and over the cliff where Reynolds's mansion rested. The view was unbelievable. The magnificent architecture of the huge estate surrounded by the natural beauty of the ocean and surf of the Malibu coastline brought an involuntary gasp from Mark. Tracy watched his reaction, smiling.

Luis slowed the chopper, hovering for a brief moment over the main helipad before gently touching down. Coming out the front door of the mansion to meet them was Jason Reynolds himself.

Tracy opened her door on the right side of the helicopter as Mark unbuckled and followed her. Tracy hugged her grandfather before turning toward Mark and making the introductions over the noise of the turbine winding down.

"It's a pleasure meeting you, Mark," Jason said with an outstretched hand. He towered over Mark by a good four to five inches, leaving Mark feeling a bit over-powered by the man's presence.

Mark shook the hand firmly. "Nice to meet you, sir. This is quite a place you have here."

"Thank you," Jason replied. "Please come inside. I know you have a schedule to keep."

GLENDALE
12:04 P.M. PACIFIC

Samantha looked at Peter's business card then back up to the numbers on the buildings as she drove down Sonora Avenue. She needed Peter's help to make sense of the survey results. Her only hope was to catch him at home. Maybe his phone was out of order.

She knew she was getting close as she passed the 1000 block. Ahead she noticed a couple of Glendale police cars blocking the right lane with lights flashing. She eased into the left lane and passed the cars slowly, catching a glimpse of the yellow police tape noting the location of a crime scene. As her eyes scanned the area, she realized that 1241 was Peter's address. This was his duplex. She pulled her car to the curb and rushed to the front door, having to duck the tape as she did.

"I'm sorry, ma'am, you can't come in here." An officer stopped her.

Over his shoulder, Samantha was stunned at what she saw. The room was a mess. Somebody had demolished Peter's expensive computer equipment. Glass, broken components, and cables lay all over the desk and room. Her eyes caught site of a white sheet that appeared to be covering a body.

"What happened officer?" she asked, afraid of the answer.

"Homicide," he replied flatly. "The occupant was shot, sometime last night."

Samantha's knees buckled, her hands covering her mouth, "Oh, God, no."

A woman detective stepped away from the desk and walked over to Samantha. "Excuse me, ma'am. I'm detective Shelly Morris. Did you know this man?"

"I think so. Peter Lovil?"

"It appears so," the detective answered.

"Is he dead?" Samantha asked even though she knew the answer.

"Yes, ma'am. How do you know Mr. Lovil?"

Samantha shuddered, the shock settling deep down within her. "He was help-ing me with a story I'm doing. He's my computer expert."

"And you would be?"

"Samantha Steel with National Studios."

"Oh yes, I thought I recognized you," the detective responded flatly. "Would you mind taking a look at him? We need to make a positive I.D."

Samantha took in a deep breath and lowered her head as she prepared herself. She stepped over to the corner of the room with the detective. Morris crouched down beside the body and gently lifted the sheet up.

It was Peter. His lifeless eyes stared straight at her, his face frozen in that last moment of terror. She dropped her head, only nodding recognition as she started to weep.

NATIONAL STUDIOS
12:15 P.M. PACIFIC

"I've got an idea," Rick exclaimed as he returned to Cassie's desk. The two had spent the last half-hour alternating between praying about Mark's dilemma and dealing with issues about the upcoming show.

"What?" Cassie wanted to know.

Rick searched through the report Mark had printed for Russell. "Here it is. Chicago."

"What about Chicago?"

"While we were praying, the thought struck me to look where Dawkins was supposed to have been the night he died. His wife thought he'd gone to Chicago." Rick looked down at the paper in his hand. "The Drake Hotel."

"That's right. But she said he was found the next morning in his office, in New York."

"Yeah, I know," Rick muttered as he dropped the papers. "But there's something about Chicago. You'd think a wife would have some idea when her husband was going to be traveling. It doesn't make sense to me that he could just die in his office working late. Was his wife right, that he was supposed to have gone to Chicago but never made it?"

"Or what if he did go," Cassie responded excitedly, "but came back that same night?"

Rick laughed. "Now that's an interesting theory. We need to find out if Dawkins ever checked in that day."

"Plus check the airlines, for Dawkins and maybe the other names on that list. I wonder where Mr. Reynolds was that day?"

Rick's eyebrows went up as he nodded. "That's a good question. I think I know just the guy to handle this for us. A good friend from my UCLA days, Tim Green. He's a producer at the PBS station in Chicago. He'd—"

Cassie's phone interrupted him. She picked it up and listened for a moment.

"Yeah, right away.

"It's the stage. They need you—something about where the backup singers are supposed to be placed."

"OK, I'll head over there and call Tim from the booth."

"Sounds like a good idea to me," Cassie said. "Maybe he'll come up with something to help Mark."

"In the meantime, we'd better keep praying." Rick headed for the door. "Mark should be having lunch with Reynolds right about now."

MALIBU
12:21 P.M. PACIFIC

A buffet that would rival the Sunday brunch at the Beverly Hills Hilton was waiting by the pool for Mark and Tracy when they made their way back to the house.

"This is very impressive," Mark whispered to Tracy as he handed her a plate.

"He's pulling out all the stops for you."

"That doesn't mean I'm going to go easy on the questions." Mark belied his nervousness with a twisted grin as he plucked a couple of shrimp off the serving table.

"He wouldn't have it any other way," Tracy replied.

After choosing from an array of salads, appetizers, hot dishes, and pastries, the two made their way to a table in the gazebo, overlooking the spectacular Malibu coastline.

"You know, I could get used to living out here," Mark said as he took his seat.

"It's a view I never grow weary of," Jason Reynolds remarked from behind Mark as he joined them at the table.

"Aren't you eating, Papa?" Tracy asked.

"Sure, I was just letting you two go first. Please go ahead and eat. Phillip," he called to one of the men gathered around the table. "Bring me a plate of whatever you think is best."

Phillip dutifully complied while Jason turned to Mark.

"How are you handling . . ." Jason paused searching for the right words, ". . . your celebrity status?"

Mark laughed, "It's a challenge." He studied Jason's face as he continued. "I'm frankly surprised that I'm being allowed the airtime."

"Ah," Jason smiled, "but it's probably going to give you the biggest rating that *Across the Nation* has ever had—maybe even the largest audience the National Studios has ever seen. You can't buy that kind of publicity."

But you can manipulate it, Mark thought. "Don't you mean *your* network can't buy that kind of publicity?"

Jason paused, looking intently at Mark as he contemplated his response. Phillip reached in and set a plate of food in front of him. Finally, Reynolds nodded. "Yes, my network."

Tracy stared at her grandfather—her mouth open in shock. She would never have believed Mark had been right about the companies he owned. Jason smiled reassuringly at her. "This friend of yours must be pretty good at what he does to have dug that up."

Mark was shocked at the admission. "I'm most amazed at the attention the big three networks are giving this—"

"You're thinking that they'd want to ignore any mention of media bias?" Jason interrupted.

"Exactly. I can't believe they're giving me this platform."

"Then you really do believe in what you're saying?" Jason asked pointedly.

"Of course I do." Mark was taken aback. "Do you think this is all some publicity stunt on my part?"

"No, I'm sure that it is not." Jason smiled. "If it had been, we could have planned ahead and had everything lined up to make an even bigger splash."

Mark shook his head, comparing Tracy's quiet tension to her grandfather's smugness. "This is all just a game to you, isn't it?"

Jason laughed good-heartedly, attempting to diffuse the rising irritation he sensed in Mark.

"Not at all. Yes, I'll admit the network is grabbing every bit of publicity that we can. Why wouldn't we? But it's created a dialogue within the media that I frankly think needs to be addressed, thanks to you." Jason punctuated his words with a warm smile. "And it certainly isn't hurting your career, is it?"

"That remains to be seen," Mark responded quietly. He was confused. Reynolds wasn't reacting at all as he'd expected.

"Look at it this way, Mark," Tracy said, reaching over and touching his arm. "You're passionate about what you feel, and now with all this publicity, you've been given the chance to get your message across to millions of people."

Mark looked into her eyes. The compassion he saw touched him as Tracy continued, "I know what you've said has certainly impacted me."

"There's no question you're touching people," Jason said. "It doesn't matter how or why this happened, Mark. Jump on the bandwagon and ride it for all it's worth. You can make a difference. Get your message heard, and make a name for yourself all at the same time."

Mark rubbed his eyes, not sure how to respond. "You're assuming that people will want to listen to what I have to say," he finally responded.

"We can make them listen, Mark—that's the beauty of it," Jason said. "Do you think this national fever over the crisis in India just sprang out of nowhere this weekend?"

"No." Mark wondered where Reynolds was going with his question. "The hostility between the Hindus and the Muslims goes back centuries, but the drought and the massive earthquake that struck India have everybody worried about Pakistan aggression."

"But you're missing the point," Jason explained. "The drought's been going on for years, and the earthquake was weeks ago. Why all the attention now—every network doing in-depth coverage of Pakistan and India over the weekend, even your own show? It's because the press decided it was time to make it an issue. The politicians don't set the national agenda; the media does. We decide what issues the American people need to be concerned about."

As Mark contemplated Reynolds's words, he thought back to a journalism professor in college who had made nearly the same statement. At the time, Mark thought he was just exaggerating to make a point with the students. Now he wasn't so sure.

"Use the power of the media for yourself, Mark," Jason continued. "You're in a perfect position to do it. I'll back you 100 percent."

Mark glanced over Reynolds's shoulder and out into the beautiful Pacific Ocean, unsure of how to respond. It was getting late. He would have to fly back to the studio. The three ate in silence for a few moments.

"Mr. Reynolds," Mark spoke, "I have some questions I wanted to ask you."

"Go right ahead, and please call me Jason."

"All right, Jason," Mark agreed. He glanced at Tracy, wondering how she'd react to the questions he wanted to put to her grandfather. "In researching the story I'm doing on the influence the polling process is having on our country, I came across some information that surprised me."

"Such as?" Jason asked calmly.

"How is it that out of ten research companies I looked into, you either own or are connected in some way to eight of them? ARI, Nationwide Polling, Chicago

Institute of Research, North American Statistical Analysis, The Billings Institute—"

Jason stopped him with a wave of his hand and a flash of his million-dollar smile. "So you're the one who's been snooping around our computers. I guess that's how you dug up my connection to National."

Mark waited, keeping his expression neutral.

"Yes," Jason confessed, "I won't deny that those companies are mine as well."

"Then why do you hide it so deliberately?"

Jason thought for a moment. "For the precise reason that you are here with me now. It raises questions that are running through your mind at this moment—conflict of interest, monopoly, manipulation—am I right?"

Mark grinned. "The thoughts have crossed my mind."

Tracy's head moved back and forth between the two men as if watching a tennis match.

"Nothing as sinister as that, Mark, I assure you." Jason said warmly. "The collecting, recording, and dissemination of information are a passion for me. It started as far back as I can remember, reading newspapers and magazines—listening to the news broadcasts on the radio before the first television signals ever made it into somebody's home."

Mark reached for a sip of water, listening intently.

"Even during my high school days, instead of running for class president, I was going around surveying the kids, making predictions of who was going to win and by what margin. And I was right. I learned back then, knowledge is power.

"So when my father passed away—I was only twenty-five at the time—I sold off his coal-mining fortune to acquire radio and television stations and newspapers; then I began building from the ground up the finest polling companies in the nation. ARI was my first, and the only one I kept my name on as part of Reynolds Industries."

Mark nodded, then asked, "You don't think the public has a right to know that you own what amounts to a monopoly on the public opinion firms in this nation?"

Reynolds chuckled. "It's hardly a monopoly. There are thousands of polling companies—more springing up every day."

"But you control eight of the top ten, and from what I can gather by my research, you are in some way connected to Richard Adler, who owns the other two—"

"You've done a good job of investigating so far, Mark, but don't let your imagination lead you to erroneous conclusions. Richard is an acquaintance of mine, but to suggest there is some kind of collusion going on between us is preposterous."

"Think about it from my perspective for a moment," Mark argued. "Here are two media moguls, owning numerous media outlets covering radio, newspaper, and television. You just highlighted for me the great power of the media that's at your fingertips, and yet these same two people also own or have controlling interest in the top polling companies in the United States. You can't tell me there isn't ample opportunity to use those resources and that power to manipulate this nation."

"Something like what *Pravda* was to Russia?" Jason laughed. "It would be impossible here, Mark. We still have a free press, with thousands of outlets—television, radio, the print media, why, even the Internet. No one person or two people can control that. I've had these companies for over forty years—working through Democratic and Republican administrations, being in competition with ABC, CBS, NBC, now CNN, and all the other cable upstarts. I strive for excellence in the companies I own, especially when it comes to measuring public opinion. You don't think I control some of the top companies because of a lack of accuracy, do you?"

Mark didn't have an answer for him.

"Of course not. It's because of that accuracy that we are the most sought after. I knew long before Bill Clinton ever showed his face in Washington, the power of knowing the American people's opinion. We're not in the business of propaganda. We're in the business of scientific analysis, recognizing social movement, accumulating knowledge—that's what it's all about. Knowledge is everything."

Mark looked at his watch—after one o'clock. He needed to head back to the studio for the 1:30 interview. There was so much more he wanted to address with Reynolds, but there wasn't time.

Jason noticed the glance. "Yes, we need to be getting you back, don't we? I hope I've answered some of your questions. We're not adversaries, Mark. I want you to succeed. The potential is there for you to have a huge influence on the nation Wednesday night. You have the country's stage—it's a powerful platform. Think of the impact you can make on the issues you have a deep passion for—the bias of the press, the abortion debate. Take the spotlight and run with it all you can."

"You're not going to try and stop me?" Mark asked.

"My heavens no. I'm not about any particular social agenda; I'm just zealous about the process. What you're advocating is good medicine for the media. I think we need to hear it. I would ask though, as a personal favor, that you not report anything about my . . . diverse holdings, shall we say."

Mark thought carefully before responding. "I promise I'll speak with you before I say anything on the air about it."

"Agreed," Jason said, reaching into his pocket and pulling out a small box. "Here, I want you to have this."

Mark took the package. "What is it?"

"Just a small token of my appreciation," Jason answered. "Open it, please."

Mark opened the box. The sunlight reflected off the gold of a beautiful Rolex watch. He was speechless. It was such an elaborate gift, so unexpected.

Mark looked up to Jason, "I don't think I can accept this—"

"Oh, nonsense. As an executive I don't think we appreciate the really talented people who make the network operate," Jason explained. "It's just something that will let you know how much I appreciate your contribution to *Across the Nation*. Think of it as a late Christmas bonus."

"I'm not sure what to say," Mark said as he tried to think of a way he could refuse the gift without offending him.

Jason stood. "You don't have to say anything, but it'll help you realize you need to get back to the studio. It's been a pleasure, Mark. I think we need to get together again in the near future and continue this discussion. I'll be interested to see how Wednesday night goes."

Mark accepted the handshake. "Thank you, Jason. You've been most gracious. I'll definitely want to take you up on that offer to discuss this further."

Jason turned toward his granddaughter. "Are you staying a bit longer, or heading back to the office?"

"I think I'll head back with Mark," Tracy responded. "I'll have to say though, having lunch with you two is certainly an event."

The three laughed as Jason led them to the waiting helicopter.

CHAPTER 28

CHICAGO
3:13 P.M. CENTRAL

Near the crowded northern border of the city limits nearly within the boundaries of Lincolnwood, WTTW, Chicago's PBS station, stood out among the rows of apartments and small homes making up the neighborhood. The glass and brick building was covered in snow, and the wind howled through the streets as another February storm raged.

Tim Green walked through the studio, protected from the bitter cold outside but not from the headaches a heavy winter storm brought to his schedule. The stage was ready, the lights were set, the crew was waiting in the cafeteria. For that he was grateful. The staffers had all been called in at seven that morning, before the snowfall had covered the city like a blanket.

The problem was he couldn't get the musicians to the studio. They were stuck at the hotel, ten miles away. And even if he could get them out here, he would still be without an audience, not a good thing for a performance in the round by John Tesh.

He stepped into the hallway, trying to come to terms with the obvious decision before him: cancel the show or at least delay it if he could move everything to tomorrow night.

292

"Tim Green, call the operator," he heard come through the speakers in the false ceiling. He continued to the end of the hallway, up the circular stairway, and into his office on the second floor. He slumped into his chair, picked up the phone, and called the reception desk.

"Green here."

"Tim, you have a call from Los Angeles. I'll put it through."

He tensed. It was probably the callback he'd been waiting for from Tesh's management.

"Tim, you old dog, how are things in Chicago?" The familiar voice on the other end brought a smile to a face that needed one.

"Other than being snowed in by the worst blizzard of the year, having John Tesh and his band stranded downtown with no chance of an audience showing up for our concert in the round series, I'd say life couldn't be better," Tim laughed. "Tell me how sunny and warm it is in LA, Rick, and I'll reach out over this phone line and strangle you."

Rick Treadway burst out laughing. "OK, I won't tell you it's seventy-five degrees out here. But you were the one who didn't want to make a go of it here in lovely California. No, not Tim Green. Chicago was the city. You just had to go back."

"I'll take my winters here any day compared to your smog, mud slides, brush fires—oh, and did I mention earthquakes?"

"Touché, old friend," Rick responded. "I'm sorry to hear about your concert. What are you going to do?"

"I don't think I have a choice but to cancel or at least try and move it to tomorrow. I'm waiting for a callback from Tesh's management to see if he can stay over an extra night."

"I hope it'll work out for you. Do you need to go?"

"No, there's nothing I can do until that call comes in anyway." Tim settled into his chair and propped his feet up on the desk. "What's up?"

"Well, I've got a mission for you, if you're up for some investigative footwork."

Tim was puzzled. He'd never heard a request like this before from Rick. "What are you talking about?"

"I've got a friend, Mark Taylor—"

"The same Mark Taylor who's all over the news right now?"

"Yeah, that's him."

Tim lowered his voice. "Everybody out here is talking about how nuts that guy is."

"I would expect nothing less from PBS," Rick laughed.

"Yeah, you got that right. I've been quietly cheering the guy on—very quietly if you know what I mean."

"I know exactly what you mean."

"How can I be of help?" Tim asked.

"Well, he's been working on this story, and we need somebody in Chicago to check out whether or not a person was scheduled to stay at the Drake last week. Do you know anybody at the hotel who might be willing to check for us?"

"I've spoken with the manager several times today alone. We've got Tesh and his band there right now. Give me the information, and I'll see what I can come up with."

"Great!" Rick exclaimed. "We really appreciate this."

SOMEWHERE OVER HOLLYWOOD
1:20 P.M. PACIFIC

Mark looked out the window over the city as they flew back to the studio. The beauty of the Malibu coastline was gone, replaced by miles of concrete, asphalt, and buildings as far as the eye could see. It flowed by in a blur as Mark's mind reeled with everything Reynolds had said.

Tracy's voice came over his headset as she reached out and grabbed his hand. "I think my grandfather really liked you."

"I liked him too. He wasn't what I expected at all."

"I knew he'd be able to answer your questions." Tracy smiled at him.

Yes, Reynolds had been able to handle all the easy questions Mark had put to him, but what about the ones he hadn't asked—about Dawkins's death, Kevin's accident, the gay poll, the list of seven names. Mark wasn't sure if it hadn't been the right time to bring those things up, or if he had blown it by not asking? Maybe he was grasping at straws. Dawkins's death could have been a heart attack and Kevin's a legitimate accident—there was no way to know. There was no law against owning multiple polling companies and television networks. Maybe he did have it all wrong.

He returned her smile as he continued in thought.

"Who's your next interview with?" Tracy asked.

"I don't remember. I just know it's at 1:30."

"I'll have you down in three minutes," Luis said through the headsets.

National Studios was coming into view over Tracy's shoulder as she turned to him. "Just remember what Papa said—this is your moment. Take it and run."

Mark looked at the beautiful face before him, smiling so sweetly, her hazel eyes sparkling with life. Could Reynolds really be the monster Mark had thought him to be and still be related to this wonderful woman? Jason Reynolds was the main reason Mark was being allowed the national stage to speak out for what was most dear to him. How could that be if he was so evil?

"How about meeting me for dinner tonight?" he asked.

Tracy's smile broadened. "I'd love to. Tell me where and when."

"My place. I'd just like to be alone with you. We'll order Chinese or something." Tracy squeezed his hand. "I'd love that."

Luis broke into a grin in the front of the helicopter as he gently guided them toward the executive landing pad.

CHICAGO
3:25 P.M. CENTRAL

Things were finally starting to come together for Tim Green. The call from Los Angeles had finally come in, and John Tesh and his band were available to stay one more day. Everything was in the works to keep the show a "go" for tomorrow night.

He picked up the phone and dialed the Drake Hotel.

"Jack Cummings please," he said as the operator answered.

Within a few moments he heard, "Cummings here."

"Jack, hi. It's Tim Green at WTTW."

"Yes, Tim, how can I help you?"

"We're moving Tesh's concert to tomorrow because of the storm. Is there a possibility of keeping him and the band over one more night?"

"Hold on, let me check." Jack quickly searched the computer's reservations for the suites that he'd placed Tesh's group into. "I'll have to move a couple of things around, but it looks like we can accommodate you."

"Great, it'll really help me out."

"I'll get it all set up here, Tim."

"Thanks, I appreciate it," Tim responded. "Oh, one more thing. Could you check a past reservation for me?"

"Sure, something to do with the station?" Jack asked.

"No, it's a favor for a friend. A week ago Monday, a Leeland Dawkins was scheduled at your hotel. Do you have any record of that?"

There was a pause over the line, Tim was afraid Jack wouldn't do it. "This is a highly unusual request, Tim. Why are you asking?"

"You wouldn't be revealing anything private, Jack. Mr. Dawkins passed away either that night or early Tuesday morning. A friend of mine is trying to track down his movements prior to his heart attack."

Jack thought it over for a second, then punched the name into his computer.

"Yes, he was scheduled in that night. Let me see—there's something weird here. It looks like he checked in—my, that is odd. He checked out an hour later. It looks like he didn't even spend the night."

Tim grabbed his pen and started writing. "Are you sure? That sounds strange."

"It is strange. But that's what's in the computer."

"Could you check out some other names that I have, to see if they were there that night?"

"I don't think it would be appropriate—"

"Please, Jack, it's very important."

"Give me the names and I'll check it out. If something turns up I think would be OK to pass on to you, I'll give you a call."

Tim knew that would be all he could ask for. "Thanks, Jack. I'll owe you one."

He gave him the list of names Rick had supplied him. After profusely thanking Jack for his time, he disconnected the call. As soon as he hung up, his phone rang.

"Tim Green."

"Mr. Green, this is Jayme at Chicago Limousines returning your call."

"Yes, I wanted to change the order for John Tesh's pickup at the Drake Hotel to tomorrow, same time."

"That's hoping that the roads are clear by then?" Jayme laughed.

"They should be; I hear the storm should pass us by late tonight."

"I hope so. We've had to cancel all of our service today. We're thinking about getting four-wheel-drive limousines for this time of year. Last week we almost had the same problem when the other storm blew in here."

Mentioning the other storm gave Tim an idea. "Jayme, did you by any chance dispatch limos to the Drake Hotel last Monday night?"

Jayme didn't take long to answer. "I remember that night very well. We sent all seven of our stretch limos out there. With the exception of one, they all made the run from O'Hare to the hotel and back that same night."

"Wow, you're sure it was seven limos?"

"Yes, I remember they all had to be stretch limos, and that's all we have."

"I need to know the names of the clients, Jayme."

"Hold on, that won't be hard." Tim could hear fingers tapping on a keyboard.

"Here they are—no, wait a minute. There aren't any names in the computer. I remember now. We were just given the flight information for each occupant. Our instructions were to have the limos at the airport for each pickup with our driver holding a number."

"A number?" Tim asked.

"Yes, the numbers one through seven. No names were ever given to us."

"Do you still have the flight information?"

"Yes, it's right here."

"What cities were they coming in from?"

"Let's see, we have two from Los Angeles, one from Dallas, two from New York, one from Washington, D.C., and the one local pickup here in Chicago."

Tim scratched more notes. Rick was really on to something.

"Would it be possible to fax that list over to me, Jayme?" Tim asked.

"Well, I guess I could. I hope I'm not doing anything illegal."

Tim let the comment slide. "Can you tell me who ordered the service?"

Jayme looked at the screen in front of her, "Let me see here—a company called Entertainment Enterprises out of Dallas wired the money to us, but there's no listing of any phone number."

Probably not a real company, Tim thought. "You've been a big help, Jayme, thanks."

"There's one more thing, Mr. Green," Jayme said. "I remember one of our drivers that night talking about having trouble with one of the passengers on the return to the airport."

"Trouble, what do you mean?"

"I don't remember exactly, but I can let you talk to him. He's right here, stuck in the snow like the rest of us. Hold on."

NORTH HOLLYWOOD
1:27 P.M. PACIFIC

Samantha pulled her car into the visitor's parking space at Vanessa's apartment building. She didn't remember making a conscious decision to make the trip. It was all too much for her—the Internet story, Peter's death, but especially the churning within her ever since the first talk with Vanessa.

Samantha stepped out of her candy-apple red Mustang convertible and willed herself to take the steps toward Vanessa's door. *Maybe she isn't even home,* Samantha hoped.

She knocked and waited.

Vanessa opened the door. "Samantha, what a surprise. Come on in."

"I'm sorry to bother you," Sam said, "but I was driving by and decided to stop."

"Oh, you're not bothering me at all. I just put Shelby down for her nap, and I'm not working tonight. So I'm all yours. Would you like some coffee?"

"Yes, that would be nice," Samantha said as she sat at the kitchen table.

Vanessa poured two cups and brought them to the table. Taking a seat next to Samantha, she poured some milk in hers and offered some to Samantha.

"No, thanks, I like it black."

Vanessa set the milk aside and sipped her coffee, waiting for Samantha to begin, while praying earnestly.

"I'm not even sure why I'm here," Samantha began.

"Take your time. Whatever's on your mind will come out," Vanessa said.

Samantha looked up at the caring woman—a stark contrast to the one she'd seen on the video she'd rented Saturday night. The images flooded Samantha's mind. It had been so strange to sit in her living room alone, watching the tape. She'd seen adult videos before but never of anybody that she knew personally. Maybe that was why she'd reacted the way she had. It disturbed her, making comparisons between her Web site and pornography, fighting the arguments Vanessa had made to her that afternoon. It'd taken her several seconds to recognize the old Vanessa. Something about her eyes—dull, lifeless, without hope—that made the Vanessa on tape look so different than the one she'd spent the afternoon with. She had stopped the movie after Vanessa's first scene.

Then Samantha's mind pictured Shelby laying in her crib—Vanessa's lifeline. That moment had reached deep into her soul and pricked a distant memory—one she'd attempted to bury forever.

"I had an abortion three years ago," Samantha confessed, staring into her cup of coffee.

Vanessa set her coffee cup down and took Samantha's hand. She kept the moment quiet, waiting until Sam was ready to continue.

Through tears she finally did. "I was just getting my career going, doing the newsmagazine show on Channel 7. I couldn't have gone through with it; it would have stopped my career dead in its tracks." Tears began their slide down both cheeks. "I didn't even think twice about it until Saturday night when I saw one of your videos."

Vanessa was shocked. "You rented one of my old videos?"

"Yes," Samantha smiled through the tears. "I rented *Feisty Flight Attendants.*"

"Oh, great." Vanessa sighed with a slight smile. "How did that lead to your remembering the abortion?"

"The image of Shelby came to my mind after I watched one of your scenes and thought back to what got you out of that life. That's when it hit me like a ton of bricks—the memory of what I'd done when I was pregnant."

"Oh, Samantha, I'm so sorry."

The two were silent. Then Samantha looked up and caught Vanessa's gaze. "At the time it seemed like the only thing to do. I bought into all the arguments about it being my body, my decision—just a mass of tissue. I remember a couple of days of questioning my choice—feeling a tug at my conscious. But that faded quickly as the people around me reinforced what I'd done. But after looking at Shelby—and—and what you did with the same—how could I have done what I did?"

The quiet reserve that had been holding Samantha together broke down. Vanessa reached over and wrapped her arms around the woman as she sobbed.

"What can I do now?" Samantha asked when she regained control.

"Nothing, Samantha, except the simple act of asking forgiveness," Vanessa responded.

"I don't know how to do that."

"I didn't either," Vanessa replied.

"But you didn't abort your—"

"Not about the abortion, about my life. The mess I'd managed to make of it. All the sexual sin, the rebellion, the selfish life I'd led. I needed to be forgiven too. We all do."

"I'm not sure I'm ready for your religion," Samantha whispered softly.

"I'm not talking about religion," Vanessa countered. "I'm talking about forgiveness from an all-loving, all-powerful, and all-forgiving Father who loves you. It's not religion, Samantha; it's a relationship that God wants with you."

"I don't know—I'm scared."

"That's perfectly natural," Vanessa said. Then she pulled out her Bible and began going over the Scriptures that Jill had shared with her when she'd made the decision to start her life over with God. At least Vanessa had been introduced to the things of the Lord at a young age by her grandmother. For Samantha, everything was new. She'd never heard of original sin, Christ's atonement on the cross, grace, or forgiveness.

"So all I have to do is ask Jesus for forgiveness?" Samantha asked as Vanessa completed her journey through the Scriptures.

"And give him your life. It sounds simple, but it's true."

Samantha looked down, taking in all that Vanessa had said to her. Then she finally looked up and said, "I want to do that. Would you help me?"

"Of course I will."

The two spent the next few moments praying. Vanessa encouraged Samantha to talk to God as if he were in the room with them, saying whatever was on her heart. It was hard for Samantha at first, sobbing when she asked God to forgive her for the abortion, but the words flowed a little easier as she asked Jesus to be Lord of her life.

Vanessa embraced her when she finished. Then the two separated, sharing Samantha's grin as the peace of forgiveness touched her.

"I want to share one more Scripture with you," Vanessa said. "I know with me, it was very hard to accept that I was forgiven, that I could stand before God as if I'd never done the awful things I'd committed." She opened her Bible to Colossians 1, and turned it so Samantha could see the words as she pointed to verse 21 and began reading: "Once you were alienated from God and were enemies in your minds because of your evil behavior. But now he has reconciled you by Christ's physical body through death to present you holy in his sight, without blemish and free from accusation."

"You see," Vanessa continued, "even when it comes to having an abortion, through Christ's death, you can be presented as holy in his sight, without blemish."

Samantha smiled warmly at her, the words sinking into her heart.

CHICAGO
3:31 P.M. CENTRAL

Tim Green waited patiently on the phone for the limousine driver to come on the line.

"Hello, this is Roberto."

"Roberto, this is Tim Green over at WTTW. Jayme told me about the client you had last week at the Drake Hotel."

"Oh yes, that was a weird night."

"Please tell me about it."

"Well, I picked up one of the VIPs for that night—Number Four actually." Roberto explained. "He was very quiet on the way to the Drake, didn't say a thing, but was very nervous, kind of fidgety.

"Well, I dropped him off at the back of the hotel, like everybody else, then sat out in the freezing cold. Within an hour he was the first one out, being helped by two men. The three climbed into the limo and I took him back to the airport."

"What do you mean he was helped by two men?" Tim asked.

"He couldn't walk on his own. The guys with him told me he'd had too much to drink. But that didn't make any sense. He'd been in the hotel for less than an hour."

Tim scribbled "drunk—one hour" on his pad. "Then you just returned him to the airport."

"Yes, but that was also strange. Instead of taking him to the American terminal where he'd come in, I was instructed to drop them off at the corporate terminal instead."

"That's odd, did you hear them say anything in the backseat?"

"Nothing. No one spoke at all."

"Well, thank you, Roberto," Tim said. "You've been very helpful."

LOS ANGELES INTERNATIONAL AIRPORT
2:08 P.M. PACIFIC

Vince Sinclair stepped outside the United terminal and into the Los Angeles mixture of sunlight and hazy smog. It was a pleasant change from the New York winter. He took off his leather jacket, revealing the short-sleeved Hawaiian shirt he'd put on in anticipation of his trip. He slung his duffel bag over his shoulder, anxious to unpack and get his handgun back under his belt where it belonged. He stepped over to the curb and thought of his next move. He'd have to find a hotel, then make contact with Number One through E-mail, and see if he could arrange a meeting.

He was excited. After over six months of work, he was finally getting close.

CHAPTER 29

"Britney would like to run the number again." Debbie, the stage manager, forwarded the message to Rick through his headset. Spears had just rehearsed her song for the second time. Usually, that was all Rick required to be ready for the show that night. But sometimes, the artists themselves wanted another rehearsal.

"That's fine, we've got the time," Rick said from the control room. "Let's run it one more time, everybody."

The third pass did the trick for Britney and the band, so Rick called a five-minute break for the crew.

"There's a call for you, Rick," the production assistant reported.

Rick grabbed the line. "Yeah, Rick here."

"Rick, it's Tim in Chicago. I've got some news for you."

"Already? Wow, that's great Tim."

"First, from the hotel, Dawkins was expected to stay at the Drake that night."

Rick started making notes as Tim filled him in on the details.

"So you're saying that the guy checked in but checked out an hour later." Rick summarized the call from Tim. "Then he's carried into the limo, unconscious and taken to the private air terminal."

"That about covers it, Rick," Tim said. "I'll fax this list of airline connections from the limousine service."

Rick had an idea. "Was your contact at the hotel pretty helpful?"

"Somewhat. Why do you ask?"

"Could you call him back and ask if there was some kind of meeting room set aside that night. If the limo company said they're delivering seven people to the back of the hotel, even though they didn't register as guests, there must have been some room reserved for them."

"Good idea, Rick. I'll call them back and check on it."

"Thanks, Tim. You've been a big help."

"My pleasure. It's helped add something intriguing to an otherwise bad day."

Rick hung up and immediately dialed Mark's extension. Mark answered after the first ring.

"Mark, it's Rick. How did the lunch go?"

"It went pretty well," Mark returned brightly. "Reynolds wasn't what I'd expected at all. It's made me rethink some things about this whole investigation."

Rick was surprised at the tone in Mark's voice. "I've got some news from Chicago."

"Chicago? What are you talking about?" Mark asked

"I had a friend of mine do some checking on your Mr. Dawkins at the Drake the night of his death—"

"This sounds fascinating, Rick, but I can't talk right now. I'm scheduled in the studio for another interview in two minutes."

"But you've got to hear this. When are you free?"

Mark looked at the schedule in front of him. "I'm clear at four."

"Great, that's when we're on our break. Come over to the control room. I'll be working on my script. You've got to hear this."

"I'll be there."

That was strange, Rick thought. Mark didn't seem interested. But he knew Cassie would be, so he left the booth and headed toward her office.

Mark nearly ran over Frank Russell as he stepped out of his cubicle, heading toward the studio.

"Whoa there, big fella." Russell laughed, catching his balance.

"I'm sorry, Frank. I'm running late for the Larry King interview."

"Oh, that's right." Russell looked at his watch. "Look, I won't hold you up. I'll walk with you over to the studio while I share the good news."

"What good news?"

"We're killing the fluff piece on *The Single Life*. We'll run that Sunday night. The top brass is pulling out all the stops promoting the show with your controversy. We're still going to open with Sam's story, but we want to close with a segment that's all yours."

"I'm not sure I understand."

"Your reaction to the attention—a chance for you to put a tag on this whole affair. Give it some thought and let me know how much time you want. It's your moment—go for it!" Russell slapped him on the back as he opened the door into the studio.

Mark walked toward the waiting stool in the center of the room. His own segment? Instead of having to run that fluff piece on the stupid sit-com, he was being given the closing segment, as much time as he wanted? A week ago, if people had told him he'd be in this position, he would have laughed them out of the room, but here it was. Mark chuckled and shook his head as he took his place on the stool.

"What's so funny?" the audio technician asked as he helped place the microphone on Mark's shirt.

"Oh, nothing."

Rick made his way quickly through the production office and walked up to Tina, Cassie's assistant. "Is she available?"

"I think so—let me check." Tina picked up her phone. "Cassie, there's a handsome director type out here who would like to see you." Tina eyed Rick up and down. "Sure, it looks like him . . . OK." Tina hung up. "She said you can go right on in."

"What else did she say?" Rick asked.

"Nothing," Tina smiled at him. "Just girl talk."

Rick stepped through Cassie's door, "What was that all about?"

Cassie laughed as she stepped around her desk and gave Rick a hug. "Just having a little fun. I was describing to her the love of my life, and she said you fit the description, so I let you in."

Rick smiled, then gave her a kiss on the cheek. "It's great working with you."

"What's up?" Cassie asked.

"It's about Mark. I just got a call back from Tim in Chicago."

"What did he find out?"

"Well, I'd say it looks like Mr. Dawkins did go to Chicago, checked into the Drake, went to some kind of meeting, checked out within an hour, then was carried or dragged back to his limousine and taken to the private airfield. That same company had a total of seven limos out that night, all delivering to the Drake within ten minutes of each other."

"And you say Dawkins was carried back into the limo? How did you find that out?"

"Tim was able to talk to the driver. They made up some excuse about having had too much to drink, but he was in the hotel for less than an hour."

"Maybe he was already dead."

"Do you think that's possible?" Rick asked the same question he'd been asking himself. "Then they flew him all the way back to New York to stick him in his office to be discovered?"

"Why not? If they've got a corporate jet, what's to stop them from taking the body back to New York? There'd be no witnesses," Cassie answered.

"Wow! Whatever Mark has gotten himself into is getting a little weird."

"It sure is. How did he respond when you told him."

"That's one of the reasons I wanted to talk with you. He didn't want to hear it. He had another interview to do, but I could hear it in his voice. It sounded like he's given up the story altogether."

"He can't do that now," Cassie said. "He's so close to getting some real answers. Maybe he's just overwhelmed by all the media attention."

"Remember what you said last night. That's their plan—to keep him so busy he won't have time to care."

"It sure seems like that's what's happening, doesn't it?"

"Let's pray for him," Rick offered. He took her hands as they sat on the edge of the desk. "Lord, we come to you on behalf of Mark. We don't know where his head is right now, but you do. We pray for clarity in his mind, for your thoughts to be ever present, and your wisdom to be what he follows.

"Father, block any attempt by the enemy to confuse him, to distract him from whatever purpose you've established in his life, his career, even his walk with you, Lord. As you gave me that verse for him a few days ago, strengthen him, dear Jesus, and protect him from the evil one. If he's ready to give up the fight, restore him. Bring back the passion I saw in him Sunday when he returned from New York.

"And, Lord, I pray that whatever else is hidden would be brought out in the open. If people have been murdered by this group, we pray they'd be exposed, and justice, by your standard, would be the victor. In Jesus' name."

Cassie looked up at her fiancé and smiled. "As we prayed, I felt like God showed me Mark is at a real turning point in his life right now. He's coming up against some decisions that are going to be difficult. We need to continue praying for him, and ask others to join us."

"I'll call the prayer chain from the home group. That'll get Gary and Jill and some of the others praying with us."

"I'll do the same with my group," Cassie said. "I know that God is in control, but there are some fierce battles ahead for Mark."

"That's funny," Rick held Cassie close to him as he responded. "I had the same thought."

"Go ahead, caller," Larry King said, looking directly into the camera in front of him.

"I take offense to what your guest is saying, Larry." The voice came through Mark's earpiece as he sat in the Hollywood studio, three thousand miles away.

"He's listening," King said with a smile. "Fire away."

"I saw him on *The John Harold Show*," the caller continued. "I don't think he knows what he's talking about."

Mark smiled and looked straight ahead. It was hard to connect with someone who could see him—on TV—while he had to look at the hard, cold glass of a studio camera lens.

"That poll that John Harold quoted last night on the abortion issue had a margin of error of plus or minus 3 percent. How can he argue with that?"

Larry King kept his gaze steady into his camera. "Mark, how do you respond?"

"Most of us don't understand this sampling margin of error. I know I didn't until just a few days ago. Take the survey quoted last night: it stated that 64 percent approve of abortion on demand. Most of us erroneously take that to mean that if we could actually poll the entire nation of over 275 million people, we'd get between 61 and 67 percent of them saying they agree with abortion on demand. But that's wrong."

"What do you mean?" King asked

"All that margin of error really means—and this is important for our nation to understand, Larry—is that if you conducted the same flawed poll, with the exact same biased questions, to a random audience selected in precisely the same manner and did it an infinite number of times, you'd end up with the same mean-ingless results within three percentage points. It only validates your sampling technique, not the research itself or the results, for that matter. It does not reflect on the truth or the validity of what you're trying to research at all. If you polled with biased questions or to an unscientific sample, what does plus or minus 3 percent really mean if the research is flawed?

"But we never hear that from the pollsters, do we? It's become the common misconception that these numbers scientifically reflect the opinion of the entire nation, and nobody is standing up to point out the error."

"Until you came along." King interjected. "Boise, Idaho, you're on with Mark Taylor."

MALIBU
3:12 P.M. PACIFIC

> To: CoSN1@csi.com
> From: Vsinclair@researchinternational.org
> Topic: Let's Meet
>
> Number One,
>
> I've done all I can do to help you from the East Coast. If you choose to continue on with Palmer, there's not much more I can do. You need another new Number Four. You could have done better in replacing Dawkins.
>
> I am in Los Angeles and would like to meet with you to prove to you that I can be trusted and be included in the seven.
>
> Vince

Jason Reynolds stared at the computer screen. So he was in town. The man was brave; Jason gave him that much. But how much did he know? Did he know his identity? Doubtful. Was he a threat, or a friend, as he claimed? He knew enough to be dangerous so Jason felt a meeting would be prudent. If he turned out to be an adversary, Luis would quickly take care of him. If he could prove his loyalty, per-haps there was room in the group to start an apprentice program. In either case, it sounded as if they'd made the wrong choice in Dawkins's replacement. Palmer was making too many mistakes.

Reynolds picked up the phone and dialed Luis's cell number.

"Where are you?"

"Downtown," Luis responded.

"Come out here. There's something I want to show you."

NATIONAL STUDIOS
4:15 P.M. PACIFIC

The control room was quiet as Rick sat at the console, making notes in his scriptbook. The door opened behind him. He turned to see Mark. He looked exhausted; his posture was slouched and his head down.

"How's it going, Mark? Getting tired of being the one answering the questions yet?"

"I haven't been this tired since boot camp." Mark flopped into the chair next to Rick. "But it's been so incredible to be able to talk about these issues."

"Yeah, but it can't be easy on you. Especially trying to stay sharp as you're being interviewed by those who disagree with you."

"Yeah, Larry King wasn't exactly an easy sell."

Rick laughed. "No, I bet he wasn't."

"So what'd you find out?"

Rick proceeded to fill Mark in on the details surrounding the night in Chicago. He gave Mark the list Tim had faxed with all the flight arrangements from the limo company for the drivers that night.

"I can't believe you did this, Rick."

"It just kind of came to me after Cassie and I looked over your report. Do you have any flight information from Mrs. Dawkins concerning her husband?"

"No, and I'm not sure she will either. She thought she'd just made a mistake."

"Well, I'd say it looks like your suspicions were correct. I've got my friend checking back with the hotel to see if he can confirm the rental of a meeting room of some kind. I wonder what you'll get if you checked those flights with the names on your list?"

"Yeah, I was wondering the same thing." Mark looked at the cities involved—Dallas, Los Angeles, New York, Washington, D.C. "But there's really no point. I've been ordered off the story—threatened would be more accurate. So there's nothing I can do."

Rick studied his friend. In the short time they'd known each other, this was the first time he sensed any defeat. He'd given up.

"You've finally got some outside source of evidence, Mark. You can't turn your back on it now."

"You don't understand, Rick. The only thing I could do now would be to turn it all over to the FBI. Even if I followed up on your leads, I don't have an outlet for it anymore. If I do any legwork on this story, I'll be fired. It's that simple.

"Besides, after meeting with Reynolds today, I really can't picture the man having anything to do with Dawkins's or Kevin's death. Maybe it was just a heart attack and a car accident."

"That sure doesn't sound like the Mark I talked to in the commissary last week. You had a passion for this story. What happened?"

"What happened is I got a dose of reality, Rick. Besides, I've moved on. Having a chance to speak out on these other issues is where I need to be. This story doesn't seem all that important anymore."

"What do you mean?" Rick asked.

"Don't you see?" Mark pleaded. "God has to have his hand on all this publicity I've received since the show Sunday night. Why else would the networks and all the cable shows be clamoring to hear my story? I'm speaking out for our pro-life position like it's never been spoken about before. The industry is listening to somebody expose the bias we've all been bullied by in the past several decades. Don't you see that as the work of the Lord?"

Rick didn't respond right away, praying for wisdom and words from the Holy Spirit before he spoke. Then he looked up and pierced Mark's heart with his words. "Right now, I see a Christian brother who can't see the forest for the trees. Don't let the fact that Reynolds is throwing you some crumbs from the table of his media empire distract you from the evil that you saw in him earlier."

Mark lowered his head as Rick continued. "What's it to him if you have your fifteen minutes of fame? Sure a discussion flares up for a few days, but then it's relegated to the late-night hours of Fox News and CNBC while the nation forgets it ever happened. We certainly won't see any headlines in the *Los Angeles Times* or the *New York Post* about it. The networks won't lead the evening news with your story. It'll all blow over, the bias won't stop, the pro-life cause will continue to be given third-class treatment, and Reynolds will have won and continue to hold his death grip on the mind of our nation."

Mark didn't respond.

"I read your report, Mark. So did Cassie. You're onto something that needs to be exposed. For heaven's sake, don't give up now. With what you've got from Chicago, there's got to be enough to get the FBI to notice. Dawkins was at the Drake. If we match the flight numbers, get the limo driver to ID him, we can prove it."

Mark looked up, catching the fire in Rick's eyes. "You weren't there, Rick. Reynolds is so—I don't know what he is—but I don't see being able to prove anything against him. He's got all the answers."

"Have you even asked the right questions? If he's done what it looks like he's done, he's got at least two deaths to answer for." Rick slid his chair closer to Mark's. "You can't let him get away with that."

Mark shook his head and calmly took the faxed list from him. "I don't know what I can do, Rick. I just don't know."

Without another word, Mark got up and headed out the door.

MALIBU
4:52 P.M. PACIFIC

Luis leaned over Reynolds's shoulder and read the latest E-mail response from "Vsinclair." He grunted as he finished the last sentence.

"You're not going to meet him, are you?" Luis asked.

"No, you are," Jason answered flatly.

"Are you crazy? Who knows where this guy is coming from? How could he know as much as he seems to know? He could be a Fed or something."

"No, if he was FBI, I'd know about it, plus we'd be swamped by subpoenas. I want to find out more about him. Set up a meeting. You can be me for a while, until we check him out."

"OK," Luis said reluctantly, "I hope you know what you're doing. Send him a reply—tell him to meet me at the entrance to Balboa's golf course in the Valley—nine o'clock tonight."

Luis started to walk out of the office, then turned back to Reynolds. "Oh, by the way, first report back from Taylor's watch. I was told it looks like he's giving up the hunt. Some friend is trying to convince him to keep at it, but whatever you said at lunch seems to be working."

Reynolds grabbed a cigar out of his humidor and leaned back in his chair as a broad smile spread across his face.

NATIONAL STUDIOS
6:00 P.M. PACIFIC

The last credit rolled by, leaving the copyright for National Studios keyed over the shot of John Harold chatting with his guests, Britney Spears and Michael J. Fox.

"And fade to black," Rick called as Chad reached the end of his countdown. "Great show, everybody. Enjoy your day off tomorrow. We'll see you all Thursday."

As Rick was removing his headset, the phone in the control room rang. The script supervisor picked it up, then turned to Rick. "It's for you."

Rick grabbed the phone by his chair. "Yeah."

"Rick, it's Gary. I'm glad I caught you."

"Good timing, Gary—we just finished the show."

"I tried to time it that way. Hey, listen, do you have any plans tonight?"

"I don't think so. Cassie and I were just going to grab a bite to eat."

"Great! Bring her with you."

"To where?"

"Our house. You'll see why when you get here, but you have to come. We've got dinner all ready."

Just then Cassie walked into the room—satisfied with another completed show. She saw Rick's strange look and raised her eyebrows.

"Hold on, Gary. Cassie just stepped in." Rick put his hand over the mouthpiece. "It's Gary. He's got something going on, but he won't tell me what. He wants us to come by his house tonight for dinner."

Cassie grinned. "Sounds good to me. We wanted to get them to pray for Mark anyway. This way we can make sure."

"OK, Gary, we'll take the bait. We'll be over there in about a half an hour to forty-five minutes, if traffic will allow."

"We'll have dinner ready."

Mark hung up. "I wonder what that's all about."

"With Gary and God—it could be anything," Cassie laughed. "I can't wait to find out."

CHAPTER 30

Mark was running through his apartment like a madman as Peter Jennings's voice rambled on in the background with another story on the continuing crisis in India; this one focused on President McNeil's push for international involvement and the need for Congress to approve his UN appropriation bill.

Tracy would be there any minute; Mark didn't have time to think about Pakistan or India. The living room and kitchen looked all right, but his bedroom and bathroom were a mess. He quickly slammed his shaver, toothbrush, toothpaste, and hair dryer into different drawers, wiped the counter with a washcloth in a hit-or-miss attempt to clean, and made sure no towels were lying on the floor. He headed for the bedroom as the doorbell rang.

Without missing a beat, he opened the closet and in one blur of fast motion threw everything on the floor into it and shut the door. He ran back through the living room, shut off the television, and took one last look to make sure the place was presentable. He drew in a large breath and let it out slowly as he walked toward the front door, hoping his breathing appeared normal.

"Hi, Tracy—" But it was dinner being delivered from the Golden Dragon down the street. He retrieved his wallet and was paying the deliveryman as Tracy came up the steps.

"Looks like I'm right on time," she said, entering his apartment and glancing around.

"Make yourself at home," Mark said as he took the food into the kitchen. He smiled as he walked past her; she looked beautiful. Mark felt a brief moment of insecurity, remembering that she was socially on a much different level. Tracy, the granddaughter of the richest man he'd ever met—a man who could donate fifty million dollars at the drop of a hat and who lived in that unbelievable mansion in Malibu. She probably had a trust fund worth more than he could make in his entire lifetime.

But today had been a landmark day in his career, in his life. If he could take this moment and run with it, as Jason had said, maybe he could rise to the level he needed to attain her. Surely the elite in his profession fit that category—Malibu homes, money to throw at their favorite causes. He just needed to use this week as a catapult. Everything he'd ever dreamed of could be attained—and what a wonderful platform he'd have to continue with his bold statements for God.

"I love your apartment," Tracy said. "It really feels homey."

"Thanks, but it's nothing like your grandfather's place."

"Oh, Papa's place is nice, but I'm glad I don't live there."

"Where do you live?" Mark asked, realizing he didn't know.

"I have a small apartment in Westwood I've kept since my UCLA days, but I do spend a lot of my weekends in Malibu."

"I can see why." Mark put the food on the table. "I couldn't believe how beautiful it was out there. I wish we'd had more time."

"So do I. It was fun to watch you and Papa go at it." She grinned mischievously.

"I tried, but I couldn't hold a candle to him. He had me so flustered, I didn't even get to the tough questions like I promised you. What would you like to drink? I have iced tea, water, Pepsi, coffee."

"I'd prefer water, please."

"Water it is," Mark said filling two glasses with ice and Sparkletts from the container by the sink. "Chopsticks or a fork?"

"I'm game for chopsticks, if you are."

Mark brought the water to the table with two sets of chopsticks. "I hope this is OK. The restaurant makes great chicken lo-mein, and I love their shrimp."

"This looks wonderful. I haven't had Chinese in months."

"Good. Well, have a seat."

The two sat down. Tracy kept her hands to her side, politely waiting for Mark to jump in. He was wrestling with the decision to bless the meal or not.

Tracy noticed his hesitation and placed a hand on his. "Are you all right?"

"I'm sorry." He shook his head. *You idiot, you're making a fool of yourself.* "It's just that normally I pray before the meal—"

"Well, go ahead." Tracy smiled, thinking his shyness was sweet. Her reaction relieved some of Mark's tension. "I want you to just be yourself. That way I'll get to know the real you."

"Then let's give thanks," Mark said, taking her hand in his. He bowed his head slightly and closed his eyes. He bowed his head slightly and closed his eyes as he began. He didn't see Tracy keep her eyes on him a second longer before closing them as the corners of her mouth remained raised in a slight smile.

"That wasn't so hard, was it?" she asked when he'd finished.

"Not for me. How about you?"

"I kind of liked it. It gives me a little deeper glimpse into that feeling you and Rick have of God being with you all the time—like we talked about Sunday."

"So you were listening—good."

Tracy took a bite of the shrimp. "This is excellent."

"Wait until you try the lo-mein," Mark said as he dabbed his chopsticks into his plate. "So how was it at the office today?"

Tracy relayed the events of her day, then it was Mark's turn to reciprocate. He began to relax and open up.

Downstairs in the parking lot, the man in the van was finally entertained. He'd been bored watching an empty apartment all day. It was about time something was happening.

When they had finished eating, Mark carried their plates to the kitchen. Tracy followed with the glasses. When he'd cleaned the plates and placed them in the sink, he turned around to find Tracy behind him.

"You don't have to do that," he said, reaching to take the two glasses from her hands. The touch sparked something between them. Their eyes met and lingered. Mark placed the glasses on the counter, then turned back and placed his hands around her waist.

Tracy kept her eyes locked on his as Mark slowly brought her body closer to his. He lowered his head. Their faces were now inches apart as he closed the gap and gently brought his lips in contact with hers, and they shared their first kiss. It was tender, a sweet moment as they took their first step past friendship.

Mark loosened his hold on her waist and raised his arms, to caress the back of her neck. Tracy responded by placing her arms around his shoulders as the kiss lingered. Then their lips parted, but the embrace continued. Mark smiled as he looked up at the ceiling in elation.

Then he saw it.

The light from over the kitchen table hit it just right as Mark's eyes were in a daze. But the reflection caught his attention. He recognized the small lens within the air-conditioning grate.

Tracy noticed the reaction as his body tensed. "What—"

"Shhh," Mark whispered as quietly as he could into her ear as he seethed inside. "We're being watched." He cleared the rest of the table, whistling as he did so. Tracy, although confused, fell into step with his plan and worked with him.

"What do you say we take a walk?" Mark asked as if it was the most natural suggestion he could make.

"That sounds great. It's beautiful out tonight."

"I'll grab a sweater. Be right back." Mark entered his bedroom, trying to get a glimpse into the grates there to see if he could spot another camera without being too obvious. Nothing there, but in the bathroom, the light once again reflected off the lens, and Mark could tell at least two rooms were bugged. The bathroom! Mark was furious. He grabbed a jogging suit top out of the drawer and headed back to the kitchen.

Tracy waited patiently while Mark opened the front door. He was about to lead her out when he thought of the Rolex watch on his wrist—given to him by Jason Reynolds. He turned back, removed the watch, and set it on the kitchen counter.

Mark led Tracy down the steps and headed through the common area of the complex toward the pool. Once he felt like they were far enough from the apartment, he lashed out.

"I can't believe this! How could I have been taken in by that? How does he think he can get away with it?"

Tracy kept her distance, not sure what was happening. Mark noticed her reaction and walked back toward her.

"I'm sorry, Tracy. You were great up there. You catch on quick."

"What was that all about, Mark?" she asked.

He opened the pool gate and led her toward a couple of lounge chairs as he tried to suppress his anger.

"After we kissed, I looked up into the ceiling—in wonderful bliss I might add." Mark smiled at her as his temper subsided. She shook her head, feeling more comfortable and returning the smile.

"I noticed light reflecting off something in the air-conditioning grate in the ceiling. It was a lens. Somebody's got a camera in my kitchen. When I went back to get the sweater, I noticed one in the bathroom as well. I'll bet every room in the house is wired."

"Who would do that to you?" Tracy asked concerned.

Mark paused. He knew who it was, without a doubt. There was only one investigation he'd started that would give anybody cause to be concerned with his movements. That one person was Jason Reynolds. But what should he tell Tracy? She wouldn't believe him. Things were going so well, and now this.

Suddenly, an image flashed through Mark's mind—a picture of Jesus after fasting for forty days in the desert, standing on the pinnacle of the barren land as Satan showed him the kingdoms of the world and offered it all to Jesus if he'd bow down and worship him.

Mark sat down in a daze. Tracy followed his lead, wondering what he was thinking.

The image of Jesus was gone in a flash—replaced by Reynolds standing on the top of his mansion in Malibu. Only this time Mark was with him. The vision was so real, Mark felt as if he'd been immediately transported there. He could smell the salt air, feel the cool breeze blowing against his face; he even felt slightly dizzy as he looked down at the cliffs below him. Jason Reynolds turned away from him, opening his arms toward the horizon in a gesture that indicated to Mark all that he could see could be his. In that direction, Mark saw the mansions of Malibu along the beach. In the distance he could see Hollywood, and somehow he was able to make out the major studios—National, Paramount, NBC, CBS—the buildings sparkled as if they were made of gold. He turned back toward Reynolds, but he was gone, replaced by a huge cobra, leaning back, ready to strike . . .

Mark flashed back to reality. The information Rick had discovered from Chicago raced through his mind, illuminating the true nature of what Mark was facing. How could he have been so deceived, so enticed by what Reynolds had to offer. The vision, or whatever it was, propelled Mark out of the delusion and knocked him to his senses. He followed the conviction of his heart and quickly repented before he responded to Tracy's question.

When he finally looked up, his eyes were filled with tears.

"Are you all right?" Tracy asked.

"Yeah, I'm sorry," he said as he composed himself, then he stared into her eyes. "Tracy, do you know where your grandfather was a week ago Monday?"

Tracy's eyes darkened. That was a strange question, but as she thought back, she did know. On his way to Washington, D.C., he'd planned to stop overnight. "He was in Chicago."

Mark shuddered. Rick's evidence was too strong to ignore, and the image of Reynolds on the Malibu cliff was still powerfully etched in his mind. Mark's anger returned.

He took hold of one of Tracy's hands. "There's only one person I can think of who would have any reason to bug my apartment—your grandfather."

She opened her mouth to speak, but no sound came out.

"Before you think I've jumped off the deep end, there are some things you need to know," Mark continued. "I think the cordial lunch we had today was just an act. I think Jason's been using my newfound fame to distract me from the story I was working on."

"Mark, I can't believe what you're saying."

"Just hear me out first, then see if you feel the same way. I have some pretty good evidence that in Chicago that night, Jason met with a group of six other men at the Drake Hotel. One of those men, a Leeland Dawkins—"

Tracy interrupted. "I knew Leeland—the president of Research International. He died that night but in his office in New York City."

"No, that's where he ended up. Earlier that night he was in Chicago with your grandfather. His limousine driver took him to the meeting, but he was carried out by two other men, taken to a private air terminal, and, I believe, flown back to New York already dead so his body could be placed back at his office."

"This is preposterous, Mark. Leeland and my grandfather were friends."

"There's more. I also believe that Kevin Spencer's death wasn't an accident."

"You're not serious."

"I am. Kevin contacted me after I was at your office last week."

She blinked in surprise but said nothing.

"He found out that the gay poll your company did was greatly flawed—biased questions plus a computer program that routed over half of the random calls to pro-homosexual cities like San Francisco and Miami. He turned the information over to me Thursday night. Then two days later he turned up dead. And now I've got video cameras all over my apartment. It has to be your grandfather."

"I can't believe my grandfather would have anything to do with Kevin's death." Tracy shook her head. "I loved Kevin. He was part of the family at ARI."

"But he was also investigating a very sensitive matter—the manipulation of survey data, rigged polls, biased questionnaires. Look at the media giant your grandfather has control of to assimilate the false information. The other six members of his little group control an incredible amount of the print media, radio stations, and TV markets in this country. They have ties all the way to the White House."

Tracy was at a loss for words. She couldn't believe what Mark was telling her, yet she knew him well enough to know he wouldn't be saying it if he didn't believe it.

"That's why you took the watch off. You think it's bugged too?"

"I didn't want to take any chances."

"Is there some way you can prove all this?"

"Only circumstantially so far, but we're getting close to some hard evidence," Mark answered. "Is there a way you can find out what flight your grandfather took to Chicago that night?"

"I'm sure he would have taken the corporate jet," Tracy said.

"How could we find out for sure?"

"I think they keep a copy of the flight plans at the office. But how would that help?"

"I have a list of the limousine pickups for that night in Chicago. If we can match the time and place of your grandfather's jet to one of the limousine pickups, we can tie him to Dawkins the night he died."

The silence hung between them as Tracy took in all the information. Eventually she looked into Mark's eyes. "Will you help me get to those flight records?" he asked.

Tracy held the gaze, then lowered her head as she thought. Her heart was torn. She wanted to help the man sitting beside her—the man who for the past several days had shown her a passion for life and a commitment to a higher ideal that she'd never seen before. He had captivated her heart.

But could she betray her grandfather? The man who had nurtured her from birth and been the father that her dad had never been. But if he was behind Kevin's death, she had to know. Maybe the flight record would prove that he couldn't have possibly been involved. If she helped Mark, it would help her find out one way or the other.

"I'll help you, Mark," she finally whispered. "But I'm not saying I believe all of your accusations. It might just prove my grandfather's innocence as well."

Mark nodded. "Fair enough, Tracy. Let's get those records, and we'll see what's there."

"Can you stop by my office sometime in the morning?"

"I should be able to. I'll leave the studio right after the production meeting." He kissed her lightly. "However it comes out, I don't want you to get hurt. I nearly dropped the whole thing today—not believing that anything as evil as what I was thinking could be tied to you."

Tracy smiled, then turned back toward the apartment. "What do you want to do with our spying-eye friends back in there?"

"You want to have some fun?" Mark asked, allowing a mischievous grin to form.

"What do you have in mind?"

"Let's go back into the apartment, then we'll . . ."

WESTWOOD
6:42 P.M. PACIFIC

Rick and Cassie were excited when they pulled up to Gary's house. It was unlike Gary to be mysterious, and while riding there in Rick's Jeep, they couldn't figure out what could be awaiting them.

They walked up to the front porch and knocked on the door. Jill was before them a couple of seconds later with all smiles. "Come in, come in."

Gary was waiting for them in the living room with Vanessa and Shelby.

"Vanessa!" Rick exclaimed. "Good to see you again." Then he turned to Gary. "Is this the surprise?"

Gary laughed, "No, not quite."

Rick and Cassie waited. Vanessa, Gary, and Jill all looked like the Cheshire cat from *Alice in Wonderland*.

"Well," Rick finally had to prompt them, "what's going on?"

"Do you want to tell them, Vanessa?" Gary asked.

"All right, I will," she said. "We wanted to introduce you both to the newest member of our Christian family."

Rick and Cassie looked at each other, puzzled.

Then Rick saw Samantha Steel make her way around the corner of the hallway, a huge smile adorning her face.

"Samantha?" Rick asked. "Is she talking about you?"

Sam just nodded. She was sure if she tried to say something, tears would start again.

Cassie was the first to compose herself and firmly embraced her. "Welcome to the family, Samantha. That is so good to hear."

"Yeah," Rick tried to find the words. "I'm thrilled for you, Sam. But how? When? Let me hear the details."

"It started with Mark suggesting I speak with Vanessa," Samantha smiled toward Vanessa as she began her story. They all settled around the room as Samantha related the past couple of days—the awful feeling she'd had while posing for the photographer, her talk with Vanessa, the haunting memory of her abortion, and finally the shock of discovering her computer expert had been murdered.

Cassie felt something stir within her during that part of the story. Her mind wandered as Samantha continued, describing the second conversation she had with Vanessa.

"I am so amazed," Rick confessed. "I've been praying for you ever since we did that infomercial together."

"Well, it finally paid off, thanks to Vanessa here."

"Yes," Gary said, "but also thanks to your willingness to open up and let somebody break through the walls you'd built up."

Sam blushed, not sure how to respond.

"We don't mean to embarrass you," Rick said. "We're just excited for you, and I hope you'll let us help you grow in your new relationship with the Lord."

"I'm sure I'll need a lot of help."

"Well, there are several Christians on the lot now," Rick added. "Cassie and me obviously, then there's Mark Taylor, Reggie, one of our security guards, several camera people, and other technicians. We may be the minority in our business, but you're not alone."

"For the first time in my life, I don't feel alone," Samantha proclaimed.

Rick studied the serenity on her face—something he hadn't seen before. It fit her nicely. "May I ask you a question?"

"Sure."

"How will this affect your story on the Internet site tomorrow night?"

"Good question," Samantha laughed. "I'm not sure I know the answer yet. I've been so wrapped up with these three—learning more about what I just committed to—that I haven't really thought about it. I need to get home and do a whole lot more research."

"I have some material on the negative effects of pornography," Gary offered. "You're welcome to take it with you."

"I will. Thanks Gary. That could be very helpful."

"May I ask you something, Samantha?" Cassie asked suddenly.

"Yes?" she responded as all eyes in the room turned to Cassie.

"The computer expert that you found murdered this afternoon . . . would you happen to know if he was the same person Mark was using to do some research for him?"

"Yes, I believe he was."

BURBANK
7:30 P.M. PACIFIC

Mark opened the door to his apartment for Tracy.

"That was a wonderful walk, Mark, thanks."

To make sure the cameras would catch everything, they'd decided to sit at the kitchen table, directly in view of the lens Mark had seen in the kitchen.

"I'm glad you enjoyed it. The view certainly doesn't match the one in Malibu, but it's home," he said.

"It was great having you out there for lunch. I really think Papa liked you." She tried to make her voice and inflection sound as natural as possible. She felt like an actress in a stage play and nearly giggled.

"He really impressed me." Mark played along. "Here I was ready to pounce on him with the questions I've been milling around in my head, then he practically gives me all the answers before I even get to them. I can't believe I was suspicious of your grandfather, Tracy. He's really a great man." Mark turned his head slightly away from the camera aimed at him from the kitchen. He tried to hide his smirk.

"It's definitely not a story that's worth putting my career on the line for," he continued under control again. "I hate to admit it, but Russell was probably right. Kevin must have had some grudge against the company and was stringing me along."

"And then that horrible accident. I feel sad for Vickie," Tracy said.

"And Kevin was much too young with so much ahead of him to end up dying in that car like that," Mark added.

The two let the stillness linger, realizing they weren't acting anymore.

"Are you up for a movie or anything?" Tracy asked, trying to break the uncomfortable silence.

"I wish I was. I'm really beat though. With all the interviews they've thrown at me and the two hours sleep I got last night, I just need to crash. I hope you understand."

"I forgot about all that. You must be bushed."

"Come on, I'll walk you to your car."

As they made their way down the stairs, Mark started to laugh, then Tracy burst out laughing.

"I don't know how convincing we were," Mark whispered to her as they walked, "but it should give a little breathing room tomorrow."

"And it was fun. I can't believe we did that. What if it's not my grandfather behind those cameras?"

"Then somebody's going to be scratching their heads, but it can't be anybody else. I'm sure of it."

As Mark opened the car door for her, he spotted the white van toward the back of the parking lot. "You know what, that van's been parked at one end of the lot or the other ever since I got back from New York. I'll bet that's how they're monitoring the apartment."

"What are you going to do?"

"Nothing. I'd be just asking for trouble to go over there and confront the guy inside."

Tracy was relieved.

"I'm going to do exactly as I said, go back inside and crash. I'll see you tomorrow morning, as soon as I can get over there."

Tracy smiled. "I'll be looking forward to it."

"You know, when this is all over, I hope we can spend some time together without having this between us."

"I would like nothing better."

Mark put his hands behind her neck and pulled her close. He kissed her and lingered in her fragrance.

BALBOA GOLF COURSE
9:10 P.M. PACIFIC

Through night-scope binoculars, Luis kept his eye on the mysterious Vince Sinclair. He'd arrived right on schedule, but he could wait. Luis was in no hurry to make contact.

An hour earlier, Luis had pulled his car up against the brick wall that separated the walkway to the clubhouse from the practice putting green. It was a perfect hiding spot, leaving the parking lot entirely empty of vehicles. Luis had stationed himself near the clubhouse where he could keep his eye on both the north and south parking lots. Ten minutes ago, a Camry had turned off Balboa Street, driven slowly up the hill along the front of the clubhouse, and stopped in the north parking area.

Now hiding behind a large oak tree on the north side of the brick wall, Luis continued to scan the area to make sure Vince hadn't brought along any "friends."

He waited another five minutes.

Vince was getting nervous. He hoped he hadn't overplayed his hand. He wanted to be on the inside but didn't know any other way to break in. He looked at his watch—fifteen minutes late. He'd give it another five minutes. Then he saw headlights pop on behind him.

Vince got out of the car. The headlights blinded him. Luis stopped the car about ten feet behind Vince's. He turned off the motor and opened his door but left the headlights shining in Vince's eyes.

"So you wanted a meeting—here I am. Talk," Luis called out.

"Are you Number One?" Vince yelled.

"Keep your voice down," Luis instructed. "Just tell me why you want to meet me."

"I know what you've built up over the past years," Vince answered, "and I want to be a part of it. I can be of great service to you."

He paused, waiting for some kind of reaction from beyond the headlights.

None came, so Vince continued. "You've given the Number Four position to somebody who is going to screw up everything for you. Palmer is inept. He's more interested in getting a little something from the female account managers than he is in taking care of your business."

"Go on."

Vince took a step toward Luis's car.

"From where you're standing," Luis ordered.

"He's careless. How do you think I got the E-mail address? His recklessness will be your nemesis. I saw the instructions for the abortion poll. I know about the homosexual poll. I know you had to take care of the old Number Four and elevate Palmer, but I'm telling you it was a mistake. I can help you."

Luis turned and whispered into the car. "What do you want to do, boss?"

"Make sure he's not carrying a gun. Then let him in," Jason answered from the back seat.

"Come on over here," Luis instructed. "Slowly."

Vince walked cautiously toward the glaring headlights. A nervous flutter tickled his gut. Luis met him in front of the car, turned him around, and patted him down from head to toe. Then he led him back to the side of the car and opened the back door. "He's clean, boss."

"It's an honor meeting you," Vince said humbly as he climbed into the seat.

"Yeah, let's just hope for your sake it doesn't turn into your death sentence," Jason countered. "You've got about two minutes to convince me of why I should take a chance on you."

BURBANK
9:23 P.M. PACIFIC

It was a strange feeling for Mark to get ready for bed, knowing his every movement was watched and recorded. Mark even felt self-conscious about how long he brushed his teeth and how many times he should spit into the sink. He chose to use the toilet with the lights off.

He wanted to call Peter to see if through his computer magic he could match the flight times from the limousine company in Chicago with the seven names and cities from their list. But he couldn't chance contacting him from the apartment. He'd try to reach him in the morning.

Settling into the bed, he pulled out his Bible. He wanted to read a few Scriptures before conking out. He knew tomorrow would be a battle when he went back to Russell and tried to sell his story one more time.

As he opened the Bible, the phone rang.

"Hello," he answered.

"Mark, I'm glad I caught you. It's Rick."

Mark panicked, he couldn't let Rick say anything that would be picked up by the surveillance. "Look, Rick, it's not a good time right now—"

"But listen to me, you've got to hear this—"

Mark could hear the urgency in his voice; Rick had learned something. Mark made a quick choice. "No Rick!" he interrupted forcefully. "I told you I'm done with it all. Whatever it is, you can wait and tell me tomorrow at the studio."

Then Mark reached over and placed the phone back into its cradle.

WESTWOOD
SAME TIME

Rick placed the phone down and looked up in shock at Cassie, Gary, and Jill. After Samantha and Vanessa had left, Cassie and Rick filled them in on where Mark was, and the four had decided he should be told about Peter.

"I've never heard him act like that. He just cut me off and refused to listen to what I had to say. I'm afraid that Reynolds has won. It sounds like Mark has totally given up on his investigation—content to ride out his newfound fame."

"We need to pray," Cassie interjected.

"I agree," Gary added. "It's not over. God has a plan. We can't lose hope. Let's pray for Mark right now."

BURBANK
SAME TIME

Mark was about to pick up where he left off reading the night before, but he stopped. He was dealing with numerous emotions—the professional rush from having his name and opinions beamed all over the country, the despair from realizing that he was being given the opportunity only because Jason Reynolds was orchestrating the entire event, the thrill of the hunt returning after finding the surveillance equipment in his apartment, and the fear when he thought of the deaths of Kevin and Dawkins. And the emotional high of his feelings for Tracy conflicted with his hesitancy to get involved with somebody who wasn't a Christian.

He was tired. He thought of a passage of Scripture—something about running the race. He sure felt like he was in the middle of a marathon and just didn't have anything left to finish. He found the word "race" in his Bible's concordance. There it was, Hebrews 12.

> Therefore, since we are surrounded by such a great cloud of witnesses, let us throw off everything that hinders and the sin that so easily entangles, and let us run with perseverance the race marked out for us. Let us fix our eyes on Jesus, the author and perfecter of our faith, who for the joy set before him endured the cross, scorning its shame, and sat down at the right hand of the throne of God. Consider him who endured such opposition from sinful men, so that you will not grow weary and lose heart.

Mark read the words, but no feeling of relief came. He just wanted to quit, to go back to the way life was a little over a week ago. He reread the verses and something caught his eye: "Jesus, the author and perfecter of our faith, who for the joy set before him endured the cross." He hadn't noticed the wording before: "for the joy set before him endured the cross." Mark closed his eyes, trying to visualize Jesus submitting to the torture and death of crucifixion because of the joy set before him.

Knowing that soon he would once again be at the right hand of God, his Father helped Jesus endure the terrible pain and suffering of the cross.

So I guess I don't have a right to complain, Mark thought. *I just need to catch a glimpse of the joy set before me and be able to endure whatever comes my way tomorrow. Besides*—he remembered the Scripture he read the previous night—*so what if they kill me, then what else can they do?*

Mark smiled, in spite of his exhaustion. He set his Bible aside and closed his eyes as he brought his concerns and fears before the Lord. He closed with thoughts and prayers for Tracy, praying that the events of the past week would bring her to her own relationship with Jesus, before he was too far gone in his feelings for her. His last thoughts before he drifted off were of the softness of her lips and her silky hair flowing through his fingers.

CHAPTER 31

Rick waited outside the *Across the Nation* stage. He wanted to talk with Mark before the meeting. It was getting late and he hadn't shown up yet. He paced back and forth in front of the building as he prayed.

"What are you doing on this side of the lot, Rick?" Reggie, the former football player and now security guard, asked as he strolled around the corner.

"Hi, Reggie. I'm directing *Across the Nation* tonight while Terri spends some time with her dad."

"I didn't know that." Reggie laughed. "I'll make sure I'm hanging around here this afternoon then. You never know when you might need me around."

Rick smiled in spite of his anxiety about Mark. "You're always welcome around my shows, Reggie."

Reggie continued down the alley as Mark finally rushed around the corner.

"Mark, I've got to talk with you."

"I'm glad you're here, Rick. I've got to talk to you too. I tried to call you on my cell on the way in, but you beat me here."

"What was with you last night?"

Mark looked around the alleyway. A few other staff members were coming toward the door, "Come over here." Mark pulled Rick around the corner.

"I couldn't talk last night. My house is bugged. I didn't want you to say anything that would put you in danger, so I hung up. I'm really sorry."

"No, it's all right. Now it makes sense. But it sure made a bunch of us spend a lot of time in prayer for you last night."

"That's great. I'm sure I can use it. What did you want to tell me? It sounded urgent."

"Mark," Rick couldn't think of a gentle way to break the news, "Peter's dead."

"No!" Mark cried. "Not him too! How?"

"Samantha couldn't reach him all day yesterday, so she went to his house and found the police already there. He'd been shot."

"I can't believe it," Mark said, shaking his head. "How did you find out about it?"

"Samantha told me last night. And the good news side I wanted to tell you: she's made a decision for the Lord."

Mark froze. Unbelief filled his face. "You're kidding."

"No, I'm not. Vanessa really had an impact on her, and I think some of the things you said to her had something to do with it also."

"Wow, that's incredible." Then he again struggled with his grief. "I can't believe Peter's gone. Reynolds is going to pay for this."

"Then you're back in the fight?" Rick asked.

"I was back in the fight as soon as I saw the camera in my kitchen," Mark replied. "I can't believe I was ready to drop the whole thing.

"I had the most incredible experience last night—some kind of vision where God showed me that what Reynolds was offering me was very much like what Satan offered Jesus in the desert after he'd fasted for forty days. I'm sorry I fell for it, Rick. Please forgive me."

"That's the old Mark I've come to know."

"I may be back, but I'm not sure what to do about it. We need to really know God's direction."

"I agree, and I'm with you through this in whatever I can do," Rick said. "We'd better get in there. We're late."

Rick and Mark stepped into the production meeting while Russell was speaking.

"So tonight we're going to give our new celebrity—oh, here he is now."

The staffers laughed and whistled, and a few clapped as Mark made his way to the table.

"I was just telling everybody about the close of the show tonight, Mark," Russell continued. "We're going to let you have the last segment all to yourself—kind of a monologue when you can respond to how this entire controversy is playing out."

"So what about the *Single Life* piece?" Jennifer asked.

"It's killed. We might run it Sunday night."

Jennifer did nothing to conceal her contempt for the decision as she stared at Russell.

"Have all of you seen the promos the network is running for tonight's debut?" Russell continued, ignoring Jennifer's reaction. He nodded toward a production assistant standing by a TV and VCR. Moments later, the set came to life as pictures from Sam's Internet site floated by the screen.

Samantha closed her eyes, lowering her head as the men on staff whistled and cheered. Strip-show music and the announcer's voice-over accompanied the pictures.

> You've seen her weekly on *Across the Nation* but never like this. Tonight, National Studios presents *Across the Nation: Wednesday Edition.* See Samantha Steel as she uncovers what's behind the scenes of adult Internet sites. Tonight, nine o'clock, eight Central, *Across the Nation: Wednesday Edition.* Put the kids to bed early.

Samantha shuddered, sensing a struggle within her. Part of her was excited about the promo—the attention it would bring, how well it was done, and how she looked—but the new Samantha was embarrassed at the images, wishing she'd never started this story. A few days ago, she would have been thrilled with the promo.

"That alone will get us the biggest audience ever," Winston, the production executive said.

"Where were my pictures?" Tad complained.

Samantha looked up at the group and smiled weakly. Russell laughed as he brought the meeting back to order. "So, Samantha, is your piece ready to go?"

More snickers could be heard from the staff. Samantha ignored it. "I think so, Frank. I need to go over some things about it with you today if you've got the time. It's kind of taken a different direction than I expected."

Russell raised his eyebrows, glaring at her over the top of his glasses. "I'll bet I find this interesting."

"Oh, you will," Jeff, her producer chimed in.

When the chuckles died down, Russell continued the meeting. "OK, let's go through the rest of the show."

AMERICAN RESEARCH INSTITUTE
9:07 A.M. PACIFIC

Tracy sat with her back to the desk, staring at the downtown traffic circling the Reynolds building. When would be the best time to get into her grandfather's office to look for the flight log? Probably fairly early, in case he decided to show up at the office for a change. She was so deep in thought that she jumped six inches in the chair as she heard a man clear his throat behind her. She turned and looked into the face of Luis standing with a man she didn't recognize.

"Ms. Reynolds," Luis smiled, "sorry to startle you, but your grandfather wanted me to make sure I introduced you two. This is Vince Sinclair. He'll be taking over Kevin's duties for us. We were able to steal him from Research International."

Tracy tried to hide her surprise. How could her grandfather have a replacement for Kevin already? He just died Saturday.

Vince approached the desk with a friendly smile and an outstretched hand. "It's a pleasure to meet you, Ms. Reynolds. I'm excited to be with ARI."

Regaining her composure, Tracy stood and accepted the handshake. "Please call me Tracy, and welcome to the team."

MALIBU
9:15 A.M. PACIFIC

Jason Reynolds strained through the last few minutes of his treadmill workout. His legs ached, and sweat dripped off his forehead. The video screen in front of him gave him a wondrous view of the Swiss countryside surrounding Lake Geneva, but he knew the hill coming toward him meant the platform he was jogging on was about to incline, making it harder to keep up the pace. He looked at the timer on the panel in front of him—just a few more minutes to go, if he could hold out.

"Excuse me, sir." Griff said.

"Not now, Griff!" Reynolds grunted.

Griff dutifully waited the remaining three and a half minutes for the program to end. Reynolds gasped for breath and grabbed a towel as he stepped off the platform. His legs were unsteady as they hit the unmoving ground. "Now what is it?"

Griff held up a videotape. "Luis wanted you to see this—it's Taylor's tape from last night."

"All right, put it in."

Griff walked over to the corner behind the video screen, ejected the workout tape, and inserted the surveillance video.

Reynolds stretched his legs, waiting for the burning to subside as his attention was drawn to the screen. He could see Mark and his granddaughter stepping into frame and sitting at a table in what looked like Mark's kitchen. "Turn it up," he ordered.

Griff obliged, and the room filled with the words Mark and Tracy had orchestrated the previous night. Reynolds watched intently, at first his mood darkened at the sight of Tracy in Taylor's apartment. But as the conversation played itself out, he smiled at times and nodded as he heard Mark explain that Kevin had probably just been an employee with a grudge.

Reynolds waited until the conversation ended and the two had walked out of frame. "Thanks, Griff. I think we have Mark Taylor right where we want him."

NATIONAL STUDIOS
9:23 A.M. PACIFIC

Mark was watching Russell's door as he perused the morning edition of the *Los Angeles Times*. As soon as Samantha made her way out, he was ready to make his way in. His eyes scanned the front page, a blurb at the bottom caught his attention:

Senate Leadership Approval Ratings Drop
In an apparent backlash to the attempt to block President McNeil's UN appropriations bill, the Senate leadership's already low approval ratings dropped seven percentage points in the latest CNN/*Time* poll.

Mark skimmed the rest of the story, looking for details about the poll. His search was fruitless.

His stomach churned as he thought about what he should say to Russell. He silently prayed, knowing the risk involved. He'd been warned off the story twice already. He didn't know how Russell would react when he broached the subject again.

The door opened and Samantha stepped out. Mark got up and headed toward the office.

"May I talk with you for a minute, Frank?"

"Sure, come on in. Have a seat."

Mark took the chair closest to Russell's desk.

"You wouldn't believe the direction Sam's going with her story. I don't know what's gotten into her."

I do, Mark thought. "Maybe as she got into the whole thing, she just had a change of heart."

"Boy, did she! But either way, those pictures will still get the audience we need. Now what's on your mind?"

"Some new information has come to me about the polling story," Mark said.

"Correct me if I'm wrong," Frank countered, "but didn't I tell you on more than one occasion to drop it?"

"Yes," Mark replied, "and I did. But this information came to me—I didn't search for it."

Russell sat back and looked at his watch. "You've got two minutes. We've got too much work to do to sit here and waste time talking about a story that will not air on this show."

"OK, I'll be brief. There was one part of the report you didn't see—a list of names that were found at Dawkins's house last weekend. Seven names—influential people from the polling companies, major media conglomerates, and financial institutions, and even one name tied to the White House. The reason you didn't see them was because Jared Winter was on that list."

Russell looked at Mark. "You're trying to imply that Jared Winter, the head of our studio, is somehow involved in your polling conspiracy? You're nuts, Taylor."

"Hear me out, Frank," Mark pleaded. "It's not just Winter. Did you know that Jason Reynolds owns National Studios?"

Silence hung over the room.

"Where did you get that information?" Russell asked.

"From my computer expert who helped me put the pieces together," Mark said. "He's also turned up murdered yesterday, which makes three deaths surrounding this group. Dawkins in New York, Kevin Spencer, and now Peter Lovil."

"Do you have any proof?" Russell bellowed.

"It's coming together. I can now place Dawkins in Chicago, which, according to an eyewitness, is probably where he actually died. But then his body was found the next morning in his office in New York City. I think I can also place the other six members on this list, including Winter and Reynolds at the same location in Chicago."

Mark waited for Russell's response. None came. He just kept staring at Mark.

"Put aside all my interviews, all this media attention, Frank. That's just fluff. This story is huge. We've got a group of people controlling the polling data—killing anybody who gets in their way. They've got the media outlets to release whatever percentages they want—manipulating public opinion, keeping the politicians jumping through whatever hoops they design for them—and you sit there with no response? Where's the journalist in you, Frank? Has it been killed by the corporate giant?"

"This isn't about me," Russell replied coldly. "This is about you."

"Exactly. Remember the speech you so eloquently gave me last week, about hanging in there until the story comes along, the one that will sit and burn in my gut? You know, the one you can't put out. Well, here it is for me, Frank. What are we going to do about it?"

"What do you want me to do?" Russell jumped up from his chair and went to Mark's side of the desk. "You paint this wild tale of conspiracy—one in which you say the head of our network is smack dab in the middle of. That same person who has already given me the order that if you even mention a word about this story again you are to be fired on the spot. Fired, Mark, do you get the message?

"So what can I do? Let's see, if I go in there pleading your case and you're wrong, then you obviously don't have a story anyway, and you've just lost your job. If I go in there and, let's say, you're right, then I get canned right along with you, and we're both out of jobs. If I let you keep investigating against Winter's orders and you do come up with enough evidence, then what do we do? Go to a competing network to get a time slot? There is no way to win this one, Mark."

Russell sat dejectedly on the edge of his desk. "Is there any way I can talk you into giving whatever you have to the authorities and dropping this whole thing?"

Their eyes met. Russell saw Mark's determination. "No, I guess not," he concluded.

Mark sat quietly as Russell struggled with his decision.

"You're fired, Mark," he finally said.

"He fired you?" Rick asked as the two talked in the darkened control room.

Mark nodded. "I left Frank no choice. He couldn't go to Winter with any of it, and he already had his orders."

"Are you sure you did the right thing?"

"Of course not! I went with my gut, but I have no idea if I did the right thing." Mark started to pace. "Maybe I should walk right back in there and tell him I'll play along—no, I can't do that."

"Man! Talk about a tough situation," Rick said. "I'm sorry I encouraged you back into this fight."

"No, don't be. It's not your fault. If this is God's doing, we'll just have to play it out and see where he has it end."

"Maybe if you give it some time, Russell will cool off, and he'll be reasonable," Rick offered.

"That may be, but I'm not going to hang around and wait for it."

"What are you going to do?"

"Keep searching. I've got an appointment to keep."

"Mr. Winter, I've got Frank Russell on the line." Jared Winter heard the amplified voice of his secretary through the intercom. He set aside the budget figures for the next feature National Studios was going to produce and picked up the phone.

"Yes, Frank. What's up?"

"It's about Mark Taylor," Russell said. "I just fired him."

"You what?" Winter was shocked. They'd poured so much publicity into him and the midweek show was about to debut. "What possessed you to do that?"

"He wouldn't drop the polling story like you instructed. I had no choice."

Winter remained silent. What should he do? He was under the same instructions. If Taylor went back to investigating, he would have to be eliminated, or the Circle could be compromised. He'd have to inform Reynolds and quickly.

"Did he tell you why he's willing to jeopardize his career for this one story?" Winter asked.

Russell considered giving him all the details, including the fact that Winter was one of Taylor's suspects but thought better of it.

"No, just that some new information came his way," he finally answered.

"Where is he now?" Winter asked.

"I'm not sure. He left the office. We can always reach him by cell phone. Why? What do you want to do?"

"Nothing yet. I'll get back to you." Winter hung up and dialed the private line to Malibu.

CHAPTER 32

Mark walked through the lobby of Reynolds International, merging with a group of businessmen heading for the elevators. He didn't want to get stopped by security and have to sign in.

By the time he got to the sixty-fourth floor, just he and the attendant were in the elevator. He stepped into the spacious lobby of ARI, walking quickly past the receptionist while she was distracted with a phone call.

He made his way down the hall to Tracy's office.

"May I help you?" Brenda, Tracy's secretary asked.

"I'm supposed to meet—" Mark began but stopped as he spotted Tracy coming out of her office.

"I'm expecting him, Brenda," Tracy said as she took Mark by the arm and led him down the hallway.

"We're going up to the executive offices," she whispered as they walked. "I've been trying to get up the courage all morning. Earlier, I was sitting there thinking about it, and Luis sneaked up behind me to introduce me to Kevin's replacement. I nearly jumped out of my skin."

"They've already replaced Kevin?"

"Yeah, can you believe it?"

"No, it seems awfully fast."

"That's what I thought," Tracy returned.

"Guess who's out of a job as of this morning."

Tracy stopped in the hallway. "You? What happened?"

"I went to Russell's office, asking to keep on the story. We didn't see eye-to-eye on the issue, and I wouldn't back down."

Tracy resumed walking. "I hope you know what you're doing, Mr. Taylor." She turned the corner, leading Mark into the elevator.

"Sixty-six please," she instructed the attendant.

The three rode in silence, traveling the few floors to the top of the building. The doors opened up to an even more impressive lobby than Tracy's floor. Dark-green marble tiles led to a receptionist.

"Hi, Tracy." The woman smiled. "Your grandfather isn't in today."

"I know, Rhonda, thanks."

She led Mark right past her, toward a row of plush offices. Another woman sat at a desk outside Reynolds's office. Mark assumed she must be his personal assistant.

"Hi, Carla," Tracy greeted her. "My grandfather asked me to get something out of his office for him. Could you let us in?"

"Sure, Tracy, I'd be happy to." Carla grabbed a set of keys in her desk, then ushered the two into the office suite. "Can I help you find what you're looking for?"

"No, I think I know where he keeps it. But I need to check a file as well, so it could take a couple of minutes."

The phone in the outer office rang as Carla was about to respond. "Excuse me then, I need to grab that call." She left the two alone.

Mark was standing closest to the door and quietly shut it. "Where do we start?"

"Check the filing cabinets. I'll check the computer," Tracy said, walking over to her grandfather's desk. She touched the mouse and the screen flared to life, showing numerous files. She searched through them looking for something that might have the company jet's flight logs.

Mark opened the top drawer of the cabinet, searching through the alphabetized files. He wondered silently if there might be any trip alarms or security cameras that were monitoring their work.

"Have you found anything yet?" he asked, growing more tense.

"No, how about you?" Tracy replied nervously.

"Nothing."

Tracy opened a file labeled "Corporate Assets," and she saw "Lear jet."

"I may have something here." She opened the file and saw a folder labeled "Flight Logs."

MALIBU
SAME TIME

The private line in Reynolds's office rang as he worked at his computer terminal.

"Yes."

"Your granddaughter and Mark Taylor are in your office," Luis said.

"What are they doing?" Reynolds asked calmly, not surprised. He'd received the call from Winter earlier. Confused by the discrepancy of what he'd seen on the tape and Mark's refusal at the studio to drop the story, Reynolds had just waited. He knew sooner or later, Taylor would make his move.

"Searching for something. Tracy's on your computer, and Taylor is looking through your files."

"Well, that's a waste of their time. There's absolutely nothing in that office that'll incriminate me."

"What do you want me to do?"

"Nothing. I don't want to frighten Tracy. Keep your eyes on them. I may want to talk with Taylor shortly."

AMERICAN RESEARCH INSTITUTE
SAME TIME

"Here it is, Mark," Tracy said. On the screen was the record for that Monday.

Mark read the information. "The jet left Los Angeles airport at 2:15 that afternoon, arrived in Chicago at 7:56 Central time. Look, the flight plan originally called for the plane to fly the next day to Dulles airport in Washington, D.C. But the plan was changed to fly to La Guardia, they left Chicago at 10:49 that night, arrived New York early Tuesday, after two in the morning. But it was only on the ground twenty-seven minutes, then it left for Dulles."

Tracy looked at Mark as he finished reading. "Is that what you were looking for?"

"Yes, it puts your grandfather in Chicago at the same time as Dawkins. I'm sure they used the company jet to get his body back to New York."

She lowered her head, trying to grasp what it meant.

"Let's get out of here before we get caught. Is there any way to print that information?" Mark asked.

"Yeah. Turn on the printer over in the corner." Mark did so, then she hit print.

"Twenty-seven minutes—plenty of time to have a body removed from the plane, wasn't it?" Tracy asked, her mind beginning to open to the possibility that Mark was right.

"Yes, it was, Tracy. I'm sorry." Mark answered softly.

She walked over to him. He opened his arms to her as she laid her head softly on his shoulder. He held her gently, caressing her hair as they waited for the printer to spit out its piece of paper.

"I don't know what to believe," Tracy confessed. "I feel like I'm betraying my grandfather by even bringing you in here." She pulled back and looked straight into Mark's eyes, tears forming in hers. "He's been more than my grandfather—he raised me since I was nine. I can't conceive that he could have done the things you claim."

"I understand, Tracy," Mark said, "and I'm sorry. I didn't want to shatter your world. I'm just looking for the truth."

He couldn't deny the incredibly strong feelings he had for Tracy. Causing her this pain felt like a knife stabbing into his own heart. Without thinking, Mark reached out to help. "Just say the word, Tracy, and I'll drop the investigation."

Tracy tilted her head, the tears now sliding down her cheeks. "You'd do that for me?"

Mark didn't respond. Inside, he was struggling with what he'd said. If God had indeed placed him on this path, how could he say yes to Tracy and no to God. He prayed she wouldn't take him up on his offer. "I can't stand seeing you struggle with this, Tracy. I never intended to hurt you."

Tracy gave a meek smile. "I couldn't let you do that," she said, touching his cheek lightly with her hand. "Would being ignorant of the truth be better than facing reality? Maybe for a few days, but how long would it take for the fantasy to unravel? We've come this far—I want to see it to the end. I want to know what kind of man my grandfather really is and what kind of man you really are."

"You're one incredible woman, Tracy Reynolds."

"Let's get that paper and get out of here."

"You're on." Mark turned and headed for the printer while Tracy tried to return the computer to the way she had found it. On the way out of the office, Tracy asked him one last question.

"Mark, would you have really quit?"

He paused, looking down at the floor, then back into her eyes. "I meant it when I said it, but to be honest, I don't know. My heart was sincere. I wanted to stop whatever it was that was causing you pain, but if I really knew God was telling me to continue, yet I had promised you I'd stop, I'd have a real dilemma on my hands."

NATIONAL STUDIOS
1:05 P.M. PACIFIC

Rick sat in the unfamiliar control room. He had at least an hour until he had the show's final rundown for the staff. Rick had met with the graphics and virtual set crew, making sure everything was ready.

He picked up the phone and dialed Cassie's office. He figured she'd be in today, even though they weren't taping.

"Tina, is Cassie available?" Rick asked.

"Hold on, Rick."

Within a few seconds, Cassie was on the line. "How's it going over there?"

"Not good, Cassie," Rick answered.

She could hear the despair in his voice. "What's wrong, honey?"

"It's Mark—they fired him."

"Oh no!"

"Yeah, he went in to try and get Russell to let him continue his story and got the ax."

"Oh, Rick, I'm so sorry. How did he take it?"

"Actually, really well. He was determined to get to the bottom of it all. I feel bad. I don't know if he would have pushed it without our Chicago stuff."

"That's understandable, but I don't think it would have made any difference. Mark couldn't tolerate being manipulated by Reynolds and his group. He needs to get to the truth."

AMERICAN RESEARCH INSTITUTE
SAME TIME

Back safely behind the closed door of her office, Tracy and Mark went over their options.

"I don't want you to go to the police," Tracy pleaded. "Not yet anyway. Maybe there's some other answer to all this. I'd like to hear what Papa would say first."

"I don't think the police or the FBI would even listen to me yet anyway," Mark muttered. "It's all circumstantial. There's not even a suspicion of foul play with either Dawkins's or Kevin's deaths, and I have no idea how they found out about Peter. Wait a minute." Mark paused as something came to mind.

"Who's Peter?" Tracy asked.

"My message machine—that's it." Mark exclaimed, then turned to answer Tracy's question. "Peter was the computer expert I had look into the stuff Kevin gave me. He left a message the other day on my machine at home. I just found out this morning he was murdered yesterday."

"I'm sorry, Mark."

"I'll bet the surveillance was there when I came back from New York."

"So you think my grandfather's people traced him down and had him murdered?" Mark nodded his head.

Tracy wanted to change the subject. "Now tell me again, how do you think the polls were rigged."

Mark sat down, looking intently at her over her desk. "From what Peter found out, it looks like the computer program has a subroutine that can be accessed by a code word. When implemented, the subroutine alters the random selection of telephone numbers and instigates calls to numbers from selected data bases with known political leanings."

Tracy nodded. "We've always prided ourselves on being the most scientific and accurate polling company in the country. It's incredible to think all this time, we've been rigging the results of our polls."

"Have you seen the gay poll that caught Kevin's attention?" Mark asked.

"No, I never got the time to look at it. I do remember when I heard the results I was surprised as well."

"Can you look it up on your computer?"

"Sure, I've got access to every survey we do here."

Tracy spun her chair to the computer side of her desk and started opening files. Mark walked around the desk to look at the computer screen.

"Here it is—" She clicked on the results page. "Wow, 81 percent approval rating for special protection in the workplace. That's incredible, not even equal protection, but special."

Mark leaned very close over Tracy's shoulder. She shuddered slightly in pleasure as his breath lightly touched the back of her neck.

"I can see why these results attracted Kevin's attention. But you say RI was doing the same thing?"

Mark was silent.

"Mark, did you hear me?" But he was deep in thought.

"I just remembered something Peter told me the last time I talked with him." He stared into the screen, then he looked down directly at her. "What's a weigh-factor?"

Tracy was surprised by the question. "It's a device used to keep a particular sample within required parameters. Why?"

"Explain it to me," Mark pressed.

"Well, say for instance to have a scientifically accurate sample for an election, you have to have so many responses from the state of Rhode Island, let's say twenty calls out of a thousand. But when your polling is complete, you only have seventeen responses. When you publish your results, you'd have a bunch of footnotes by all the graphs and percentages, saying, 'We did not attain a minimal sample size in this cell.' To avoid that, a pollster can implement what's called a weigh-factor. In this case you can add a weigh-factor to the geographic category of this poll, so that all of the Rhode Island surveys will be counted as if twenty were received. Then you have just one footnote added to the conclusions, instead of on every graph and percentage listed. It's used quite often in demographic categories as well to even out a sample, like if you don't have enough women in the twenty-five-to-forty age range."

Mark kept his gaze intent on Tracy as he asked his next question. "Is it ever used with a response?"

Tracy shook her head, "No, never. It would taint your whole survey. No one would ever think of using it in a response category. It'd throw your percentages off—you'd end up with more than 100 percent responses."

"What do you mean?" Mark's mind continued to spin.

"If your survey had a 50 percent positive response, but you added a weigh-factor of 1.2, it'd give you a 60 percent positive result, but you'd still have the other 50 percent negative to deal with, and the total survey results would now be 110 percent. Not possible."

"But what if there was also a counter weigh-factor for the other percentage, say of 0.8, wouldn't you get back to 100 percent"

For a few seconds, Tracy stared at Mark blankly. Then her eyes widened. "Oh, man! I never would have thought of that—using a weigh-factor to change a response category. In that case you can name any stinking percentages you want, no matter what your data says. It goes against everything I've ever been taught about making our polls accurate. How did you think of this?"

"It was the last thing Peter said to me. He found two lines of language in the latest polling program code that Kevin had placed on the disk—something to do with weigh-factors. After hearing your explanation, I think one line implements the weigh-factor and the other the counter weigh-factor so that you can name your final percentages before you even take the poll. He found that after the program ran, it would delete the two lines of instructions, leaving the final results with the weigh-factors figured in, but not accounted for in any of the results. Do you think you could find those lines of instructions in the program?"

"If it's there, I'll find it. I didn't spend four years at UCLA in computer science for nothing."

Mark leaned over and kissed her. "You're too much."

"If you're right," she shuddered at the thought, "you're too much."

Tracy turned her attention on the computer again, looking for Bob Carpenter's latest poll. The cell phone in Mark's pocket rang. While Tracy continued, he answered the call.

"Hello."

"I think we need to talk again." Mark recognized Reynolds's voice.

"Hi, Jason," Mark responded. Tracy turned around, eyes wide in surprise. He nodded.

"I agree. Name the place."

"Do you think you could find the house by driving out here?" Reynolds asked.

"I can find it."

"Then please, come join me," Jason said. "I know you don't have to run back to the studio."

Mark felt his stomach drop. It hadn't taken Jason long to find out about his meeting with Russell. Should he risk meeting him face-to-face? Mark needed the chance to confront Reynolds with what he had, but was a meeting at the mansion wise? He prayed intently as the seconds ticked by.

"Well, Mark, what is it going to be?"

"I'll come," Mark answered. Tracy looked up at him, fear striking her face, but she couldn't say anything, afraid to reveal her presence with Mark to her grandfather.

"Good, I knew you'd see the light," Reynolds chuckled. "Come with an open mind, Mark. There's a way out of this for both of us, trust me. I don't want to lose a valuable reporter."

Mark shook his head. "We'll see, Jason. I'll make it out there as soon as I can."

"I'll be expecting you. Now may I please speak to Tracy?"

Mark's eyes closed. The sense of being sealed in a maze enveloped him. He sighed and handed Tracy the phone.

She took it in her hands. Her eyes begged for help.

"Papa?" She asked meekly.

"Yes, honey. You don't have to talk, just listen. I know you've got a lot of questions, I'm sure Mark has a lot of accusations. But don't jump to any conclusions until we can talk. Things are not the way Mark's painting them to be. Trust me, pumpkin. He's coming out to the house, and we're going to talk. Everything will work out, I promise you."

Tracy was too stunned to ask how he knew they were together. What about Leeland Dawkins? Did he fly to New York to deliver the body? There was so much running through her mind, so much she wanted to say, but the warmth and gentleness of his voice kept the questions unasked.

"I understand."

"Good. I'll call you as soon as Mark and I have met."

She handed the phone back to Mark, her eyes in a daze.

"What did he say?" Mark asked.

"Just not to jump to any conclusions until we talk. Are you really going to see him alone?"

"I don't think I have a choice," Mark answered. "He said there's a way out of all this for us. I've lost my job, he's in danger of losing everything. It's time we talk."

"But if he's killed three other people, as you claim . . . " The words were heavy on her tongue. "What's to stop him from hurting you?"

"I'm too high-profile right now for him to try something stupid like that. I'm sure he wants to convince me of his innocence. Plus, you know I'm going out there. He won't be able to do anything to me and expect to get away with it. It just might be the opportunity I need for him to slip up." Mark reached into his shirt pocket and pulled out his recording pen. "This will record whatever he says. You never know what he may confess to in the heat of the moment."

Tracy fought back tears as she walked Mark out of her office and toward the elevator. It'd taken her the better part of an hour to delve deeply enough into the program to identify the two lines of code that Peter had found. It was devastating to face the reality that Mark's theories about her grandfather could be true.

As they reached the elevator, he placed his arm around her waist.

"I'm sorry, Tracy. This must be incredibly difficult for you."

"I just can't believe my grandfather could do this. I don't want you to go out there."

"I'll be OK. God wouldn't have brought me this far to leave me stranded now."

She smiled. "I know you feel that way. I wish I had the faith you do."

Mark grinned. "You can."

She pinched his hand, laughing through the tension.

The elevator door opened, and Vince Sinclair stepped out. He stopped short as he recognized Mark. A brief flash of fear crossed his face. Mark hadn't noticed him until he paused.

"Mark, this is our newest employee, Vince Sinclair." Tracy introduced the duo, wondering why Vince was acting strangely. "Vince, this is Mark Taylor."

"It's nice to meet you," Vince said, lowering his head.

"Have we met—" Mark reached out his hand as his mind raced. But before he could finish the sentence, Vince made a quick turn and headed down the hallway.

"That was strange," Tracy commented. "He sure was in a hurry."

"I've seen that man before, Tracy," Mark said, "but I'm not sure where."

"My grandfather just hired him today."

"Watch yourself with him. I don't trust him." Mark gave Tracy a warm hug. He turned and stepped into the elevator.

"Right now, I don't trust anybody around here. Be careful, Mark." And the elevator closed.

Twenty minutes later, Mark was in his beat-up Honda Civic, heading toward the coastline. He picked up his cell phone and dialed the production office.

"Rick Treadway please," he said, trying to disguise his voice somewhat so the receptionist wouldn't recognize him.

"Hello."

"Rick, it's Mark."

"How's the hunt going?"

"I'm headed to the lions' den right now," Mark replied.

"Mark, are you crazy? You're going out there?"

"Tracy and I found the last piece of the puzzle. We know how he's rigging the polls, and we can place him and the corporate jet in the same location with Dawkins."

"But you can't confront him alone like this. We need to have the FBI or somebody with you."

"There isn't time, and he's ready to talk. He admitted to Tracy that we're going to meet. I don't think he'll try anything. I just wanted you to alert the gang and get them praying for me."

"That we'll do, but are you sure this is what you're supposed to be doing?"

"Yeah, I think so. I've got to get him to slip up and confess something. Otherwise, everything is all circumstantial."

"Boy, Mark," Rick shuddered, "I sure hope you're right. Call me as soon as you can."

"I will." Mark hung up the phone and slowed as he came to the end of the freeway in Santa Monica. From there, he'd take Highway 1 to Malibu.

NATIONAL STUDIOS
2:30 P.M. PACIFIC

Rick and the associate director went over the rundown. The door opened behind him.

"Rick, could I talk with you a minute?" Samantha asked.

"Sure, Sam, come on in," Rick responded.

"I'll grab a quick lunch and be back in a few minutes, Rick," the associate director said as she left.

"Did you hear about Mark?" Samantha asked.

"Yeah, he spoke to me before he left."

"How was he?"

"Doing OK, for somebody who just got canned."

"Frank's not talking about it. Do you know why he was fired?"

Rick thought for a second; there was no reason not to tell her. "It's that polling story he's been working on. He'd been warned to drop it. He was even threatened with losing his job if he didn't. Mark found some new information and went in this morning to ask Russell to let him keep at it, and he got fired."

"Wow!" Samantha gasped. "With all the publicity surrounding him right now, Russell is crazy. Half the country will be watching because of Mark tonight. What are they thinking?"

"They're trying to get the dog off the scent, that's what." Rick then told Samantha where the investigation had led.

"I can't believe it!" she exclaimed. "Is it really possible that the polls have been rigged?"

"Mark seems to think so."

"That would be the biggest story the network has ever covered, and they're killing it to protect themselves. How ironic."

"Yeah, Mark is in a tough spot. So pray for him when you think about it."

"I will, but I'm still learning how to do that," Samantha replied.

Rick smiled. "It's not hard. Just speak to God like you're talking to me. Now what can I do for you?"

"A couple of things." Samantha said nervously. "I wanted—wow, this is hard for me."

"Take your time."

"I feel like I need to ask for your forgiveness," Samantha said as she dropped her head. "You know, for how I treated you last year."

"Thanks, Sam," Rick responded with a smile. "I forgive you."

She looked up as Rick continued. "But I haven't held a grudge against you. I was being arrested. You were just doing your job, although a bit too well I thought at the time."

Samantha grinned.

"Remember," Rick said, "I was the one trying to get through to you to apologize for the way I had acted. We just got off on the wrong foot. Do you forgive me?"

She nodded "Yes. Boy, all this forgiveness stuff is new to me."

Rick laughed. "You'll get used to it. Then it's the most marvelous thing in the whole universe. What else is on your mind?"

"It's this story on the Internet," Samantha said. "I'm not sure what to do. I just saw the video we're going to roll into the show, and it's—how do I put this?— pretty spicy."

"I figured it would be," Rick thought. "A lot of the pictures are of you?"

Samantha's face reddened. "Just like we promoted."

"Well, that's a tough one. The Bible says that once we've received Jesus, we're new creatures—the old has passed away and everything is new. We're forgiven by the Lord, but we still have to live with the consequences of our past actions."

"Part of me still doesn't see what the big deal is with the nudity, but then the other half . . . Well, I'm embarrassed and don't want my body to be used as Vanessa talked about."

"I understand, Sam. There will be many struggles between your new spiritual life and the way you used to think. But you're not alone. Let the Holy Spirit guide you."

"I'm trying, but it was so hard after seeing the tape. I looked at my eyes and it scared me. They were as lifeless as Vanessa's were in a video I saw of her."

"They probably were, Samantha, but they're not anymore."

She smiled. "Thank God for that, huh? I want to get the Web site shut down. With Peter gone, I'm not sure how to do that."

"I know who could probably help you—our off-line editor. Let me give him a call."

"That'd be great. Once I get this story over with, I want it behind me."

"I know you do, but this is one area that will probably not be that easy to get away from," Rick said as he picked up the phone. "Once those pictures are out there in cyberspace, they're impossible to get back."

Samantha nodded. "I know, and that really bothers me. But you know what? I'll just have to go on the air tonight and make it all worth it."

"That's the spirit."

CHAPTER 33

Mark pulled into the circular drive outside the mansion. He turned off the motor and prayed for God to give him the confidence and peace he needed to confront Reynolds.

He pulled the MPR-1 recording pen out of his shirt pocket, hit the record button, and put it back. Then he stepped out of his car and walked to the door.

It was opened by Luis, whose eyes reminded Mark of a black hole. "Come on in. Mr. Reynolds is expecting you."

Mark stepped into the foyer, where Luis stopped him. "If you don't mind."

Mark stood still with his arms up while Luis searched him for any kind of weapon.

"He's in his office. Follow me."

They walked up two flights of the circular staircase and then walked down the hallway to the office. Luis opened the door, ushered Mark into the room, then left, closing the door behind him.

"Well, Mark," Jason said, "it's come down to this. Please come in and have a seat."

Mark stepped farther into the room, struggling to appear confident, but also fighting the urge to turn and run.

"Now what is so important about your investigation that you're willing to give up your job and everything you've worked so hard for, Mark?" Jason asked.

"I think I've put it all together, Jason," Mark answered. "You do still want me to call you Jason, don't you?"

"Please do. I think we can come out of this still friends, Mark." Jason flashed his patented grin. "So tell me what you think you know."

Mark couldn't sit still so he got up and paced the room. "I know that you are rigging the polls in all your companies and probably a few you don't own. Through your many media holdings you disseminate the false data to the nation, thereby shifting the direction of the country toward whatever twisted goals you think are important."

Reynolds didn't react, so Mark continued. "I know that you were in Chicago the night that Leeland Dawkins was murdered."

"Murdered?" Jason interrupted with a smile. "He died in New York, of a heart attack, I believe."

"No, he was murdered in Chicago. You had his body flown to New York."

Reynolds's expression darkened, but he stayed silent. Mark approached the desk, placed his hands on the counter and stared right into Reynolds's eyes.

"I know that you're the one behind Peter Lovil's murder, and that Kevin Spencer's death was no accident."

"If you had any proof of these wild accusations, you wouldn't be here alone. What would stop me from having the same fate befall you?"

"I'm too visible right now. How could you explain my death so closely tied to the others who were searching into your empire? Besides, there are people who know I'm here."

"Like Rick Treadway? Maybe even his fiancée Cassie?" Jason suggested. Mark shuddered, concerned that he had put his friends in danger. Reynolds continued, "Next you're going to tell me you have all the evidence left at some lawyer's house ready to turn it into the police if he doesn't hear from you in the next fifteen minutes. Come on, Mark, you don't have anything but theories and insinuations."

Mark was about to respond when a door opened across the room and his producer, Jennifer Williams, walked into the room.

"You see, Mark, there isn't anything you know that I don't know," Jason said as Jennifer walked over and stood beside him. "I've watched your every move, been two steps ahead of you wherever you go. I've even got a copy of the report you wrote for Russell."

Mark recalled the moment he came out of Russell's office and Jennifer had been leaving his desk for the copy room. His screen saver had not been activated when he got to his computer. It all made sense now.

"No one is waiting for your call," Jason said. "Rick has your information and my computer disk." He snapped his fingers in front of Mark's face. "And just like that I can have that problem taken care of."

Mark kept his gaze on Jennifer, shaking his head. "You've really made a pact with the devil, haven't you, Jennifer? I'm not surprised."

She stepped behind Jason and rubbed his shoulders as she flashed Mark a wicked smile.

NATIONAL STUDIOS
SAME TIME

Rick left the stage area and headed toward the *Harold Show* offices. He wanted to pick up Cassie and break away for a bite to eat. He looked at his watch. He was sure by now Mark would have talked with Reynolds, and he wondered how the meeting had gone.

As he approached the building, he saw Cassie coming out the front door.

"Hello, beautiful," Rick called. "How about lunch?"

"I was just headed your way."

He gave her a warm hug, followed by a quick kiss. The two walked toward the commissary. Cassie took his hand as she asked, "Have you heard from Mark?"

"No," Rick answered. "It's been nearly an hour and a half. I'm starting to get worried."

"Is there anything we can do if we don't hear from him?"

Rick had been mulling this over ever since Mark had called him. "I don't know. We've got all his documentation, but I don't know what to do with it."

"How about the detectives who worked with us on Bennett's murder? They cover Malibu."

"That's a good idea, but let's give Mark more time to work things his way. For now, I'm just going to keep praying."

MALIBU
2:54 P.M. PACIFIC

Mark thought carefully as he faced Reynolds and now Jennifer. If she'd given him a copy of the report, then Reynolds knew nearly everything. "I know about the seven."

Reynolds flinched for the first time and Mark jumped on the reaction. "Dawkins was stepping out of line; he had to be eliminated. That still leaves you with Winter, Capshaw, Davidson, Adler, Fisher, and probably somebody to replace Dawkins—like Mike Palmer, the new president of Research International? Your little group has had a long run, Jason, but it's over."

Jason's face hardened. In all his research and surveillance on Mark, nothing had come across his desk that he'd broken the Circle. He leaned back in his chair, forcing a smile before he looked up to Jennifer. "You better get back to the studio—it's getting late."

Jennifer's eyes darted between Reynolds and Mark, trying to make sense of what Mark had said. She didn't want to leave.

"But, Jason—"

"Now, Jennifer," Reynolds spoke quietly, but firmly. "I want to talk with Mark privately."

She leaned over and gave him a kiss on the top of the head before turning and making her way out of the room.

"How did you get the names?" Jason snapped as soon as the door shut behind her.

"Let's just say Dawkins made a death-bed confession."

"Your trip to New Jersey turned up something we didn't find," Jason thought out loud as he processed the new information. "And you left that out of your report, didn't you? Probably because Winter's name was part of it. I have to hand it to you, Mark, you've done your homework, but you've got one conclusion that's in error."

"Enlighten me."

The door opened again. Luis held a gun aimed squarely into Mark's chest. "The one that made you think you were—how did you say it?—too high-profile for me to do anything about."

Mark lowered his head, acting defeated as he weighed his options. Could he react fast enough to disarm Luis before the gun would go off? Doubtful, and perhaps Reynolds had a gun in his desk too. He'd have to play this out, he decided, as he prayed as he never had before.

"Mark, you should have left well enough alone." Jason walked around the desk toward him. "You are just at the beginning of your life, with no limits in sight. I set you up with all the publicity anybody could hope for to springboard your career into the superstardom. You'd stopped reporting the news and were making it. I even gave you a platform for your idiotic, right-wing ideology, and you had to throw it all away, and for what?"

"How about the truth?" Mark responded.

"You want the truth?" Reynolds's voice strained as he nearly shouted. "OK, young man, here it is. Dawkins had to be taken care of; he was setting himself up to turn on the Circle. Yes, that's the name of our little group—the Circle of Seven. We've been together a long time. I learned years ago of the power of propaganda. I studied Hitler, Mussolini, and Stalin. I saw in the infant stages of our technology how this country could be led. I couldn't let one mentally deranged person throw it all away."

Mark felt the evil pouring from Reynolds as he went into his tirade. He knew the MPR-1 was recording every word, but with the confession came the clear understanding that Reynolds would never allow Mark to walk off his property alive.

"And through the past five administrations, we've been behind the scenes, prodding and pushing—opinion polls, focus groups, approval ratings. We've fixed it all."

Reynolds turned and paced the room. An evil, proud smile appeared as his rantings continued. "Do you know how easy it is to sway a congressman, a senator, or even a president when he's confronted with a batch of percentages on how his constituents feel? It doesn't matter if the numbers aren't real. He'll respond—they all do. The real power isn't in the White House; it's right here—in my office." He slammed his hand on the desk to emphasize his point.

"I told you yesterday the issues of the day aren't decided by the politicians. They're certainly not decided by the electorate. They are decided by the media.

"And when you consider my influence in the media, combined with my control over the polling companies," Reynolds continued, "I not only determine the issues of the day; I decide what the nation thinks about them."

Reynolds took a deep breath. His passion had surprised him. He'd held his emotions captive through so many years of controlling from behind the scenes. It was such a rush to release them.

Mark wanted nothing more than to be able to get up and walk out of the room. The evil emanating from the man was making him nauseous.

"Is that why India's in the news right now?" Mark asked. "Is that your doing?"

"Yes!" Reynolds proclaimed boldly.

"And what are the American people supposed to think about that?"

"They're supposed to be compassionate toward a state devastated by famine, drought, and earthquakes. They're supposed to demand that the UN step in and do something about it, and they're supposed to pressure Congress to pass the UN appropriation bill."

"And what do you hope to gain?"

"You're a fool, Taylor." Jason began to pace again, switching the subject. "You can be part of the solution, not part of the problem. It's your choice."

"How do you fix elections?"

"Oh, we haven't figured that one out quite yet." Jason laughed. "Whenever it gets close to an election, we have to be very accurate. We'll push and manipulate as much as we can before the primaries, then do it again up until a couple of months before the national election to position our candidates the best we can. And if we've done our job right, the people will vote the way they've been programmed to, but for the actual election our polls have to be right on.

"You see, the one true test of the polling industry is during an election. That's the only time that the populace is ever really counted, and when those come up, you can bet we're as accurate as scientifically possible. But in between, and in social opinion surveys, there's no accountability. What outlets we don't control in the media we usually share in what I would call an ideological monopoly, so I found we can run with whatever percentages I want. We've been doing it for a while now, and nobody's caught on. It's perfect." Jason beamed with pride at his own propaganda machine.

"How long have you been using the weigh-factor?"

Jason nodded with raised eyebrows, surprised by Mark's knowledge. "That's something we're just implementing. A stroke of genius in its simplicity actually. I realize now we should have used it on the gay poll; then you wouldn't be standing here right now. I don't know what Bob was thinking . . ."

Jason paused, glancing back up at Mark smiling. "You have impressed me, Mark. It would be a shame to lose you, but as I was saying earlier, there is a way out of this for both of us, if you'll listen to reason."

Having nothing to lose, Mark held his hands out by his side. "I'm listening."

"I doubt you have enough on me to ever convict me in a court of law, but you can still make trouble for us, and we certainly don't want any light shining on our operations. So here's what I'm offering you: you can have your job back, along with a hefty salary increase. I'm sure with all the publicity you've brought to the network we can justify raising you to the status of a Diane Sawyer or a Ted Koppel.

"I'm talking in the seven-figure range here. We'll build *Across the Nation* around you—the straight-talking, no-nonsense reporter who tells it like it is. You can still have your platform for the causes you want to champion even if I don't agree with your politics. You'll be a household name, and the way things are looking, you might get my granddaughter as a bonus."

Mark smiled as his mind flashed back to his vision of the cobra on top of the Malibu cliff. "And all I have to do is promise to drop the investigation—forget everything I know about the Circle of Seven, ARI, Leeland Dawkins, Kevin Spencer, and Peter Lovil."

"That pretty much sums it up. Think of the power, Mark, the position of influence you'd have in this country. What I'm talking about here is real. Don't throw it all away. You won't get another offer like this one."

"And how would you explain my demise if I don't take your offer?" Mark asked.

"That'll be easy. You came out here to discuss your being fired, and I talked you into coming back to work. Our meeting ended too late for you to drive back to the studio in time for the show, so I sent you off in one of my helicopters. Unfortunately, there was a mechanical failure, and the helicopter crashed into the Pacific Ocean. An expensive loss, but one I can write off."

Mark shook his head. Reynolds just might be able to pull it off.

Reynolds continued, "I know from the foolhardy decision you made with Russell this morning that when it's only your neck on the line, you may not choose in your own best interests. So Luis is going to take you downstairs before we finalize our deal. We'll finish this up in a few minutes."

Mark had no choice but to walk the direction Luis pointed with the gun. They used the elevator this time, down the hall from Reynolds's office. Luis kept the gun aimed at Mark the whole time, not getting too close to him during the ride down. Mark sensed that behind the cold black eyes Luis would be a formidable opponent in hand-to-hand combat. He'd play along for now but continue to look for an opening.

"Let's have the cell phone," Luis said, holding out his left hand.

Mark reached into his pocket and handed it to Luis without comment.

They exited on the lowest level, which Mark remembered led to the beach. But instead of going out the glass door, Luis led him to the other side of the room. He unlocked a door near the large-screen TV and walked him down a hallway. They came to another locked door. Luis opened it and pushed him in, quickly shutting the door behind him.

He heard the lock snap into place as he glanced around the room. It was like a studio apartment. A bed in the middle of the room with a dresser and television set, a small table next to a kitchenette, and a door that he assumed led to a bathroom. No windows or any other exit that he could see except the one he'd just been shoved through.

He heard the sound of a toilet flushing. Somebody else was locked in here with him. Moments later, the bathroom door opened, and the person stepped into the room.

Mark's mouth opened in shock.

AMERICAN RESEARCH INSTITUTE
3:01 P.M. PACIFIC

For the third time, Tracy tried to reach Mark on his cell phone but just got the voice-mail recording. Her simple nervousness turned into a gripping fear. He would have had plenty of time to get there and talk with her grandfather by now. Why wasn't he answering his phone? Should she call her papa? What would she say?

She couldn't sit still any longer. She grabbed her purse and headed out of her office.

"I'll be out the rest of the afternoon," she told Brenda.

"What about your appointments?"

"Cancel them with my apologies," Tracy yelled without turning back.

MALIBU
SAME TIME

"Kevin! You're alive!" Mark shouted.

"Mark, what are you doing here?"

"Evidently, the same thing you are." In spite of having met only two times, they embraced.

Pulling away from the hug, Mark noticed bruises and cuts on Kevin's face.

"What happened?" Mark asked.

"Have you met Luis yet?" Kevin responded, touching his blackened eye. "He's very handy with his fists."

"Kevin, I'm sorry."

"It's a lot better than it was. How's Vickie? What have they told her?"

Mark shook his head, "She thinks you're dead, Kevin—we all did."

Despair overwhelmed Kevin. His only hope of getting out was that Mark had somehow put all the pieces together and come to rescue him. But now it appeared hopeless.

"Your car was found Saturday morning. It had crashed into the LA River and caught fire. A body was found inside, burnt to a crisp. It fit your general description. Everybody just assumed it was you. I wonder who it was."

"Poor Vickie, she's got to be beside herself."

"She took it pretty hard, but think of the joy of the reunion when you see her again," Mark said.

"I've thought of nothing else for the past five days. I couldn't figure out why Reynolds kept me here—alive."

"I think it's for my benefit."

"What do you mean?" Kevin asked.

"He made me an offer he hopes I can't refuse," Mark explained. "Apparently, you're the wild card."

NATIONAL STUDIOS
3:30 P.M. PACIFIC

"OK, gang, listen up," Russell yelled above the clamor of the production office. The staff members quickly quieted and looked over their cubicles to see the executive producer. "I know it's been a hectic day, but there are some last-minute changes. As most of you probably know, as of this morning Mark Taylor is no longer with us. We can all talk about this tomorrow when we don't go on the air live in two and a half hours. For now, let's just keep the show going. His monologue segment is out, but we're going to act like he's still on staff for the show. That way the open is still good, and we'll deal with his firing and the press stuff after our debut. We're going to roll in his piece on *The Single Life*. Jennifer—" Russell looked around the room. "Where's Jennifer?"

No response. "Somebody get Jennifer in here," Frank yelled. "We have a show to do." The crew in the studio heard Frank's voice through the soundproof wall.

REYNOLDS MANSION
4:14 P.M. PACIFIC

Mark and Kevin had spent the past hour reviewing the details of what Mark had uncovered over the past five days.

"I can't believe they'd use a weigh-factor to rig the results. That's unconscionable," Kevin said.

"That's probably why they did it—nobody would ever analyze the program so closely. Even when Peter found it, he didn't know what he was looking at. It took Tracy to put the pieces together."

"Well, it looks like nobody's ever going to find out about it either," Kevin said gloomily.

"Don't give up yet, Kevin." Mark, paced the room, looking for a way out.

"I've spent five days in here doing what you're doing. I haven't found any outside access, except through that door." Kevin's hand still pointed at it when they heard the lock give way and it opened.

Luis stepped in first, still holding the gun, followed by Reynolds.

"Well, have we had fun catching up?" Jason asked.

"It's been pleasant," Mark answered. "Thanks."

"So you see why your decision should be made very carefully," Jason looked at Mark. "It's not just your life hanging in the balance."

Mark smiled. "For my own edification, just how will you explain Kevin suddenly turning up after his car was burned with a dead body inside?"

"Oh, that one's easy," Jason leered. "I've got a doctor who'll swear he's been treating Kevin for the past week for amnesia. His car was hijacked, and his wallet and all identification were taken. The nasty criminal who stole the car must have had the unfortunate accident, while poor Kevin here's been under the care of a physician, working hard to restore his memory."

Jason stepped in front of Kevin. "I'm sure Mr. Spencer would be happy to get his life back if all he had to do was forget this ever happened, wouldn't you, Kevin?"

Kevin turned his head toward Mark, his eyes pleading.

Jason turned back to Mark. "So you see, Mark, there isn't much choice here. You know I have the power to do what I'm saying. Sure, it'll be a bit uncomfortable explaining your accident in the helicopter as well as whatever we devise for Rick and Cassie, but in time it'll all be forgotten."

Mark stared into the lifeless eyes. Reynolds talked about ending life as casually as he bought and sold stock.

Jason paced the room as he spoke. "But the easiest solution for all concerned would still be for you to come to your senses. You'd be an asset to the network and go on to live a happy and meaningful life."

Mark swallowed hard, fighting to find the courage. "I wouldn't call submitting to you a meaningful life."

"Be careful what you say in the next few minutes," Jason snapped. "I have the power over you to not only decide Kevin's fate and your fate, but also how slowly I allow you to die."

Griff poked his head into the room. "Mr. Reynolds, your granddaughter just pulled up."

Jason swore. "Keep her upstairs. I'll be right there."

"And how are you going to explain to Tracy that you had me murdered?" Mark asked.

"I won't have to—she'll be overcome with grief like the rest of us when the helicopter crashes. It looks like you've been given a few more minutes to make your decision Mark. I suggest you use them wisely."

"Tracy darling, what are you doing out here?" Jason said with a smile as he reached out to hug her. She stepped back, avoiding the contact.

"Where's Mark?"

"He's thinking over my offer," Jason explained. "We're still in negotiations."

"For what?" Tracy asked. "His life?"

"No, no, dear." Jason spoke calmly, trying to ease her fears. "Please don't jump to any silly conclusions."

"What other conclusions are there?" Tracy said coldly. "I've seen the program myself—you're fixing the results. That goes against everything I learned in school, not to mention everything you taught me, Papa. How could you?"

Reynolds sighed. Mark had gotten to her, and getting her back was going to be more difficult than he'd thought.

"Tracy, give me the benefit of the doubt until I can explain."

"I'm listening."

"It all started years ago, when a group of us found a way to steer the country in the right direction. It started small, nudging a poll here—or fixing a focus group there—and we found out that we could make a difference." He looked into his granddaughter's beautiful face, his heart breaking. If he lost her, all he'd built—all that he'd dedicated his life to—wouldn't matter. "It's all been done with the country's best interest at heart—bringing about positive social and political change. We've never abused the power."

Tracy was repulsed. How could the man she had held in such esteem—even worshiped—suddenly appear to her as the vile person standing before her at this moment? "I don't understand, Papa. How could you?"

"Pumpkin, you've got to look at what I've accomplished," Reynolds pleaded. He saw the disappointment in his granddaughter's eyes, and it hurt—more deeply than he could have imagined. "Without me, we'd still be having back-alley abortions, science classes would be teaching creation, censorship would be stifling the creative minds of our time, gays would still be hiding in the closet, the right-wing, religious warmongers would have probably started a nuclear war or two by now. I've brought our nation forward into the twenty-first century, saved it from those who would shove us back into the dark ages. You, as a woman, should appreciate that."

Tracy was frightened; she'd never seen her grandfather like this. She knew of his distrust of religion, but his unveiled hatred now took her breath away. She never would have dreamed he used his vast empire to manipulate the national social climate. She was speechless, and her lack of words distressed him to the core.

"I need you to understand. I can't lose you Tracy."

She finally asked, "Why, Papa? Why?"

He had run out of words to convince her. Time, he decided. It would just take a little time to bring her back. But he'd have to have Mark on his side, or at least make it appear so, or he would lose her forever.

"You'll understand, pumpkin, soon." He placed a hand on her shoulder, attempting to maintain the connection between them.

"I want to see Mark," she demanded.

"That wouldn't be wise," he answered. "We're at a delicate spot in the negotiations—"

"What negotiations? Your company fired him six hours ago!" She hit her words hard. "I want to see him."

"No, Tracy!" Jason shouted. "He doesn't want to see you until we're finished. And I need to get back there if he's going to make it on the air tonight."

Tracy cocked her head. At the mention of Mark's going on the air, she wondered if there was some hope that there could be a compromise between the two. But she couldn't see how.

"Give us a little time," Jason said, his voice calming. "I'll have him call you as soon as we're done."

He gently took her arm and led her to the front door.

"That's it? You're asking me to leave?" She pulled her arm back from his grasp.

"It's better for both Mark and me if we aren't distracted right now." Jason knew full well he couldn't let her see Mark ever again.

Tracy couldn't believe he was kicking her out. "But—"

"I promise he'll call you in a few minutes."

She looked straight at her grandfather; he paused before closing the door. Her expression softened. For a moment she reflected the little girl who had worshiped him all her life.

"Promise me you won't hurt him in any way," she pleaded.

Reynolds nearly lost his resolve. He had always struggled in denying her anything she asked, but this time he had no choice.

"Honey, you've been watching too many movies. Trust me. I want him back on the air more than you realize."

Jason walked back to the apartment where Luis still waited. His gun still targeted the center of Mark's body.

"Where's Tracy?" Mark asked.

"I told her you and I needed more time to finish our negotiations," Jason answered.

"And she bought it?"

"Yes!" Jason answered coldly, not wanting to discuss his granddaughter. "Now what's it going to be?"

"I have a counteroffer for you," Mark said.

"It's a take-it-or-leave-it proposition, Taylor."

"You told Tracy we're negotiating, so let's negotiate. Let Kevin go—show your good faith. His wife thinks he's dead, for goodness sake. Then promise me that Rick and Cassie are left alone, and I'll do whatever you want."

Reynolds studied Mark's face. It was too easy—he expected more resistance. "What's the catch? You said we were negotiating."

"No catch. After that I'm yours. I don't want anybody else hurt—too many have died already."

"I agree," Reynolds responded, then reached into his pants pocket and pulled out his cell phone. He punched in a couple of numbers before raising it to his ear as he grinned. "Winter, it's Jason. Mark Taylor is back on the show."

Kevin glanced over at Mark, a hopeful smile creasing his lips.

"Yeah, I know what I'm doing," Reynolds continued after a brief pause. "Don't worry, he's on board. Call the producer and let him know. I'll have him flown over later." He flipped the phone shut, then looked up at Mark, "It's a done deal. But Kevin stays for one more night." Jason winked toward Kevin, then gave Mark his trademark smile. "I want to see your broadcast first, before he goes home. I don't think I can trust you without keeping some leverage." He turned toward his security chief. "Let's go, Luis. We've got work to do."

Reynolds and Luis left the room, and Kevin and Mark once again were locked in.

"Thanks, Mark," Kevin said. "I appreciate your trying to get me out of here."

"I didn't think he'd go for it, but I wanted to try."

"Do you think he'll honor the agreement?"

"Not a chance."

Tracy drove away from the mansion. She turned the first corner on Highway 1 and quickly downshifted, bringing the Miata to a stop on the side of the road. She looked to see if anybody was behind her. It was clear.

She agreed to leave for only one reason. So she could sneak around the house without being watched by Luis or her grandfather. She had to find Mark.

She jumped out of the car and began her trek back to the mansion, finding herself praying to a person she had never seriously considered real before. *God, if you're listening, Mark and I really need your help here.*

In the elevator on the way up to the main house, Luis turned toward Number One. "Are you serious about letting him back on the air?"

Reynolds smiled. "Of course not. I just need him to believe it long enough to call Tracy and tell her we worked out a deal. I don't want her blaming me for his death."

Luis chuckled, relieved. For a minute downstairs, he'd started to lose faith in his boss.

Chapter 34

"All right, everybody, listen up," Frank Russell called out to the stage as the staff gathered around him. "Somebody get the control room people out here."

A production assistant ran into the booth and grabbed Rick and the crew. When Russell saw them enter the studio he continued. "We've got a new rundown coming out. Mark is back in the show."

The staff erupted in cheers. Russell held up his hands to regain control. "OK, settle down. These changes put us with a lot of work to do in just a few minutes. I don't have to remind you how important this night is to all of us. Let's get moving!"

The staffers dispersed quickly back to their positions. Rick saw Cassie walk in the stage door. He waved her over.

"What's all the excitement about?" she asked.

"Russell just announced that Mark's back on the show."

362

MALIBU

THIRTY-TWO MINUTES TO AIR

Mark sat on the edge of the bed while Kevin reclined with his back against the headboard.

"They're going to have to get you over to the studio pretty soon," Kevin said, looking at his watch.

"That is, if they're going to keep the deal," Mark responded.

"Do you think they—" Kevin stopped when he heard rustling near the door.

Mark heard it too. He tiptoed over, placing his ear against the door. He heard a voice on the other side.

"Mark, are you in there?"

It was Tracy.

"Yes, Tracy. I'm in here and so is Kevin."

"Kevin's alive?" Tracy asked in a loud whisper.

"Yes. Can you get us out of here?"

"I'll try." Tracy attempted several keys until finally one worked.

Mark flung his arms around Tracy. "How did you get the key?"

Before she answered, Tracy turned to Kevin, embracing him. "I'm so glad you're alive, Kevin." Then she turned to Mark. "I sneaked into my grandfather's office and stole a set of keys. I didn't know if one of them would work or not."

"You really are amazing, aren't you?" Mark beamed. "Let's get out of here."

"What about your deal with Reynolds, Mark?" Kevin asked.

Mark looked at Kevin. "You don't really think he was planning to keep his end of it, do you?"

Kevin looked at Mark earnestly. "What other choice do we have?"

Mark grimaced. "Think about it Kevin—he's held you here for over five days, just in case I got too close to him. He's killed at least two other people that we know of, three counting whoever was in your car. In his mind we're just two more statistics. As soon as enough time has gone by so that he won't be under any suspicion, we're both dead along with my two friends as well."

"Isn't there any way to ensure against that?" Kevin pleaded.

"Only to get out of here with his confession," Mark said.

"What confession?"

"The one recorded by this," Mark answered, holding up the MPR-1.

"He confessed to you?" Tracy gasped.

"Not to everything, but I've got enough," Mark said. "We just need to get out of here."

"My car's just down the road," Tracy offered.

"No," Mark said. "I've got a better idea. Follow me."

Mark grabbed Tracy's hand and started toward the door.

"Just where do you think you're going?" They stopped in their tracks as Vince Sinclair appeared in the doorway, gun in hand.

"Vince!" Tracy was shocked as she stood before the new employee with his gun trained on her. "What are you doing here?"

"I might ask you three the same question."

Kevin sighed, once again dejected. Mark tensed, getting ready to make his move. It was now or never.

Vince moved the gun, pointing it right at Mark's chest. "I wouldn't, Taylor. You don't know what you're dealing with. Besides, I'm on your side."

Mark's eyebrows rose in shock. He looked at Tracy, who shrugged her shoulders. She was as confused as he was.

Mark turned back to the mysterious gunman. "What do you mean 'on our side'?"

"I'm an agent with the Justice Department. My real name is Vince Cross," he explained, lowering his pistol. "I've been undercover for a few months at Research International."

"That's where I saw you—last Saturday," Mark exclaimed.

Vince nodded. "I was afraid you were going to mess up the investigation, or at the least do something stupid and get yourself killed—looks like I was right about both."

"So you thought your warning was enough to send me running with my tail between my legs?" Mark asked.

"I didn't know who you were at the time. I thought I could scare you away." Vince looked at Mark with admiration. "I was wrong. Look, they're going to be coming back down here any minute. We've got to move."

"Do you have a plan for getting us out of here?" Mark asked.

"Not yet."

"You mean you don't have the cavalry outside the house, ready to bust in?" Tracy asked.

"No, I wish I did," Vince said, glancing down the hallway to make sure nobody was coming. "I've been ordered off this investigation three times already. Reynolds's connections go way up—"

"All the way to the White House," Mark agreed.

"That makes sense." Vince nodded to him. "I can't wait to hear what you've figured out. I've been operating on a leave of absence. I was hoping to get some evidence that my superiors can't ignore."

"That's what I was afraid of," Mark said. "Anywhere I go with this, Reynolds could squash it—and our lives will still be worthless."

"Well, the first thing to do is get out of here," Kevin said from behind Tracy.

"He's right," Tracy said. "My grandfather could come back down here any second."

Mark looked at his watch. "Tracy, what's the best way to get to the front of the house without being seen?"

NATIONAL STUDIOS
THIRTEEN MINUTES TO AIR

"Let's take a look at Sam's tape," Rick called out from the control room. "Roll B."

The screen lighted up with images from Samantha's Web site—mostly pictures of her. Rick blinked, then shook his head. The network was certainly pushing the limit on how much of her body it was willing to air. Rick wished he had more control of the show. If he wasn't just the fill-in director, he'd go to Russell and try and get this tape killed.

Frank stepped into the booth while Rick was watching. "We're going to get the ratings tonight, aren't we?"

"You're probably right, Frank," Rick returned. "But I wish you'd left a little more to the imagination with some of Sam's pictures."

Russell laughed. "Are you kidding? They're perfect. Are you set, Rick?"

"I think I'm ready—just looking over the playback tapes." Rick said as the images continued on the monitor.

"Good. We're happy to have you with us." Russell slapped him on the back. "You may have to be on your toes tonight. Mark isn't back yet—he might be cutting it real close to making his segment."

"We'll be ready for him," Rick assured him.

MALIBU

TWELVE MINUTES TO AIR

Mark poked his head around the corner of the house. This was the perfect spot. To remain hidden, Tracy had led the tree men up the stairway outside the mansion and around the guest quarters.

The outside of the mansion was lighted up like a theme park. As soon as they moved, they'd be in the spotlight.

He turned back to the group hiding in the bushes. "OK, here's the plan," he whispered. "We're going to take one of the helicopters—"

"Are you crazy?" Tracy asked. "Who's going to fly it?"

"I am," Mark said, "I flew some in the Gulf. We'll make it."

Kevin sighed. "Oh, boy, this is just great."

"Don't we need a key?" Tracy asked.

"Not with the Jet Ranger," Mark said. "If the doors are open, it's ours."

"You three go ahead," Vince instructed. "I'll provide cover for you until you take off."

"That'll leave you here alone?" Mark protested.

"How quick can you get that bird in the air after you crank it up?" Vince asked.

"Thirty seconds."

"They'll nail you before that unless I slow them down," Vince argued. "It's your only chance. I'll be able to take care of myself."

"Where are we going to fly—to the nearest FBI office?" Tracy asked.

"No, I don't know who we can trust. Our only chance for survival is to get me to the studio. I'll broadcast what we know."

"You're going to go on the air with this?" Vince asked.

"Our only chance for survival is to go public," Mark insisted.

Vince laughed. "You're probably right—for me as well. But, talk about due process."

Mark laid out his plan, making sure they all knew their parts.

"Vince," Mark said as he finished, reaching out his hand. "I hope to see you again, and thanks."

Vince received the handshake warmly. "Oh, you will see me again," he promised.

"OK, gang," Mark said. "Wait here for my signal."

He stepped out of the bushes, turned the corner of the house and ran toward the two choppers, keeping his body low and as much out of sight as possible.

Tracy glanced around the corner of the house to see if he'd been spotted. So far so good.

Mark went directly to the back door of the second chopper and opened it. He leaned inside, pulling out a screwdriver he'd taken from the pool shed as they made their way past the guest house. He used it to open an access panel on the broom closet, a column between the two front seats. He grabbed a crescent wrench from his back pocket and worked feverishly to unfasten two control rods, scraping his knuckles several times against the metal as the wrench slipped. By the time he got them free, his right hand was bruised and bleeding. He reversed the rods as quickly as he could, then began reconnecting them while he mentally tried to calculate how much time had passed.

"Where did Vince go?" Reynolds asked as he and Luis relaxed upstairs in the family room.

"I don't know. He went off looking for a bathroom a few minutes ago," Luis answered.

"Is everything ready on the cliff?" Jason asked.

"Griff is all set. But I'm not sure how you'll avoid an investigation."

"We'll figure that out later. I don't have time to sabotage a helicopter. This is the only way we've got to take care of Taylor. Have Ray get the chopper ready, then go downstairs, and bring them up here. It's time Mark made that call to Tracy."

Luis put down his beer. "OK, I'll be right back."

Reynolds smiled. In a few minutes his biggest problem would be on its way to the bottom of the Pacific Ocean.

NATIONAL STUDIOS
THIRTY SECONDS TO AIR

"Thirty seconds," the associate director to Rick's left counted off.

"All right, everyone, have a good show," Rick encouraged. "Welcome to Wednesday nights."

The countdown continued, both from the associate director and from the stage manager on the floor. Samantha sat in her seat, wearing one of her most conservative outfits, a high-necked cream blouse under her dark blue jacket. She couldn't remember when she'd been this nervous before a show. Then she did something that would have never occurred to her before today—she bowed her head and asked God for help.

"Stand by the opening tape on A," Rick instructed as the countdown hit ten. Eight seconds later he completed the direction. "Roll A."

The monitor came to life in front of him as the show began.

MALIBU
6:00 P.M. PACIFIC

Tracy nervously kept hidden behind the house with Kevin and Vince, waiting for Mark's signal to move out. She looked at her watch—it'd been nearly ten minutes. Then she saw Mark close the door of the second helicopter and head for the one closest to them as he waved toward them.

"Let's go!" she whispered, leaving the safety of the bushes in a dead run. Kevin followed right behind as Vince headed for the spot he'd picked out to give them cover.

"Did it work?" Tracy asked as she jumped in the front seat beside Mark.

"We'll know if they try and follow us," Mark said, hoping that what his buddy in the war told him was true. "Let's get this baby in the air before they realize we're gone."

Mark reached above his head and turned on the master switch. He checked the collective, holding the throttle release button down and rotating the throttle back and forth. He held down the starter button, keeping his eye on the gas producer meter—looking for it to climb to fourteen. He hoped he remembered right.

Luis ran back into the living room. "They're gone!"

Reynolds swore, throwing his glass of scotch into the fireplace. "Well, find them!" he yelled.

"Let's torch it up," Mark said as the meter hit the awaited number. While keeping his finger pressed down on the igniter button, Mark cracked the throttle, now feeding fuel into the cell. The familiar whine started low in frequency but quickly built in pitch and noise level as the turbine kicked in. The main rotor started spinning above their heads. Tracy's and Kevin's eyes shot toward the house. They were certain someone would run out any minute from the noise. Mark kept his eye on the control panel. As soon as everything was in the green, they'd be off.

Help me to be able to fly this thing, Lord, he prayed.

Jason heard the whine of the turbine from inside the house. "The helicopters!"

Luis was already on his way toward the front door. Reynolds hurried right behind him.

Mark was watching the meter—20 percent, 25. He needed 60 to lift off.

"Here they come!" Tracy screamed out as Luis ran out the front door, his gun drawn. Suddenly, he stopped, ducking behind one of the front pillars. She couldn't hear the gunshot Vince fired just above Luis's head. Reynolds appeared in the doorway for a second, yelled something, then ducked back into the house.

"Whatever Vince is doing, it's working!" she shouted.

Mark kept his eyes glued to the control panel—40 percent, 45.

Luis jumped out from behind the pillar.

"He's coming again!" Tracy screamed.

"Get your headset on!" Mark ordered as the whine grew into a loud thunder.

Luis was trying to get a shot off at the helicopter as he ran a zigzag pattern across the lawn. Vince aimed and fired but couldn't get a good shot off at the moving target. Reynolds poked his head out of the doorway looking directly into the helicopter—his eyes locked on Tracy. His expression of shock quickly turned into outrage as he ran toward them yelling, "No!"

Luis fired as he ran toward the helicopter. The glass windshield cracked as a bullet hole appeared right between Mark and Tracy.

"Fifty-five percent—good enough," Mark proclaimed as the needle was millimeters away from the green line. He pulled up on the collective, causing the main rotor to change pitch and grabbing more air above them. The craft began to wobble. Mark gently moved the cyclic between his legs, trying to get a feel for the craft.

Tracy's scream came through loud and clear in Mark's headset. Luis was getting closer, bringing his gun up to fire another shot.

Mark pulled back on the stick, lifting the chopper into the air. He pushed in the left peddle and moved the stick, spinning the craft around and bringing the back of the helicopter in line with Luis's attack. Luis dove to the ground, the tail rotor barely passing over his head. Reynolds hit the ground right behind him.

"He's got Tracy in there!" Jason screamed over the noise. "You can't let Griff bring them down!"

It wasn't the smoothest takeoff, but the chopper was airborne. As soon as Mark had gained enough altitude, he tilted the craft forward and sped away from the mansion.

In all the commotion, Ray had made it to the second helicopter and was rushing through his warm-up sequence. Luis noticed the rotor spinning, then looked back at Reynolds. "I'll try and force them down," he said as he scrambled for the chopper.

"Don't hurt my Tracy!" Reynolds yelled from the grass.

Luis jumped in the backseat as Ray brought the craft to full power and started lifting it off the ground.

Mark was still having trouble controlling the helicopter, overcorrecting with every movement as he gained altitude over the Malibu coastline. Tracy was trying to keep one eye on the house, either through the side window or the back, depending on which way Mark was pointing the helicopter at the time. She could see her grandfather lying on the grass, while Luis made his way to the second craft.

"It looks like they're taking off in the other helicopter," she said.

Kevin, sitting on the other side of the chopper, saw something more troubling. "Check out the guy on the cliff," he yelled. "It looks like he's pointing something at us."

Mark saw a man standing on the cliff side. He was silhouetted against the illuminated landscape and holding a device on top of his shoulder. Mark's mind flashed back to his last mission over Iraq.

"That looks like," he started to say before a bright flash nearly blinded him, "a missile launcher."

NATIONAL STUDIOS
SAME TIME

Samantha looked nervously to Stan Jeffries sitting beside her. He was opening the show, just about ready to introduce her.

"We'll have Mark's exclusive reaction to all he's been through the past couple of days, later in the broadcast. But first up, we have Samantha Steel—"

"Take two!" Rick commanded from the control room. The shot changed from Stan's close-up to a shot of Samantha and Stan just as he turned to bring her into the conversation.

"Samantha, I understand we had a lot of interest in the Web site the past three days."

Samantha smiled. "The response was incredible, Stan. At last count we had over two hundred thousand hits."

Stan chuckled. "Which means our viewing public got to see you in a whole different light."

Samantha laughed for the camera—inside it hurt. "As well as our own Tad Forrest, who volunteered for our female viewers."

A shot of Tad appeared on the air as he responded, smiling, "It was for science—an experiment into the naughty viewing habits of our audience."

"And our public thanks you, I'm sure," Samantha said as the shot of her and Stan came back on line.

"I never thought the experience would affect me the way it did, Stan." Samantha turned to her close-up camera as the light flashed on. "But as you'll see in this report, I stepped into a world I didn't know and got more than I bargained for."

Her image was replaced on the screen by the beginning of the taped piece. Samantha was clear for the next four minutes and thirteen seconds.

MALIBU
SAME TIME

"Hang on!" Mark cried as he forced the stick forward and left. The helicopter banked hard, dropping like a stone. He didn't have that much altitude to play with. Mark hoped he could keep the chopper under control before it either crashed into the cliffs beside them or into the ocean below. The center of his eyes ached, trying to fight off the burned-in image from the flash of the surface-to-air missile. *Lord, be with us now,* he prayed.

Griff hadn't expected the sudden move when he'd shot. The missile passed inches above the main rotor before heading harmlessly past them and out into the Pacific.

"Here comes Chopper 1!" Tracy screamed from beside Mark.

Mark couldn't look up. His full concentration was on the controls to keep the craft in the air. He was only the emergency pilot on the extraction runs he'd made during Desert Storm. That hadn't amounted to much flying time—just enough to be dangerous. He pulled out of the bank just twenty feet away from the cliffs with the ocean dangerously close below them. He gently nudged back on the stick. The huge bird shuddered before it started to climb again.

"Whew!" Mark sighed, as his vision began to return to normal. "At least we know how Reynolds was planning to cause the helicopter crash."

"What about the other helicopter?" Tracy asked.

"I don't think it'll be a problem," Mark grinned. He just hoped whoever was on the cliff didn't have time to reload before they were out of range.

The chopper climbed above the cliff line, once again revealing the well-lighted mansion. The second helicopter was coming right at them, ready to give chase as Mark pointed his bird away from the house and toward the lights of Los Angeles.

Luis had his headset on and had grabbed an AK-47 automatic rifle from behind the backseat. "Get me closer!" he yelled to Ray as he stuck the barrel of the gun outside the window.

"There's something wrong!" Ray shouted in frustration.

"I don't want to hear it!" Luis ordered. "Follow that helicopter. We can't let them get away."

Ray moved the cyclic to the left as he gently pushed down his left leg, planning to turn the craft that direction and head toward the escaping helicopter. But the opposite happened—the helicopter rotated right.

"You're facing the wrong direction. I can't get a shot off!" Luis yelled.

Ray couldn't figure out what could be wrong, and his instinct told him to give it more. He applied more pressure on the stick, but that only increased the right turn.

Panic set in as Ray fought the controls. He adjusted, moving the cyclic left. The chopper straightened out for a second, but the feeling was too awkward. He started making drastic movements with both his hands. He was losing control.

Mark's flying improved as he started getting used to the controls. Tracy kept her eye on the other helicopter from her window. "It looks like he's flying drunk," Tracy said.

"That's probably about how he feels right now!" Mark chuckled in response.

Ray started swearing. Nothing he tried could make the helicopter do what he wanted. The craft started tilting on its side, spinning uncontrollably as he fought to keep it level.

"Get it together, Ray!" Luis yelled from the backseat. Then he started shouting every filthy word he knew as they edged closer to the cliffs.

Jason Reynolds watched in horror as the craft spun wildly out of control. Just over the edge of the property, the helicopter's main rotor hit the Malibu cliffs, hacking away at the rock and dirt before dropping the bird out of the air. It crashed to the sand below in a fireball on Reynolds's private beach.

He turned and headed back into the house, quickly suppressing any sense of loss for Luis or Ray—he still had a plan to stop Mark.

"Oh my!" Tracy gasped as the fireball rose in the sky. "They're down!"

Mark could tell from her voice they hadn't landed smoothly. He felt a twinge of guilt—not for Luis, but for whoever might have been in the chopper with him.

"Everybody OK?" Mark asked as kept the helicopter aimed toward Los Angeles.

"I think so," Tracy answered. "I hope Vince is OK down there."

"I can't believe we got away," Kevin said in his headset. "That was some nice flying, Mark."

"Yeah, I guess that Marine training comes in handy sometimes," Tracy laughed.

"Let's just hope I can remember how to land." Mark was only half joking.

"What?" Tracy turned toward him.

Mark kept his eyes forward, grinning as he searched the sky for any other aircraft.

CHAPTER 35

"We're coming out of the tape in ten seconds," the stage manager yelled in the quiet studio. Samantha straightened up in her chair, took a deep breath, and exhaled it slowly.

When the cue was given, she looked right into the lens, ignoring the TelePrompTer words in front of her. She felt like a tightrope walker stepping out over the great abyss onto just one inch of wire.

"When I suggested we do this story, it was in hopes that it would be tantalizing enough to get this show more viewers—and I imagine it probably worked—the Web site drew a lot of interest. Now I want to let you in on a valuable lesson that I learned in the last few days.

"I interviewed a young woman as part of my research. She declined to be on camera, and I understand why. She opened my eyes to a side of the pornography business I never realized before—yes, I said the word pornography. Most of the staff here will be shocked to hear me use the word in this context. But you see, whether we admit it or not, what we just saw was in fact pornography. Sure, we casually look at nudity in our culture as no big deal. Careers are made now by doing a spread in *Playboy* while TV shows stumble over each other to be the first to air the pictures. Our society has slid a long way down this path in which the word *pornography* is now used to describe only the most despicable video and pictures imaginable.

"But that courageous young woman showed me where that path ends up. It starts simply—a young woman taking her clothes off for some extra money. For me, posing was difficult at first. I felt dirty—my conscience tried to speak to me. But at the encouragement of the photographer, it did get easier. But at what cost?

"For this woman, it nearly cost her her life. For many young teenagers, the slide down into prostitution and drugs starts with a simple film-shoot, but the end of that can be total destruction. Thank God my new friend made it out of that life and is doing wonderfully well—raising her infant daughter. It isn't easy for them, but they have a new start—a happy one."

Samantha paused, looking down at her notes and taking a quick breath. *Be with me, Lord,* she prayed. Then she looked back at her audience through the camera lens.

From the control room, Rick saw her pause. He prayed silently for her as she collected her thoughts.

"Wow, what's gotten into Sam?" the associate director questioned.

Rick chuckled. *The Holy Spirit,* he thought.

"That same woman also taught me about the other victims." Samantha reached beside her and held up a small portion of the surveys that had been answered. "We included in our site a voluntary survey to which thousands of people responded, anonymously. Would you believe that in spite of the full-page warning that our site was only for adults over eighteen, over half of those who answered our survey admitted to being under that age?"

Samantha paused, letting that sink in. "I think the youngest that I saw was from a thirteen-year-old boy. What do we say to that young boy who gets his first idea of sexuality by looking at pictures on the Web? And believe me, our site is nothing compared to some of the filth I came across in my research."

"Think about the days before the Internet—young boys would get their hands on a *Playboy*—or maybe it was a *National Geographic*—to satisfy the curiosity of what the female body looks like. If that boy wanted to go deeper into pornography, he'd have to search it out, go through the embarrassment of asking at the drugstore counter or sneaking around somewhere else. But now, if a curious teenager goes to the Internet, everything is at the touch of his fingertips without any of society's safeguards to protect him—from simple pictures of nude women and men, right on down the gutter to fetishes, S&M, bestiality—you name it—it's only a mouse click away. Nowadays, instead of a youngster's first image being a naked woman in a magazine, it could easily be full, hard-core graphic sex or something even worse.

"Am I calling for censorship? To be honest with you, I don't know yet. But what I do know is that we all need to call for responsibility. The images rampant on these Internet sites are dangerous for adolescent minds just getting their first taste of what human sexuality is all about.

"In the last few days my research took a different path than I expected. I looked into the addiction side of pornography and found very disturbing trends. Attempting to satisfy sexual desires through pornography leads men and even some women down a path that never ends. They may spend some time at each plateau, but soon it ceases to satisfy their hunger—so they go a little further, dig a little deeper, and there's always something more intense waiting. Before long, they're viewing things that would have disgusted them just months before. But it's now driving their obsession.

"I want to offer you my apology for not researching the subject more before I started this story and the Web site. To the parents whose young children accessed the site, I apologize. I'm sorry. I want you to know this has become more than a story for me—it changed my life.

"I hope all of you who visited our Web site at samsnudes.com will view it one more time. We've changed it. It now has an 800 number people can call to get help with pornographic addiction, as well as a list of books and articles on the subject and recommended software that can limit access to these adult sites for your children. I hope we have two hundred thousand more hits over the next three days. Maybe that will make up for what I've done." She paused, then added, "We'll be back after this."

"Cue music, dissolve to graphic." Rick nearly couldn't speak after Sam's emotional pitch. The screen changed to a full-page graphic of samsnudes.com along with the 800 number.

Jared Winter sat in his plush executive office at National Studios, shaking his head irritatedly. What had gotten into Samantha? It was as if the tag to the tape was made by a totally different woman. And did he hear another "apology" from her? *Across the Nation* was going to be the laughingstock of the Hollywood community. After Mark's outburst Sunday and now this, he might as well call it *Apologize to the Nation*.

His private phone rang, interrupting his thoughts.

"Winter here."

"Jared, it's Jason. We've got a problem." Reynolds shouted over the line.

Winter had expected the call. "Calm down Jason. I'll have a talk with her—"

"What are you talking about?"

Winter sat up, confused. "What are you talking about?"

"It's Taylor. I think he's on the way to the studio by helicopter."

"I know," Winter said. "That's what you set up over an hour ago."

"You don't understand—he escaped. If he gets there and gets on the air, he'll spill everything."

"Don't worry," Winter promised. "I won't let him get anywhere near that stage. What do you want me to do with him?"

"Whatever it takes to keep him off the air!" Jason spat out. "Just make sure you don't let anybody harm my granddaughter. She's on board with him."

MALIBU
SAME TIME

Jason slammed down the phone. He poured himself a double scotch. He looked outside the glass doors and saw Vince coming in from the backyard pool area.

"Where have you been?" he asked sharply.

"Taking care of something," Vince answered calmly. He'd taken the precaution of making sure the man on the cliff with the missile launcher wouldn't outflank him. Griff was currently tied up and gagged in the pool house.

"You sure didn't come through when I needed you," Reynolds spat out. "Everything turns bad, and you're nowhere to be found. Some way to prove your loyalty to the Circle!"

"Would it be all right if I use your phone?" Vince asked.

"Is that all you've got to say for yourself?"

Vince walked over and picked up the handset, dialing 911. Reynolds's eyebrows went up when he heard only three numbers punched. "What are you doing?"

Vince brought his hand up from behind his back, revealing his pistol, pointed right at Reynolds.

Jason swore, pitching the glass across the room. "I guess I was a fool to trust you."

"No, you were a fool to think you could get away with it," Vince answered.

Reynolds shook his head as it lowered down to his chest. His lawyers could get him out of this, if only Winter took care of Taylor.

"All I have to do is make one phone call and you're a dead man!" Reynolds threatened.

"You can make it the one call you're allowed in prison if you wish," Vince smiled as he waited for the 911 operator to answer the call. "You have the right to remain silent. . . ."

SOMEWHERE OVER LOS ANGELES
SAME TIME

Mark navigated toward the Hollywood city limits, carefully letting the helicopter descend as he neared National Studios. He saw the landing pad, marked by a circle of red lights atop the executive building.

"Brace yourselves—we're approaching the studio," he announced. He wasn't sure how gently he'd be able to set the chopper down.

"Mark," Tracy pointed out, "there are a bunch of security guards on top of the building."

NATIONAL STUDIOS
SAME TIME

"We're back in two minutes," the associate director called as the control monitor stayed in black. The commercial was rolled in from the master control studio in New York.

Rick looked back at Cassie, sitting behind him. "I'm proud of her."

"Me, too—that was pretty gutsy."

The door opened, and Russell stuck his head in. "I just got a call from Winter. Mark's out of the show. We're back to running the piece on *The Single Life*. Tad will introduce it for the last segment."

The door closed, and he was gone. "I wonder what's going on?" Rick asked.

"I don't know. I hope he's OK."

They heard the muted sound of a helicopter overhead. Rick took his headset off and stepped back to Cassie sitting on the back bench. "Reggie's outside our studio door. Ask him to check on who's in that helicopter."

"I understand." Cassie headed for the door.

Mark continued his descent, preparing to land on the roof. He wasn't concentrating on anything but keeping the huge craft level as he manipulated the controls.

Tracy studied the security guards as they descended. "Mark, they don't look friendly. I've never seen National security with guns before, and they've got them drawn."

Mark didn't need any confirmation. He brought the collective back up toward him and pulled back on the stick. The chopper backed away from the executive office building, banking hard to the right as it changed course.

"Where else can I set this thing down?" he asked.

"There's some grass over there." She pointed to the right.

"That's the park for the day-care center," Mark exclaimed. "It's perfect, right next to our studio. Hold on."

He kept the chopper low as he aimed toward the grass. He wanted to set it down quickly before the guards could get to his new landing site.

Reggie sprinted around the corner on the back side of the stage just as the helicopter reversed course and flew overhead. He stopped short, turned back and headed the opposite way down the street, trying to determine where the chopper would land.

"We're back in five, four, three . . ." the associate director called. Rick refocused on the show and tried to put Mark and his problems at the back of his mind.

"Roll A," he called, bringing the videotape up online as the show continued. "Stand by on the set. This is Tad's segment. Here we come, everybody."

He heard the chopper fly back over the studio—only lower and louder this time. He wondered what was happening above them.

Mark nearly clipped the trees as he headed for the grass. He knew he was cutting it close, but he didn't want the security guards to catch up with him. The skids hit hard, but the softness of the grass helped to compensate. Even so, the three bounced inside the huge craft as it settled back to earth.

Mark shut the turbine down as soon as the skids touched. "Be careful! Don't run out toward the back of the craft!" he warned.

Tracy saw another guard running toward them. "Here they come," she warned.

Mark opened his door, preparing to fight the huge guard running their direction. Then he looked up into Reggie's smiling face.

"What's going on, Mr. Taylor?" Reggie asked.

"No time to explain. You've got to help us get into the studio."

"Follow me." He led the three of them around the corner and into the back of the stage.

Reggie grabbed his radio once he had them safely inside. "Emergency lockdown for *Across the Nation.* Nobody gets in without my approval."

Reggie locked the door behind him, knowing that his counterparts were doing the same to every door into the studio. "That should give us some time. Let's go!"

Mark led his group toward the control room, then stopped at the head of the hallway. He grabbed his MPR-1 pen and handed it to Tracy. "Go into the door marked 'Audio' and give this to Steve. Tell him to download it, and cue it to where your grandfather says 'you want the truth'—that's important—'you want the truth.'"

"Got it." Tracy grabbed the pen and headed for the audio door.

"I've got to talk with Russell. Reggie, come with me," Mark said. He stepped through the studio doors to the stage area. Tad was center stage, reading the TelePrompTer as he introduced his videotape. Russell was sitting at a table surrounded by his four producers just off stage, listening to Rick call the show on his headset. Mark walked up behind him and tapped him on the shoulder.

Russell turned around, and shock registered on his face. He dropped his headset on the table, got up, and turned toward Mark. "What are you doing here?" he whispered.

"I've got the complete story, Frank," Mark whispered back. "I have to get it on the air."

Jennifer turned around and saw him, her eyes opened wide in shock. "You can't listen to him, Frank—"

"Shh," everyone at the table responded to Jennifer's outburst.

"Reggie," Mark whispered with a smile, "would you please take Ms. Williams and hold her somewhere? And call the police too. I'm sure they'll want to talk with her after the broadcast."

Reggie stepped next to Jennifer, dwarfing her by his six-foot-seven-inch frame. She started to protest, but one look from Reggie kept her quiet.

"What's that all about?" Russell asked.

"I'll explain. Come on." Mark grabbed Russell by the arm and led him to the hallway between the stage and the control rooms.

Once the door closed to the stage, Russell turned to Mark. "What are you talking about?"

"I've got the evidence—everything I need to bust the story wide open. I've even got Reynolds on tape confessing."

Russell shook his head. "I can't let you go on the air with wild accusations. Both our heads will roll."

"I don't have a choice," Mark pleaded. "This thing goes so high up, Frank, if you don't let me get this story out on the airwaves right now, I'll be a dead man before the sun comes up tomorrow."

Russell looked into Mark's eyes. He could sense Mark's intensity and the fire in his gut. Russell contemplated the situation. The phone calls from Winter had him worried. Why would Winter tell the crew to prepare for Mark's return, then just after the show hit the air, call back and change his mind? Something wasn't right, and it was time to find out what.

"Tell me everything quickly."

Rick stretched his arms. Only one more segment to go, and the show would be over. He wondered what had happened to Mark.

His question was answered when Russell came charging into the room with Mark and Kevin right behind him.

"Here's what's happening, Rick," Russell instructed. Rick listened intently. He smiled at Mark, thrilled to see him alive.

"Mark is taking the last segment solo. Kill the tape we'd planned. He'll have an audio cue to roll in—they should be downloading the sound bite right now."

"Understood," Rick said. "You better get on stage, Mark."

"On my way." Mark tried to organize his thoughts for the broadcast. Tracy met him at the door and enveloped him in a big hug before letting him out the door.

"What's going on, Frank?" Rick asked.

"We're about to make TV history, Rick." Frank beamed. He hadn't felt this alive since he had reported from the battlefields of Vietnam for NBC.

"We're back in one minute," the associate director called out.

Jared Winter paced his office. Not a word from his security team. He couldn't let Taylor get on the air. He grabbed his phone and punched in the numbers for the control room.

"Get me the director."

"We're on the air," the production assistant politely reminded him.

"This is Jared Winter!" He cursed. "Put the director on the phone, now!"

The production assistant held the phone away from her ear. "Rick, it's for you."

Rick turned to remind her they were back on the air in less than a minute. "It's Jared Winter."

He looked at Russell, who reached for another extension and picked up the line to New York, nodding to Rick to take the call from Winter. Rick answered, "Yes, Mr. Winter."

"Is Mark Taylor in that studio?" Winter asked.

"Yes, sir."

"Under no circumstances should he be allowed on that set. Is that understood?" Winter yelled.

Rick paused, thinking he could buy time if he stalled. "But, Mr. Winter, I've got orders from Frank Russell to do just that."

"I don't care. I'm the president of this network, and I'm ordering you to keep him off the air."

Rick smiled as the tirade of curses continued over the phone line.

"Thirty seconds," the associate director announced.

"We're coming out of the commercial, Mr. Winter," Rick interrupted him. "I'll let you talk with Russell—hold on."

"Wait—" Rick heard through the phone as he hit the hold button. Everyone in the control room looked to Russell.

"Yeah, who's this?" he was saying into the phone. Russell had contacted the studio in New York where commercials were integrated into the show before it was sent up to the satellite. "Mike, good to have you with us. Listen, we've got a situation here. This is Frank Russell, the executive producer for *Across the Nation*. We're about to put somebody on the air with an incredible story—one that's got to be aired. But you might get a call from somebody asking you to pull the plug on us. It might even be Jared Winter, the president of the network. I'm asking you please, don't listen to him or anybody else. It's a matter of life and death. I'll take the heat for any trouble you might get into—I'll even authorize a raise for you if you do what I'm asking." He paused, listening to the response. "Good, Mike, I'm glad we can count on you."

Russell hung up the phone and shouted to the room, "We're on!"

"Fifteen seconds."

In the back corner of the room, Kevin found an extra phone. He punched in his home number. "Vickie, honey, it's me. Yes, I'm alive—"

Rick laughed as he now realized who the stranger was in his control room. He pulled on his headset. "Stand by, everybody, we're coming back. Is Mark ready?" He asked the stage manager.

"He's getting his mike on now," a voice said through his headset. "He'll make it."

Over his shoulder, Rick heard Russell pick up the phone with the network president. "Russell here, Mr. Winter."

"Frank, keep that idiot off the air. He's crazy!" Winter screamed.

"No, Jared, I'm not going to do that," Russell told him with a smile breaking out on his face. He couldn't figure out if it was the adrenaline rush or the fact that he was willing to put everything he'd worked so hard for on the line for one good story, but Frank Russell felt like a newsman again.

"What do you mean you're not going to do that?" Winter snapped. "He's fired. Keep him off that set. Do you hear me, Frank? You're fired! I'll have your neck if he gets on—"

The associate director was calling out the last five seconds to going live again.

"Not this time sir, I'm sorry," Frank said calmly even though Winter continued screaming.

Rick called for the bumper tape as the show faded back up on the line.

"I suggest your next call should be to your lawyer," Frank said, then hung up the phone, excited to hear what Mark had to say.

MALIBU
SAME TIME

Vince sat on a barstool, keeping his gun trained on Reynolds while waiting for the police to show up. He'd set Jason in front of the television tuned to the National East Coast feed so they could view *Across the Nation*. Vince didn't want Reynolds to miss a moment of Mark's report.

The television came to life with the bumper tape and show's logo, then dissolved to Mark's image sitting at the desk. He began his report as Reynolds grimaced and lowered his head. *All you had to do was stop him, Winter.*

NATIONAL STUDIOS
SAME TIME

"A lot has happened this week, since my," Mark smiled to the camera, "outburst on the air last Sunday night. A lot of you may be tuning in because of the promos we've been running about it, or maybe you're watching because of the sensational story Samantha was covering this week. In either case, I welcome you to our show.

"If you're looking for me to analyze my belief in the bias of the press, I'm afraid you'll have to wait for a later date, but one I'm sure we'll get to on this show. Tonight, I have a more pressing report to make."

"Stand by, graphics," Rick announced. "Go, graphics. Camera 1 pan left."

The virtual set behind Mark animated. A graphic representation of a computer with an operator sitting beside it appeared over his shoulder as the camera adjusted. Then the words "Polling: Accuracy or Fallacy?" appeared.

"Where did that come from?" Russell asked over Rick's shoulders.

Rick smiled. "I spent some extra time this afternoon with your graphics people."

Russell patted Rick's shoulder. "Good work, son."

Mark continued, "For the past week, I've been doing some research behind the scenes of the polling industry, as I sought to understand the enormous weight our political leaders, the press, and now our society as a whole have chosen to give them. What seemed like a simple look at a political process turned into an incredible story of murder, abuse of power, the flagrant rigging of national opinion polls, and the amazing hold a group calling itself the Circle of Seven, led by media mogul Jason Reynolds, has had over this country. My story starts at one of the top polling companies in the nation—The American Research Institute where an amazing young man by the name of Kevin Spencer had the courage . . ."

Jason Reynolds listened to Mark's report and stared into the television screen. His analytical mind raced, thinking about which parts of the story Mark could prove and which accusations were merely circumstantial. A highly paid defense team could pick Taylor's story apart.

"It's ironic, isn't it?" Vince pointed out "To have your network be the vehicle to bring down the Circle of Seven."

"It'll take more than one reporter shooting off his theories and insinuations to bring me down," Reynolds spat out viciously.

"What I'm saying is not just the excessive imagination of a young reporter," Mark continued. "The best way you can grasp that is to hear the words from the man himself. Analysis by the FBI will confirm that the voice you are about to hear is that of Jason Reynolds, owner of Reynolds Industries and the actual head of this network." Mark looked up above the camera, "Roll it please, Steve."

Rick confirmed the order in the booth. "Roll the tape, Steve."

Reynolds's voice played in the control room, in the studio, and to millions of households across the Eastern and Central time zones, including one house in

Malibu, California. Jason Reynolds screamed out in front of the television, covering his face with his hands. "No-o-o!"

> You want the truth? OK, young man, here it is. Dawkins had to be taken care of; he was setting himself up to turn on the Circle. Yes, that's the name of our little group—the Circle of Seven. We've been together a long time. I learned years ago of the power of propaganda. I studied Hitler, Mussolini, and Stalin. I saw in the infant stages of our technology how this country could be led. I couldn't let one mentally deranged person throw it all away. And through the past five administrations, we've been behind the scenes, prodding and pushing—opinion polls, focus groups, approval ratings. We've fixed it all. Do you know how easy it is to sway a congressman, a senator, or even a president when he's confronted with a batch of percentages on how his constituents feel? It doesn't matter if the numbers aren't real. He'll respond—they all do. The real power isn't in the White House; it's right here—in my office.
>
> I told you yesterday the issues of the day aren't decided by the politicians. They're certainly not decided by the electorate. They are decided by the media. And when you consider my influence in the media, combined with my control over the polling company, I not only determine the issues of the day; I decide what the nation thinks about them.

Reynolds dropped to his knees in front of the television, shaking uncontrollably. "You're a dead man, Taylor! You can't do this to me!"

Mark kept his gaze straight into the lens, addressing the millions across the nation. "That recording was made just a few moments ago while I was being held captive along with Kevin Spencer at Jason Reynolds's mansion in Malibu. With the help of a government agent, we were able to escape by helicopter and make it to the studio to give this report."

He decided to keep Tracy out of his story, hoping to protect her as much as he could from the descent of the press that would follow tonight's broadcast.

"Kevin is one of those great American heroes who probably won't get the credit he deserves. He risked his life when he made the decision to question the irregularities he saw in ARI's polling results. There are thousands just like him throughout the polling industry—those who have a passion for their careers—working diligently to get the most scientifically accurate research possible."

Mark looked quickly off camera, catching Tracy's reaction as she smiled before turning back and continuing. "But the process has been corrupted by others, those who control the polling companies as well as many high up in my industry—the media. When all the facts come out about this Circle of Seven and the incredible influence Jason Reynolds wielded in his social manipulation and control of the political approval ratings, our nation will be horrified. Their influence stretches all the way up to the highest office of our land. As soon as this broadcast is over, I'll be turning the seven names over to the proper authorities."

Mark explained briefly how Reynolds had been able to manipulate the polling process. After a few minutes, he could see out of the corner of his eye the stage manager signaling him to wrap it up.

"We are currently in an intense political debate in this country whether we should allocate billions to the United Nations as President McNeil has requested. In the last few days the airwaves have been inundated with compelling footage from India. Every news show, including this one, has done in-depth reporting on the crisis. That's been followed by opinion polls telling us that over 80 percent of the nation is in favor of the UN taking action, in favor of Congress passing McNeil's appropriation bill, and for the UN to be able to use those funds for so-called family planning—what some would term population control. Just today, I saw a poll saying that the senators who oppose McNeil's plan have seen a sharp drop in their approval ratings.

"The numbers are a lie—the crisis pressed upon us by the media. This is the work of the Circle of Seven. Through press reports and fake opinion percentages, they are once again trying to manipulate you and attempting to influence how Congress responds to this crisis. Don't let them succeed. Our politicians need to lead with ideas and do what is right, not what is popular. They are often not the same thing."

Mark could see the stage manager counting down the final seconds of the show. "Don't be swayed by what you've seen in the media over the last several days—don't be manipulated by this evil group. I'm sure more will be coming out soon as the Justice Department investigation continues.

"From my perspective, it's time to put the public opinion polls back where they belong—as a useful tool for analyzing our society, not as the driving force for every political decision, the headline in every newspaper, or the compulsion behind the follow-the-pack national mentality."

Mark took a deep breath and concluded. "This is Mark Taylor reporting for *Across the Nation: Wednesday Edition*. Thanks for watching."

Tracy was just off camera as Mark finished the broadcast. She couldn't wait for him to get his microphone unplugged and walk off the set. She ran into his arms as soon as the monitors on the stage went to black.

"Oh, Mark," she cried, "you were wonderful."

He embraced, pulling her as tightly as he could. After a moment he pulled back, looking into her eyes.

"I'm so sorry about your grandfather, Tracy," he said, wishing there'd been some way he could've protected her. "I'd give anything if it hadn't worked out this way."

She smiled. "I know, and I'm sorry too. It was so weird talking with him up at the house—it was as if I didn't know him."

"I wonder if you ever really did," he added.

"Maybe not." Tracy lightly touched the palm of her hand against his cheek. "I just thank God that nothing happened to you."

Mark smiled. "And just when did you start thanking God?"

"About the same moment you dropped us out of the sky to dodge that missile." The two laughed, embracing again.

"Wonderful show!" Russell called out as he stepped onto the set. "Everyone is to be congratulated! Especially you, Mark—what a great story. You thought you were the talk of the town this week—wait until tomorrow."

"Which reminds me, Frank," Mark laughed. "I wanted to talk with you about a raise Mr. Reynolds mentioned to me earlier today."

Frank laughed, slapping his reporter on the back. "You have a great imagination, son."

Rick stepped in behind him. "Great reporting, my friend," he said to Mark as he threw his arms around him.

The staff huddled in the center of the room, shaking Mark's hands and congratulating him.

Through the chaos, Cassie found her way next to Samantha. "What you did was wonderful, Sam."

"Thanks," she responded nervously. "It'll be interesting to see how I'm received by the industry after that segment."

"Well, I've been in television for three years, and I haven't had nearly the impact you just did with your first broadcast as a Christian. It must feel great!"

Samantha broke into a smile. "You know, Cassie, I have to admit, it does feel pretty good."

NATIONAL STUDIOS
7:10 P.M. PACIFIC

Reggie stepped into the group, followed by a couple of Los Angeles policemen and two FBI agents. "I wanted to make sure the police arrived before I unlocked the studio, just in case Winter decided to play rough with us."

"Good thinking, Reggie," Rick smiled.

"Where is Mr. Winter?" Mark asked.

"He was last seen speeding out the main gate, taking one of the guardrails with him," one of the agents said. "But we know where to find him. Now, Mr. Taylor, I think it's about time we spend a few minutes catching up with your investigation."

"I agree," Mark said. "But there's an agent with the Justice Department out at Reynolds's mansion that you'll need to bring in on this as well."

The second agent nodded. "We know—Vince Cross. He called us earlier. We were on our way here when Reggie called the police."

Mark smiled at Reggie, then turned to the agents. "Let's go into the conference room," he suggested to the detectives. "I've got a lot to tell you; this could take awhile—"

"What about my grandfather?" Tracy interrupted.

"You must be Ms. Reynolds," the agent closest to Tracy responded. At her nod, he continued. "He's fine. From what I understand, after you fled the mansion in the helicopter, Mr. Cross took your grandfather into custody."

Tracy shuddered. She could never have imagined Papa being arrested for anything. In the past few hours, the exalted image she'd held in her heart for him for more than twenty years had been completely shattered. It was replaced by the mental picture of Vince leading him outside the mansion in handcuffs. Everything had happened so fast. Now the weight of what she'd lived through—of what her grandfather had done—was unbearable. She broke down in tears.

Rick graciously offered to escort the group to the conference room, leaving Mark and Tracy alone in the emptying studio.

Mark placed his arms around Tracy just before her knees buckled. He squeezed tighter, supporting her weight as he whispered into her ear. "It's OK, Tracy. It's OK."

Epilogue

Thursday, February 15
Federal Bureau of Investigation
Los Angeles
4:10 p.m. Pacific

"Ms. Reynolds, just a few more questions. Did you have any knowledge of your grandfather's trip to Chicago a week ago Monday?"

Tracy sighed. She sat at a conference table in a small room, surrounded by two FBI agents and one federal prosecutor. After answering questions for the past three and a half hours, she was tired, thirsty, and wanted to go home.

"I told you before," she answered through her exhaustion, "I knew he was heading for Washington and I thought he mentioned something about stopping in Chicago overnight for a meeting. I didn't know for sure until Mark and I saw the flight logs for the corporate jet."

The agent continued with a string of related questions. Tracy wasn't sure if she was a witness or a suspect. The line had grown fuzzy over an hour ago.

The door opened in front of her and Vince Cross stepped in. One look at her demeanor and he cleared the room. "All right, I think she's had enough. Give me a few moments alone with her."

The other three men left the room without arguing. With the publicity generated by Mark's sensational exposé, Vince had been assigned to head the investigation. Jason Reynolds, Jared Winter, Albert Fisher, and the rest of the Circle of Seven were all in federal custody, compliments of the Justice Department.

"You look like you've been run through the wringer," Vince chuckled.

Tracy looked up at him without a smile. "If this is how you treat those who are cooperating with you, I'd hate to be on your bad side."

"I'm sorry, Tracy. I should have stayed in here with you. I guess my colleagues were being a little overzealous."

"Do they think I'd be stupid enough to be involved, yet be the one to free Mark, the only man who could bring down my grandfather?"

"No, Tracy, they were just trying to be thorough. Everyone within the circle is not saying a word. This is going to be a tough investigation, but that's not your problem. It's mine," Vince admitted. "Again, I'm sorry. You're free to go."

Tracy sat there without reacting for a moment. She was still having trouble coming to grips with the scope of what her grandfather had done. She'd been allowed to spend a couple of minutes with him—a supervised visit—prior to her interview with the agents. Her heart was torn by the love and respect she still held for the only real father she'd ever known, yet repulsed by his loftiness and arrogance. All she could get out of him was a strong rebuke for being a part of his demise, how she'd been set up by Mark's boyish charm and used to get to him. No hint of remorse for what he'd done or the lives he'd destroyed.

Her current state of exhaustion increased the doubts her grandfather had planted in her mind. She was weakening. Could Mark really have used her? Did she supply the final pieces of the puzzle for him, betraying the man who had raised her since she was a child, only to be betrayed herself?

Tracy was drained; she didn't know what to think anymore. She looked up at Vince, and a slight upward curve appeared on her lips as his last words finally sank in. "I can go?"

"Yes, Tracy," he repeated, "you can go with my utmost thanks. I'm sorry for what you must be going through."

She lowered her head. "I'm sure it's nothing compared to what Papa is probably going through."

Vince nodded, reached into this jacket, and pulled out a white envelope. "I was asked to give you this."

He placed it into her hands, then opened the door, turning back to her one last time. "If there's anything you need, Tracy, give me a call."

Vince stepped out the door, allowing it to close behind him. Tracy sat inside the room alone, wondering what was inside the envelope. She opened it slowly, pulling out a piece of notebook paper as she began to read the handwritten note.

> Tracy, it's hard to believe what we've gone through in the past seven days. What do you say we give it a fresh start—no investigation, no interruptions—just a nice dinner. Meet me in Fellini's when the Feds are finished with you. I'll be waiting. Mark

Tracy felt a tear slide down her cheek. Her doubts seemed to weaken. She smiled, picturing the lunch they'd shared last Friday. Her heart leaped as she remembered sitting across the table from Mark when he had asked her the series of personal questions, totally unrelated to his story. Her excitement increased at the thought of their relationship continuing. Fellini's was the perfect place to start over.

She folded the note, stuffed it back into the envelope, and placed it into her purse as she got up to leave. She opened the door, shocked to see Mark standing in the hallway in front of her.

"You wouldn't happen to be related to the man who gave away fifty million dollars last week, would you?"

Tracy laughed, releasing much of the tension that she'd kept bottled up inside her. The same question that had gotten him off on the wrong foot over a week ago.

His hair was only half-combed, and his shirttail was hanging half out of his pants. He looked as if he'd been through the same process that she'd just experienced. But his eyes hadn't changed. Their intensity and passion spoke volumes to Tracy as her doubts completely vanished.

"Maybe I am, maybe I'm not," she teased as she took a step toward him. "If you were any good as an investigative reporter, you might know the answer to that yourself."

"If I were any good at being an investigative reporter, I wouldn't have nearly gotten both of us killed."

He took her hands and brought them up to his chest. "How are you doing?"

She grinned. "Better now. My last few hours haven't been so good."

"Mine either," Mark confessed. "After having a taste of what it's like being a cooperating witness, I sure hope I'm never a suspect."

Tracy laughed. It felt good.

"Are you finished here?"

"Yes, I'm free to go, as Vince put it."

"Did he give you my note?"

"Yes," she answered, pulling it out of her purse. "Right here. So why aren't you waiting for me at Fellini's?"

"I couldn't leave. I didn't know after all that's happened if you'd—"

"Still want to see you?" Tracy finished for him.

"Yes." Mark lowered his head.

She smiled, touching his chin with her hand as she brought his head up, and kissed him lightly on the lips. "Yes, I would love to have dinner with you, Mark Taylor."

He grinned, tilting his head back with a long sigh. "Thank you, Jesus."

Tracy laughed. "You can say that again."

Mark placed his arm around Tracy as he led her out of the building. As they walked, she placed her head close to his shoulder.

They made their way outside, deciding they could walk to the Reynolds building and pick up Mark's car later. They stopped at Grant Street waiting for the light to turn green when Tracy noticed the *Los Angeles Times* in a newspaper rack next to her.

"Mark, look at this," she gasped, pointing to the headline.

Mark leaned over her shoulder, his face immediately turning beet red as his eyes scanned the heading:

Americans Stand by Their Media

In response to the recent attention focused on the perceived bias of the media, an overnight poll conducted by AOL/Time Warner and CNN revealed 78 percent of Americans say they are strongly confident in the accuracy and fairness of the press.

If you would like to communicate with
Clay Jacobsen, you may E-mail him at
laskocj@aol.com